THE LIBERATOR

THE LIBERATOR

A Psychic-Spiritual History of THE ORION EMPIRE

LIANNE DOWNEY

Jolibro

Jolibro Publishing
La Mesa, California

THE LIBERATOR: A Psychic-Spiritual History of the Orion Empire
 For information, please contact Jolibro Publishing:
www.jolibro.com
info@jolibro.com

Visit the author for news & events at www.liannedowney.com

Cover painting by Douglas Taylor, www.douglastaylorvisionaryart.com
Cover design by Damonza

Library of Congress Control Number: 2009906876

ISBN 978-0-9824691-0-1 Hardcover
ISBN 978-0-9824691-9-4 Paperback
ISBN 978-0-9824691-6-3 eBook

Jolibro Publishing

Dedication

To Uriel, with humblest appreciation.

1

The Visit

As I settled back in my chair, the Light Being dipped his Mind into mine. His pure Love oscillated within my thoughts, answering the unasked questions residing there, awaiting his arrival in Consciousness. "How did we begin?" I wanted to know. "Why are we so lost?" Immediately, he pressed the tale into my mind…

SHE COULD SEE THE planet looming into view through the window of the starship. It hung there in space like a brown globular mass, desolate, alone, abandoned on the outer reaches of the Milky Way Galaxy.

How very sad it looks, she mused. *How dark and dim its aura! Truly, there is almost no light remaining—nothing to burst from its surface with the radiance of life in regenerative motion!*

Reluctantly, Uriel turned away from the view stretched before her. Her eyes, gleaming with great Intelligence, took in the forms of her space crew. Alinora, Darkohn, Borabia, Coran, Leeza, Machuta, and young Zortarian were clustered around the circular tabletop viewing screen at the center of the starship. It illuminated their faces with a slight green glow.

"Uriel," Zortarian exclaimed, "we have found it!"

She smiled at him, nodding slightly her acknowledgement. Yes, of course she already knew that they had located the site where their ship would hover above this desolate world that so desperately needed their help.

"Shall we enter the proper coordinates?" Coran asked.

"Yes," Uriel replied. "Do so."

Her heart was filled to overflowing with compassion for the many billions of souls trapped on the surface of this dying planet. They were so immersed in their sea of self-pity and greed that they knew not how serious their circumstances had become.

She, Uriel, had taken on this physical anatomy for one singular purpose: she was leading a starfleet into the aura of this planet. Her own ship, the Celestonn, would enter the lower atmosphere, hovering above the surface of the planet for some length of time so that they might recharge the very ions of the planet's atmosphere with a higher-frequency beam of Radiant Intelligence. Their presence would not be known to the majority of the inhabitants of this world.

There were, living upon its surface, those individuals who were sensitive enough to view—psychically—the presence of these Lighted Ones in their atmosphere. However, their viewings would not be believed by most of the inhabitants of such a world, who were living in a state of numbing ignorance that had blocked all higher sensing capabilities. Their minds were like gluey masses, incapable of extending themselves in any form of mental growth. They had become contented, as a people, to live out their lives in a robotic fashion, carrying on from dawn to dusk in the same routine motions, repeating their conversations from days prior and lives previous. They routinely ate, slept, worked at their mundane, purposeless tasks, and argued amongst themselves over the smallest fractions of Infinity that they so hopelessly desired to possess. To one whose mind had grown well beyond such a lower state of existence, this was a most horrendous state of affairs.

The Mind of Uriel was not singular. It was joined by countless others of far-reaching mental development who had linked themselves in a compassionate Brotherhood of Intelligent Minds. They had served their time on such worlds, gained the lessons that one might gain thereon, and moved themselves out of this lower-dimensional state of existence by adding to their own mental structures those elements of life experience which were constructive in nature. They actually built vehicles of thought or consciousness by which they propelled themselves into higher-dimensional states of existence. As they lived life after life on such planets, eventually evolving unto worlds whereupon a more progressive state of life was expressed, they continually developed this inner Intelligence, and as they did so, they were joining themselves with Higher Minds who likewise passed through this evolutionary progression.

Although it was grossly concealed and largely indiscernible among the peoples of the planet Uriel's starship now approached, they too carried this same potential to expand their mentalities and become a part of this conjoined Creation known to the Higher Ones as the Infinite Mind, or Infinite Creative Intelligence. That is why Uriel and her crew—indeed, the entire fleet of starships—was readying its descent unto this lower-dimensional world. As all are joined, so does the progression or regression of any individual soul or any individual planet affect the mental state of all infinite beings, for truly each individual soul possesses an infinite potential.

"We have readied our descent," Borabia announced.

"Very good," Uriel responded. "Now lend your minds to we Brothers of Light, that we can direct your course in a true fashion."

The crew settled into reclining chairs made of a substance that glowed with a soft, blue light. As they leaned back and closed their eyes, this glow seemed to increase in intensity.

Uriel, too, seated herself in this circle of individuals. She wore a gleaming white suit of what appeared to be sparkling crystal facets. With each breath, each rising and falling of her chest, these crystalline facets reflected a multitude of rainbow colors. The tiny beams of colored light shot forth in all directions, penetrating the atmosphere of the ship's interior.

Her crew was garbed in a similar material but of different colorations. Each individual wore a particular shade of pastel: coral, lavender, powder blue, pink, soft green, yellow, and an opalescent shade that defied any static description.

As they attuned their minds to those of more advanced mental development—Beings of pure Light-intelligence who were not visible to their physical sense structures—a beam of pure white intensity began to form in the midst of this circle of starfleet officers. Several long moments passed, and the beam oscillated in continuous motion from floor to ceiling, glowing brighter and brighter as the frequency increased. If the ship were viewed from some exterior vantage point, it could be seen to glow throughout the surface of its exterior form, until the intensity became so stepped-up that the brilliant white light burned the retina of any physical viewer and eventually disappeared from view.

Through this process of opening their minds to a higher Source of energy-intelligence, the crew had actually raised the frequency (rate of vibration) of the atomic structure of their starship. It transformed and transcended into a higher-dimensional rate of vibration, thus allowing its immediate transference unto the lower atmosphere of the planet toward which they had directed their course. They had instantaneously relocated themselves across the stretches of what appears to be vacant space. It is filled with oscillating energies of vast frequencies. Their knowledge of interdimensional physics allowed the crew to use their minds as a propulsion factor, joined as they were with those Minds that supplied the added force of their own Intelligence.

As the ship reappeared in a stepped-down or demodulated state of oscillation, the crew one by one blinked open their eyes. Slowly they rose to their feet and gathered around the central viewing screen once again. The light beam which had appeared in their midst diminished to a pencil-thin streamer of light that rotated in the very center of the ship. It was actually oscillating from the north to south magnetic poles of the starship; that is, from floor to ceiling in a constant phase-reversal process.

From the scenes depicted on the viewing screen, Uriel could see that their presence was even more desperately needed by these lost souls than she had previously imagined. One after another, they viewed scenes of horrible mass killings, tortures, starvation, wanton destruction of the landscape, and other, more subtle derelictions of mind that were being expressed among the peoples of this turbulent world.

"We must not remain long," she told her crew. "Our very presence here is, even now, penetrating the lower structures of this atomic world with an increased radiation of life force. This will be sensed as a gradual stepping-up effect by the people who now reside here."

"Will they feel this difference within themselves?" asked Alinora.

"Some, perhaps," Uriel said as she turned back to the window. Beyond its transparent surface she could see a dim landscape of green and brown, undulating into the distance in monotonous shades of the same dark colors. "Most will be totally unaware of the change that is occurring within them. It will seem as if their own thoughts have shifted, so subtly that they will not recognize the added clarity by which their minds are beginning to function. But this is only a slight beginning."

She turned back to the questing faces of her crew members, all of whom had proven themselves through countless lifetimes of self-mastery. They would, on a world such as this, be regarded as god forces, yet none among them would ever allow such a circumstance to occur if it were in their power to halt such misconceptions, should they choose to incarnate on a planet for the purpose of lending their minds as teachers.

"We will live many lifetimes among these people," Uriel declared. "I see now that it is the only way they can be reached! We shall enter this world through the vehicle of the womb, and live as these individuals live, in a physical anatomy in this hell world!"

Uriel's words rang out with a hollow yet resounding commitment.

The faces of her crew were solemn, and knowing.

Uriel spoke truth, they knew. She could not do otherwise, for hers was a Consciousness that functioned in vast galactic swirls of intelligence. They held her in the highest regard as their teacher.

"If this is what must be done, then so be it!" proclaimed her first officer, Machuta. "We shall carry out your wishes, dear one, to the utmost of our capabilities. Your Light we shall carry with us in our hearts and minds, never allowing this radiant source of Infinite Intelligence to dim, no matter what fate may befall us!"

"It is true, Uriel, what you say," added Darkohn. "We too can sense within our very beings the pressing need that even now threatens to engulf us in a vacuum of despair as we oscillate here, in the atmosphere of this forlorn world! Yes, we shall carry out this plan to rescue these lost minds! They are our brothers and sisters. How can we ignore their need?"

"Well said, Darkohn," Uriel replied. "We cannot. They are a very part of us. As they live and breathe, so do we, and as they succumb to this downward spiral in which they are totally engulfed, so do they threaten to draw in upon this abyss the consciousnesses of countless souls, existing throughout Infinity! We must take strong measures to halt this regressive motion. We will enter into this very whirlpool of hellish descent and, by the strength of our inner awareness and our attunement with one another, we shall reverse the direction of this vortical motion. We shall redirect the momentum of the joined consciousnesses of all souls living on worlds such as this one!

"We shall, through our mind forces, joined in a legion of great strength, reshape the very atmosphere of such planets!

"You will see, dear ones, that this world shall glow with a great Light in future eons of time. That Light will be the regeneration of the very substance of our minds, our very selves, which we shall give unto this world!"

"So be it," they said in unison. "So shall it be."

"Now let us depart," Uriel said, "before we too are swallowed whole by this downward current."

Instantly the ship vanished from the planet's atmosphere.

Later, in a quiet moment in her private chamber, Uriel opened her consciousness to those of similar mental development—her own polarities or soul-mates with whom she was joined in Consciousness.

Dear ones, I fear our task is much greater than we had envisioned.

Yes, dear Sister, came the immediate reply within her consciousness. *It is so. But we shall overcome this blot upon the Infinite horizon!*

Beloved Michiel, Uriel replied in her thoughts. *Heart of my heart, soul of my soul, this shall be a very long endeavor that we undertake.*

Yes, Beloved One, so it shall be. But there is no other option, is there?

No, dear one, Uriel replied. *We cannot abandon these dear children of our Minds, who have stranded themselves through the misuse of that Infinite*

Spark of Intelligence which they have been given as embryonic beings of this never-ending expression of life force…

So we shall do what is necessary to be done, Michiel completed her thought. *We shall take on physical anatomies once again and live among these peoples on these thirty-three planets that you have, in your expedition, pinpointed as the roots of this negative force which has been instigated among the worlds of this particular galaxy. We will be joined by our many Brothers and Sisters of Light who have pledged themselves to this healing mission. We shall not be alone, and though we must part, our Minds, dear one, are ever joined in Love! Nothing—not time nor space of a physical world—can come between us, for we are One!*

I do feel your love, beloved Michiel, and it fills me with hope that we can be successful in this mission. With your love to comfort me and warm me to the depths of my soul, I feel I can accomplish anything!

Indeed you can, dear one. Your Mind extends beyond a thousand universes!

So you tell me, Uriel thought, *so you say. But as I peer out through these physical eyes at the gross distortions of human expression that we have discovered on our expedition, I feel very small, indeed. It is a monumental task that awaits.*

We cannot despair, Michiel responded. *We must never lose sight of our goal! We shall carry on, until that time when each individual being has been reformed in his ability to think as we do, with an open, inner contact with Higher Minds—those who always aid their younger brothers and sisters with this added, higher-frequency Intelligence. Once restored, their minds will begin to function progressively and we can take our final departure.*

How long, dear one, do you suppose we will need to carry on?

We cannot know, beloved Sister, we cannot know. But we sense that many millions of lifetimes must be lived before our work is done on all of these thirty-three worlds. You have now polarized the darkest of these dim reflections of Infinity. The initial work has been done.

For this I am grateful, Uriel replied. *I can now return this starship to its home base on the planet Axiahn in the Pleiadean constellation, and there we shall regroup for our next foray unto the first of these planets to experience our direct, physical contact. Have you selected this world in your mind?*

Yes. We do believe that your first contact shall be with the planet Tyron, whereupon reside those individuals who are responsible for this massive aberration of human consciousness.

And do you, dear Brother, know where our Mission shall experience its completion?

It is far, far into the future and we could not foresee this end. We must merely live each day in anticipation of that which can be accomplished at any given moment, wherever our thoughts reside. Do take my Love and the Love of all your Brothers and Sisters with you on your return flight.

This I shall do, and please, accept my extensions of Love unto you, and all those Lighted Ones who have made our journeys possible!

Uriel sat quietly for a moment, thinking of the magnitude of the mission upon which she had just embarked.

No, she thought, *I cannot think thusly or I shall never be able to carry on!*

In the central control chamber of the starship, the crew sat quietly entertaining their own thoughts about all that had been seen and experienced. They were aware through their own psychic attunement of Uriel's projections of Mind—both to her polarity, who was not residing in a physical anatomy at present, and to each one of them, as she regenerated their minds with this higher force of Intelligence which they, in turn, regenerated to countless souls with whom their minds were in contact.

Each one of these Brothers of Light would live many lives as man or woman on Tyron, on Vixall, Anzea, Basis, Endinite, Shunan, Din, Emil, Ballium, Dal, and so on—and on Earth, the very darkest world of all. They would be known as philosophers, scientists, artists, musicians, spiritual teachers, even as "gods" to the primitive minds who would at first be unable to correlate their presence with any previous understandings they had held about the nature of a human being. Their minds were so far in advance and so much more sensitive to the higher frequencies of Infinite Intelligence that these aboriginal beings would, at first, be incapable of relating to them in any intelligent manner.

Each of these Brothers, being of this advanced mental acuity, would understand and express only compassion toward these younger souls.

They would do all possible to carry out this Plan without interfering in any direct way in the lives of these lost peoples. Yes, it would be possible, they knew, to merely present ideas, concepts, and the means by which these peoples could heal their own minds and awaken themselves to the interdimensional reality of their own energy selves. This could be and would be done, no matter how many times the Brothers were forced to return to the confines of a physical anatomy—a torturous experience for one of such advanced development who had already graduated from this limited state of existence. But they cared not for their own discomfort, nor whatever calamities they might experience while engaged in this nearly-impossible task. They merely desired to give of their mind structures unto their fellow beings.

Such is the nature of compassion. Such is the nature of Love.

2

Axiahn

After a brief rest so that I, trapped in a physical body on a physical world, could eat and sleep, the Lighted One continued his story:

THE LIGHT THAT RADIATED from Uriel's starship burst upon the horizon of the planet Axiahn. It was a symbol of triumph for the Axiahnites, who had lent their minds in great anticipation to the expedition undertaken by Uriel and her crew of seven. A great welcoming celebration was staged for the return of these interstellar travelers.

But Uriel's mind was preoccupied. Indeed, her entire crew seemed somewhat removed from the joyousness being expressed by the citizens of Axiahn. Not all—in fact, few among the Axiahnites were of the mental development of these eight individuals.

The Axiahnites did indeed live a more progressive lifestyle than found on the planets Uriel and her fellow star travelers had just visited. They were open to Higher Minds and were engaged in a study of their own spiritual evolution. They knew of the continuity of life. They knew that each individual lived many more than one single lifetime for the purpose of self-education. They knew, as well, that everything they thought or did would remain a part of themselves throughout eternity; that is, until they had some recognition which changed their attitude about life and rebuilt certain energy structures within their own mentalities. One could not erase one's past mistakes but could take measures to correct previous misconceptions and to remove the debris accumulated by these past mistakes—the psychic debris. This debris became a form of mental blockage if one did not do this periodic mental housecleaning in subsequent lifetimes.

This is how the mind grows and renews itself with new information, and this is what the peoples of the planets in the Milky Way galaxy so sorely lacked—the knowledge of the scientific principles by which their very selves functioned. Without this knowledge, a soul is truly lost, indeed, for he cannot renew himself and replenish his mind with more expanded concepts of life. And one's mental concept determines precisely the nature of the life he lives at any given moment in his time spent on a physical, atomic world.

The Axiahnites knew all this, and they lived by it. Their children were brought up to understand that they each held a certain responsibility for their actions. No one served as judge, jury, or executioner for the Axiahnites. They governed themselves individually, from within, through their knowledge and understanding of these principles of the continuity of life and the awareness that they were permanently inscribing their very deeds into their own psychic anatomies, that eternal, soulic structure which is one's vehicle of consciousness throughout many lifetimes.

The Axiahnites knew much, as well, about the spiritual, non-atomic worlds to which they traveled between lifetimes to enhance their understanding of these infinite principles of energy. They knew of the Higher Brotherhood, those Lighted Ones who had gone before and paved the way by their examples of how a mind can expand infinitely. So they had recognized in the body of this one whom they called Uriel the oscillating Consciousness of a very highly developed Master, a Master of Masters, a gigantic force of Intelligence which provided the substance of life for countless dimensional worlds. Their understanding of this One extended beyond words to describe. They also knew that her seven officers, handpicked, had incarnated with her on their planet for this particular purpose. They were aware of the Mission this One had initiated with her three polarities—Michiel, Raphiel, and Muriel—even as it presently existed in its gestating form on their world.

Yet they had no concept whatsoever of all that Uriel and her fleet of starships had encountered. They could not have believed the desolation and decline of their brother worlds. Their own lives were too filled with joy and contentment! It would not be believed that so many trillions of individuals could have allowed themselves to decline in such an overwhelming, all-permeating manner that they took with them many billions of unsuspecting souls in this mental reversal. Truly the people of the dark planets of the Milky Way were insane, for they had lost the full functioning capability of their minds.

All these awarenesses occupied the thoughts of Uriel and her crew members as they sat through the welcoming presentations of the Axiahnite officials. The officers were of course gracious to their hosts and did appreciate their added extensions of love. It was a welcome return to a more normal state of life. But the crew knew, deep within their hearts, that they could not remain in this comfortable existence for long—not while so many of their earth brothers and sisters suffered from ignorance!

In the weeks and months that followed, Uriel met many times with the several hundred individuals she had drawn to her prior to her incarnation on this atomic planet in the Pleiades star cluster. Before they incarnated in physical anatomies, these souls expressed a highly developed state of consciousness in their pure energy form on a non-atomic world known by the name Aries. They had served for eons of time—although this concept had no meaning to these developed Minds—as Light Bearers for souls living within the confines of a physical anatomy on countless worlds. They might be termed Angelic Forces or Beacons of Light who constantly shone their Intelligence to light the way for younger souls while maintaining their impersonal yet compassionate stature among the peoples of lower worlds. Most of their recipients living in physical bodies knew not of this inner help, which was ever forthcoming.

But truly the events which had catapulted Uriel and her entourage back into physical bodies on this relatively lower-frequency world of Axiahn was unprecedented in the annals of humankind. One single, solitary Being of Light had stumbled in his Consciousness and fallen to the depths of an earth world. His fall affected many others. They tumbled behind like scrambling mice pouring overboard from a sinking ship. Many Lighted Minds were lost in this devastating turn of events.

How could this be? How could one Mind be allowed to create such a cataclysmic circumstance? Each individual soul is free to shape his own destiny, whether he be living in his first embryonic, aboriginal form as *Homo sapiens* or whether he has evolved well beyond the atomic life to take up his position as a Light for many, many souls. There are always those more advanced and always those of lesser development with whom one can share that which he has gained.

This individual Light Being, Antares by name, was carrying out his duties as a server of humankind. Yet there was a weak point in his mental development, some miniscule portion of human ego which had not been fully resolved by this one, and when it arose within his consciousness, he was incapable of rectifying this mental aberration, even though his own spiritual teachers alerted him to this fact. They did all possible to avert this disastrous fall unto the lower-dimensional worlds, but he did not heed their warnings. Instead he descended into a physical anatomy on an earth planet to—he believed—"help" these souls avoid a natural disaster which was threatening their physical planet.

This he did, but in the process he violated a very important principle of life: he interfered in the lives of those whose minds had not yet formed to their full development, to their broader understanding of the principles of interdimensional physics by which Antares' own mind functioned. He was to them a god, and he did not discourage this perception.

Indeed, he grew to thrive upon it, and throughout the course of millions of years of repeated incarnations in physical anatomies upon this and other worlds, he reversed his entire mental development to become an extremely powerful, negatively-biased force. He became opposite to all that which is growing, thriving, expanding, and progressing. He symbolized the demolition of human consciousness—and the force of his previous development was turned inward upon itself, to become a cannibalistic expression of energy that affected, eventually, many trillions of souls who fell under his influence.

This was the state of affairs in existence as Uriel, a teacher of Antares, made her determination—with the help of her polarities, Michiel, Raphiel, and Muriel, who together formed a quadrocentric Hierarchy of Intelligent Force—to follow this one's descent and heal his mind. Once his own mental fabric had been restored, then the legion of Light Forces could heal the minds that had been destroyed under his dominating power!

His name on the earth worlds was feared far and wide. Tyrantus became the first "tyrant" known on many planets throughout the galaxy. Thus far, over one hundred planets had fallen victim to his negative hordes—individuals who had pledged themselves to this now-demonic mind force. Those who did not willingly join his growing empire were eliminated. Entire planets had been disintegrated with the press of a button. This demonic mind was capable of such massive influence due to his previous development as a Light Being, a wielder of the Infinite Intelligence which passed through the developed lens of his consciousness. Now, however, he used this development for his own personal gain and glory, and many of those former Light Beings with whom he had been associated and who joined him in his descent unto these hell worlds were likewise using their previous mental acuity for destructive and selfish ends!

That is why Uriel and her many Brothers of Light knew that they must enter into this battle of "good" and "evil." Without a counterbalancing, positive force instigated by those of equally accomplished mental ability, the lesser-developed minds that were succumbing to this encroachment of evil would have no chance for survival. They would continue in a declining, regressive motion until they had completely unraveled their intelligence. They would ultimately be reabsorbed as the raw material of Infinity, to be born again at some future time as a new spark of life. Their individual natures would be lost, and any developments which they had made would be for naught. They would experience the only true death: that is, a total and complete reabsorption into the Source of Life.

In the meantime, they were living in a most horrendous state of life. They fed off one another like the lowest animal forms. Yet the intelligence of Antares and his cohorts, applied in a destructive fashion, had created a highly sophisticated technological system which was implemented among these hundred planets that had fallen under his banner of dictatorship.

Orion was the name inscribed upon this flag of evil. The Orion Empire was centered in the star systems of the Orion constellation. That is why Uriel chose the planet Axiahn in the nearby star cluster Pleiades for her home base as she created this physical anatomy through which to present herself to the earth peoples. The Axiahnites' progressive development could serve as a positive reinforcement of her momentum.

"Dear Brothers and Sisters," Uriel addressed the gathered Axiahnites, who had been awaiting some word from the starship commander. "We have seen much to turn our hearts inside out, and we regret to report to you that the need is great for our assistance upon the many worlds that we have visited. We had hoped to discover more Light glimmering within the minds of these tormented souls. We had hoped that the advancement of the Orion forces had not done the damage that we discovered!

"But we must be accepting of the reality that presents itself to us. We have determined through our introspection and with the great help of the higher forces that our mission shall begin at this present junction of consciousness. We shall, each one, pledge ourselves to carry out this healing plan for the peoples of the Milky Way galaxy in all ways and means which present themselves as opportunities for our projection of Light unto these needy worlds!

"You, our brothers and sisters, have lent your minds to us in your positive understanding of this dire circumstance. We deeply appreciate your expressions of love unto us, for they do help to carry us forward on this wave of Infinite Love, which is ever-regenerative and supplies the very force of our lives, and the lives of all Infinite creations. We do intend to see that shining future day when all souls now living upon these lost planets shall likewise lift their faces unto this Infinite, Inner Sun—the very Fountainhead of Infinite Creation which supplies the sustenance of their lives! We shall not give up, nor shall we allow ourselves to succumb to whatever malformations of consciousness will present themselves as we descend in force unto these lower worlds—and we shall indeed do so, for we have determined the need for our presence among these peoples in physical anatomies!"

A slight rustling gasp arose from the gathered citizens.

"Yes, dear ones, we know the magnitude of this statement, and we are fully prepared to take on this responsibility. We have long passed that time when it was necessary for our incarnation in physical anatomies for the purpose of our evolutionary growth. We do know that by returning to the worlds of karma, we shall incur negations within our own psychic anatomies which will need to be resolved in future lifetimes and evolutions. Nevertheless, this is the only way by which this infusion of Light-intelligence can reach these lost souls. They have declined to such a state that they are presently incapable of finding the inner access to this Life Force, which they severed over the course of many lifetimes lived ignorantly and under the influence of the dominating, negative legions and hordes who are obsessing them from both the astral and physical dimensions.

"It is a gross entanglement of aberrant mental formations that we must extend our Minds to aid these ones in disentangling and rectifying. They will be required to rebuild their minds from those first elemental states of consciousness. We believe that, with our help and constant assistance, this will be possible—but it shall not be easy, neither for ourselves nor for them!

"Yet, as you well know, we cannot turn our backs on our brother beings! They are a part of the fabric of our own selves. We must not turn away in despair or disgust, but must extend our compassion in their direction. This will mean *life* to them! And it will encourage our own continued progression unto Infinity.

"Therefore, we hold your support of our mission in the highest esteem. Your steadfastness of purpose in your own maintenance of a progressive way of life does serve as an example for many more souls than you can yet recognize. Hold firm in this determination! Do not allow yourselves to succumb to whatever negative influences may come your way! In future lifetimes, you may discover yourselves taking up a portion of this healing Mission of the Light Forces and you, too, shall join in lending your minds, yourselves, and yes, your physical bodies to this purpose. Nothing shall stand in our way, and *we shall be victorious!*"

A great wave of love and approval rose up from the Axiahnites as they extended their minds in deepest appreciation for the depth of compassion displayed by Uriel and her starship crew. They had never seen such a demonstration of Power, although Uriel had lived on their world in preparation for her expedition throughout the course of her thirty-some years.

She had emerged as a great intellect among the Axiahnites, and was directed from her own higher mind unto the fields of endeavor which would serve her larger purpose. It was only within the last few Axiahn years that the full picture had formed in her consciousness. She was awakened through a series of dreams and psychic attunements to the reality of her mission. Michiel had appeared within this mental attunement and Uriel immediately recognized his Presence.

She had been preparing herself as a starship pilot and had quickly proven her excellence among the ranks of starship commanders. She was given increasing responsibility, until that time when many individuals served under her command. As she then saw, in dream state, all of these individuals had likewise incarnated for this purpose. They had been her students and fellow Light Bearers on Aries and they, too, had traveled to Axiahn through the vehicle of the physical womb, born into the tall, slender, fair-complected forms native to this planet. They had studied and mastered the disciplines of physical life, until that time when each held a particular expertise which would be required by Uriel and her fleet of Light Bearers—for truly that was their purpose.

The expedition undertaken to the earth planets of the Milky Way was merely the first stage of this historical advancement of Light Forces unto the lower worlds. As Michiel communicated to his polarity on Axiahn, she would soon travel to a particular planet, that world upon which Tyrantus now resided and from which he controlled the lives of countless trillions of souls through a devious system of electronics. She would confront her former student, face to face. He had not heeded her warnings or the warnings of any of the Spiritual Hierarchy before his fall, *eighteen million* Earth years previous. But now the cycles had swung for this momentous confrontation.

It would be a battle for the lives of an infinite number of souls, but Uriel knew she would be victorious! Her war would be fought with Love, not destructive weaponry! There is no force more powerful than Infinite Love for it is the Creator of life itself. It is that Essence of Consciousness which breathes life into the newborn babe, and ascends unto the higher dimensions as that babe's life progresses to its end and returns the embryonic soul unto its true home amongst the stars, there to gain new knowledge before, once again, returning into a physical anatomy.

Love, then, is the very foundation of life! Love is Infinite Intelligence.

Tyrantus could *not* resist this compelling Force, which he himself had once shared among humankind. Uriel would speak to *Antares*, who lay dying within the mind of this demonic tyrant. It was Antares that she would awaken, and it would be Antares who would in turn awaken those whom he had condemned to eternal mental sleep!

With these words still ringing in my consciousness, the Storyteller departed. He left no name by which to call for his return—but I knew now that he would return. His tale had not ended! I closed my eyes more tightly and basked in the radiating warmth left by his embrace of Consciousness. Such is the nature of compassion, I thought. Such is the nature of Love.

3

A Circle of Light

The Mind of Uriel, when joined with a physical consciousness, was capable of accomplishing great deeds for the benefit of humankind. Of course, this Mind functions at all times in all dimensions to maintain the progressive motion of Infinity. It supplies the directive maintenance of the ever-regenerative flow of intelligent energy from that Cosmic Fountainhead which supplies life for all Infinity. But when associated with the atomic anatomy of a physical earth person, this Mind has then been given a means by which to perform the necessary physical tasks required to bring this Infinite Intelligence, in a more direct fashion, into the reach of souls living in a lower state of evolutionary development.

The souls incarnated on the earth planets that had fallen under the influence of the encroaching Orion forces were in much more serious need than those who had merely not yet developed their minds. These Orionites, as they were called, had been deterred from their evolutionary mental development. The electronics implemented by Tyrantus and his minions were quite pernicious in their effect when used upon the minds of hundreds of millions of individuals living on these numerous planets. Generated wave forms of energy-intelligence were used to interfere with the natural thought processes of these individuals to make them submissive and pliable to the wants and needs of the Orion leadership. They became puppets to this Orion Empire. Their thoughts were no longer their own. They could not express a progressive state of life, as they were no longer thinking their own thoughts but were being fed from a vast, computer-like structure that had been built as a "brain" of the Orion leadership.

This "brain" generated and regenerated the information fed into it by these devious minds, who had taken their previous mental development and reversed its impact. What was being laid out as a scheme of life for all Orion citizens was merely a gigantic, machine-like state of expression. All the many people were but parts of this electronic machine. They supplied the motivating force necessary to carry out the work required to feed, clothe, and arm the Orion forces so that more planets could be drawn into this web of a robotic existence.

Why? For the further glory of those who had attained power over this sprawling system of planets. It was for their own ego-satisfaction that they continuously made their aggressive approach unto new worlds and acquired them as one acquires a piece of property. They made these planets succumb in a variety of ways, through military force or more devious techniques of propaganda or certain mental manipulations.

In all cases, the electronic influence of the Orion brain was implemented and began to generate false thought structures into the minds of these unfortunate souls, who had no idea that they were being so influenced. It was as if massive dosages of drugs had been supplied to them, unknown to them, and they were subtly taken over and were no longer capable of thinking clearly or attaining any expansionary insight through the association of their minds with Higher Forces of Intelligence.

This severing of their connection to Higher Minds was the circumstance which brought Uriel and others of the Spiritual Hierarchy into their midst. If they were no longer capable of receiving inner, inspirational help through their mental attunement—which is a natural process of the mind of *Homo sapiens*—then the legions of Light Force would come to them in a more direct way, to alert them to the danger lurking among these planets in the form of the Orion Empire!

Without this inner sustenance, a soul will die. No man nor woman can survive without this creative source of Infinite Intelligence. They can live for a time, perhaps, surviving on the mental momentum that has already been established through their existence in physical anatomies; however, this momentum will soon subside, and they will be left in a lifeless state, spiritually speaking. Eventually, they will no longer be capable of maintaining any physical anatomy and will exist within the astral and subastral dimensions as mere blobs of energy which have lost all intelligence. These energy blobs will still, for a time, be motivated with various thought-forms that they had created in their physical lives—certain desires or habits of expression that they will attempt to recreate through their attachment to the physical bodies of others.

Yes, they will become like leeches upon the minds of those still living in atomic anatomies, and they will attempt to sustain their existence through this process of living as a parasite upon the consciousness of others. These lost and broken souls are known as astral obsessions, and they were clinging to the Orionites in massive hordes, for they were associated with these individuals, as they had once lived among them.

One by one, the Orionites were deteriorating unto this state of near non-existence and eventually, even those obsessing blobs of energy would be entirely disintegrated and their energy force of life reabsorbed into the Infinite Fountainhead to be reformed and redesigned into the embryonic state of a new soul. Their previous mental development or personal, individual imprint of Intelligence would be entirely erased.

This is true death! It is not a part of an individual's evolutionary life cycle. The true plan, if such a term can be used, for any individual facet of Infinite Intelligence is one of constant growth and expansion of intelligence. The Mind of Uriel, Michiel, Raphiel, or Muriel provides the highest example of this mental attainment that can be approached in conception by earth peoples who are not yet capable of expression from this higher vantage point of development.

Uriel's plan was to reverse the trajectory of these trillions of souls. To do so, she would first need to unlock the hold upon their minds being maintained by those negative perpetrators who had fallen from higher states of awareness. Only when these minds were freed of the electronic influence of the Orion brain could they begin to be rebuilt, and that would be the required process: they would need to be helped by the Higher Ones to shear away the dross influence of Orion propaganda and technology and begin, again, in a lower evolutionary state of expression, as aboriginal man and woman.

But this would be a future development and Uriel could not think beyond her present need: the plans which must be carried out immediately if this future restoration of minds were to occur.

"My dear brothers and sisters," she addressed her gathered crew members. "We have been waiting here on Axiahn for that proper cycle when we might make our next approach unto the lost worlds of Orion. I feel that time is nigh. We shall prepare ourselves then—mentally—for all that which shall bombard our senses as we descend unto the surface of these many planets.

"Our first entrance into the Orion Empire shall be into that very den of iniquity, the planet Tyron, whereupon resides the negative force Tyrantus, the one who has masterminded this entire, horrible state of affairs. He must be the first to recognize the truth of the vast harm which has been inflicted upon Infinity itself by the detouring of so many trillions of soulic expressions of life! He does still have within him, I feel, some inkling of his previous development. If I can reach that last dim spark of Intelligence, then we shall be successful!

"But, dear brothers and sisters, this will not be an easy accomplishment. I did wish you to know this and to keep yourselves alert to the fact that we may fail many times before we achieve our ultimate success."

Uriel glanced at the faces of those who had gathered to hear her address. Their countenances were serious now, and yet there glowed within them a Light that stemmed from their inner link to a higher source. They expressed this Light in great unity among themselves, causing it to regenerate and fill the large room in which they were seated with a higher frequency than normally found on the planet Axiahn.

Uriel was well pleased with their development. None among them had failed to gain the expertise required for these missions unto the earth worlds. They had carried on in a most integrated fashion since their birth on this Pleiadean planet. She felt that they were indeed ready for the next stage of their advance upon the negative forces.

"But dear ones, do not allow any fear whatsoever to creep into your thoughts. As you well know, this would cause an immediate failure of our individual and joint efforts to overcome the negative forces. Fear is the manna upon which they feed! So fear not, and remember that you are not alone. Your minds are filled with an Intelligence which will guide your every action and give you the information required to carry out the task that you have, each one, set up for yourselves as you contact the Orion citizens. We all, together, will be able to reach many, many individuals. Any one of us single-handedly could not have this overall effect. But as those many who are so joined in Consciousness, we can extend our efforts over broad geographical and mental levels of attainment.

"As you know, each of these Orion citizens has come from a different evolutionary background. Many of these planets which have been attacked and overtaken by the Orion forces were existing at a much lower state of development than others. These aboriginal souls have been the most deeply affected by the influence of Orion technology, particularly this electronic control under which they now function. Other worlds were of a more advanced technological and even spiritual development, and those are the planets that can become key factors in our mission. Once restored to their true state of evolutionary expression, they can become guideposts for the many forays we shall make unto these worlds. They can lead the way for others to overthrow this negative influence and restore their growing ability."

"Uriel," a voice called from the rear of the room, "may I ask a question, please?"

"Yes, of course. Please do," she replied.

"How long will it be before we begin to see some progress in this mission?"

"That is a question that cannot be answered, but we know that every step taken with a positive intent moves Infinity forward, if we can use this imprecise terminology. We cannot concern ourselves overly much with our results. We must merely undertake each individual task as it presents itself, accomplish that particular end, and move on to the next cycle of attainment. One by one, these progressive tasks shall join together to form the whole of this Mission. There is much that we cannot foresee at this juncture, but we shall be quite busy with the immediate needs and our minds will be fully occupied. We need not dwell, then, upon tomorrow while we have today yet to complete!"

All nodded in agreement. Of course. Yes, they should have realized this. One cannot live in past or future but only in the present moment.

"Now let us adjourn to our individual quarters to make that necessary attunement. Each one individually will need to strengthen his bond with Infinity. This journey that we are beginning will test your strength to its utmost limits. Trust me in this, for I know whereof I speak. So strengthen your resolve, and know wherefrom stems your own intelligence! We are not alone, nor should we ever be. Go in peace."

The gathered crew members rose as if in one motion to salute their commander. She returned their salute, an open palm raised upward, symbolizing the reception of Higher Intelligence that characterized their mental joining with one another and with the Brotherhood of Higher Minds.

As they lived through physical anatomies, even on a more advanced world such as Axiahn, they were already at risk. That is, at any given time they might begin to degenerate their mental development through the overemphasis of this physical life in their own individual minds. They could easily forget and return to previous mental states in which they, too, had lived the majority of their expression in a physical anatomy, with only brief interludes spent in higher-dimensional worlds between physical lifetimes. Therefore, they were already practicing great restraint and caution as they lived in these physical bodies. They did, of course, live in the same fashion as the Axiahnites, but with a vastly increased sensitivity to all sensory input. This increased sensitivity could become quite discomforting if they had not already determined within themselves, as they prepared for this descent into physical anatomies, that they would undergo this discomfort for the purpose of helping others.

For Uriel, this discomfort was increased multifold. Her mind, being of an Infinite nature, was capable of feats that her crew members had yet to develop. She could, if she wished, perform among them that which might be termed miraculous; however, with her great intelligence and wisdom she knew that such interference in a lower dimension cannot be instigated by One who is desirous of maintaining his advanced development.

This is where Antares had erred so dismally. That is the instant at which his mind began to unravel, when he chose to express so-called miracles among an earth people for the purpose of "saving" them—and now his purpose was to maintain his dominance over them by constantly dazzling them with his mental trickery.

But Uriel knew all of his tricks quite thoroughly. She would not be deterred by any obstacle which he might throw up to stop her closer approach unto his consciousness. She knew how to penetrate that shield of ego, and she would do so!

The starships, then, were readied for their next flight, with the planet Tyron as their destination. One thousand individuals were awaiting their time of departure. This huge entourage was relatively small in the minds of these ones who were accustomed to functioning in a broad expression of consciousness. To the Orionites, however, they would appear as an immense fleet of starships.

There were thirty-three ships all together, each one symbolic of the thirty-three levels of attainment a soul passes through in a certain phase of his evolutionary development. These crystalline starships, which were directed by the minds of their crew members, gleamed with a brilliant, golden hue under the rays of the Axiahn sun. Their coloration would change as their frequency was stepped up to activate their alignment with the electromagnetic lines of force that constantly oscillate among the planetary and solar bodies, which are parallax points of the infinite, creative, intelligent energy of life. These are the roadways by which the starships criss-crossed the universe, as their designers knew quite thoroughly the principles by which these electromagnetic lines of force were created and maintained. Joining themselves, then, with Infinity, they were capable of spanning great distances in very brief periods of time.

Their journey to Tyron was accomplished in a momentary flash of joined mental attunement, as the frequency of each ship was increased through the mind expressions of their crew members. They became one with the electromagnetic force fields and could be translated to any location within the galaxy—or galaxies, if need be.

This science of interstellar travel was yet unlearned by the Axiahnites when Uriel and her Brothers from the planet Aries incarnated on their world, but through the course of their adult years on Axiahn, the Arians had been teaching the Pleiadeans this spiritual technology, if it can be termed as such. The Pleiadeans were most grateful for this instruction, for it advanced their own civilization light years into the future. Of course it could not be otherwise. No planet could experience the Presence of these Lighted Ones without expanding its global expression through the stepping-up of its own base plane rate of frequency oscillation. The Intelligence added unto the lives of these Pleiadeans was immeasurable!

Such as Uriel and her Arian Brothers and Sisters cannot do otherwise than to give of their Intelligence in this fashion. They would leave Axiahn in a much more progressive state than that in which it was found by them. This was the same effect that they would have upon the Orion planets. However, that effect would be long in its gestation, and at this particular moment of introspection, it could not be determined how long that progression of time would be.

Like streaks of starlight, the fleet of Arians translated themselves into the upper atmosphere of the planet Tyron. They remained there for some time, undetected by the defensive technology of the Orion headquarters for the negative leaders, as they were oscillating at a much higher frequency than Orion technology was capable of detecting. They were able, from this vantage point, to observe the activity on this planet from a much closer perspective. This was valuable information for Uriel and her crew members, for they would need to know as much about this civilization as possible in order to determine the correct approach to take unto these peoples, who were so capable of annihilating their brother beings—and so willing to do so with the slightest provocation!

The Arians were shocked at what they saw. Crawling upon the surface of this world were human beings who had been reduced in intelligence to something lower than the lowest earthworm, for even that earthworm has a connection to its higher, directive force of Intelligence! Yet these individuals were attached to a mechanical device, an electronic computer composed of endless tangles of hardware that had been programmed by devious minds bent on the total domination of Infinity!

Tears streamed down Uriel's face as she viewed the scenes presented on the screens of the ship, Celestonn. Deep silence reigned among her crew members as well. They too began to cry with an overwhelming feeling of compassion for their brother souls.

These were no longer human beings! There was no life remaining, no light that could be detected within their faces. They had become machines. Whatever spiritual Intelligence they once possessed was completely obscured by their encasement in an electronic web of controlling signals. They could not think. They merely reacted to the exterior impulses projected constantly from the Orion brain. Day and night they were bombarded by this controlling force, and they were, unbeknownst to themselves, groveling at the feet of their Orion masters.

"It is much worse than I feared," Uriel said very softly. "I do not know if they will be able to see us. Their minds have been so severely damaged. Their higher senses have been completely destroyed. They do not exist!"

This brought a new wave of compassion to the gathered officers. They could not imagine the pain of life lived without knowledge of any creative purpose.

"I believe that we should return to Axiahn at this present time. But before we depart, we shall create upon this planet some means which shall facilitate our return. Let us join our minds in a great bond of unity, dear ones."

Uriel reached to a golden button by her seat. As she depressed this circular knob, thirty-two screens around the room lighted with the faces of the crew members gathered around viewing screens on each ship in the fleet.

"Dear brothers and sisters, you can see that this is a circumstance of utmost seriousness and it is imperative that we act wisely. We cannot make a hasty approach unto this planet. It would serve no purpose, for our projections of consciousness would roll off the minds of these individuals like so much water poured onto a metallic surface. We must, then, revise our plans. We shall join ourselves in Consciousness at this moment."

Uriel paused as each one visibly relaxed his physical features, closed his eyes, and breathed more deeply.

"As we link with our Brothers on the higher world of Aries, we are being given a vast surcharge of energy. Feel this vortex surrounding you, each one, and we all together as one whole. We shall make of ourselves a glowing orb of Light; we shall become a Sun unto this dark, metallic planet!

"Let this Sun regenerate as we step up the frequency to higher and higher oscillations of Infinite Intelligence. Now this high, high, healing frequency is regenerated among us as it encircles and encompasses and oscillates back and forth, from positive to negative, each one adding a greater charge of Intelligence through his own attunement.

"Let us, with our minds, direct this Radiant Sun to thoroughly encompass the planet Tyron!"

Uriel paused again.

"Now we see within our minds that this golden, penetrating energy is completely encasing this world of lost souls. These energies penetrate the lower atmosphere, radiating and regenerating as they are demodulated unto the atomic surface of the planet. They interpenetrate and interweave within the atomic structures of each individual living thereupon, and now are interpenetrating the very surface of this world, recharging and stepping up the frequency oscillation of each particle of dust that forms this planetary body.

"Let us remain thus in consciousness."

For seven long moments Uriel and her fleet maintained this energy projection. The planet was saturated with Light. If it could be seen psychically, it would have taken on a golden glow; however, as the energy beams approached the surface of the planet, they were diminished in their brilliance by their absorption and dispersal into these lower atomic structures, which were incapable at the present time of fully accepting and regenerating these energies.

Nevertheless, they were impinged within the psychic anatomy of the planet itself. New Intelligence had been added unto the physical expressions of this psychic source, the energy body that sustained the physical appearance of the planet.

This higher frequency would serve as a carrier wave to bring Uriel and her entourage to the surface of this world at a future time. For now, however, they knew that these energies would need to be solidified, so to speak, in their interpenetration with the planet Tyron.

As the Orionites lived upon the surface of this world, they would be incepting some miniscule measure of this new Intelligence which had been infused into their own psychic anatomies. They were distinctly unaware, of course, of this new development. They were incapable of sensing any such higher oscillation. Nevertheless, this oscillation would regenerate within their minds, even as they existed in their broken states. It was this relative frequency which would be required for Uriel and her Brothers to make contact with these individuals. There would need to be some remaining essence of expansive Intelligence within them for any possibility of their recognition of their true spiritual selves, which had been obliterated by the Orion electronics.

"Now, dear ones, we have done all that is possible to help these souls at the present time. Let us encircle their world with our starships, for this shall create a further establishment of positively-biased energy forms as we interact with this physical planet through our physical anatomies and starships. We shall be engaging ourselves with these atomic structures and we will therefore form some relativity with this world for our future access.

"So let us engage our minds in this dispersal, as we encircle the planet."

Each starship commander programmed the necessary information and directed his or her mind to follow Uriel's command. The crew members stationed themselves in their flight positions and instantaneously this mental repositioning of the thirty-three starships occurred. They oscillated in a ring around the planet, still invisible to its inhabitants.

"Now," Uriel commanded, "let us dip lower into the planet's atmosphere, and as we do so, some light from our ships may become visible to these Orionites. However, I doubt if there are any capable of perceiving even this demodulated frequency, which is so far advanced from their present state of existence."

Slowly the band of starships began to descend, like a circle of light contracting toward the center of this globe. Great streamers of Intelligence were radiating into the atmosphere of Tyron. The fleet remained thus suspended in the lower atmosphere of the planet for a few moments. Then, at Uriel's command, they vanished.

So has begun our work, Uriel mused. *And my dear Brothers, I thank you for your Wisdom and guidance.*

4

Into the Lion's Den

The Storyteller took my hand, mentally, and led me deeper into Orion. "You must know the full story," he conveyed to me. "This is the only way for you to understand." He drew me down a dark tunnel but there was no light at the other end. We had emerged into a city of darkness. "From here you will see the tragedy as it presented itself to the Lighted Ones . . . "

A THOUSAND YEARS HAD PASSED since Uriel's starships first graced the upper skies of the planet Tyron, unperceived by those who lived below—those whose minds were encompassed in darkness. Life propelled the people forward in their continual drudgery. They had no spark of joy to keep them buoyant, no hope for tomorrow, no wish for yesterday. All their tomorrows and yesterdays were blended into one long, gray smear of mere existence. They had lived this way from the time of their birth, and they could expect to continue in the same routine, robotic tasks until they finally left the physical anatomy.

No possibility existed for their ascension into a higher spiritual world between their dismal lives in Orion. They had no relativity to such higher worlds and they would not be capable of gaining access to these higher-frequency dimensions. They merely floated in a jelly-like state of consciousness in some subastral realm that was very similar to the physical life from which they had just departed. They were not conscious of the separation from this physical life to the non-physical state of consciousness; they were not conscious of anything at all except the seemingly continuous stimulation of their "physical senses" which truly no longer existed! These were but thought-forms of consciousness replaying themselves like old tapes that had been rewound and replayed, over and over again.

This haphazard oscillation of consciousness drew them hither and yon as they attached themselves to those still living in their physical anatomies, and very soon they were attracted to some gestating human form, drawn back into their physical life on an Orion planet with very little time of spiritual refreshment. Indeed, they had no spiritual refreshment whatsoever. This was one of the most criminal acts that had been perpetrated upon these people: the removal of their ability to ascend to higher worlds to gain new Intelligence and to learn about life under the auspices of their spiritual teachers. They had lost all connection to the higher reaches of Infinity.

The daily life of the Orionites was quite dependent upon the outside directives received from the Orion brain. Each individual citizen began his day with orders received from this central, computer-like machine and carried out his tasks dutifully, for he knew no other way of life.

There were those living on Orion worlds who did know better, but they had been totally suppressed, and in many cases, tortured beyond recovery, their minds destroyed by a variety of demonic, diabolical techniques that had been developed in Orion laboratories for making those "difficult ones" more submissive and pliant to the wishes and needs of the Orion government. These individuals filled many so-called hospital wards and asylums. Those who could be trained to perform some useful task were reintegrated into the Orion society; those who had lost all functioning capability were farmed out to these institutions or, indeed, taken to outlying planets where they soon became the actual food devoured by the Orion elite!

It is nearly inconceivable, but this was the state to which these people had degenerated themselves. When they lacked food, when a famine tore through certain Orion planets, or when the ever-pressing need for fuel to propel the warships of Orion grew to increased levels, this means of using the human anatomy, like an animal substance to be preyed upon by carnivorous beings, was undertaken.

No depth was too low for the Orion leaders, who had truly lost their sanity. They had no compassion. They were unfeeling machines, and they were entirely motivated by an aggressive, egotistical nature that had replaced their previous benevolent qualities.

It does seem impossible to consider this circumstance, but it is truth. A developed mind, when reversed in its motivation, is the most destructive weapon that can be unleashed on humankind. Tyrantus and his cohorts were proving this beyond doubt! This group of elite—the twelve council members of the Orion central government—had once been Advanced Beings, leaders of humanity from higher dimensions, what some have called "angelic" in your histories. But as they fell into this animalistic state, they took with them many more individuals with whom they had been associated in a positive way.

They were vicious beyond belief. They cared not for any other living thing, human or animal; indeed, they treated all things as if they were mere fodder for the egos of these individuals. They were subhuman, in that all positive mental bias had been relinquished and replaced by a driving force of destructiveness. They longed only for greater powers, wider influence, and more souls to bow down to them as gods.

This they did achieve, through the conquest of many, many planets.

To journey into the heart of Orion was to take one's life in one's hands. Only Uriel would have the courage to face the lion in his den. She knew the strength of his physical accomplishments; she knew that her physical anatomy would be at a disadvantage when presented with the destructive technology of Tyrantus and his Orion bureaucracy. But she also knew that the power of Spirit oscillating within her consciousness would be undiminished by anything these Orion leaders could present to her.

Nevertheless, she felt it would be wisest to first appear to these individuals in the form of a man—a tall, strongly built, striking man who presented an imposing figure to any other physical being. His eyes were clear, yet penetrating. They saw with the vision of a Mind that spanned universes—they saw with the Mind of Uriel. His hair fell about his face like a gleaming halo of golden light. All who looked upon the face of this Benevolent One were struck by the compassion radiating there, in the countenance of this strong man. It was not what they expected—such a strongly dominating individual might have as easily been fierce in his gaze. Yet that power and strength which encompassed the presence of this One, whose name was Dalos, came from an Infinite Source. It had no personal emotion attached. It was pure, radiating, Infinite Intelligence; indeed, it was love that permeated the expressions of this man from the Pleiades, as he came to be known by those whose planets he visited in his many travels throughout the galaxy.

As before, Uriel had allowed herself to extend her Consciousness into a physical dimension through the normal process of incarnation. She was born into the form of this male body and grew into adulthood in the usual fashion, although she/he did exhibit his precocity at an early age.

Dalos lived on that world that has been introduced to you as the planet Axiahn. Many cycles had passed since Uriel's first incarnation upon this Pleiadean planet. Now she had returned and again was accompanied by two hundred individuals from her true home of Aries, who likewise returned in physical anatomies for the purpose of completing Dalos' entourage of Lighted Ones. The Axiahnites well remembered Uriel and, as Dalos grew into manhood, they recognized the spiritual force that he carried with him.

As before, Dalos became aware of his higher purpose at the appropriate junction of cycles and he gathered about him those who had prepared themselves to serve under his command. This time, however, they were fewer in number, yet no less devoted to their purpose and to the commitment toward this healing mission.

Great seriousness played upon the faces of these ones as they made their initial journeys from the surface of the planet Axiahn. These first travels through space were directed toward planets within the Pleiadean constellation. It was an opportunity for Dalos and his followers to strengthen their consciousness as Light Bearers and to gather into this consciousness the minds of many souls who had not yet been affected by the Orion negative forces. It was extremely important to Uriel that she establish this contact with many thousands of souls who might have otherwise been lost, if the Orion warships had suddenly attacked these thus-far-untarnished worlds. This was no less a part of her mission than the actual rescue of those souls who had already been lost.

Dalos, then, became known throughout the Pleiadean constellation as a teacher of great wisdom, a bringer of Light, Love, and Peace. He was highly respected and revered for his wisdom, yet not worshiped, as this would be his careful purpose: to deflect any intimations of such worship on the part of the peoples of these planets. They were given a clearer understanding of their own position on the ladder of evolutionary development, and they saw themselves, not as inferiors to this great Mind, but as facets of it that carried the full potential to grow into such as the one called Dalos. They too might one day serve as a "Sun" to many physical worlds.

But the time eventually came for the descent into hell.

With his brothers gathered in harmonic association, Dalos prepared his single starship. This huge, lighted vehicle was outfitted with many examples of technological developments based upon the Axiahnites' understanding of the principles of Infinity that had been instilled within them during Uriel's prior visit and developed over the course of the ensuing thousand years before Dalos appeared among them. He now had helped them to refortify their understanding and to advance their expression of life to another degree.

Life on their planet was truly a joyous proposition, containing all the benefits of the knowledge they held of their true nature as Infinite beings engaged in a progressive development of consciousness. They supplied many new inventions for Dalos' journey to the planet Tyron. These inventions would help in his demonstrations among the Orionites to prove to them the reality of the interdimensional qualities of life, this knowledge of which the Orionites had become so ignorant!

As the morning sun streaked across the planet Axiahn, Dalos gathered with his two-hundred-member crew beneath the shimmering structure of his interplanetary craft. He gave his love and projections of Consciousness unto his brother Axiahnites, who received his words with love in their own hearts—and a touch of sadness at the departure of their beloved teacher, for he had become most valuable to the entire world; indeed, *worlds* of the Pleiadean star cluster. But they knew that the time had arrived for this next phase of his spiritual mission and they would not dream of expressing any form of resistance through their desire to keep this One to themselves.

"Hail to thee, beloved Dalos!" they cheered. "Our love goes with you!"

Dalos returned their mental embrace with a radiating smile and extension of his hand, palm upward in the now-traditional Axiahnite "salute of humility." This they returned with a great surge of consciousness. To the best of their ability, they lent their minds to the success of Dalos' journey.

As he disappeared into the ship, Dalos felt a twinge of warmth pass through his body.

Yes, dear one, he thought, *I know you are with me, as we are always together.* It was Michiel's presence that he felt. *We shall now, at last, meet our foe and make certain that he becomes friend once again!*

With a brisk nod, Dalos directed his flight crew to elevate the starship from the planet's surface, which they did through their mental attunement. Once freed of the gravitational pull of Axiahn, they then linked themselves to the electromagnetic force fields and slipped through the cosmos to their destination.

This time the Arians—for that was their true home—made their presence known to the Tyronites. They halted their approach some distance from the planet, establishing themselves in an orbital path around the globe that was clearly positioned in a non-aggressive stance. Their immediate contact with the Orion defensive forces was to inform the Orionites that Dalos' ship approached in friendship from a distant location and wished to communicate freely and openly with the leadership of the planet Tyron.

This message was received with startled attitudes by the operators of the Orion monitoring systems. They had detected no approach of a foreign spacecraft! They could not explain to their superiors how this ship had arrived in their midst without their previous knowledge. Many individuals were immediately dismissed from their positions at the monitoring screens and replaced by others. There was no room for error or miscalculation in the Orion society, and there was no hesitation to take swift action to replace one "machine" with another, for that is how human beings were regarded: as mere parts in the larger machine, strictly replaceable and at all times dispensable.

Tyrantus was immediately informed of this development. He was not pleased. He did not take kindly to surprises of any kind whatsoever. His total obsession was for absolute control and domination over every movement of life in this vast territory which his empire now encompassed. He was the supreme ruler and commander of all things; therefore, a solitary starship entering his defensive air space was immediately considered to be a threat, and those who reported this information were, likewise, removed from their positions. Many heads of departments were taken to the rehabilitation wards as a result of this circumstance.

Meanwhile, Tyrantus directed his aides to present him with all details known about this foreign ship. He was given a complete readout of information received through the Orion computer systems and was given printed copies of the message that had been received from this ship. So far, no reply had been given by the Orion communications network.

Dalos was not surprised. He imagined the effect his sudden appearance would be having on this world of ultimate control. He knew well that his ship was oscillating at a frequency that was untouchable by the Orion warships. He simply awaited Tyrantus' reply. He was in no hurry; he knew that his mission was one of long duration. He had infinite patience to guide his actions.

On Tyron, there was a flurry of scrambling activity as orders were given and rescinded. Much confusion reigned. Tyrantus was so thoroughly unaccustomed to any intrusion on his smooth, orderly operations of life that he was personally disconcerted by the entire affair. He did not know how to respond, but he dare not allow any individual to recognize his momentary confusion and mental turmoil! He immediately ordered all individuals from his presence. He commanded that a communications device capable of reaching the distant ship be brought to him, with the bearer dismissed the moment his apparatus had been delivered.

This was done with great fear on the part of those serving Tyrantus in this closer fashion. They had never seen his face so livid with rage! They knew that he would sooner strike them dead than give them a second look when he was in such a state.

Once alone, Tyrantus tried to calm his thoughts. He failed and tried again—to no avail. Still shaking with anger, or perhaps a fear that he would never admit, even to himself, Tyrantus placed his hand over a smooth square on the surface of this device.

"This is the Supreme Emperor of Orion. You are invading our territory! You must depart at once, on peril of death," he commanded.

Dalos expected such a response. He knew that this one could only respond according to his present nature: he was snarling like a cornered animal. There was only one answer that could be made. Dalos motioned to his assistant to open the communications circuitry.

"Yes, Emperor Tyrantus, we know your identity and we respect your planet's defensive shields. We shall not make any aggressive motion to advance toward your world until we receive your permission. Our purpose is not to harm or infringe upon your lives. We merely wish to share with you knowledge that we bring from other planetary systems. We do so in friendship and peace."

These words were quite strange to the ears of Tyrantus. No one had ever offered friendship to the Orion forces! He was taken aback, and did not know how to reply for several long moments.

"What is your origin?" he demanded. "How is it that you have—" and he stopped. He did not want to reveal to this intruder the fact that their approach took the Orionites by surprise! "Of course, we have been monitoring your approach to our planet and we have you under our full surveillance. You have only reached your present position due to our benevolence. We have nothing to gain from you."

Dalos caught the shift in Tyrantus' tone.

"Perhaps that is so, but we do believe that you might wish to determine this after examining the many technological advances that we have made on our worlds. We believe that you will find them to be of great interest and benefit to your many peoples. We know of your empire, of course, and we know how greatly you yourself admire new technological devices. Please consider our offer to share our knowledge with you."

Tyrantus was extremely suspicious of this seemingly benign voice that irritated him greatly. He could not explain why, for no one had irritated Tyrantus for many hundreds of years. He had been in his present physical anatomy for over three hundred years and any irritation that he had ever felt was immediately dealt with in a most decisive and determinate manner.

But he could not resist this offer of some new technological development. After all, this ship *had* appeared in the upper atmosphere of Tyron, escaping all detection of the most sophisticated defensive systems that his empire possessed. Perhaps there was something to be gained from these foolish peoples who so willingly placed their lives in his care. He wondered if individuals possessed of such advanced capabilities could truly be so stupid as to believe that he would allow them their lives once he had gained all that he could from them—and what was it that they wished to gain from the Orion Empire? No doubt they were seeking some protective security. That is what all foreign worlds desired, he assumed, a stronger force to keep their enemies at bay.

Very well, then. He would allow this ship a cautious entry into the lower atmosphere of Tyron so that it could be fully inspected by the probing electronics of the Orion brain. But he must not appear in any way too anxious for what these foreigners had to offer. They might become greedy in their desire for his return of gratitude!

"I have determined," he spoke sternly into the communicator, "that you may descend into a closer range for inspection. If you wish to land on our planet, you will first be required to submit to our full electronic survey. Do you agree?"

"Agreed," Dalos promptly replied. "We have expected this and we shall oblige all your requests."

Instantly the Axiahn ship vanished and reappeared several miles above Tyrantus' headquarters.

Immediately alarms sounded throughout the defensive positions of the weapons systems scattered throughout the planet. Footsteps pounded through the metallic hallways outside Tyrantus' quarters, as piercing tones penetrated what had been a deadened and fearful silence.

Tyrantus jabbed at a button. "Halt all alarm systems," he barked. "We have given the command for this ship's descent."

Startled personnel throughout the globe heard Tyrantus' order. They froze for an instant, then desperately reached to follow his command before his wrath was further fueled.

Had he known of the next developments that would occur on his world, Tyrantus might not have been so quick to allow Dalos' entrance. But of course these circumstances were the result of that penetrating Intelligence that had already begun to tap the deepest reaches of Tyrantus' mind. He was being affected by factors that he did not suspect, as he felt himself to be in full control of the situation. This was not the case but he need not know this, for Dalos had no desire to prove his superiority over the mind of Tyrantus. Dalos merely desired to save the consciousness of Tyrantus—and the consciousness of many trillions of souls—from total annihilation. Dalos would not stop until this had been achieved.

As Tyrantus' many thousands of technicians scanned their monitoring screens, attempting to make sense of the information pouring from the Orion computer, Dalos relaxed in his seat aboard the starship. His crew settled in peacefully, knowing that their lives would soon become encompassed by scenes which would tear at their consciousness and challenge each thought with new input.

Dalos' eyes closed. "So it shall be," he whispered to himself. "So it shall be."

5

The Power of Love

Dalos was a strong man, tall, well-proportioned, the epitome of human perfection. His lean, smooth cheeks surrounded the most penetrating, deep-blue eyes that one could imagine. His chin was solid, yet relaxed in an assured, friendly manner, his lips ready to break into a radiant smile or formed in an attitude of seriousness of purpose. He was tall yet not intimidating, strong but not domineering. He was, in fact, a magnificent specimen of humanity to behold, and he was held in the highest respect by all those who had made his acquaintance and those, of course, who served under his command on this starship.

They knew his true Mind as their leader and teacher. They knew their own Higher Minds, therefore it was easy for them to accept the mental development of this eloquent man and to respect his greater wisdom and intelligence as they respected themselves. And they knew that he represented their future development.

Dalos taught by example. He was a benevolent, kind, compassionate man who could be stern and direct when necessary. His entire motivation was to help others through the illumination of their own minds. He could not personally do anything to change their thinking, but he could illuminate for them the irrational or illogical ideas that they had maintained within their modes of thinking. This he did quite frequently, for his starship crew as well as those individuals whom they encountered in their many travels. He did this in a kind and loving yet direct and intelligent fashion, penetrating to the core of any given circumstance with his piercing knowledge of the human mind. This sometimes left the individual in a state of mental disarray until they could collect their thoughts and piece together the complete picture that Dalos had made apparent to them. Inevitably, such individuals recognized the truth of his words and appreciated his clear insight.

There were those, however, who could not accept this deflation of their personal egos and they were incapable of incepting the lesson that was being delineated for them by this more advanced Intelligence. They were the losers in this particular set of circumstances, for they were then unable to receive any additional help from this One, as their minds would become blocked and closed by their reactionary states. This was a common occurrence among earth-world peoples, and it was quite familiar to Dalos and his entourage. Many times in their visits to Pleiadean planets they had seen this situation occur among lesser-developed minds. They learned, then, that man is not always wise in the desire to refresh and refurbish his mind. This was a lesson that they had so long ago mastered within themselves that they had nearly forgotten how easy it is to succumb to certain emotional reactions, fears, resentments, and angers.

They expected that the Orion peoples would be no different. They assumed that these individuals would have their share of emotional reactions to the truth that Dalos and his Brothers of Light would be bringing to the forefront of their consciousness.

They had no idea how extreme these reactions could be in one who has deteriorated his mind into an animalistic state of fierce competition for survival and superiority.

Such a mind is incapable of deciphering anything that might be beyond its limited capacity. Such a mind fears all new experiences as a threat to its existence. Such was the mind of Tyrantus and such were the minds of his many followers.

Tyrantus was already immersed in a fear for his life that even he himself did not detect. This appearance of a starship from an unknown planet had completely disrupted his routine. Yet he could not tear himself away from this matter, even in his moments of private thought. He was obsessed with the desire to get to the bottom of this situation and to resolve it quickly and effectively. Something about this particular starship commander threw his thoughts out of their normal, so-called, equilibrium and he did not like this individual, although they had not yet met face-to-face.

As the surveillance of Dalos' ship was completed, the starship was given clearance to land in a designated area not far from Tyrantus' headquarters. The Pleiadeans complied with all instructions, to the letter. They did not wish to cause any further annoyance to their hosts; they knew that they were treading on dangerous ground to begin with and they did not need to stir the hornets' nest.

As Dalos emerged from the starship, he was greeted by a sight that stunned his eyes. Gathered below were hundreds of thousands of steely faces. At first he thought the people were all wearing masks of some sort; then he realized that this mask was the encasement of a physical anatomy that bears no life within. Indeed, it is the spiritual Essence of a human being that enlivens the physical anatomy with a dancing oscillation of intelligence, light, and animation—but he could detect nothing of these qualities among this sea of plastic-metallic faces that gazed upon the Pleiadean starship as if it had suddenly sprouted from beneath the soil of their planet!

These faces were hungry, Dalos decided. Hungry for life itself!

Yet they are totally ignorant of this strange feeling that must certainly be coursing through their beings at this spectacle they now see before them! How to begin? How to reach and touch these souls without causing harm, or overburdening their robotized minds with too much, too soon?

"Greetings, citizens of Tyron!" Dalos began.

Immediately a piercing sound broke through the deadened atmosphere. A large commotion drew Dalos' attention to his left, where Tyrantus approached.

He was not alone, of course. He was surrounded by a V-shaped formation of fierce-looking armed guards in stiff metallic uniforms. They broke a passage through the gathered Tyronites, with no concern as to whether anyone might have been hurt by their abrupt movements.

Behind this arrowhead wedge of brutal bodyguards strode a

dark-cloaked man whose face was cold and angry. He was moving toward the base of the ramp extending from Dalos' ship to the floor of the planet.

Dalos descended further down this ramp, his crew assembled quietly behind him. He raised his hand in a salute of peaceful respect.

"To you, Tyrantus, we extend our greetings," Dalos said in a calm but strong voice.

Tyrantus gave a sharp wave of his hand and his bodyguards parted, forming a tight half-circle behind their Emperor and keeping a clear distance between him and the assembled crowd.

There was no threat from this crowd, however. These people had lost all willpower and were merely standing with their arms at their sides, gazing in confusion at the sight before them. They could not have moved if they had wished to do so, but they would not dream of raising an aggressive hand toward their Emperor! They would not bite the hand that fed them! Neither did they show any outward signs of obeisance or demonstrations of love or respect.

Tyrantus did not seem to take notice of this lack of demonstrative affection on the part of his supposed subjects. If he had desired, the slightest command on his part would have sent them to the ground in a form of worshipful adulation but no such command had been given. Therefore, the people did not move. They would not move unless commanded to do so. They had been allowed to emerge into this public area from their work stations as a demonstration of strength and false respect for these visitors.

Tyrantus felt it wise to begin with some show of the sheer numbers that gave his empire its power. These people would shortly be dismissed and redirected to their places of work, for the Orion machinery could not continue without each of its many billions of "parts," that is, the human workers who kept this empire functioning.

Dalos and his crew took in these facets of life on Tyron with a clear perception that went beyond the sights presented to their physical eyes. They understood all the nuances of Tyrantus' acts. He had no secrets from them, particularly from Dalos.

Tyrantus made no reply to Dalos' greeting and merely stood staring at his new adversary—for in Tyrantus' mind there was no such thing as friend, only foe, an unknown force to be defeated and forced into submission. He looked upon the face of Dalos with a startled realization that this man—for he did appear as such—was not at all concerned or apprehensive about the situation into which he had placed himself! He was a foreigner in a strange land, yet he showed no indication of fear or doubt. Tyrantus was puzzled by this but he could not allow himself to be concerned with these thoughts for right now. He must attend to the matter at hand.

"I am known as Dalos to my crew," Dalos continued. "Please feel comfortable to address me as such."

"I shall address you in my quarters," Tyrantus barked. "You have disrupted our routine here and we must dispatch with our business in all due haste! My guards shall accompany you all to an appropriate sector for our formal reception."

With that, Tyrantus turned on his heel and strode off toward a waiting transport vehicle.

Dalos was disconcerned with his rudeness. He smiled to himself with the realization that Tyrantus had only appeared to greet them personally due to his overwhelming curiosity to see these "intruders" first hand, before anyone else had done so. Yet in his insecurity he brought with him, not only his dozen bodyguards, but a large portion of his adherents!

These poor souls were waved away by several mean-looking individuals and they turned, slowly disappearing into surrounding buildings, all of which were identical in their gray-faced exteriors which had no windows and very few doors. Another group of guards advanced to surround the Pleiadeans as they disembarked from the ship, directing them down another ramp into a subterranean space where a shuttle vehicle awaited their departure.

Tyrantus, of course, had taken his own route to the preplanned meeting area. He made his grand entrance once the Pleiadeans had been settled into a circular room that was designed as a council chamber. Twelve individuals were already seated upon a curved platform behind a panel containing a boggling array of electronic gadgetry. They were very different from those Orion citizens who had been dragged out to greet this foreign starship.

These twelve individuals still had life in their faces, albeit a life that was defiant and visceral in its expression. They appeared capable of ripping the throat of their enemies with their very teeth.

A slight shudder passed through one of Dalos' crew members, whose response drew the immediate attention of her fellow star travelers. She took a deep breath quickly, realizing that she must not allow herself to react in this manner to her new hosts! She had for a moment forgotten herself and allowed her mind to sink to a lower-frequency level, whereby she was affected by the sight of these mad dogs, as they appeared to her.

Dalos, who was standing near, placed a firm hand on the arm of this young woman. Immediately she felt a radiating warmth pass through her and the tremor of fear left her completely. She looked into Dalos' eyes and found there vast pools of Intelligence that reassured and dispelled any qualms that had arisen in her consciousness. She accepted the deflationary realization of her mental slippage instantly; no words were needed. There was an exchange of thought between Dalos and this one that rejoined them in consciousness, and that consciousness was immense, indeed!

At that moment Tyrantus burst through a rear entrance, still surrounded by his noisy bodyguards whose armor-like suits made a harsh scratching noise with each movement. They fanned out to stand at attention behind this Council of Twelve while Tyrantus took his position at the center peak of this angled and curved arrangement of seats. To his left and his right spanned a descending half-turn of his closest associates—although they were not close in any sense of mutual appreciation. They were bound by their need for one another, but they would as soon tear the life from each other as from a platter of meat placed before them.

Dalos stepped forward but he did not speak. This time he awaited Tyrantus' first words.

"So," the dark-haired leader spat, "you have something you wish to give to us?"

Dalos returned Tyrantus' gaze as long as possible but Tyrantus quickly looked away. A tense moment of silence hung in the room. All the council members' eyes were upon Dalos but he paid them no heed. It was to Tyrantus that he directed his response.

"We have come in peace and brotherhood to your world. We wish you no harm. Indeed, have we not placed our lives in your care?"

Tyrantus shot a glance at Dalos. *He is not stupid, then. Of course not!* Tyrantus thought. *But why have these strange people ventured into the heart of my empire? Do they have some concealed plan to destroy me? He felt the blood rising in his cheeks.*

"Speak plainly! State your business with us for we have no time for your foolish games and pretty words! We demand to know your intentions and yes, your lives *are* in our hands, so do not attempt any trickery or deception!"

Dalos noticed that a few of the council members' faces twitched at this outburst from their commander. They clearly feared him. He wondered what hold Tyrantus had over these poor lost souls who were tearing the fabric of interdimensional life to shreds as they carried out his orders.

"We have spoken plainly, Emperor, although we understand your need to protect the lives of your subjects and we understand that there are many trillions who fall under your direct control."

"That is true," Tyrantus barked, "and so you see the power we wield! You would be wise to take heed of this fact!"

"We do respect your defensive and offensive capabilities, sir. We also know that we have much to give you, many insights into your own minds which will perhaps provide you with a new way of life!"

These were bold words for Dalos to speak to one who believed that he had mastered the physical life. Tyrantus stuttered in anger for a moment, while a sharp gasp rose from a few of the council members. No one dared question his great mastery of life like this! Particularly no solitary representative of some distant planet who was only surrounded by the unarmed members of his crew, and they did not appear to have any physical strength whatsoever!

In fact, this assemblage seemed quite pitiful in the council members' opinions, as they bore no arms and bore no means of protecting themselves. They were quite effeminate in their appearance, even the male members of this starship crew. How dare such a one address their Emperor in this fashion! One member of the council rose to his feet in anger.

"What gives you the right to speak so in our presence?" he shouted.

"Hear, hear!"

"True!"

"Well said," the others concurred, raising their fists or pounding the panels before them.

"Do you not realize where you are and to whom you are speaking?" the council member continued.

Dalos paid him no mind.

"Emperor Tyrantus," he said, "we repeat that we have no desire to interfere in your life, merely to offer you the option to peruse that which we have to share. This can be done at your convenience, in the manner in which you choose, if you will only allow us to elaborate."

"Sit down," Tyrantus commanded his aide. "I will handle this myself!"

The man immediately sank into his seat, somewhat humiliated by the reprimand, but he would *not* show his emotion.

"I have decided," Tyrantus announced, "to speak with this individual privately."

The others were shocked.

"Do not question my authority!" he boomed. "I dismiss you all—and to you, Dalos, if that is what you are called, I command that you remain while your aides are removed to a suitable waiting area. I promise you that they shall be made comfortable."

"This is agreeable to me, Emperor."

Dalos was pleased with this turn of events. Now he would be able to speak directly to Tyrantus without the Emperor's need for performing or maintaining any façade for the benefit of those who fell under his command. It would be one on one, man to man—spiritual teacher to fallen student! He wondered, how faint were those memories in Tyrantus' mind?

Dalos knew that if he could present to this one a picture of his former self, the mind of this man now known as Tyrantus would explode in grief. Such could not be done. This was a very delicate operation of surgical repair that Dalos had undertaken, but he knew that progress was already underway. He had not expected Tyrantus to so quickly agree to this private meeting, which had been Dalos' wish from the beginning!

"Dear brothers and sisters," Dalos addressed his crew, "I shall return to you shortly."

With that the Pleiadeans were directed out of the council chambers and the council members rose begrudgingly, saluting their master and departing through separate doorways, each of which led to a private area in which they all maintained a complete staff of servants and aides. They also kept their private vehicles in these secluded areas so that they might leave and return undetected, to carry out their many nefarious deeds.

Of course, Tyrantus kept a close watch on their every move; there were no secrets from Tyrantus in his empire. But he wished to have the opportunity to probe the mind of this one who called himself Dalos without the prying eyes of these too-ambitious council leaders. Tyrantus trusted them less than they trusted him, but he held the upper hand. He was always one step ahead. This situation was no different. He would discover for himself the true motives of these foreign star travelers, and he would maintain his superior positioning among these council members—any one of whom would gladly have removed and replaced Tyrantus long ago if they felt this could be accomplished, and many had tried.

Countless were the assassination attempts and coups that Tyrantus had squashed beneath his iron fist, and he doubted not that there would be many more such attempts on his life. But these twelve were idiots in his mind. They were crude and unschooled in the ways of political expediency. They operated by brute force, and Tyrantus knew the workings of their minds as well as he knew his own!

From Dalos' perspective, Tyrantus knew not his mind at all! But it would take time to reveal this important fact to this demonic one. He had become the driving force of evil for more planets populated by more individuals than Dalos cared to recall at this moment. Dalos' entire Consciousness was directed into the present moment. He did not make a single move without the guiding directives of the Cosmic Intelligence through which flowed the energy force of the very Fountainhead of life.

This Power was true power—the Power of Love!

Tyrantus had finally met his match.

6

The Confrontation

My life is in your hands," Dalos repeated to Tyrantus. "How can you doubt that I have no ulterior motives here? We are a brotherhood of beings whose purpose is to serve mankind. We do not choose to interfere or intercede in the lives of others, but we do offer our knowledge if it can be of benefit and is desired by other-planetary dwellers whom we encounter on our travels throughout the cosmos.

"We have come to your world because we believe that we have information that will help you to live your lives in a more fruitful manner."

Dalos chose his words carefully when addressing Tyrantus, knowing that the slightest additional irritation to this man, who had already been pushed to his limit of tolerance—which was very small indeed—would result in a ferocious explosion on his part. Dalos knew that should this occur, no further progress would be made. All barriers would be thrown up to block Dalos' efforts and none of the teachings he sought to bring to these Orion citizens would ever reach their ears. No, he must bide his time, choose his words wisely, and be patient.

Tyrantus was pacing back and forth in the now-vacant council chamber. Dalos had been offered an empty seat in the middle of the room. The guards who had accompanied Tyrantus were now reduced to a single individual posted just outside the doorway. They were, to all intents and purposes, alone in this control room—for that was the reality of its purpose. From here, the Orion Council managed the affairs of all planets in the Empire, and in this room they fought among themselves for superiority, when not joining their minds in some devious design to overtake more populated worlds throughout the galaxy.

This was Tyrantus' lair. Here he ruled supreme over these battling functionaries. Certainly they controlled large portions of the Orion Empire. Each one had a responsibility for a particular facet of life in Orion, whether that be transportation, education, communication, or military operations, but it was Tyrantus who kept them strictly within the bounds of his own decisions. He gave them just enough power to keep them contented and to reduce their attempts to overthrow his rule. No one knew all that Tyrantus knew; he was the only individual who had access to all information regarding the daily operations of this gigantic, seething mass of robotized humanity. He kept it that way deliberately, and there were fierce battles fought among the Orion leaders to gain access to much of this information. However, thus far, Tyrantus had succeeded in keeping them in the dark as to the full operations of the Empire.

That is why he realized that he must speak with Dalos privately. Perhaps this individual did bear some valuable information—would he be so foolish as to allow his natural enemies, his supposed supporters and council aides, to get their hands on this?

No, he would not! But this Dalos individual was causing him much unrest within his thoughts. He seemed to be speaking in circles, Tyrantus thought. *Why does he not come directly to the point? What does he want from us in return for his offerings?*

"No, Tyrantus, there is nothing that you can provide for us, although I realize that is difficult for you to believe," Dalos responded as Tyrantus shot him a startled glance. Dalos could see that Tyrantus was not accustomed to having conversations with one whose mind was as quickened as his own, and as capable of discerning his thoughts as Tyrantus was of monitoring his opponents'! Dalos, of course, used no electronic gadgetry to attune to Tyrantus' consciousness. He didn't need such third-dimensional assistance. Dalos' mind—the Mind of Uriel—was all-wise and all-seeing in a dimension such as this. He knew the underpinnings of Tyrantus' thoughts far more thoroughly than Tyrantus himself knew them!

"Why do I find it so difficult to accept that statement, Dalos?" Tyrantus uttered. "You realize that there is nothing given for nothing. You have traveled a great distance to reach our world, from your description of your home planet. One does not cross the galaxy without some sense of his own reward!"

"That is how we differ from you, perhaps," Dalos ventured. "We do cross the galaxy routinely to reach distant worlds that can use our assistance and who have asked for this help."

"We have not asked for your visit to our world," Tyrantus blurted, "so why have you come?"

"As I said," Dalos repeated patiently, "we have been called here by the cry of your people as a whole. You may not realize that they have made this cry, for it is their very existence that cries out to us to help them live fuller lives, more complete and certainly more contented!"

"How dare you insult my people thusly!" Tyrantus boomed. He stopped a few inches from Dalos, who did not move a muscle. "Our people are quite contented with their lives! They have the riches of the Orion Empire to enjoy, and they are very fortunate, indeed, that we rescued them from their sad little lives that they were living in some primitive state on dusty planets scattered around this constellation!

"You do not know what you are saying. Perhaps *we* should show *you* something before you leave—perhaps *that* is what you need from us! I will show you how happily an individual can live in our world. I have discovered the secret of this happiness and I have freed these people from all burdens of want or need! They have everything they could possibly desire, and they are rewarded plentifully for their dutiful loyalty to our cause! Any individual living anywhere in this universe would be proud to become a part of this Empire!

"I do not understand your way, sir, to insult your very host and to claim your superiority when you are stupid enough to present yourself in an unarmed fashion in our very midst and make these preposterous claims. You are fools! What could you possibly, possibly have to show us that we do not already know? I am tempted to destroy the lot of you! You have caused me enough bother!"

Dalos sat calmly through this tirade. He had expected it. When it seemed as if Tyrantus was running out of words to fling across the room—for he had stomped to a corner of the seating platform—Dalos quietly interjected. "We are different, that is apparent. But perhaps you would like to view some of the devices which we have on our starship, which will explain much more clearly our purpose in coming to you. If you desire, we can proceed to the ship and I will arrange a demonstration for you of a particular instrument which I think you will find most interesting!"

Tyrantus did not like losing control, as he just had. He knew it was a sign of weakness and this Dalos had not shown any such weakness! He was relieved that his opponent had not taken some undue advantage of his weakened state of mind.

Tyrantus composed his thoughts and briefly considered Dalos' offer.

"I *shall* do so," he finally said. "Yes, you must prove to me that you come in peace. Show me your gadgetry—but do not attempt any deception with me, for I cannot be deceived!"

"Of course not," Dalos agreed. "Shall we proceed?" He rose from his seat.

For a moment Tyrantus was struck with a sudden feeling that he could not define as he glanced at this tall, handsome individual. Immediately he shook off this discomfort, turned, and barked an order at his waiting guard. "Ready our transport," he said. "We are leaving now." The guard hurried off to comply as Tyrantus gestured to Dalos. "You will travel in my personal vehicle."

Dalos nodded and followed Tyrantus from the room.

Of course, Tyrantus had no intention of venturing onto this stranger's ship unaccompanied. He reminded Dalos as they made their way to the waiting shuttle that he held Dalos' crew under his close guard. But this was not sufficient precaution for Tyrantus, who himself would have quickly sacrificed a crew ten times that in number if it would mean the achievement of some goal that he had set for himself, such as overtaking the leader of an entire empire of worlds! No, Tyrantus ordered his bodyguards to stay at alert and they followed the two leaders to the starship.

As Dalos commanded the opening of the ship to their entrance, Tyrantus gestured for his guards to follow.

Dalos turned to face the Emperor. "I do not believe you would wish them to share in our total conversation, do you?" Dalos said in a level tone. He knew that Tyrantus was greedy for information that would help him to maintain his superiority over these poor individuals.

Tyrantus did not say a word. He turned and, with an abrupt gesture, directed his guards to maintain their position outside the starship.

"You need not fear, Tyrantus. I would *not* leave my crew stranded on your world."

Tyrantus looked for an instant into the eyes of this astonishing man. In that millisecond, he was struck by the full force of the Infinite Intelligence that beamed forth from Dalos' eyes. The Emperor could not speak for a moment. Again, a strange feeling passed through his being, this time causing him to shudder from head to toe. Quickly he threw off his concern and answered Dalos, "Yes, I believe you would not."

Together they made their way to the central, open area of Dalos' starship. Tyrantus was immediately impressed; however, he gave no indication of his true feelings. He had never seen a ship of such design and he was quite taken by the warm radiance that seemed to bathe the interior of this starship in a glow of sunlight—however, there was no window through which some physical sun streamed.

"You perhaps feel some difference, Tyrantus, as you entered our ship?" Dalos said. "This is due to the nature of our propulsion system. We do not use fossil fuels; we travel by our mind projections."

"Surely you do not believe that I will take this idiotic remark seriously! What kind of fool do you take me for?" Tyrantus boomed. "If this were possible, we would have mastered it long ago! Everyone knows that the human mind is only capable of a limited set of functions. It requires a vast array of computerized circuits to enhance its abilities. Granted, once it has been linked to such a computer the human mind does then take on new capabilities. But I do not believe that your minds have flown this ship from one side of the galaxy to the other—no more than my decision to walk across the room propels my feet!"

"That is exactly how we travel," Dalos replied. "It is our decision to journey to a particular destination and with our knowledge of interdimensional physics, we are able to position ourselves to take advantage of certain electromagnetic lines of force which criss-cross the universe, as you no doubt know," he continued. "We steer our ship by our directive thought. We need no mechanical device to intercede between our thoughts and our actual motion."

Tyrantus was beginning to think that these people were not fully possessed of their minds. It sounded like a badly written story to him. But he decided to keep these thoughts to himself. He would humor this individual to see what further information he might glean from this Dalos' willingness to talk.

For three hours Dalos spoke to Tyrantus, while those awaiting Tyrantus' return speculated as to the nature of this conversation. They had no way to know how far this exchange of words had gone.

First, Dalos explained to Tyrantus that he, Dalos, had incarnated in his physical anatomy for a particular purpose: to travel through the galaxy and to contact those civilizations which, as he had described previously, needed the assistance of a Mind more intelligent to help them along their way.

This Tyrantus heartily agreed with! In fact, as he pointed out to Dalos, he himself had done this very thing, and he was glad that Dalos appreciated the need for a superior mind to direct the lives of its inferiors.

Dalos rejoined this response with the information that his way of aiding others of a lesser development was considerably different. Dalos and his entourage did not ever attempt to take over any particular planet, and did not wield weapons of force. They merely presented themselves and their knowledge and offered to share it with these other worlds.

"But what do you gain in return?" Tyrantus wanted to know.

"We gain the satisfaction of knowing that we have served our fellow man," Dalos replied. "This is payment enough for any soul."

At one point, Dalos noticed that Tyrantus was sinking lower and lower in the soft blue reclining seat. His eyes were beginning to droop and Dalos knew that he was being infused with the higher frequencies of the surrounding ship. This step-up in consciousness had such an effect upon many individuals. Their desire—and very often they did so—was to leave their conscious minds behind and drift off to sleep. While their physical bodies slept, they were then free to attune to higher-frequency dimensions, and much teaching and learning went on in such states of consciousness.

Dalos paused in his discussion, hoping that Tyrantus would indeed drift off into such a productive sleep. But as soon as his voice ceased, Tyrantus' eyes jerked open and he roused himself from his semi-transcended state.

"You promised to show me some equipment," he reminded Dalos. "That is why we came to your ship. I've heard enough words for now—I want to see a demonstration of these things you are describing to me!"

Tyrantus' tone had changed considerably. He was now much softer in his demeanor and seemed genuinely interested to learn that which Dalos had to teach. This was a good sign. Dalos was very pleased. He immediately stood and gestured toward a sliding door. "Let us go, then, to our on-board laboratory."

Tyrantus rose and followed Dalos to the next room. There he saw a baffling array of devices that were quite unfamiliar to him. Dalos drew him to a particular apparatus that was composed of several screens and a bank of dials. He directed Tyrantus to place the palm of his hand on a particular sensing area.

Tyrantus hesitated for a moment. He had forgotten his earlier fears about following this stranger to his starship without any protection against his possible kidnapping. He stole a sideways glance at this starship commander. No, Tyrantus did not believe him capable now of any underhanded activity. He could not explain his feeling of comfort in the presence of this man, but for some odd reason he trusted him. Still, it would not hurt to ask—

"What is this device? And what will it do to me?" Tyrantus wanted to know.

Dalos smiled. "You need not fear it. It cannot do you any harm. Indeed, it is one of the most helpful apparatuses that has been brought into existence on the planet Axiahn. You shall see." Dalos' eyes twinkled.

Reassured somewhat, Tyrantus reached a hand hesitatingly toward the panel. At the last moment it occurred to him that he should have drafted one of his guards to be the subject of this demonstration, but his momentum had already been set and his curiosity overpowered him. He settled his palm into what turned out to be a surprisingly warm and pliable substance.

"What is this element that appears hard, yet feels so soft to the touch?" Tyrantus asked.

"It is a crystalline substance," Dalos replied. "It oscillates at a slightly higher frequency than you are accustomed to, and it does adapt to the formation of your own physical anatomy. It is now interacting with the atomic structure of your physical cells."

Tyrantus was alarmed. He was not accustomed to being a guinea pig and he would have withdrawn his hand immediately if it had not been for his rigid self-discipline, which did not allow him to show any sort of fear when in the presence of a potential enemy—and Dalos was still that, to him. So Tyrantus had no choice but to leave his hand in position on this strange machine.

The screens of the device suddenly came to life as Dalos flipped a switch and adjusted three or four dials. On the top screen, Tyrantus saw numerous wave forms of energy oscillation. This was no different than the common oscilloscope. In the small screen at the bottom of the device, he noticed a pattern of oscillating colors that were something like cloud formations, constantly changing, intermingling, appearing and disappearing. The colors were quite distinctive, with several areas of dark brown bleeding across the brighter reds and oranges.

But it was the image on the large center screen that caused Tyrantus to jerk his hand away.

"What are you trying to do?" he shouted. "What is the meaning of this?"

Dalos turned to face Tyrantus. "We call this the psychic anatomy viewer," he explained calmly. "It gives us a complete read-out of the psychic structures of any individual so that they can detect the cause for any present problem they may be having, whether it's physical, mental, or some other fluctuation in their daily lives."

"Where did you get that videochip?" Tyrantus wanted to know. "How have you tricked me into this? What spies have been feeding you information?! I demand to know immediately!"

Tyrantus' guards, alerted by the sound of his shouting, stormed aboard the ship. Dalos raised his hands in a motion to calm their aggression.

"Peace, Emperor," he said. "I mean no disrespect! You need not call your guards upon me—I am but one man here and I have no aggressive weapons. You have merely viewed a scene from your own past-life history. You are of course aware that the individual lives many consecutive lifetimes, are you not?"

"Certainly," Tyrantus said. "We have already discussed this matter. But what difference does that make? You have stolen information from my archives and I demand to know how you came to have access to this information!"

"You misunderstand, Emperor, with all due respect. This image that you have seen is not a recorded replay. It is the actual recreation of those energy wave forms residing within your own consciousness."

This was gobbledygook to Tyrantus. He could not make sense of these words, he was so thrown into confusion by the image that had suddenly appeared on the screen. It was a total shock to his conscious mind. He was unable to think clearly, and knew only that this man who called himself Dalos had witnessed a very private and incriminating scene from Tyrantus' earlier life. He must get to the bottom of this, once and for all!

"Seize him!" Tyrantus ordered, and the guards immediately took Dalos by each arm. "Place him in maximum security until further orders," Tyrantus commanded.

"I am now in possession of your ship, yourself, and your crew, and I shall have the answers I seek!"

Dalos did not say a word. He knew that any further resistance on his part would only bring a greater force from this demonic mind, which had now recoiled upon itself when confronted with a certain truth.

The scene that had illuminated the screen of the psychic anatomy viewer was one of battle. Tyrantus was piloting a starship. His face was twisted in a terrible grimace. Behind him burned the reflections of a great inferno just beyond his ship. The scene had shifted to show the immense explosion that ripped apart an entire planet. Huge flames, many thousands of miles in length, seared through the atmosphere as atomic debris burst in all directions. Again, Tyrantus' face appeared on the screen. It had suddenly lost all its color. In a final, lingering image, tears began to stream from his eyes.

It was at that moment that Tyrantus blew up and jerked his hand from the psychic viewer. Immediately, all screens went dark.

No one but Dalos and Tyrantus knew this secret. Tyrantus was determined to insure that Dalos had no contact with anyone so that he could not relay any information to them about this terrible event. Tyrantus had never, *never* shown any weakness! One small leak of information like this would easily destroy him and his empire!

7

Psychic Shock

As Dalos was led down an endless white corridor, his thoughts were with his crew. He knew that they were unaware of his imprisonment and his concern was to, some way, let them know of the developments that had taken place during his meeting with Tyrantus. It was, in Dalos' mind, an unmitigated success. He had reached that portion of Tyrantus' consciousness which was not yet totally diminished in its capacity to receive a higher-frequency input.

That spark of Intelligence that still remained within the mind of this fallen one was Dalos' only hope for the rescue of the countless souls who had fallen under the influence of this single individual. He must re-ignite this spark into that larger Flame which had once encompassed the mind of this former Advanced Being.

Dalos cared not for his own fate. His mind was thoroughly involved in the work at hand; that is, the helping of many other souls, and those souls included the members of his own entourage, for they too were his students and his responsibility.

They had been taken to a room not too far from the council chambers. It was a large enough room so that they were not cramped; their discomfort came mostly from their inability to know that which was taking place with their starship commander. As they attempted to rest or to keep their minds occupied in a constructive fashion, the Orion guards kept a watchful eye upon these strangers.

The Pleiadeans made no attempt to communicate with these Orion citizens. Instead they maintained their own mental oscillation with one another. This they did quite purposefully, in order to maintain a higher-frequency state of awareness. There would come the appropriate time when they would involve themselves with the citizenry of this planet and this would be done in a carefully prescribed manner, in the appropriate way.

For now, however, their immediate need was to maintain the unity of their joint consciousness and to keep their positive charge in order to be of assistance to Dalos, who was, at that time, carrying the forward thrust of their mission to this planet. Their efforts would always be joined in this carefully planned and orchestrated fashion. No one individual would allow his or her mind to stray from this focus of purpose. If one was designated to carry out a particular function, then all added their minds to that individual in a positive, conscious awareness of his actions and needs. Thus they helped to supply the energy force for that individual's accomplishment. They would not push nor pull against one another by diverting their minds to some other activity at the inappropriate time.

So their conversation was kept to a minimum and largely concerned the activities of Dalos. To the best of their ability, they maintained their attunement to the Higher Mind of this One, that is, the Consciousness of Uriel, and to the entire Brotherhood of Beings who were supplying them with the energy force for the mission that they were now representing.

This was a great responsibility that each one carried. They were the banner carriers for this healing plan for countless trillions of souls, and they were only two hundred in number. Therefore, each one's individual responsibility was that much greater. Deep within their hearts, they knew the seriousness of their purpose. They had been preparing themselves for such tasks as this throughout countless millions of lifetimes. They had developed their minds to be capable of receiving and transmitting the Higher Intelligence that they carried into this lower-dimensional world. Theirs was a development similar to that of Tyrantus and his twelve council members—that is, before those individuals relinquished their positions as Light Bearers.

That is why, perhaps, the crew member who shuddered at the sight of the Orion Council felt such a deep shaking within her very psychic structures. She knew, consciously, that she was looking at the reversal of a mind such as her own. She was viewing the negative effects of the fall of one who has achieved a greater development of his intelligence and has made of himself a propagator of life. Yes, that was the function of these individuals as they joined with an infinite number of similarly developed Minds: they served as the Source of life sustenance for countless lower-dimensional worlds and creations of Infinity.

Although they had spent much time preparing themselves for the sights they would see on this regressive world, still the actual, physical reality of these individuals was quite overpowering to the senses of the Pleiadeans!

After several hours of waiting with no news from their commander, the Pleiadean crew was informed that they were being directed to a new location. They were given no news of Dalos, but a tremor of concern passed through the group. They knew that all was not well.

They were led to another, adjoining building, down a series of long hallways and into a barracks-like building. Each one was assigned his or her own quarters. This was a huge complex of living quarters for visiting dignitaries and others who came to do business with the leadership of the Orion Empire. They were not jail cells, but these living spaces were under very detailed surveillance and all activities within these quarters were monitored throughout the day and night.

The Pleiadeans suspected that they did not truly have any privacy as long as they were on this world of ultimate control. They graciously accepted this hospitality. Although they made inquiries of those who had directed them to these quarters, no one could or would provide information as to the whereabouts of their leader. They agreed among themselves to carry on in the most positive manner and to keep to themselves for the time being, until they finally learned how Dalos' encounter with Tyrantus had concluded—if it had concluded at all! It was quite possible, they realized, that these conversations were still ongoing, and this would be a most positive development, if it were the case.

Dalos, meanwhile, had been taken to a specially designed room. It too was not a prison cell—in appearance, anyway. It was outfitted with the physical comforts provided by Orion technology. He was not subjected to any form of physical abuse, other than the rough handling of Tyrantus' guards, but he was not free to leave these special quarters. He was not allowed communication with his crew.

This, to Dalos, meant that his hands were tied for the time being. His entire function and purpose was to communicate, and without this opportunity, he could find no comfort in these supposedly highly-valued accoutrements of Orion technology. As he reclined in one of the seating arrangements in this closed room, Dalos opened his consciousness more fully to the Minds of his polarities, who never truly left his consciousness.

Dear Ones, I know that you are with me, and that your Wisdom shall guide my actions. I do feel that we have had some success with our contact, do you not agree?

Yes, Beloved One, we hear your call and we do see that this one known as Tyrantus has been touched most deeply by your words and, most importantly, your projections of Consciousness. He is at this moment in a state of great inner turmoil. You have stirred the embers!

That was our purpose—and I am very glad to know that I have been successful in this, although I am presently held captive and unable to carry on.

Do not be alarmed, came the inner reply from Michiel. *This is a temporary circumstance. Tyrantus will soon enough desire your presence. He cannot let go of the tail of this tiger which has pounced upon him! He will not be satisfied until he knows what it is that is now tormenting his mind. You have made him aware of layers of his own consciousness which he had deeply buried and suppressed. You have touched the feeling nature of this individual which he believed himself to have torn from him many hundreds of years ago.*

This could not have been accomplished if it were not for your great Love and endurance, your willingness to confront him on his own territory. We here are applauding you and are always, of course, adding our own Love to further your ability to carry on.

These words are precious to me, Dalos replied in his mental oscillation. *They are the only comfort I require! And so I shall find patience to await the return of our Brother—who shall soon learn the reality of that truth. We must never let him forget that he has been our Brother of Light! This knowledge cannot be allowed to die. It is his only hope, and the only hope of all those souls whom he has blinded to the truth of this Light that exists within them, as well.*

We shall not fail! Michiel responded. *We cannot fail.*

So be it, Dalos agreed. He closed his eyes and lay his head upon a soft cushion, drifting off to sleep.

Many hours passed before a loud crashing startled Dalos awake. The door to his chamber burst open and three guards strode abruptly into the room. Tyrantus appeared behind them.

"So," he said. "You have had plenty of time to think. Are you now ready to cooperate?"

Dalos righted himself and gazed directly and serenely into the eyes of Tyrantus, who could not return his gaze. Immediately, Tyrantus turned away, walking to the opposite side of the room in a great show of flashy command.

"Have you finally lost your ability to speak? You seem to be quite fond of words," Tyrantus spat out.

Dalos could see that he was greatly disturbed and was snarling like the cornered beast. "I am always at your service, Emperor, to respond to any questions you may desire to ask. I would request, however, that before we carry on with our interview, you allow me to inform my crew that I am well."

Tyrantus whirled around to face Dalos. "This cannot be! You will answer my questions first!"

"Very well. Shall we speak here?" Dalos inquired.

"Do not speak to me in an insolent tone! Bring him to my quarters," Tyrantus ordered, and strode back out the door. The guards immediately grabbed Dalos' arms and led him out the door.

"You need not treat me in this fashion," Dalos said to them quietly. "I am perfectly willing to follow."

They glared at him as if they did not understand the language he spoke. Truly, they knew nothing other than their aggressive ways. They had been "trained" by Orion electronic implants to serve—to the death, if need be—with no human feeling nor concerns for their *own* welfare. They could not comprehend Dalos' words, nor could they receive the radiating Force of his Higher Intelligence, which was penetrating the atmosphere of the planet itself as long as Dalos remained upon its surface.

Hundreds of thousands of individuals living upon this planet were similarly blocked from comprehending or receiving this Higher Intelligence. That, for the present, was not Dalos' concern. He knew that this situation, dismal as it might be, could not be remedied until he had broken through the armor of Tyrantus himself. First this so-called leader must be reached; then his many followers could be freed from his control. One by one, Dalos—Uriel—would reach them.

Tyrantus' quarters were much more than a simple living space. They served as electronic surveillance rooms, from which he could monitor activities on numerous planets in his empire and in all sectors of operations within his massive governmental structure. These quarters included reception areas where he met with the visiting officials who came to seek his favors and promotions, and they included a vast area designed to provide him with any pleasure he so desired.

He chose to meet with Dalos in one of a dozen reception rooms. Each one of these rooms was designed for a different purpose—to set a different tone for whatever meeting took place within its walls. Some were designed to put the visitor at ease. Others were created with the visitor's discomfort in mind. These were the so-called "fruits" of the massive research undertaken into all facets of physical life by this sprawling empire. The psychological effects of various colors, shapes, sounds, scents, and other sensory aspects of life were delved into at great length, and Tyrantus himself was the first to use the results of this research in his manipulation of those with whom he carried on his endless transactions.

He always had the advantage, therefore, in any encounter with one of his many functionaries.

The monitoring systems in these reception rooms were of the most advanced technology known within the Orion Empire. Tyrantus could practically read the thoughts of the individuals who came to his place of business—and the business at hand was the maintenance of Tyrantus' position of supreme power over all people. He cared not how this was achieved, so long as it was insured.

Here, he felt, he would be able to probe the mind of this Dalos. He would never admit it, but he recognized that he had allowed himself to be placed at an extreme disadvantage by meeting with this individual on his own territory. Tyrantus could not understand why he had suffered this lapse of mentality and had agreed to this meeting on Dalos' starship! But he was most displeased at the events that had occurred. He must learn how this one had secured the information that was presented to Tyrantus. This leak in his government must be stopped! He did not care how, and he did not care how many lives he must eliminate before he discovered how Dalos came to have access to this information.

Dalos was led into a room that was green in color, with streaks of orange zigzagging at odd angles throughout. It gave him a nauseous feeling of motion as he entered the room and Dalos immediately recognized the purpose of its design. He merely adjusted his consciousness to focus upon his conversation with Tyrantus; it was not difficult for Dalos to detune himself from his physical senses, as his Mind was of such a nature to have long ago surpassed the need for sensory input in order to experience the lessons inherent in physical lifetimes.

"Now, Dalos, perhaps you will be willing to tell me the truth," Tyrantus was seated behind a console that contained a boggling array of controls.

"I see that you have all your tools at hand, Tyrantus," Dalos replied. "They will not be necessary. I am quite willing to speak truth to you, for that *is* my policy."

"Do not be curt with me!" Tyrantus sneered. "I am quite sick of your attitude. I demand to know your sources!"

"As I explained to you, it was your own energy structure which supplied the image you viewed upon our screen," Dalos said calmly. "There is no trickery involved. It is a principle of science that we fully intend to explain to you. In fact, it is our intention to teach this science to your people, if you allow us to do so. This is the *interdimensional* science of consciousness that we believe you have yet to discover for yourselves, and it is our full desire to share this knowledge with you."

Tyrantus did not know how to respond for a moment. This was not the kind of answer he was accustomed to receiving. No matter how he treated this man, his answers were always the same! At this moment, Tyrantus could not think of another question to put to Dalos. He had difficulty understanding the motivations of this stranger from the Pleiades.

Dalos took advantage of Tyrantus' momentary silence. He knew the effect his words were having upon Tyrantus, even in this atmosphere of self-glorification that this one had created.

"Do you not desire to know more about your own mind?" Dalos proposed.

"And I suppose you are the one to teach me!" Tyrantus finally found his voice. He laughed harshly. "You, who cannot even keep your crew in hand! You have failed, Dalos. You have failed miserably. You no longer have command of your own ship. You have no contact with your crew, and you are here, in my power. *You* are going to teach me about my own mind?" He laughed again. "I believe that you had better look to your own!"

"It is my mind, Tyrantus, that tells me of your deepest fears."

Again, Dalos had pushed boldly into the forbidden regions of conversation with this powerful emperor.

Surprisingly, Tyrantus did not leap at his throat as one would expect. He sat quietly for a moment. Something in the tone of Dalos' voice had affected him. Despite himself, Tyrantus discovered that he had a certain strange interest in this man. He could not call it a "liking," for Tyrantus liked no one, least of all himself. He did not know how to describe these unusual feelings but they fully occupied his thoughts and he could not seem to divert his mind back to his own wishes and desires. Once again, Dalos had gained the upper hand in the conversation.

"What could you possibly know about my supposed fears? You have much to learn about me, Dalos. You underestimate my power. That is a fatal mistake!"

Dalos did not say a word but continued to look directly into the eyes of Tyrantus—that is, when he could gain access to them, for Tyrantus kept his eyes averted as much as possible.

"I believe we should give you some demonstration of our power. Would you like me to show you one of *our* technological advancements?"

Dalos could not refuse, although he feared the worst. He knew what sort of "advancements" were made in this hell-world, but if he was to maintain his communication with Tyrantus, then he must ride the contorting beast through to the end—and he must not allow himself to be influenced by anything which might be presented to his physical consciousness.

"Certainly," Dalos agree. "If that is your desire, then I am at your service."

"Very well, Dalos. We shall now show you what Orion stands for."

With a press of a button, one wall of the room slid to the side, revealing a large screen. Upon this screen appeared the image of a man. His head was encircled by a steel band that was filled with many colored wires. These wires led directly to a huge bank of machinery. The man was positioned in a semi-reclining angle, suspended between additional banks of equipment.

"This individual is undergoing a total rejuvenation of his physical anatomy," Tyrantus explained. "Not only are his cell structures being restored to their youthful state, but his mind is being refreshed. It will now function with the clarity of a young man."

As Dalos watched in horror, six technicians manipulated the controls of this machinery. The man screamed in agony, his face distorted by the electronic amperage which flowed through his physical anatomy. His entire body contorted in what must have been an excruciating experience. Fingers curled and stretched rhythmically with these electronic pulses; knees bent and straightened in succession, and as the power was increased, these contortions increased in their rapidity. The technicians who carried out this torturous treatment were oblivious to the man's screams and contortions.

Dalos reached for a support upon which to brace himself as he felt a wave of nausea pass through. He noticed that Tyrantus was smiling with satisfaction at the scene portrayed on the screen.

"Does he not feel pain?" Dalos inquired.

Tyrantus did not stop smiling as he replied, "Certainly. But that is of no significance. What is important here is our great advancement in this ability to extend the lives of our most valuable workers. Only those specially chosen are given the opportunity for this rejuvenating treatment. They are given this great honor by their achievements for the benefit of our Empire!"

Dalos was sickened by the coldness that he felt emanating from Tyrantus. It caused Dalos great pain to know that his Brother had fallen so far in his consciousness that he had no remaining compassion—he who had been a centrifuge of Love for many, many souls in eons past!

Dalos' knees gave way as he lost consciousness.

8

The Unseen Force

Dalos had over-extended his consciousness toward Tyrantus. So deeply moved had he been by the visible proof of the depths to which this soul had sunk that Dalos' connection to his own sustaining force was momentarily severed, and he lost consciousness. In that flash instant, his body crumpled to the floor of Tyrantus' reception chamber, crashing with a terrible sound that echoed through the metallic hall.

Tyrantus did not move. He merely turned to look upon the fallen figure with a kind of triumphant satisfaction. He had finally gained the upper hand!

His aides, however, rushed into the room at this sound, fearful that some attack had been made upon their leader.

"Halt!" Tyrantus barked. "Do not approach! I will handle this myself."

The guards immediately shrank from the room, positioning themselves nearby to lend their assistance. They were visibly startled to see the form of this stranger from the Pleiades so helpless and vulnerable. They had, despite themselves, been impressed by his overall dignity and fearlessness in the face of the one who caused them all to tremble with a deep, abiding fear for their very lives.

Tyrantus eventually broke his staring stance to stoop by the side of the fallen Dalos, who was still unconscious. It appeared that his head had struck the floor in an unbroken descent. A small trickle of blood was making its way from beneath Dalos' head toward his white-cloaked shoulder.

Tyrantus had no feeling for this man, as he had long ago dampened and most likely extinguished all compassionate feelings that had ever resided within him. He was quite curious, however, to know how this individual would handle this new circumstance when he awakened. Tyrantus was anxious to watch how this one would conduct himself now that he was definitely at a disadvantage—not only in terms of his physical confinement, for Tyrantus did plan to return Dalos to maximum security surveillance, but because he had lost face, in Tyrantus' eyes. He had succumbed to the pressure of an unfamiliar situation and had allowed himself to be defeated by his own physical anatomy!

That, in Tyrantus' book of rules, was strictly forbidden. He himself would never allow any limitation of the physical body to sway him or deter him from his projected goals—and in this case, Tyrantus' goal was to master the mind and body of his new opponent, this being who had arrived in his midst from some distant planet, bearing yet-unknown gifts of technology. Thus far, all that Tyrantus had witnessed had shown him that there was, indeed, something to be gained from these Pleiadeans and he was not about to relinquish his hold upon them until he had wrung the very life from them; that is, every possible means of gaining a new advantage over all his opponents, through some application of whatever technological advancements these Pleiadeans could offer him.

Of course, he would dispose of them in some appropriate fashion when he was finished taking all that he could from them. But this was not Tyrantus' concern at the present moment. For now, he must deliver this fallen warrior unto the hands of his best medical professionals—and now that the thought occurred to him, it would be a particularly advantageous opportunity to do some probing into the physical makeup of this Pleiadean. He did appear to be quite similar in his physical structure to the Orionites; however, this individual had displayed some impressive characteristics of bravery, emotional control, and was somewhat taller and more physically well-balanced than the Orionites.

Yes, Tyrantus thought, *now I do truly have the Pleiadean at my mercy! He is not even conscious to direct his own affairs. We shall take advantage of this development. I know the precise individual to carry out my brilliant plan.*

Tyrantus stood and returned to the control console. He tapped in a lengthy numerical code.

Instantly a voice responded, "Yes, sir."

"Take note. I command the presence of the one Bartolonias immediately in Reception Room 47."

"Yes, sir," came the prompt response.

Within moments a short, stocky man appeared.

"Bartolonias," Tyrantus greeted him, "your services are needed by your Emperor. I trust you shall carry out my orders to their ultimate conclusion?"

"At your command, Emperor," Bartolonias replied, with a slight bow. He was a rough-looking individual, with reddish-gray hair. His eyes were as cold as the gleaming steel that lined the floor of the reception chamber.

"Take this fallen visitor to your laboratory and do whatever is necessary to revive him."

"May I ask, Emperor, what has caused his present state?"

"You may ask nothing! Is it not your job to determine that? As you can see he is obviously unconscious. I am not a medical practitioner! Do not become insolent with me, for you know the power I wield and you know where you will find yourself if you continue this attitude!"

"Certainly, Emperor," Bartolonias quickly interjected. "I only meant to serve you better by using the great fruits of your own intelligent survey of this person's condition. However we do, as you know, have the finest of your technological developments to guide our examination, and I am certain we will be able to carry out the necessary treatment."

"That is not all, Bartolonias. I wish you to perform a complete scan upon this individual. He has come to us from a planet which he calls 'Axiahn,' located within the Pleiadean constellation. These peoples are unfamiliar to our data banks and we would wish to learn all that we can about their physiological and psychological makeup. Do you understand?"

"Yes, Emperor. I shall direct the procedure myself."

"Very good, and I do expect to see your results within a day's time."

Bartolonias was somewhat concerned by the demand for quick results, as he knew that if he should fall short of the Emperor's demands, not only would his position be eliminated, but quite possibly his very life, for one who failed the Emperor was deemed to have failed at life itself. Bartolonias was a shrewd man who had risen up through the ranks of medical research by his calculated efforts to gain the attention of the Emperor. He had masterminded many diabolical techniques by which to subject the Orion peoples to greater and greater technological controls. He had invented a technique by which electronic implants kept certain difficult individuals in line. Their actual brain structures were opened up and "enhanced" by this bit of Orion technology. From then on, they were submissive and obedient, for they were receiving and operating upon signals originating from the Orion computer.

Eventually, Tyrantus' plan was to perform these implants upon all of his subjects. It would become a routine operation, performed in the first two years of an infant's life. He would thereby be assured of an endless power over all!

Yes, the Orionites were aware of the continuity of life; that is, the rebirth of souls into new bodies after their termination. But their concept of this birth and death and rebirth did not allow for any spiritual factors. They believed that these souls merely served a brief transition period before finding their way back into physical anatomies through the process of birth—and in Orion, this process did not necessarily take place through the womb. Babies were often gestated in cold laboratories, where they grew in the artificial wombs developed by Orion research. They were the property of the Empire, and their lives were analyzed and directed from birth by the readouts obtained from their motor-physical testings. They were placed in the appropriate line of work, and it was believed that this is how the continuity of their many lifetimes served the Empire. Nothing was lost, as every individual would return to pick up where he left off, quickly developing skills that had been learned in previous lifetimes.

So it was an eternal damnation that all Orion citizens were truly suffering. They were not allowed to develop any new skills or abilities. They were, indeed, redirected into areas with which they had had a long familiarity and development. In this, the Orion researchers were correct.

However, they were totally oblivious to the fact that these souls should have been, had they been living in a healthy state of consciousness, spending much time between lifetimes, ascending to higher-frequency dimensions wherein they could be instructed and enlightened by the great minds of those Advanced Teachers who serve as the Benevolent Ones for all humanity—great Teachers such as Uriel and the countless Brothers and Sisters of Light who serve in this capacity as Light Bearers. The Orionites were, as previously noted, incapable of this mental growth due to the many impositions of electronic influence upon their physical life experiences. Because the mind itself is an electronic device, it is susceptible to this interference and distortion.

The Orion research laboratories, stretching across endless miles of the surface of planets such as Tyron, had achieved—if that term can be used for such negative developments—the ability to manipulate the minds of the Orion people to a great degree, and strictly for the purpose of serving the egomania and desire for supreme control of a handful of individuals, the Emperor Tyrantus and his Council of Twelve. These now-demonic minds did seem to perpetually reappear in these positions of leadership, lifetime after lifetime.

The Emperor Tyrantus, when he was not incarnated in a physical anatomy, was influencing from his subastral state whatever physical individual fought his bloody way to this position of supreme power—and there were others who held this role during his absence. They were those same individuals who could be found at different times in the seats of power represented by the Orion Council. These individuals interchanged positions from life to life, but always did they rise into these positions of power due to their now-superior mental abilities.

Initially, this mental superiority was the result of the progressive development of consciousness from which they had fallen. But as time went on, that time being the progression of thousands upon thousands of lifetimes, their mental superiority was the result of their having lived such lifetimes in power positions which kept them relatively free of the interference of electronic controls. Their past-life memories directed them immediately into these dominating positions. Yes, of course they were incurring horrendous damage to their psychic anatomies by the acts which they committed upon large masses of people, as the decision-makers and aggressive warriors who took over entire planetary systems. Yet this subtle, damaging influence had not yet become apparent to these souls, for they still lived in a society which catered to their twisted states of mind. Indeed, it was designed by them to enhance their physical desires and pleasures.

The reward systems of Orion society were replete with opportunities to gorge oneself upon the pleasures of the physical senses. All facets of physical life were distorted into gross orgies of overindulgence. Tyrantus encouraged such behavior, for it was another means by which he was able to manipulate these individuals. The reward and punishment system had been honed to a kind of devious perfection by Tyrantus' government. Greed was encouraged; lust, a most highly cherished state of consciousness. And through the control of the desired objects of these greeds and lusts, Tyrantus and his government leaders then controlled the people. They held the carrot, and were quick to wield the stick when other methods failed.

Bartolonias scooped up the unconscious body of Dalos, signaling for several of the guards to assist. Immediately, a gurney appeared and Dalos was taken to a building some distance from Tyrantus' quarters. There he was put through a series of neurological tests.

Every part of his physical anatomy was probed and prodded, manipulated and examined. It was determined that he had experienced a severe concussion upon his fall, and he was soon brought back to consciousness, only to be administered an anesthetic which took him out once again so that the more painful tests could be performed without his knowledge.

The Higher Mind of Uriel, of course, was totally and thoroughly aware of all factors of this development, but there was nothing that could be done at the present moment to halt this course of events. This was the risk that had been taken by Dalos when he willingly placed himself and his crew in the hands of Tyrantus and his minions. It was known by the Pleiadeans that much so-called "medical research" was merely a pretense for the development of controlling means by which to keep the people submissive to Tyrantus' wishes. Now Dalos' body was in the grip of these devilish workers, who could dissect a living body without batting an eye, who were capable of performing the disembowelment of a fellow human being without the slightest ripple of concern or compassion.

They had been trained to feel nothing and to regard their work as the highest achievements of all Orion scientific advancement. They were amply rewarded for their work, and each new breakthrough of this science was hailed as a great triumph of Tyrantus' superior intellect. There was much to be gained by the individual researchers in this particular field, in terms of material comfort and rewards of pleasure and travel. They could just as quickly become the victims of their own research if a particular experiment failed, and this was frequently the case. So these individuals had developed nerves of steely rigidity. They could not allow their fears to hinder or gain the dominant position over their greedy desire for promotion and reward. This system had been perfected in this particular field; Tyrantus was most pleased by the results achieved.

Dalos would find no one, then, among this crew of deviates who might lend a thought of care or even curiosity toward him. He was merely another experiment to them; he was an oddity to be explored.

What these individuals found most disturbing about the physical anatomy of this tall Pleiadean was a certain field of energy detected as a radiating projection that extended some distance from his atomic structures. The frequencies of this electromagnetic field extended beyond the ability of their instruments to measure. They did not report this finding immediately, as Bartolonias, the head researcher, was unwilling to do so until he could offer Tyrantus some explanation for these findings. He ordered further tests—tests which were quite dangerous in their potential to cause serious and lasting harm to the neurological system of Dalos' physical anatomy. Only through the intervention of the Higher Minds oscillating to Dalos through their frequency relationship as the polarities of Uriel—Michiel, Raphiel, and Muriel—were these technicians kept from the slip of hand that would have caused permanent damage to Dalos' spinal cord.

Eventually they tired of this activity, suturing their many probing explorations and allowing Dalos to return to physical consciousness by removing the anesthetizing agent which was steadily injected into his veins. He had undergone five days of this continuous testing and probing. When he awakened, in a white room absolutely devoid of any decoration, Dalos was disoriented for quite some time.

There were no human beings in sight, no clues as to his whereabouts or the many surgical explorations which he had endured. The anesthesia had a lasting effect upon him, keeping him in this disoriented state for long hours. He was unable to focus his conscious mind for any length of time. There was nothing, at this point, that could be done to help him. He was totally isolated and kept apart from his entourage, who knew nothing of the torturous experiences he had undergone.

They, too, were being carefully observed and analyzed by the Orion technicians. Under Tyrantus' orders, they were being electronically surveyed and the resultant data fed into the computer banks. Thus far, this data proved inconclusive. It consisted of similar patterns of energy oscillations which were previously unknown to the Tyronites. They had no data with which to correlate these energy patterns, as they had never before observed this high-frequency oscillation radiating from human beings. It would be many weeks, the scientists informed their Emperor, before any identifiable pattern could be determined which would allow them to draw some conclusion from this data. Because they were so fearful of revealing information that might cause their demotion, or demise, the scientists probing the two hundred Pleiadean crew members and those in the medical facility who had cut into the body of Dalos did not communicate their findings to one another. They kept many elements of these findings fearfully to themselves.

Dalos could do naught but lie rigid in his bed and stare at the blank white ceiling. He was in great pain, and yet he knew not how he had sustained these seeming injuries. He was immobilized by wrist and ankle restraints which caused him further pain. Occasionally, an attendant would appear to shift his position, or administer some intravenous liquid. His questions to these individuals were ignored, as their expressionless faces turned away and they carried out their duties as if they were mere machines programmed for a particular function. Indeed, that was the sorry state of their damaged minds. They were capable of little else.

The pain that Dalos felt, then, was much greater than any physical agony. He felt the pain of a Being whose very existence represents a radiating Force of Love. He had no way to express this Love to these individuals who kept their distance from him, and when they did appear, were incapable of sensing the higher oscillations of the Mind of this Being who had fallen into their care, whose only desire was to see them become free and whole once again.

As he passed the long hours of solitude and pain, Dalos' thoughts extended to his Brothers on Aries. Their returned Love flooded his consciousness with hope and a rekindled desire to complete his mission on Tyron. But without access to the people themselves, particularly to Tyrantus, Dalos was truly bound and gagged.

All that could be done was to wait and hope for that opportunity. He would never allow himself to sink into any form of despair or abandonment of his purpose.

Yet even as Dalos remained in this confined and isolated state, and even as his entourage was kept in their restricted quarters, a new energy force was interpenetrating the world of Tyron. That field of Higher Consciousness detected by the Orion instrumentation was but the lowest frequencies of this Infinite Power Beam that was radiating into the atmosphere of this third-dimensional planet from the very presence of the developed minds of the Pleiadeans, particularly that of Dalos himself. Their minds had served as capacitors for this radiating force, charged with their own advanced development and now discharging into the negatively-biased atmosphere created by the people of Tyron.

So although the mission of Dalos appeared to have reached a standstill, the most important work was ongoing. Unseen, unheard, and as yet unfelt by the Orionites, this interpenetrating Light began to infiltrate and heal the lost peoples of Orion.

9

A Plan Unfolds

A MIND THAT IS FILLED with the hectic debris of a material life cannot be receptive to the highest reaches of its potential. Always are there opportunities for an expansion of thought, but it takes the willingness of the individual to dream beyond his present reality—for there is no such thing as a dream, and "present reality" is only that conception of life which has been formed from his previous experiences.

Dalos was an example of the manifestation of dreams come true. He was an individual being, yet his own mind was interlinked and joined with a network of Higher Minds that gave him access to all Infinity. There were no limitations for a Mind such as that of Dalos!

That is why the higher-frequency radiations permeating his very being were so baffling to the Orionites. They themselves never experienced such higher attunements. They were now incapable of making that inner and higher contact, so immersed had they become within the confines of their material lives. They were completely encased in their day-to-day activities, totally inhibited in thought by the steady commands oscillating into their every moment from their originating source at the heart of Orion—that is, the Orion computer. Even those who were not linked to this electronic command center by actual, physical implants within their physical anatomies were, nevertheless, directed by the commands of their superiors and the entire structure of Orion life that had been set up and was maintained by Tyrantus and his slew of close associates. *They* determined the nature of life on the Orion planets. They had become the designers and creators for what should have been an individual prerogative; that is, the free use and growth of one's own vehicle of consciousness.

The Orionites' habit was not to use their mental capabilities. They no longer had any need to strive or struggle, for so much had been provided for them in a material way that they were numbed to their lack of inner, personal growth.

Dalos longed to reach these poor souls. He knew that if he could merely address them, speak to their hearts, to that inner spark, they could still be awakened to the dire nature of their coma-like existence. Yes, they were capable of responding through their five physical senses, yet this automatic response was robotic and meaningless. There was no purpose to this physical anatomy for, truly, it had been created by the Infinite Mind as a vehicle for learning, a tool of consciousness, a mere extension of the true being, so that individual sparklet of Infinity could learn of itself and its association to all of Infinity. Without this use, however, this physical anatomy, this vehicle for learning, became a useless, robotic, mechanical device operating out of control. Oh, yes, Tyrantus believed that he himself had everything under control. But he had no true idea of the profound aberrations that he had set in motion among these trillions of souls! He could not have believed, nor did he even desire to begin to conceive of the havoc that had been unleashed among these third-dimensional worlds.

Dalos' only means of maintaining his consciousness within the now-tortured physical anatomy that he inhabited was the slight hope that there was yet a crack within Tyrantus' consciousness through which Dalos might penetrate with some Light. That opportunity did finally come to pass.

For many weeks the situation had continued in this stalemate of constant probings of Dalos' physical body for some clue to those enigmas which the Tyronite researchers were incapable of resolving. That included the intelligence that was expressed by this one, the true Intelligence, in terms of his balance of all factors of his personal expression—in addition to the great, high-frequency radiations that the Tyronite technicians had detected emanating from Dalos' physical anatomy. Similar radiations of higher frequencies were detected surrounding the physical bodies of the entire Pleiadean entourage, but not to the great degree that had been detected with Dalos.

They made no mention to Dalos himself of their findings. He was merely a guinea pig, a subject to be probed and prodded and not one to be communicated with. However, at each instance when he was not under sedation or completely removed from conscious awareness by a wide variety of anesthetizing agents, Dalos spoke to the technicians and medical researchers with whom he was in contact.

A few among this group of individuals had become curious to hear his words, but they were extremely fearful of allowing their supervisors to see that their interest had been sparked. Such interaction with the patients was strictly forbidden for it was known that, if allowed to continue, there was some remote possibility that some element of sympathy or concern might interfere with the duties these individuals were required to carry out. Therefore, any expression of human feeling was highly discouraged by the strict system of control under which these individuals were forced to operate.

Dalos sensed their fear and did not press too hard to convey his messages to them. But whenever a particular circumstance gave him an opportunity to speak directly to one of these individuals, especially when he was alone with a single technician, Dalos did speak. It was his nature to teach, and it was his mission to reach these poor humans who had forgotten to live as such!

"Do you realize what you are doing here?" he said to one young woman on a particular day. She was administering yet another intravenous feeding, for Dalos had been so thoroughly debilitated by the constant explorations of his physical form that he was unable to take food in the normal way. "Do you know that you are causing yourself great harm?"

The young woman was surprised by these words. She did not understand what Dalos was referring to. She had been told to expect this Pleiadean to say anything or do anything and she had been strictly advised to ignore any speech directed her way. Yet something in his tone of voice caused her to desire to hear more. She nervously glanced back at the monitoring devices which were constantly in operation in Dalos' quarters. She could not speak to ask Dalos to continue, but she looked directly into his eyes.

Dalos knew her thoughts immediately. Very few of the Tyronites returned his gaze in this fashion, and rarely were their eyes as open and questing as those of this young woman. A warmth flooded his being and great compassion flowed from him to this one. She had been touched! She wanted to understand.

"Dear soul, do not be so fearful! I cannot harm you, nor would I wish you to be harmed by anyone! My words will not cause you any conflict with your superiors. I merely wanted you to know that everything you do has an effect upon you, yourself. This is most important for any individual to realize, that you are shaping your own life by your very deeds!"

The young woman still did not grasp Dalos' meaning, but something about him was very pleasing to her. She looked at him with a puzzled gaze. But what she saw returned in his kind look she could not have described. She had never, in her entire life on Tyron, experienced such! She would never be the same again, although she had no way of knowing this. It mattered not that she did not understand the principle that Dalos was alluding to; she had received a tremendous projection of healing energies through the focusing of his consciousness upon her.

As she left the room, Dalos fell back with an expulsion of breath. He was so weak he could barely lift his head. He knew not how he would continue but only that he would give it his every ounce of consciousness until that time when he could no longer carry on.

I must maintain my alertness, he told himself again. *I must keep my mission uppermost in mind. If only I could reach many more like this one, who does show that there is a spark remaining to be rekindled within the minds of these people! Perhaps if I make some form of commotion, Tyrantus will be alerted—perhaps I can devise a way to gain another audience with him. I must not give up! I must make further contact with the one who has caused this terrible situation in which so many, many souls are being kept from their true identities, their true purpose!*

Dalos' mind churned in this fashion for hours on end until, exhausted, he lapsed into a deep sleep. While in this state, he was freed of the pains of his physical body, which had sustained so much abuse from the cold, unfeeling treatment of the medical practitioners. What they practiced was the processing of body after body through their research mills, taking whatever they desired, changing at will the physical structure, and discarding their mistakes like so much garbage. They were not dealing with other human beings; in their minds, these bodies had become the property of the Orion government. They were objects to be used and manipulated into promotions and rewards for themselves!

Thus far, the Pleiadean entourage had not been subjected to this physical abuse. They were being irradiated day and night with bombarding frequencies that were, up until that time, not extremely harmful; yet they did set up a great static field which caused some mental unrest among the Pleiadeans. They were aware that they were under surveillance; however, they knew not the extent to which the Orionites had taken their science of electronic controls.

Periodically one among the Pleiadeans would approach the few Tyronites with whom they were allowed to commune. These were individuals who made certain that the Pleiadeans' needs were fulfilled, that they had sufficient food and access to Orion forms of entertainment. However, the Pleiadeans had shown little interest in the endless broadcasts of information which were relayed throughout the entire Orion Empire. They did partake of the food offered, of course, because it was necessary to sustain their presence; however, the Pleiadeans kept close to one another in their conversations and activities.

At those times when they did speak to the Tyronites, it was largely to inquire as to when they might again see their commander, Dalos, and as to what events might have been taking place with their leader and the Emperor. Nothing was conveyed through the Orion communications system about the presence of the Pleiadeans or their leader—not since that first day, when their arrival had been greeted by the workers on Tyron and the Orion peoples were informed that an entourage from a distant planet had been welcomed by Tyrantus, who expected to enter into fruitful trade negotiations with these individuals.

Of course, Tyrantus did not need to communicate anything at all to the peoples under his control. Only those details of life which would serve some purpose by being brought to the attention of these populous worlds were allowed to be released in a form of newscast. Other programs of so-called entertainment were diversions that kept the workers in their state of numbed satisfaction. Many subliminal messages were inserted into these endless programs of sight and sound.

The Pleiadeans were sensitive to these lower-frequency projections and did not allow themselves to become absorbed by the glittering surface presentations of music, dance, or drama. They sensed that this would cause them a drop in consciousness, a loss of their own inner connection with one another and with the Higher Minds who were guiding their every action in this mission to the earth worlds.

Their inquiries about the present status of negotiations between Dalos and Tyrantus were met with steely stares and uncomprehending looks from their Orion overseers—for truly they had now become the unwilling captives of these individuals. Although their quarters were spacious and extremely comfortable by Orion standards and they were allowed access to certain open areas of entertainment and recreation, they were not free to leave nor to roam the planet's surface at will—and the Pleiadeans understood this fact. It did not trouble them unduly, for they did not allow themselves to become overly fearful. This would have been a negative emotional state that could prove fatal to their mission!

Still, as the weeks passed and no word had been heard of the whereabouts or condition of Dalos, fear did begin to grow among the Pleiadeans. At first these individuals did not express their underlying fears to one another. They did not wish to give strength to what they knew to be an unproductive state of mind. Those who had begun to have this creeping sensation of unrest quickly averted their minds from these thoughts as they rose to the surface.

But eventually such thoughts became so frequent that one of them spoke out.

"Do you not think," this man said to one of his brothers, "that we need to do something to find Dalos? I fear that he has fallen into ill hands! We are not being told anything at all, and we must do something to carry out our mission here. We cannot sit upon our hands forever! We must *do something!*" His voice had risen considerably, now that his true feelings had been released.

"Dear brother," said Korion, the tall navigator to whom these words were addressed, "calm yourself! You know the risks that we take here if we allow ourselves to become so emotionally biased. We must keep our minds clear! We will know how to proceed. Perhaps you are correct and our commander Dalos has fallen into difficulty; yet what can we do from here to come to his aid, except to keep our thoughts attuned in a positive way? If he needs our assistance, we will know. If there is anything at all that can be done, we will be alerted through our inner contact with Uriel. You realize this, of course?"

"Yes," sighed Turanarian. "I know this—but I cannot stand this waiting! I feel that I have already failed and that I must do something to redeem my mission! Do you not have these same feelings?"

Korion placed a hand on the shoulder of his distraught brother. "Peace, dear one; be at peace. This will lead us nowhere but into the darkness of this void to which we have brought ourselves. This world is full of such blackened thoughts; don't allow them to take over your own mind! You must not do so, else you will be swallowed whole by this Orion monster which seems to devour its people in massive quantities. Let us wait until we receive an inner prompting that guides us to take some action."

Turanarian kept his silence but he was not appeased. He could not sit by idly while his fellow Pleiadeans deceived themselves with some sense of stubborn calm, when all indications were that they had been thoroughly foiled by Tyrantus and his entire system of control!

Truly what was affecting this individual was something far more devious than the Pleiadeans had yet realized. In the many-frequency radiations bombarding them from the Orion computer systems, they were under the influence of a drug-like, extremely low frequency that would eventually have a deteriorating effect upon their states of mind. Only the most highly developed Consciousness of Dalos could survive this constant influx of negative beat frequencies without some undue effect.

Several exchanges took place among the Pleiadeans such as that between Korion and Turanarian. They were kept in strictest secrecy. But as time passed these fearful conversations became more frequent, and eventually the entire Pleiadean entourage was permeated by a smog of doubt and agitation.

This, of course, was detected by the Orion sensing devices. The supervisory personnel were alerted to this change in attitude among the Pleiadeans. This pleased them greatly and a flurry of reports were dictated for Tyrantus' viewing. Finally they had good news to convey to their Emperor and this was a great relief among the Tyronites! This turn of events was something they could understand. These Pleiadeans were not perfect masters of their own emotions, and in Tyrantus' mind a new thought brewed.

If the entourage had been so affected, then Dalos himself must be susceptible to these penetrating frequencies. Instantly upon reaching this conclusion, Tyrantus ordered a new series of electronic projections to be directed to Dalos in his quarters.

Such low-frequency, generated wave forms were often used against the Orion citizens. It had been determined that one who was kept off balance by some underlying disturbance which he could not quite define for himself was easily influenced by certain brainwashing techniques. That was Tyrantus' plan—to insure his superiority over the mind of Dalos by putting him in a further situation of mental imbalance. Already, Dalos was crippled by his physical state, which had deteriorated considerably at the hands of Tyrantus' butchers. Now he would be an easy prey, Tyrantus calculated. His mind was already addled by the drugs injected into his veins.

We shall see how he responds to our electronic treatment, Tyrantus thought. *This will tell me what kind of man I have in my cage! And when he has become totally submissive to my desires, then we shall discuss his technological advances. Then he will most gladly tell me all I need to know, with no further deceptions such as he attempted in our first meetings. I shall learn how he came to own a portion of our historical archives! I have time. And I know that he will turn to jelly, just as his crew is now doing!*

No, these Pleiadeans do not impress me. They are like all the rest: fallible, breakable, and pliant to our needs.

Dalos, meanwhile, had hit upon an idea to gain a face-to-face meeting with Tyrantus. His higher senses told him that time was dwindling. He must arrange such a meeting soon if his mission on Tyron was to be successful.

The next attendant who came to administer a drug to Dalos was greeted with shocking words.

"Do you wish to know something about your Emperor that no one else knows?"

The attendant froze in his tracks. Fear ran a shock from the soles of his feet to his prickling scalp. Terror was evident in his eyes. No one spoke this way about the Emperor! It meant instant death!

"Have you lost your ability to speak? I say, would you like some news about your Emperor that I'm sure will serve you quite well in your desire for promotion?"

These words were quite foreign, coming from the lips of this Pleiadean who had seemed so calm and submissive! The attendant did not know whether to stay and listen or turn in fright and flee the room.

Dalos knew the effect he was having upon this individual and he felt sorry for a moment that it was necessary to cause this one some inner turmoil. But the larger need must be served, and Dalos knew that these tremors of fear would soon be allayed.

"Very well, then, if you do not wish to hear what I have to say, perhaps your supervisor would like to know that I have information about your Emperor's past that he would find very valuable. I suggest that you could win great favor if you alert him to my willingness to speak. I have told no one this information, and your Emperor would dearly like to hear these words!"

The attendant took Dalos' bait. Without a word, he dropped the instruments he was holding upon a table and left the room. He went immediately to his supervisor, trembling in fear, his face ashen.

"What is it?" the man commanded to know. "Why do you barge into my quarters this way?" The supervisor saw that this attendant had sustained some form of shock. He quickly pressed a button and two other attendants entered the room. "Help this man," the supervisor ordered.

They took each arm of the young man and began to guide him to a nearby seat.

"Not here!" the supervisor responded. "Take him to Treatment Room 35. You know the procedure."

"Wait!" the young man finally blurted. "I must speak …"

"Yes, yes, of course," the supervisor said. "Speak all you like." He motioned conspiratorially to the other two, who began to remove this one from the room.

"No! I have news of Dalos!"

"Hold it," the supervisor said to the two. "Let him speak." He sat behind his desk while the attendants stepped back to allow their fellow worker some room.

"Thank you," he said to them. "Dalos has been making strange statements, sir. He, just this moment, said things about the Emperor which I believe you should be alerted to—I dare not repeat them! I do believe—that you should see to this matter personally. He said he would tell you—certain facts that he believed you would—want to hear," the attendant related in broken speech.

The supervisor said nothing but stared at this individual, who still appeared shaken by some traumatic event. Indeed, his own stomach tightened and churned at the Emperor's name. Clearly there was something here that required his investigation, but he did not wish this mere attendant to speak further in front of others.

"Take him to the treatment room," he ordered, and the attendant meekly bowed his head, allowing himself to be guided from the chamber and down a blue hallway.

It would be a relief, the young man thought, to feel the soothing effects of the so-called "anti-stress" treatment.

Meanwhile, his superior strode down the corridor to make his way toward Dalos' nearby quarters.

Dalos had been moved to this medical facility permanently due to his weakened condition. His quarters now consisted of a jumble of tubes, vessels, pumps, electronic data recording machines, computerized probes, and a variety of restraints which were used when various treatments were performed upon the inert form of Dalos when he was rendered unconscious by the administered drugs. Now, however, Dalos was fully conscious, more conscious than he had been in weeks! His heart pounded with anticipation and, for the first time in a very long while, he felt a lift.

He knew that he would soon be confronted by the furrowed brows of this supervisory individual whose face he had seen once before, when Dalos was first brought to this facility. This was not a kind man, but he was not an intelligent man, either. He merely knew how to manipulate the system to his own benefit. He had risen to his present position through such manipulations, calculated to place himself in a moderately powerful position among the Tyronites. This was a very small-scale operation that this individual oversaw; nevertheless, he was given certain advantages and rewards that the others were not privy to. Dalos knew that this individual could serve as a conduit by which he would reach the ears of Tyrantus. He merely needed to speak the language of this man, and Dalos was capable now of using the Orionites' language quite skillfully.

The door of his room burst open. Dalos greeted the man with a smile.

He would not leave this individual without some *true* reward for the role he was about to play in Dalos' mission. This "reward" was one of Love: a radiation of Light-energy beamed into his consciousness by the Higher Mind of Uriel. Even this man, who had made himself such a part of Orion society, who had molded and shaped his mind to rise no higher than his office at the end of a long corridor, would be helped and set upon a new course of life by his contact with Dalos, the Ambassador from the Pleiades.

10

Separation

With every bit of strength that he could gather, Dalos raised himself slightly to face the supervisory administrator, whose name was Thorinean.

"At last my request has been answered," Dalos said to him. "I have been wishing to convey some information that I hold relating to your Emperor to someone of great importance. I presume that you can carry this message to the Emperor Tyrantus?"

Thorinean regarded him with a skeptical stare. He could not believe the change in this individual. Perhaps it was the drugs that were being administered on a regular basis? Or perhaps this was the effect of the treatment that Tyrantus had most recently ordered, the additional projection of electronic ray beams of a low frequency, designed to cause agitation.

Certainly Dalos now appeared to be agitated.

Thorinean knew how much difficulty this Pleiadean must be having to exert himself in this more physical way. But he was, more than anything, curious to know what information this stranger could possibly possess about the Emperor, whose every move was made in the greatest of secrecy. Only those closest aides were given access to the details of his life. Still, none of them were privy to all of the Emperor's activities. No other soul on this planet, or any other in the Orion Empire, knew everything about the Emperor's movements and activities. He kept it this way specifically to deter his enemies and to keep information from the hands of those who would gladly remove and replace him.

Thorinean decided that he would humor the Pleiadean long enough to ascertain just exactly what kind of information he spoke of.

"I am that individual you seek. I will convey your message to the Emperor, if you make yourself plain."

"Certainly," Dalos replied. "Your Emperor was confused by an apparatus he saw demonstrated upon my starship. He wished to know where I had obtained certain information about him. I am now ready to explain to the Emperor in great detail how this information was come by. I am certain he will be most appreciative to hear from you and to know that Dalos now wishes to tell all!"

"What sort of information are you talking about?" Thorinean probed.

But Dalos did not respond with full details. He knew that if he did, he might lose his opportunity to lure Tyrantus into another private meeting. Private or public, Dalos cared not, but he understood that Tyrantus would not carry on any conversation with Dalos in any way which might give others in his government access to some tidbit of intelligence that they might in the future use against him.

"I am afraid that if I gave you further detail, your life would be in jeopardy. I understand that your Emperor does not like to have his employees too knowledgeable about the details of his private life."

Thorinean flushed a deep red coloration. This was true, of course, and he himself did not have the courage to pursue any form of political blackmail against the Emperor, no matter how he might have loved to consider such a circumstance in the privacy of his own mind.

But if truth be known, Thorinean had no such privacy, nor did anyone living upon the planet Tyron or the hundred planets falling under the Orion banner. Even now, his actions and thoughts were being monitored by special security forces Tyrantus had created and kept secret from the lower echelons of his government. Only those among the Council of Twelve knew of the existence of these secret police, who constantly monitored the citizenry of Tyron and other planets.

These individuals were watching very closely the actions of Thorinean.

They knew that he had made an unscheduled visit to the quarters of Dalos—for everything in Orion functioned according to a very precise schedule of activity. They were listening in to the conversation and monitoring the emotional pulses detectable by the surface radiations emanating from the physical body of Thorinean. A slight increase in internal temperature, a drop in skin surface temperatures in the palm area, the flushed face, heart palpitations, mental stress—all were recorded in the data banks of this secret police force. When they felt they had sufficient information they would alert Tyrantus himself, for they were under strict orders to convey directly to the Emperor any information surrounding the Pleiadeans and their leader, as well as any influence they might be having upon their overseers.

These individuals, if they demonstrated any lasting effect from their contact with the Pleiadeans, were then rounded up for special "rejuvenating" treatments—purportedly as a reward for their services rendered. But in actuality, these were brainwashing techniques that supposedly cleansed their minds of any accumulated debris. It was a reprogramming session by which those thoughts that had begun to stir within them—questioning, free thoughts about the teachings Dalos and his entourage relayed by their very existence—these germinating seeds of intelligence were stripped from the minds of these individuals by the hypnotic impressions given through a variety of repetitive sensory applications of light and sound.

It was not long before Thorinean was commanded to appear before the Emperor, even before he had the opportunity to make this contact himself, which was his full intention. He had hesitated, however, for nearly thirty minutes due to his internal agitation and fear at facing his leader. Any slip of the tongue in such a circumstance could mean instant death or, at the very least, the loss of one's hard-earned position in the Orion governmental echelons.

Upon hearing the words conveyed to Thorinean by Dalos, Tyrantus sat back in glee. It was working then, he thought. Dalos was beginning to crack under the pressure of his physical pains and the electronic and drug influences that were now generating out-of-sync wave forms into his psychic anatomy.

If the Orionites had truly understood the nature of this psychic energy body, they would not have dreamed of creating this demonic tampering! Yet they had no idea of the damage they were incurring *to themselves* as they inflicted their controlling mechanisms upon others.

This was a key component of the message Dalos wished to instill within the consciousness of Tyrantus: some realization that he was sowing rotted grain that would yield a bleak harvest in future eons of time!

With the help of attendants, Dalos was wheeled into the presence of Tyrantus. This time, their meeting took place in a more spacious room, more comfortably designed. It was, in fact, a resting area for Tyrantus. He felt extremely comfortable here and he knew there was no further need to place Dalos at a disadvantage. He had already taken care of that matter quite sufficiently!

Dalos was barely able to hold his head up, but he nevertheless made that attempt from the gurney-like apparatus upon which he was brought to Tyrantus' quarters.

"I wish to remain upright," he had insisted as the attendants transferred him to this elevated, reclining, wheeled contraption. They assured him that this device could be reconfigured into a chair-like conveyance, but that his physical condition did not advise him to sit in an upright position. He was extremely weakened and might lose consciousness entirely, they told him.

Dalos was not pleased at this but nevertheless accepted their words. His main concern and desire was to speak with Tyrantus. If he must do so standing on his head, then so be it! He would not maintain any concern about his own physical status; he was focused upon this need to make contact with the fallen one.

Once he had arrived in Tyrantus' presence, however, there was no way to deter him from his insistence upon the redesign of this transporting vehicle into a more dignified position, with head held high above shoulders and feet where they should be, beneath him. Tyrantus gave the nod for this adjustment to be made, and the attendants quickly reprogrammed the transporter to give Dalos this change in position.

He was restrained in this conveyance by his arms and legs. As the complex adjustments were made to this series of maneuverable metallic plates that supported his physical body, Dalos winced in great pain but he did not cry out. Once these movements ceased, he took several deep breaths and raised his chin slightly, fixing his gaze upon the comfortably seated form of Tyrantus.

"I see that you are adapting well to your treatment," Tyrantus said with unmistakable pleasure at his visitor's discomfort. "They tell me that you have something you wish to speak with me about." Of course, he knew full well the topic that they had come together to discuss, but Tyrantus was enjoying this new advantage over Dalos and he was going to extend Dalos' torment as long as possible.

Dalos, however, cut directly to the point.

"I shall explain to you in the greatest of detail how the image of your past-life experience was obtained by the device you saw demonstrated upon our starship."

"Well, I see that you *have* had a change of heart! So, you are going to confess to your crime of interplanetary trespass—your theft of secret information dockets. You realize, of course, that there is a strict penalty enforced for this particular crime. I believe it is death, from the last I encountered any need to prescribe this remedy for one of our criminal element. This comes to mind as the appropriate law which was efficiently enforced by our judicial system."

"You will see, Emperor, that I have committed no such crime, nor have any of the members of my entourage—whom I trust you have in your safe-keeping yet?"

"You can be at peace in this regard, Dalos. Your crew is in a fine state. Indeed, I do not believe they miss their commander, for they seem to be adapting quite readily to life on our planet. You, perhaps, have been lax in your discipline among them."

This gave Dalos a slight twinge of concern. He did not like the sound of Tyrantus' words, yet he knew this one was thoroughly capable of lying to gain some insight by his opponent's reactions—or to merely throw him off guard. Dalos brushed aside thoughts of his crew for the present moment and redirected his mind to the purpose at hand, which was to begin the re-education of this sad excuse for a human being.

"You must realize, Emperor Tyrantus, that you placed your hand upon a supersensitive material that was reading and recording every experience that you, in your personal soulic evolution, have ever encountered. This sensitive material was capable of selecting that concern which created a dominating beat frequency within your present consciousness. It was a certain fear that was detected within your mind—and this fear was traced to those originating wave forms of energy-intelligence that are embedded within your personal electronic fingerprint, as you might think of it."

"What are you trying to say? That you gained access to Orion archives through the electronic impulses radiating from my hand? This is ridiculous!" Tyrantus stood in impatience. "You are once again giving me your double-talk and assuming that I am an idiot! Well, Dalos, I am not, and I have very limited patience with your elevated prose! I demand a plain explanation for what I saw on that viewing screen. I believe you falsified this information in some way. This was not truly my image! It was an electronically recreated and computed, holographic impostor!

"Yes, of course, I should have realized this at the time—this was not a true recording taken from our archival storage! It is as I suspected. You are attempting some form of trickery!"

Tyrantus was quite pleased with his own invention, the cover-up for the reality of what he had seen. He knew quite well of this particular experience the instant he saw it. It rang within him with a truth that was foreign to his present consciousness. Although the incident took place in a previous incarnation, he recognized it instantly within his very being. It touched deep, deep, forgotten memories of another self—a self that he had thus far nearly destroyed in his selfish, egocentric momentum to overtake the entire universe, if he could have his way.

Dalos continued in a calm voice. "No, Tyrantus, this was not a recreated depiction. This image was distilled from the energy structures which you yourself formed into a basic radiating frequency within you. Such is the nature of all our life experiences; they remain a part of us, and a device such as I demonstrated for you can detect these energy impingements. This is most valuable to us as a healing mechanism for through it, we can pinpoint the root cause of any problem an individual may be having. If you recall, I did give you this explanation at the time. However, you did seem somewhat distraught by that which you had seen."

Tyrantus whirled around abruptly to face Dalos. "Do not become insolent with me, sir, for as you well know, I have the power of life and death over you. It is only my benevolent concern that has allowed you to remain in a conscious state. I know you have valuable information to give to me and I am allowing you to live so that you can do so. However, we will save ourselves much trouble and I might say, you will save yourself much pain and agony if you speak plainly to me."

"I am, dear Emperor, speaking directly. I am speaking the truth to you, as clearly as I know it to exist. If you wish, I will give you a further demonstration of this device to prove to you that we have no malicious intent. We do not desire to cause any harm or disruption to you or your people. We merely desire to open your minds to certain factors of human consciousness that you have not taken into consideration!"

Tyrantus thought for a moment. Yes, perhaps another tour of the Pleiadean starship would give him some further insight into the real purpose of this strange visit from these individuals who had—as much as Tyrantus hated to admit it—confounded his scientists. Now that he was aware of the strange energy radiations that had been detected in the surrounding aura of these Pleiadeans, he was quite desirous to know of their source. But he would not allow Dalos to have this bit of information! He would not give Dalos any further information or knowledge of the extent of his desire to know all that Dalos knew. This would place Tyrantus in a subservient position—and that was an intolerable thought.

"Very well," he said, "if you believe you are capable, I shall agree. But this time, I desire to be accompanied by my closest associates, who will offer themselves as subjects of your demonstration."

"Very good, Tyrantus. I feel this is wise." Dalos knew that Tyrantus was eager enough to see what hidden secrets might be revealed about his colleagues, while concealing any of his own buried statistics. This time, however, Dalos felt certain that he would be able to awaken the Orionites to the reality of the psychic anatomy.

If only this one, single principle of interdimensional life could be conveyed to these souls, they would begin to recognize the further impact they were having upon—not only their present lives and the present lifetimes of their many subjects—but upon their own future lifetimes. He would somehow need to convince Tyrantus of his motives.

Thus far Dalos' purpose—his pure, compassionate desire to give of his Intelligence—was so foreign to the lifestyle of this individual, who had once been likewise compassionately-minded, that Dalos simply could not convey this truth satisfactorily to Tyrantus! It was an obstacle that Dalos had not counted upon. Never had he considered that one could be so backwardly motivated as to have lost touch with all instances of selflessness! But such was the case. It was a foreign element to Tyrantus, Dalos now realized. He would apply his consciousness to resolving this problem.

Meanwhile, the Pleiadean entourage was fulminating in increased agitation. The instances of friction among them had increased, much to the delight of the supervisory personnel overseeing the monitoring system that had been set up to detect the slightest changes among the Pleiadeans. It was determined that now was the time to add another element into this experimental observation that had been ongoing since the day of the Pleiadeans' arrival, several months previously.

They had thus far not been allowed to view any portion of the planet at large. They had been confined in the capital city and in this particular, expanded building, which did include all amenities that one could desire for the maintenance of a physical life. Most Orionites lived in this fashion, within the confines of a small set of buildings that contained all their needs. But the Tyronite researchers asked permission and gained the requisite authority to take several of the Pleiadeans into a new environment to see what effect this might have upon their behavior.

The Pleiadeans were the unwilling victims of a new Orion project. They had become a giant experiment in psychological/behavioral control to the Tyronites. For the most part, Tyrantus gave these researchers free rein—such as could be obtained within the controlled society, that is. He was far less concerned with the entourage of Dalos than with the information Dalos himself held.

Tyrantus knew that the separation of a leader from his troops did cause great disintegration among those who were trained to follow. In his perception, he had already won over these individuals, for he knew it was only a matter of time before they lost all sense of direction. That is always the case with those who are given a particular mission and who are detained and deterred in their ability to follow through. Tyrantus himself had witnessed this effect in the course of his many military maneuvers among the planets of the Orion constellation. He had seen it among his enemies and among his own forces, and he was wise to this need to maintain order and a proper chain of command at all times. Therefore, he knew precisely what he was doing on that first day when he separated Dalos from his starship crew. It was almost a routine matter of tactical maneuvering for a superior position.

Indeed, Tyrantus was quite surprised that Dalos did not vehemently protest this action—but then this individual did not seem to respond in the usual manner to any of the stimulus provided by the Emperor and his society!

The researchers, then, were given to understand that they could perform whatever experiments they desired upon the Pleiadeans, with the limitation that they were not yet allowed to place them under sedation and perform the kind of surgical explorations that were being performed upon the body of Dalos. This option was being reserved for some future time, as Tyrantus believed that it would be best to keep these individuals whole for their possible future use, should they prove to be possessed of advanced capabilities. He was always one to make the best use of whatever manpower was available. He was quite skilled at adapting entire planetary civilizations to suit his needs. In fact, this was a source of great pride to the Emperor.

Whole planets had been converted into colonies of workers that performed a particular kind of task. He was quite fond of creating entire worlds devoted to a particular lifestyle, and when gathered all together, they formed a more complete picture of life. One planet was devoted entirely to the operation of the Orion computer systems, the "brain" of his empire. Another world might be devoted to the agricultural activities that sustained many other planets through their production of foodstuffs.

Other worlds were strictly for pleasure and reward; some were devoted to the manufacture of a particular device or devices, and so on.

These Pleiadeans, Tyrantus considered, might then have some use to him. It was enough, he felt, to explore the biophysical structures of Dalos for now. After all, he was the prime example among them and was clearly superior to the others in his mental and physical abilities.

It did remain in the back of Tyrantus' mind that the planet Axiahn might become a larger source of Pleiadean manpower. For quite some time, he had been desirous of expanding beyond the present boundaries of his empire. This world might be the first of his planned acquisitions outside the Orion constellation.

Therefore, it was decided to allow a small group of ten Pleiadeans to tour the facilities of the Tyronite manufacturing, research, and living sectors. They were allowed to choose among themselves which of them would form this party of ten, for the Tyronites believed that they would naturally select their best specimens as representatives.

This was the case, as there were those among the Pleiadeans who served in the more outgoing roles and they were known among themselves. There was little argument or concern over which among them would accept the offer of the Orionites. However, there were those individuals who felt some concern at this change of attitude among their overseers.

Any change would have brought concern to their minds at this point, for they were on the brink of losing faith in their mission. Repeated requests for information about their commander were still denied. When this party of ten inquired as to whether they might be brought into contact with Dalos once again, the Tyronite liaisons laughed.

"You would not wish to see your leader," one of them blurted.

Instantly he was silenced by his colleagues.

That was all the Pleiadeans needed to sense the seriousness of their commander's position. They knew, then, that he was in danger and no doubt had been brought to some physical harm. The sneer upon this individual's face had spelled out for them the nature of the treatment Dalos had been receiving at the hands of the Emperor.

These ten decided that they would not relate this insight to their fellow crew members. It would only cause further unrest and concern—and fear. Fear that they could not afford to regenerate among themselves. It had already become a major factor that preyed upon their minds with each passing hour. They feared not for themselves, but for their mission, and for the status of Dalos' contact with Tyrantus.

As they embarked upon this tour in the company of a party of Tyronite officials, the Pleiadeans were silent with their own inner concerns. They barely saw the endless buildings passing by the viewing windows of the aerial transport that carried them through the city. It was not until they arrived at a particular facility that they displayed some outward interest.

This was a large auditorium in which were seated many thousands of Tyron citizens. The center of focus was a huge screen containing the image of their Emperor. He was speaking to them about loyalty and commitment to the growth of Orion. His eyes were penetrating, yet cold. The people stared up at the screen in a seemingly hypnotized trance.

The Pleiadeans could not look upon this image for more than a few instants. They exchanged glances among themselves, realizing that this projection contained the subliminal impact of robotizing frequencies. The true purpose of this gathering was to maintain Tyrantus' supremacy through the drug-like influence of these hypnotic, subliminal messages.

The Pleiadeans' guides were quite proud of this facility, to such a degree that the starship officers wondered if they were aware of this subliminal programming. Quite likely they were not, for these individuals were not of the highest echelons of Orion government. They, too, gazed up at Tyrantus' image with glazed admiration. This, they told the Pleiadeans, was one of the most recent implementations of a new program designed by Tyrantus and his assistants to enhance the lives of the Tyronites. The people thoroughly enjoyed these outings, which they were allowed each Tyron week as a reward for their diligent work performed.

As soon as possible, the Pleiadeans suggested that they be allowed to continue their tour, as they realized that there were many innovations the Tyronites might show them and could they please expand this tour, as they found it quite fascinating?

This bit of flattery worked, and they were allowed to return to the transport vehicles in a short period of time, thus escaping further subjection to these pervading lower harmonics—which they had already experienced to some degree through their captivity in the holding quarters, wherein their compatriots still suffered this insidious, undermining influence.

The Pleiadean party of ten had no idea how close they were to their commander, whose physical body at that moment was constrained within a horrible-looking contraption of steel levers and controls, in a building not far from the "Rejuvenation Pavilion." He was face-to-face with the object of his mission and he was about to embark upon a most crucial phase, one which would determine the success or failure of all their efforts to reach the lost ones.

Dalos drew into his mind the sustaining energies of those Higher Ones who never left him in consciousness. They provided all that was possible to help him maintain his functioning ability in this battered physical anatomy. He was truly displaying superhuman capabilities. The more he did so, the more determined Tyrantus became to break down his resistance and to find the source of his strength. Such was their stalemate—one which would destroy the body of Dalos, and the mind of Tyrantus, if allowed to continue.

11

The Teaching Begins

By the time they reached the Pleiadean starship, Dalos was extremely weak. For a moment it seemed as if they would not be able to continue, for he appeared to be drifting out of his conscious awareness. He returned, however, with a start, and directed the Tyronite entourage to continue toward the gleaming Axiahn ship.

During the months of Dalos' captivity, the Tyronites had attempted to gain access to the interior of this ship. They had applied many tools of intensive strength to bore into or disintegrate the surface material of the ship—to no avail. Only Dalos or a member of his crew seemed capable of gaining entrance into the sealed enclosure. There was no visible doorway in the smooth exterior surface of this starship, and the materials of which it had been constructed were unknown on any Orion planets.

This, of course, was a great source of frustration for Tyrantus' scientists, who were quite eager to please their Emperor and to provide information about this particular starship, which had appeared in their midst without their prior detection. The Emperor was quite adamant in his insistence that they continue their attempts to break into the resting ship. It still remained outside the Orion headquarters, for it was too large to transport and the Tyronites feared they might cause some damage to the ship if they used their mechanical cranes and other equipment to move the ship from one place to another—although it greatly irritated Tyrantus to have this constant reminder of his own technology's failure in his line of vision, and exposed to the public at large!

He bowed to his scientists' vehement insistence that they must not yet carry out any plan to move the ship. They assumed that it contained much sensitive and delicate electronic equipment, the slightest jarring of which could damage these technological treasures beyond repair. Tyrantus planned eventually to use his dominating techniques to force the Pleiadeans to open their ship to his staff's inspection; however, he was not yet prepared to admit his defeat to them—for it would be an admittance of defeat to let the Pleiadeans know of his inability to carry out the simplest task of opening a starship hatch!

Now, however, he was facing—in the company of Dalos himself—this particular truth. But Tyrantus was determined to brush aside this issue.

Dalos was wise enough not to focus any attention on this circumstance, which he knew must be causing Tyrantus great anger and ego deflation. Dalos had no desire to stir the wrath of this one; Tyrantus was already being shaken internally to a sufficient degree to cause irrational and defensive behavior, which could bring further harm to Dalos' own physical self and the physical lives of his entourage, wherever they may be.

Nothing was said, therefore, as Dalos directed his consciousness to command the opening of the starship, and the group of five entered the control center of the ship.

This time Tyrantus had requested the company of three individuals. They were his closest allies, three who sat on the Council of Twelve.

With no hesitation Dalos, still confined to his wheeled transport mechanism, directed them to the psychic anatomy viewer. "Who shall offer himself as our test subject?" Dalos inquired. "It is not painful, and I believe you will find it quite rejuvenating in the long run."

Fear passed through the three Council members. These words on Orion planets meant certain harm, for all known "rejuvenating treatments" were either painful reformations of the physical anatomy or numbing projections of electromagnetic fields which dulled the consciousness. These were the souls who had devised such treatments to subdue their enemies. But they were facing the amused stare of their commander-in-chief.

"Yes, which among you is the brave one? I myself have already experienced this particular treatment. I can tell you that the Pleiadean speaks true. You will find it very stimulating, I promise you!"

Nothing in Tyrantus' remarks gave the three any cause for relaxing their fears, and that, of course, was his intention. He was thoroughly enjoying their predicament.

"I shall volunteer," said one tall, stoutly-built individual. He was flamboyant in his mannerisms and could not allow such a situation to occur in which he did not display his fearlessness. "How do we proceed?" he said to Dalos.

"It is quite simple. Place your palm on this smooth panel."

The man did so, barely flinching as he reined in his fears so that they would not be apparent to the others. He was quite practiced in this technique of suppressing his true feelings. A leader who showed feeling was weak, indeed, and there had been much talk among the Council of late of the weaknesses being demonstrated by Tyrantus since the arrival of these Pleiadeans.

Very little information had been given to the Council about the research operations that Tyrantus had authorized with regard to the Pleiadean visitors. But the Council had been briefed occasionally and now, of course, these three were given access to the person of Dalos. They could see the "treatments" that he had been undergoing. They also had their own spy networks, which constantly fed them information about the activities of Tyrantus' researchers.

Tyrantus knew this, of course, but they never were quite able to gain the full story of all events that had taken place, and he had insured that no spies were able to penetrate his inner reception chambers. Many individuals had been put to death for the mere suspicion of their espionage activities, particularly those who worked close to Tyrantus. This put great fear into the minds of his aides and associates, as he knew it would. He kept his house "cleaned" in this fashion.

As Dalos reached from his restraints (which had been loosened somewhat for the occasion) to manipulate the controls, the Council member fixed his eyes in a resolute stare at the screens of this machine, which was quite foreign to him. He had never seen a configuration like it on any of the Orion planets.

Indeed, the atmosphere of the starship itself was having a similar effect upon these three as it had upon Tyrantus during his first visit. What the four Tyronites did not realize was that by their very entrance into this starship, their consciousness was raised through the interpenetrating rays of a higher-frequency, intelligent energy that permeated the ship itself. That is why the Orionites were unable to gain access to the ship. Their frequencies were quite unrelative to those of the ship's materials, and their tools and instruments could not penetrate the higher-frequency oscillations of the isotopic forms of physical matter which made up the body of the ship. These atomic structures were supported by the Higher Minds of the Pleiadeans themselves, joined with the Minds of the spiritual Brotherhood that worked with them from non-atomic dimensions at all times.

As they entered the ship, this party of individuals, by their willingness to undertake this exploration, had opened their minds ever so slightly to these higher radiations of Intelligence. This is why Dalos had proposed another visit to the starship. It was his opportunity to bring the Orionites into his domain, so to speak, wherein they would be irradiated in the opposite fashion, as they irradiated their brother beings. That is, they were being given higher-frequency beams of Intelligence that enhanced their mental clarity and, at the same time, elevated their consciousness above those electronic influences which they themselves had devised and which—unbeknownst to them—were actually affecting their creators ever as much as they affected the Council's victims, and those victims of electronic controls numbered in the many billions. So it was a case of true reversal that was occurring: just as the Pleiadean entourage was enclosed in an environment that was filled with lower-frequency radiations of unintelligent information, so were these four Orionites enclosed in the Love Radiations of the Higher Intelligences of Uriel and all her Brothers of Light!

The conversation among them, then, had taken a shift in tone. The Tyronites, including Tyrantus, were unaware of this change within themselves. They were not sensitive to the fact that they had transcended their normal states of consciousness. This is how Dalos hoped to rekindle their memories of their former existence as Light Beings—for all of the Council members had once served under Tyrantus when his name was still Antares and they lived as Arian Brothers of Light.

The Council official shuddered violently, and the wave forms depicted on the screens reflected this inner agitation. The viewing screen formed an image that was least expected.

It was a small child who appeared, holding upon the palm of his hand a clear, crystallized mineral of a pale blue color. He was offering it to a woman—perhaps his mother—and his eyes were filled with a luminosity that was quite rare among the Orionites.

The Council member did not jerk his hand from the pliant sensory material as had Tyrantus. Involuntarily, tears formed in his eyes as he gazed upon this young boy, his former self, eventually spilling over and running down his leathery cheeks. A great silence hung in the vibrant atmosphere of the starship.

Dalos said nothing. No words were required.

Finally, Dalos spoke in a gentle, soft tone. "You may remove your hand if you wish."

The Council member did not seem to hear. He was transfixed, unaware of the presence of others—those among whom he would, in his normal state of consciousness, *never* allow himself to be exposed in this way, but he seemed not to care.

"Dear one, I see that you have been touched by this experience."

The man abruptly turned his eyes from the screen, as if awakening from a dream. He looked at Dalos with a startled expression, suddenly realizing where he was and that he had made some profoundly unwise outburst. He quickly removed his hand and placed it behind a fold of his garment. "What have you done to me?" he blurted. "What is this machine that has caused me some emotional turmoil? I demand to know!"

Tyrantus, who had been watching all this with great interest—and an extreme measure of relief—finally spoke up. "It is just as I experienced, Tonar. Now you understand the seriousness of our position with this

Pleiadean, who refuses to explain the mechanics of this particular device. Yet as you can see, it does hold a powerful potential, does it not, for our future usage?"

"How is that?" said another of the Council members, who had been hanging back and hoping he would not be asked to experience this mentality-twisting machine.

"Can you not see how it weakens a strong man? I myself was nearly overtaken by the influence of this apparatus, but of course I was not defeated by it! Dalos here will tell you that I took swift action to counteract his attack upon my mind! I have allowed him to live and I have allowed his crew to live because I believe we can use their knowledge to our purposes. Do you not see the possibilities here? We can defeat our enemies without raising a single weapon! They will melt into puddles of sentimentality like small children—as Tonar here has so exquisitely demonstrated for us!"

Tonar flushed a deep, angry red. He despised the Emperor, and would as soon rip his throat as stand firm and hold his tongue, recognizing the necessity for such control. He was not in a position to physically attack the Emperor. His death would be instantaneous at the hands of, not only his two colleagues, but all those guarding forces which stood by to respond to the slightest physical signal from their leader—and Tyrantus' body was equipped with security sensing devices, so that any sudden fluctuation of his heartbeat or other internal organs would bring them instantly to his side. Tonar suppressed his hatred for now, vowing eternal vengeance. He would find his opportunity one day, and crush this Emperor like dust under his feet!

Radik, who had thus far held silent, suggested that they interrogate this Dalos further, applying more forceful techniques to elicit the precise engineering which had gone into the construction of this unique machine. It was admittedly beyond their present technology, but they could no doubt quickly adapt their manufacturing equipment to produce such a machine for their own use.

"That has been my plan, of course," Tyrantus replied, "but Dalos here has now volunteered, as I knew he would, to give us the complete information."

Throughout this exchange, Dalos had maintained his silence. He was conserving his strength, what little remained, to deliver unto these four the ultimate blow to their overstuffed egos.

"Gentlemen," he said softly, "you have thoroughly missed the value of this machine, as you call it. You have failed to recognize that it is of a far greater potential than you have yet imagined. Tonar, tell us what you felt as you gazed into the eyes of that young boy. Was he not familiar to you?"

Again, Tonar flushed. But this time it was not anger that brought the color to his cheeks, and another involuntary shudder passed through him, visible to all present.

"Speak, man! What is the matter with you?" Tyrantus commanded. "Tell us what you saw."

Tonar's eyes were averted from his colleagues. Dalos reached a hand toward Tonar and clasped his fingers in a firm grip. A wave of heat passed through Tonar's arm, spreading another form of energy throughout his being.

"Yes," he said. "I will not fear to tell you the truth." He did not know why but he gripped Dalos' hand in firm response, as if to prove that he was still alive and capable of maintaining his own consciousness. He glanced into Dalos' eyes for a split second. The Light he saw there shocked his senses once again but he did not consciously realize this. He merely opened his mouth to speak.

"It was myself. I was that young boy, and I do remember the incident quite vividly. I had found this shard of crystal in my diggings that I had undertaken as a part of my educational experience. Something about this lucent, pale blue stone fascinated me. I do not know why, but it caused me some deep feeling, some memory I cannot explain …

"It matters not!" He abruptly let go the hand of Dalos. "I do not understand why you have brought us here, Tyrantus. What is your true purpose? Are you trying to humiliate us?"

"Oh-ho, so I see we *do* have some touchy reactions there, do we not? Well, if you feel humiliated then that is your own problem, isn't it? You must gain control of yourself, Tonar. This is not fit behavior for a Council member! Dalos, tell us what you have done to our colleague here. He seems quite beside himself with childish emotions."

"Yes," Dalos replied. "I shall attempt, again, to explain this to you. But please, let us adjourn for the moment to a more comfortable environment. Let us return to the central chamber of my ship. I believe you will find it quite conducive to our conversation, which may take some length of time."

"We have the necessary time. Do not concern yourself with our personal needs—we are quite capable of managing for ourselves. We do not need you to tell us how to live our lives! We merely need you to answer some particular, pointed questions. If you wish to do so in this other section of your ship, I see no reason why not," and he directed the group to follow Dalos' lead.

Dalos was able to command the movements of his transport through a touch of a button at his fingertips. He was drained and exhausted, but he would not think of stopping now. He had reached this one, just as he had reached Tyrantus—and the other two were wide-eyed with fear and curiosity. They were going nowhere, not until they had some explanation for the strange feelings that were permeating their own selves. They would never voice these concerns, of course, not in the presence of one another, but Dalos knew of the reactions they were having, and he was gratified by this slight glimmer of progressive accomplishment. It made his weeks of suffering worthwhile. If only he could break through their mental shields in the smallest degree, he would be satisfied, for now he saw that he must limit his hopes for them somewhat. He would not be able to achieve all that had been planned for this particular phase of his mission to rescue the fallen ones. As long as progress was being made, then he would reluctantly accept this limiting reality—but he would never cease to push beyond what appeared to be possible at the present moment! He knew that there was always more that could be done, *always*—always.

The three Council members and their Emperor chose seats among the crew's flight stations and Dalos wheeled himself in close proximity to them.

"First," he said, "you must believe that I have no cause to withhold information from you. I have come to do this very thing, to teach you how to build this particular device—and many others that you will find to be of benefit. You must believe this, and if you cannot, please allow me the time to prove to you that I have no desire to fight you for some dominating position. As you can see, I am in no condition to do so!"

"Get to the point," Tyrantus interrupted. "Yes, yes, we will give you an opportunity to prove yourself. That you can be certain of! But now, tell us where these images come from that appear on the screen of this device. How did you know of the details of Tonar's childhood experience?"

"Yes," Tonar said, "how did you come by this information?"

Dalos gazed at them for a long moment. How to tell these souls of their own history? How to awaken the sleeping minds within?

"You know that your body is a pure energy creation?" Dalos inquired.

"Of course!" Radik barked.

"That is an elemental scientific understanding," said Linton, who spoke for the first time. "We are not children."

"Then do you not realize that as energy, you are constantly changing?"

"This is too much!" Linton exploded. "He has brought us here to insult our intelligence and lead us on with tidbits of child's play!"

"Be silent," Tyrantus said, "let him speak. Yes, Dalos, of course our knowledge extends far beyond anything that the physical sciences of the primitive worlds have dreamed in their most outlandish nightmares! Cells do constantly reproduce themselves, blood flows, hearts beat, lungs expand and contract—what are you trying to say?"

"That you are, at this very instant, recording intelligent information within your psychic anatomy, that energy body which is supporting your very physical self. This is a basic fact of interdimensional physics and until you can conceive and accept this fact, I cannot proceed in my explanation of all that you have seen."

The four were silent.

"Good," Dalos continued quickly. "We have now established the basic principle of the continuity of life. All experiences are recorded as permanent records in an individual's psychic structures; therefore, they can be tapped into by one whose own mind is capable of detecting this energy information, or, if such an individual is not available to provide this intelligent service, then they can be recreated through a device such as you have seen and now experienced."

"You mean," Tonar said, "that this picture came from information ..." He did not know how to continue.

"Yes," Dalos responded, "from information contained within your own self, your true self, your energy anatomy. I can see that I must illustrate this for you, because once you have grasped this principle, I guarantee that your lives on Tyron will be permanently changed."

"How dare you tell us what we shall do with this information!" Tyrantus blustered.

The others shot him a look of great impatience. They now were quite eager to hear Dalos' words and they had tired of the Emperor's constant need to assert his authoritative position.

"Please continue, Dalos," Radik urged. "I think I begin—I think I know whereof you speak. I am the sum and total of my own experiences. This seems like sound reasoning. In fact, I have been thinking along these lines myself," he hastened to add. "I suspected as much, and I was, in fact, devising some formulation of this particular theory to present at a future date."

The others looked at him with wry expressions.

"Oh, of course you were," Tonar's sarcasm matched the glint in his eye. "You had it all in your back pocket, eh? Wrapped up and ready to present to the Council?"

Radik looked at him with pure hatred. "You would be wise to keep your mouth shut," he warned. "You have certainly spilled your guts already, don't you think?"

Tonar returned his venomous look, but no further words were exchanged.

Dalos ignored this display of the lower selves of these individuals. He continued his explanations of the energy principles of life for nearly an hour. This exchange continued to be interrupted by such occasional outbursts of ego from the Orionites, but for the most part they were receptive to Dalos' teaching.

Their motivations at this point were quite mixed, however. Dalos knew this. He realized that they were listening because they hoped to gain something for themselves. Truly this was his desire as well—that they gain for themselves their own former states of Intelligence! And that is why they were able to receive his words with some understanding. They had not only learned these factors of life previously, but they themselves had been great teachers of these interdimensional principles, and now they had used their knowledge of life to create this entire, nightmarish society! But they were so oblivious to their own decline that they were functioning out of control; that is, they knew not, or they had forgotten wherefrom this information on how to perform certain tasks had come.

It would remain to be seen what kind of effect this session would have upon them.

After extending himself beyond any ability to speak further, Dalos was forced to end the discussion. "I sincerely regret," he whispered, "but I cannot continue. As you can see, I have lost all strength." His eyes closed. "You must allow me to rest," and he left them, losing consciousness to the physical world.

12

The Test of Consciousness

DALOS OPENED HIS EYES in excruciating agony. A sharp pain twisted through his spine and he drew in a quick breath through his clenched teeth, letting it out again in a cry of pain. It was one of the first to escape his lips, but there would be many more—for he had been returned to the research laboratories. This time the purpose was to break down any remaining resistance that he might have to revealing his full knowledge to Tyrantus and his associates.

Now the so-called "research" was more of a torturous nature than to discover some facts about the Pleiadean's physiological makeup. Of course the researchers involved believed that they were carrying out some exotic experiment at the risk of the Pleiadean's life. This was routine business to them. They were unconcerned whether he lived or died. To them, it was just another job to perform, albeit one that was eliciting a great deal of interest from the higher echelons of the Orion government, particularly the Emperor himself. So they were working under some pressure to perform to the best of their abilities. Many high stakes were involved, in terms of positions and rewards granted for some success in these experiments. How to measure such "success"? By the discovery of some factor of human anatomy which had heretofore been unknown to the Orion scientists.

They believed that this Pleiadean's previously excellent physical condition and mental acuity held the secrets of superhuman development, which the Orion scientists had long endeavored to create among the Orion peoples. They were constantly looking for means by which to enhance the physical anatomy and mental abilities. This involved the removal and replacement of many portions of human anatomy with mechanical parts and electronically controlled devices in an endless, diabolical array.

Of course these experiments usually resulted in failure, as far as the patients were concerned—generally, their own death.

But to the research scientists, any glimmer of progress was encouragement to continue in their fruitless striving for devices that would create super-beings. They also used genetic engineering techniques to tamper with the physical body. They were combining and recombining the cell structures in various laboratories wherein were cultured an infinite number of bacterial and viral forms of living organisms. Always were they searching for that key to life which would unlock its mystery for, although they had made substantial technological achievements through the continuity of their research in all fields, they had not yet discovered the true, overall source of life.

If only they had allowed themselves to listen to the words of Dalos and his two hundred teachers who had prepared themselves to convey this very science of life to the Orionites, they would have found that for which they so insanely searched! They were digging in the troughs of hell for the secrets to heaven, you might say. They would never find that gem of Infinity through the gross abuse and misuse of human beings. They would only find this wisdom within themselves, when they ceased to look in the exterior world for some quick and easy solutions to these questions of life and death.

But Tyrantus and his Council of Twelve had long forgotten these truths. It is true that Dalos had touched these buried factors of consciousness during his discourse on the psychic anatomy viewer, but once he lost consciousness, the four Tyronites engaged in a most enlightening conversation among themselves—enlightening in terms of their personalities, yet one which obscured their inner vision once again to the truths that Dalos was presenting before their very eyes.

"How can we listen to this man, Tyrantus, when he cannot even maintain control of his own body?" Linton exclaimed. "I believe we should immediately transfer this apparatus to our laboratories, where I will supervise the careful analysis of this equipment. We have the capability to determine how it functions and upon what basis it is able to distill these graphic images from an individual's energy emanations. I agree with Radik, that we were on the verge of this discovery ourselves, and this piece of equipment may provide us with the key to resolving the dilemmas that had presented themselves to us in our ongoing research."

"I do not agree," interrupted Tonar. "This would perhaps give Linton and his team of mad scientists the opportunity to destroy a very delicate machine which does hold great potential for us, Emperor. You know that it surpasses our present scientific understanding—that is quite obvious," Tonar directed at Linton, barely concealing his dislike for the scientific arm of Tyrantus' government. He was himself the head of all Orion communications systems, and he was quite willing to employ the results of scientific development. Yet he despised these individuals for the arrogant attitudes that reigned among them—oblivious to his own superior attitude.

"I believe we should allow Dalos to continue his explanation," Tonar went on. "From his words, we can derive the necessary information. He does seem willing to tell all, and I believe we should allow him to do so. In fact, I suspect that there are those among his entourage who, likewise, hold sufficient scientific knowledge to provide our research teams with enough material to carry on with their work, probing far beyond any achievements we have made thus far. This, to me, seems like the wisest course of action."

Tyrantus considered their words. He knew that each of them was eager to gain an advantage over the other. Wherever such a plum of scientific research landed, it would enhance the capabilities of that particular Council member under whose domain this work would fall. For Tyrantus now realized that he was in possession of some breakthrough information, all of which had been dropped into his midst by these foolish star travelers. They truly did not realize with whom they were dealing, he believed. They had underestimated his skill at eliciting whatever he needed from whomever he encountered.

"Yes, I believe Tonar has the right idea," Tyrantus said. "I have decided to continue my sessions with Dalos in private. He will be returned to the medical facility for further testing, which I think will reveal some most interesting factors."

The others knew what this meant. They knew that Dalos would be further reduced in his ability to resist the interrogations of his captors. They could do nothing to change the Emperor's mind, for to disagree too vehemently would risk many of the advantages they had been granted through his favor. Thus far, this situation did not warrant their aggressive action. They would wait to see what might develop, but each one of them had been alerted to the fact that the Pleiadeans possessed very crucial information pertaining to the future technological developments of the Orion Empire. Wherever progress was being made, therein lay the potential for one to gain greater power and influence among the Orion peoples.

Each of the three, then, silently vowed to keep his eyes and ears open to any development—and those "eyes and ears" included the hundreds of eyes and ears of the espionage agents who worked for each Council member. They would also do everything possible to keep this information from the hands of the other Council members who were not present. Of course, this decision rested within the domain of the Emperor, who could speak or not speak as he chose. If he determined to relate information about the Pleiadeans to the Council at large, then there was nothing that they could do to stop him. But in the meantime, they could speed their efforts to learn all possible, to be a step ahead of one another. So the competition to drain information from the Pleiadeans began.

What of the mental projections that they had each received from the mind of Dalos—the overshadowing Mind of Uriel? They were oblivious to this reawakening deep within their psychic structures. They were now operating with an added factor in their lives, of which they were completely ignorant. A slight pulse beat of Intelligence now oscillated within each one.

For Tonar, although he had seemingly forgotten his experience of but a few hours previous, this had become a part of his present map of consciousness, and it was this map by which he guided his actions. He did not need to be consciously aware of this experience for it to affect his decision-making process. Some facet of his human compassion had been rekindled by the sight of his own intuitive, sensitive, aware, and informed Higher Self, functioning through the body of a child.

That child who held the gleaming crystal on his small palm was remembering, reattuning to a life he had once lived, freed of the physical anatomy, a life of splendor in which the mind was creative and productive, supplying an intelligent beacon of Life Force for countless individuals still climbing the evolutionary ladder of mental development. This soft blue crystal which allowed light to enter and reflect clearly through the sensory response of the boy's eyes stirred thoughts, albeit unformed, of his previous existence as a Light Bearer. The worlds from which such a Mind functions are pure, radiant creations of the joined Minds of Higher Intellects who have learned how to use the raw material of Infinity in the creation of their dimensional environment. They lived among these crystalline creations, which might appear to one of lesser development as glistening structures of transparent material. Spired buildings, sparkling vegetation, clear, running waters—even the people themselves appeared as flame-like beings of this glittering Life Essence.

That is why young Tonar's breath was suspended when he pulled this shard of his former self from the dirt of an Orion planet. Broken, indeed, was his connection to this luminous existence! Fragmented and buried under the mounds of selfish, egotistical states of consciousness, which he had developed through the course of his lives lived in physical worlds since he followed Antares in his fall from higher states of consciousness.

Tonar was not alone in this. Even as they viewed the scene of their comrade's early life, Radik and Linton were touched by similar visions of inexplicable memory. They were not fully formed; they affected these two in a subtle, emotional way. A warm sensation that oscillated through the solar plexus, a sharp gust of cold, clear air, the scent of a flower in the rays of an afternoon sun—it truly could not be described in their language. They immediately covered their sensitive response to Tonar's experience with gruff exterior attitudes of superiority and skepticism.

But these three individuals were now as desirous as Tyrantus to truly know what had transpired on Dalos' starship.

They finally left the premises, after Dalos returned to consciousness long enough to facilitate their exit, as he alone was capable of activating the starship hatch. They had not bargained on his loss of consciousness or they never would have allowed themselves to become stranded in this situation. However, he was quickly revived by the three, who slapped his face and shook his physical body until his eyes blinked open. They were glazed and tired, yet he was sufficiently aware to recognize these unpleasant faces.

Dalos realized that he had done all that he could for now to touch their inner minds. He must rest. He longed for sleep, and he agreed to a quick departure from the starship. He did not expect the treatment that awaited him and that was just as well, for the prospect of physical torture that awaited this one would cause nearly any soul to immediately vacate the physical anatomy!

Dalos was not one, however, to relinquish his opportunity to help these soulic expressions of Infinity. He recognized them, not as the tormented, destructive, vicious creations that they had deteriorated into, but as former Brothers of the Light who still carried the potential to redeem themselves and repair the damage they had spread among so many earth worlds. This motivated Dalos' determination to remain on Tyron as long as possible, but he was faced with an army of individuals bearing the weaponry of surgical instrumentation and unpossessed of human kindness, which the Orion society had stripped from them by its very cruelty.

It was a vicious cycle that perpetuated itself through the minds and bodies of these souls. Dalos and his entourage were the only hope for breaking this momentum of cannibalistic expression. These people fed upon one another in mindless perpetuations of their robotic, consuming lifestyle. This, the Pleiadean party of ten was beginning to understand as they toured scene after scene of life among the Tyronites.

In one building, they found themselves standing in an Orion nursery. Connected to the rows of cubicles containing tiny life forms were massive tangles of electronic equipment. These newborn babies were already being scanned and analyzed by the Orion computer system. At the same time, they were being "taught," the Tyronite guides explained. Through tiny transmitters, they were bombarded throughout the day and night with information broadcast from a central source. This information was their programming into the ways of Orion life. They never had the opportunity to breathe in freedom, for at the instant of their birth they entered into a world in which the mind was never allowed to express its true function. It was constantly interfered with by the continuous stimulation of information developed to occupy the thoughts of Orion citizens.

It was believed that in this way, these young children would become more intelligent, more productive in their additions to Orion society. But what was actually occurring was their total blocking-off from the inner Intelligence which would have radiated naturally into their minds. This inner joining of consciousness with a higher source of Intelligence would have supplied them with all that was necessary to live a creative and abundant life on a physical planet. It would have been an association that they had developed with this Higher Intelligence through the course of many consecutive lives lived in two dimensions; that is, in third-dimensional, physical anatomies, and between these physical lifetimes in pure energy states of consciousness, or in fourth-dimensional realms of life. There, they would have been supplied with energy-intelligence by their spiritual teachers and guides, which would have then been proven out and made whole within themselves as they lived, subsequently, on a physical world.

This is the process of true mental growth. It is how Intelligence is made a part of oneself. But these babies would never experience this mental growth! They were, henceforth, the property of a computer system that masqueraded as a societal structure. They would only know the repetitious expression of thoughts and deeds that were guided by their overseers. No Light would penetrate this mental prison. No new insight would be allowed to flower among them. If any such blossoming of consciousness ever occurred among the Orion citizenry, it was regarded as a mental aberration that was immediately stamped out by the brainwashing treatments to which the Orion people were constantly subjected.

Innovation, independent thinking, and variety were generally unknown among the worker populations of most Orion planets. These qualities were encouraged among the scientific and governmental elite, but that which was called "innovative" or "creative" was truly a compilation of physical data and limited states of consciousness into some seemingly new formulation or combination of old ideas.

The Pleiadeans had come to provide the missing Light in the lives of these people. They were fully prepared to teach and share new ideas about life—new to the Orionites. They hoped to awaken the inner minds of these souls sufficiently so that they could carry on in their lessons through their own self-development, through the natural process which had been abrogated by Orion society. But the Pleiadeans were never given this opportunity. They had become captives, pawns in a political game being played by Tyrantus and his Council members.

The party of ten was eventually returned to the holding quarters where the remainder of the Pleiadean entourage eagerly awaited their colleagues. As the ten described what they had seen and heard, the faces of the Pleiadeans were grim, indeed. It was far worse than they had yet conceived. A sense of hopelessness spread through the group, despite their leaders' efforts to dispel this attitude, for they knew it was not constructive in nature and could cause further unrest among them.

These ten had taken on a leadership role among the two hundred, particularly now that Dalos was no longer a part of their daily lives. An entirely new structure of interaction had begun to develop among the Pleiadeans.

The Orion researchers watched this with great interest, of course. Every one of these conversations was being monitored and recorded and analyzed by behavioral scientists who specialized in group interactions. They watched as the Pleiadeans responded in what, to them, was typical group behavior: the loss of a strong leadership figure resulting in a new reorganization of the remaining individuals in which they would naturally gravitate toward the selection of a new leader to replace the one that had been removed.

This was beginning to occur. A single figure began to emerge in this stronger role over the ensuing weeks. Her name was Shimlus. She had been the polarity of Dalos, the one whose mind was most closely joined in harmonic attunement with their leader. She was looked to as the individual who would be most aware of the purpose and need of their mission at any given point, for through her closeness in mental oscillation with Dalos, it was believed that she would maintain this inner contact throughout the course of their physical separation.

Of course, each one of the Pleiadeans had his or her own inner, mental attunement with the Higher Mind of Uriel, truly the director and leader of this mission unto the earth worlds. Yet gradually, as they became more confused and fearful and restless through their confinement and lack of contact with Dalos, they began to look outside themselves for some solutions to this predicament. They gradually relinquished their own mental attunement with the Higher Mind of Uriel with each incident in which they turned their attention to Shimlus' words and expressions, hoping to find therein some ray of added light, some clear solution to this unplanned stalemate.

Shimlus was also slipping in her mental balance, yet this was undetectable to the others, just as they themselves were unaware of their own mental slippage. It occurred over such a lengthy period of time and in such subtle degrees that the Pleiadeans were losing themselves inch by inch, thought by thought, one by one. They were the victims of the steady, subversive influence of Orion subliminal electronic projections, yet they were losing their hold on their own minds through their own lack of mental vigilance. They, unlike Dalos, were weak in this ability to sustain belief and knowledge of a radiating inner source of direction and guidance. Subconsciously, they felt that it had betrayed them, for they knew of no way to resolve the present situation. Nothing seemed to emerge in consciousness as to which way they could turn, or what they might physically do to alleviate the situation.

What they did not realize was that they were doing precisely what was required. They could do no more than to await an opportunity to perform the tasks for which they had come—but to wait patiently, with a positive knowingness that, when that time arrived, they would carry out their service as Light Bearers with a full inner attunement to the very Fountainhead of Life!

Yet this attunement deteriorated with each emotional response they allowed themselves to this captivity. Frustration, anger, impatience, fear—all brewed together into a bitter poison that fouled the waters of consciousness for the Pleiadeans. Had they asked of themselves, they would have found this truth. But they were too busy looking to Shimlus, as if she were that Higher One who they began to feel—very subtly at first—had abandoned them, although this thought bore no rational characteristics. Nevertheless, it began to express a dominant frequency among many of the Pleiadeans.

Shimlus, then, had become their new leader, although this was not yet vocalized, nor outwardly symbolized. Still, more and more sought her out to hear her advice and plans for their future on the planet Tyron.

Meanwhile, Dalos suffered at the hands of the monstrous individuals who seemed determined to wring the life from his physical body.

Tyrantus waited. Soon he would conduct another interview with Dalos—a private interview. This time, he knew the Pleiadean would be asking for his mercy and Tyrantus had some idea of the bargain that he would strike—all in his favor, of course. Now he held the key to his immortality among the Orionites! Now he would become their Supreme Leader for all eternity! Dalos would give him this ability.

13

Close Encounter

THE BUILDING IN WHICH Dalos was being held was extremely large, although it was segmented into long corridors which branched off into laboratories, surgical arenas, and holding areas for the patient-subjects.

At the end of one of these long corridors, Dalos was confined to a sterile room. Lengthy tubes ran from many areas of his body and electronic sensors were attached at various intervals along the surface of his skin. They provided constant read-outs of pulse, temperature, and other vital signs. They also probed into the consciousness of Dalos, sending and receiving their electronic messages in a futile effort to discover the true mechanism by which this mind operated.

Soon the research scientists would begin layering into his brain to find the source of Dalos' intelligence—as soon as Tyrantus gave them authorization to do so. They were anxious to probe more deeply into Dalos' physical anatomy, but their hands were tied for now.

Tyrantus had other ideas about how this one could be used to the greatest benefit. He must remain whole for now. His mind was of far more use to Tyrantus if it remained functioning for the present. So, eventually, these tubes and sensors were disconnected and Dalos was once again wheeled into the presence of Tyrantus.

This time, however, he was not able to leave this medical facility. A special room was prepared by Tyrantus' security forces for the purpose of their private interview. This was not Tyrantus' first choice; however, he was informed by the technicians in charge that Dalos would not survive a move from their facility. There needed to remain some devices attached to his body that were sustaining his pulse while he was under the influence of the effects of their surgical techniques.

Dalos was barely conscious when Tyrantus entered this room. This time the Pleiadean leader was unable to maintain a sitting position. His true Mind, however, was not deterred from its full intent to carry out the healing plan of Uriel. Her compassion was such that she would never give up this plan, this mission—not so long as there remained a single soul under the influence of the negative, demonic force that had been generated by the one known now as Tyrantus!

The ashen-faced remains of what had once been a beautiful, tall, warm Being obscured the reality of the Radiant Mind that still oscillated through the physical consciousness of this One. Tyrantus assumed that Dalos was now on the verge of a total breakdown of his mental and physical capabilities. He assumed wrongly! He did not calculate the overriding influence of the Higher Mind that constantly added its Intelligence to Dalos' present existence. This Mind could not, or would not interfere in the physical circumstances through which Dalos was now living, but it still shot forth its beacons of Intelligence at every opportunity! This was such an opportunity.

Despite himself, Tyrantus was shocked at the sight of Dalos. He did not generally witness the tortures that he ordered for his political enemies. He did not generally see the effects of these experimental operations that he believed were so necessary for the continued growth of his scientific breakthroughs. He avoided this situation, although he was, of course, given full reports and extensive detail with regard to these ongoing experiments, and he was given visual access to observe these operations. He did so when required, but his natural inclination was to divest himself of any concern in this area. He rationalized that it was not a wise use of his precious time, and it was not required, so long as the job was done and validated to him that it had been carried out to the best of his workers' ability.

But this time he was forced by his desire to gain information to look upon the effects of the medical tampering that had been done to this one. For a moment, Tyrantus felt as if he, too, might lose consciousness; but he immediately gathered his strength and suppressed his emotional response. He demanded that a chair be placed near Dalos' bedside, and this was as much to give him support as to allow his closer access to the Pleiadean, who was incapable now of speaking above a very weak tone—almost a whisper.

Tyrantus considered for a moment that he may have waited too long for this interview, and he resolved to give orders to the head research team to halt their activities until further orders. He did not want to push this man beyond his physical endurance—not yet. Not while Tyrantus still needed him.

"Dalos, can you hear me sufficiently?" Tyrantus began.

Dalos merely looked at the Emperor. Great pain now clouded his eyes, yet the luminosity of true Intelligence still shone beneath this temporal haze.

Tyrantus could not return this look. It was like staring into the eyes of a wounded, innocent animal, and this, as stated, was not the Emperor's habit. He kept himself removed from the more obvious results of his dehumanizing, technological system of control. He was thoroughly capable of insulating himself in this way and merely enjoying the fruits of his powerful position.

"Now you must realize," Tyrantus said as he rose to his feet again and walked to a more comfortable distance from his handiwork, the broken body of a once-great man, "you are in a dire situation here, and if you cooperate fully with me, I will see that your circumstances are changed."

Tyrantus found it surprisingly difficult to speak to Dalos this time. He was searching for words that seemed to elude him and his thoughts were churning in a confused manner to which he was unaccustomed. A chill passed through his entire body. He was deeply disturbed, and was uncertain as to why, except that he was anxious to be done with this business and to return to his headquarters.

"Tell me, Dalos, your real purpose for coming here. Yes, I know you say you have come to give us presents, to tell us all that you know, yet I find this impossible to believe. Now speak truly. You have only your life to gain by doing so! You can see that I am determined to get to the bottom of this."

Again Dalos merely stared at Tyrantus. Words were futile, he thought. *This one cannot hear the full sound of Infinity roaring within his inner mind! He knows only selfishness, ego, and the domination of all other expressions of life. Why should I expend my strength to speak?*

But Dalos' higher Mind could not be deterred from its natural expression. "Tyrantus," he croaked, "you would not hear the truth if I spoke it plainly."

"You think so, eh? Well, what do you know? Look at you! Here is where your 'truth' has landed you—and I should say, it does not seem to serve you well! So I am done with your false truths. I want to know the answer, the real answer to my question."

"Very well," Dalos sighed. "I will give you the *real* answer. But I think that you will wish to sit down."

"Don't tell me what to do!"

"No, I cannot tell you what to do," Dalos continued. "I have never been able to tell you what to do!"

Tyrantus glanced at him.

"Yes, it is true. I have known you before, Tyrantus. We have met many, many times, in many other lifetimes."

"Why do *I* not know this?" Tyrantus said, his voice rising. "Why do *I* have no memory?"

"Because you have destroyed your mind, Tyrantus. You have abolished an entire portion of your psychic anatomy through your grievous mistakes and your onrush into the physical worlds, whereupon you have incurred a horrendous blockage of massive negation that has blinded you to Truth!"

These words tore out of the mouth of Dalos with a surprising force. Tyrantus was shaken, as much by this force as by the words themselves. He suddenly seemed meek, and gave no response to Dalos.

"You are the very Demon of demons," Dalos continued. "You are destroying the minds of trillions of souls, Tyrantus. You are destroying the lives of an infinite number of beings throughout the universe, yet you are totally oblivious to this fact! Is this not the work of an insane man—a soul so bent on its own destruction that it is destroying many others in the process?"

The words rang like bells in the hollow, steel-rimmed room. Now Dalos felt the blood returning to his face and a Power surged into his being that had seemed distant until this moment. He was finally speaking the words he came to speak to this one. There was nothing left to lose except his last physical breath, and that seemed imminent. He must speak now, or lose the opportunity which had been so painstakingly created to touch the mind of Antares!

"Do you hear me, Tyrantus? Do you remember your former self? Is there any breath of humanity left in you?"

Tyrantus began to quake, from his knees to his shoulders. He could not explain what was happening to him. He did not understand what Dalos was saying, yet it was causing him a turbulent flood of emotional thoughts unlike anything he had ever experienced. Still, he could not move his tongue to respond, and he was glad that there were no prying eyes in this particular room. He had insured that their meeting would be conducted in the utmost secrecy, arriving at this medical facility through carefully planned logistics to keep his enemies' agents from knowing of this secret visit with Dalos. Only a handful of the most trusted aides were aware of his whereabouts, and only three carefully screened staff members of this facility knew of the meeting. They knew that their lives were easily expendable if they should betray Tyrantus' secret, and he trusted that they would not do so for they treasured their lives greatly.

This was not the case with Dalos. His physical life meant nothing other than the chance to reach the ears and eyes of this demonic force, which is what Antares had become.

Now Dalos was spending that life rapidly, with each word, each breath taken to support the sound booming forth from his vocal cords. He had invested a good portion of his Higher Mind in the creation of this physical anatomy—it was his to expend as he saw fit, and now he knew, with every fiber of this being, that the time was right to penetrate the shield of Tyrantus.

"I do not speak these words in anger, or hatred, Emperor. I have come to you as your Brother of Light, *and we have been Brothers!* We have served together as Light Bearers—*helpers* of mankind, Tyrantus, not destroyers!"

A violent shudder passed through Tyrantus. He was inexplicably drawn closer to the form of Dalos, which repulsed him and yet attracted him to these words that so shattered his inner composure. He fell into the chair beside Dalos.

"Yes, well you should feel thusly," Dalos observed. "You should feel as if your entire world of illusion has crumbled. Indeed it must, if you are to redeem yourself in the eyes of Infinity, for you have become the very darkness, the blackness which is engulfing the lives of many, countless souls! Do you not feel some tremor of compassion yet remaining within you for these poor victims of your abominations? Can you not yet be touched by the cry of pain that is arising from these peoples who have been forced to conform to your ways of thinking? Listen, Tyrantus, with that inner mind! Do you not hear the massive surge of cries for mercy that are arising from the psychic selves of the souls whom you have tortured and abused?"

Dalos fell back, gasping for breath.

This gave Tyrantus a moment to contend with all that he was hearing. No one had ever dared speak a word against him! No one questioned his authority. They never even allowed such thoughts, if they were wise to the ways of his machinery of ultimate control. Certainly his enemies did entertain their opposing notions, but no one below the upper echelons of his government still maintained the mental ability to oppose him. If they did, it was quickly crushed. Their lives were ended, or their minds were dismantled in his treatment rooms.

But this one, this strange man who had suddenly appeared in Tyrantus' life, confounded him deeply! He could not raise a hand to stop him from speaking! Some morbid desire to hear more had overtaken the mind of Tyrantus. He could not voice any opposition to this one, nor could he accept that which he was hearing. All that he could feel was an agonizing cry rising up within him. Finally it broke through to the surface with a violence that surprised them both.

"Nooooo!" he screamed. "I will not listen to this any longer! What are you saying to me? Who *are* you? *Why* do you torment me so? I do not have to hear this! I can have you silenced with a snap of my fingers!"

"Yes, Tyrantus, this we both know. But I know many things that you do not. I know who *you* really are. That is the most important question that you should be asking. You, Tyrantus, are the Fallen One, the Brother of Light who relinquished his Mind to take up the robes of Emperor. You, Tyrantus, are the saddest one of all! You have given yourself away in exchange for the rewards of a physical superiority. You chose to feed, like a carnivorous animal, from the minds and bodies of your subjects, when you could have remained as a supplier of Life Essence, a bringer of beauty and wisdom to these very same souls! You could drink the waters of Infinity—but instead, you have chosen to consume the blood of your victims. You are a pitiful sight, Tyrantus. You are not fit to continue as an expression of Infinite Intelligence—yet that is what you truly are! *You are a Being of Light!*"

Dalos' voice rose, as if his very words could shatter the shield this one had built to protect himself from this truth. Indeed, they carried the Power to do so.

Dalos, with great effort, raised himself into a half-sitting position. "I have come to rescue you, Tyrantus, from yourself, before you destroy more of the very life that emanates from the Infinite Fountainhead! I am a *U*niversal, *R*adiant, *I*nfinite, *E*ternal *L*ight—I am *Uriel,* your teacher, and I have been so for countless eons of time. Yes, I now suffer in a physical body, just as do all your victims. But I have come to you in this physical way in order to speak your language. You have shut down your inner mind, your true Mind, your receiving capability, else you would have heard our messages of Love—which never ceased to emanate in your direction!

"Yes, Tyrantus, we do love you as our Brother, as we have always loved you, and it is our Love that brings me to you at this moment. I care not whether you destroy this vehicle, for my Consciousness remains true! My Consciousness envelops you in this Love Radiation, which is the most powerful force of Infinity that you will *ever* encounter! No, you cannot create it in your laboratories, and you cannot pick it apart from these bones and this rotting flesh. You will never find this Force of Life anywhere in your exterior existence. It breathes within you, Tyrantus, as it does within all beings, all expressions of Infinite Intelligence! You can only find this Life Source within your own self.

"But, Tyrantus, you had better move quickly if you wish to find any beat of true life within you, for you are dying! You are a dead man, Tyrantus. Your Spirit has been nearly stamped out by your own actions!"

Dalos could not go on. He had not the breath to continue. He sank back in exhaustion.

Tyrantus had not moved. He now looked upon Dalos with different eyes.

Yes, his true Consciousness—what little remained—had been reactivated for a moment! Long enough for a wave of recognition to pass through him.

There was silence in the room now. But not in Tyrantus' mind.

Dalos' eyes closed. He seemed oblivious to his surroundings. He gave no indication of concern as to the effect his words might have had upon Tyrantus. His consciousness now was directed to the maintenance of his own physical vitality. He had pushed himself beyond the limit imposed by his weakened condition, and a red light began to flash upon one of the nearby monitors. Instantly, the three research technicians appeared, their eyes directing a request for Tyrantus' permission to continue. He waved them on and managed to rise to his feet, turning his back upon them as they converged on the body of Dalos, using their preoccupation as an opportunity to attempt to regain his composure.

As the technicians worked to revive Dalos, Tyrantus hastened from the room, brushing past his bodyguards and storming toward his transporter.

Dalos was now fighting another battle—a battle to remain in this physical anatomy. The medical technicians were also interested in maintaining his physical life, for without this, their experimental activities would be considered to be a failure and there was now a standing order from Tyrantus to keep the Pleiadean alive at all costs.

Within a brief span of time, Tyrantus had issued another order: "Halt all experimentation on the Pleiadean known as Dalos. Place him in a recuperating room and use whatever extraordinary means necessary to restore him to some state of health."

Immediately, Dalos was moved to an environment designed to relax the patient and enhance his healing capability. Yes, such life-restoring facilities did exist on the planet Tyron. They were used for the governmental elite, and for Tyrantus himself, in circumstances in which they required some physical surgery or life-regenerating treatment. And these, too, had been developed by the Orion researchers. After all, it was their purpose to supply Tyrantus with more advanced techniques by which to sustain his own physical life and the lives of those he deemed important to his continued ability to rule.

Now Dalos was being given the benefit of the most advanced capabilities of Orion technology. When combined with the Infinite Intelligence flowing to him through his own mental development, Dalos' recovery was assured.

Tyrantus, however, had not recovered from his conversation with Uriel—for that was, indeed, the Consciousness which had reached out to him through the words of Dalos. He could not sleep, nor eat. He spent hours pacing in his quarters. He had no rational explanation for the feelings that now savaged his mind—emotions that he had not allowed himself for as long as he could remember. He actually had come close to tears in Dalos' presence! This terrified him. He was losing his mental control! He had never, never been forced into this state of mental submissiveness by any enemy! He could not forgive himself.

He did not know where to turn for help. There was no way that he could explain this situation to any other soul living on Tyron. He did not know how to regain control of his thoughts, so many conflicting ideas surfaced in his mind. Was there some truth in these outlandish statements Dalos had made? They sounded like gibberish to Tyrantus at first, but something in his mind would not let them go. Something penetrated his consciousness and gave him the feeling that he had touched upon a deeply buried secret that he himself once knew, but now had forgotten.

Still, he would not let the full picture form in his mind. He kept it at bay by his constant insistence upon the preposterousness of these notions. So Tyrantus remained in a state of mental turmoil, battling within himself against this truth that Dalos had so clearly stated. Forgotten for now were all concerns about the electronic equipment aboard Dalos' starship. Tyrantus kept to his quarters and cancelled all public appearances. He gave no reason, and he did not need to explain his actions to anyone.

The Council, however, was quick to note this situation. The three council members who had also encountered Dalos' truth-giving words were experiencing their own states of mental agitation. Each one fought a similar battle, although not to the degree Tyrantus was now experiencing. They could not explain many of their actions, but they were giving constant orders to their agents to attempt to discover the whereabouts of Dalos and the results of the interrogations they knew Tyrantus must be conducting with this one.

Linton was devising a plan by which he would gain access to the starship and probe its secrets, keeping the information he gained in this way to himself for his own future use. He saw in this situation a potential to advance himself and to gain an advantage over the Emperor. He enlisted Radik (who was also involved in the more scientific aspects of Orion research and development) to a limited degree in these plans. Thus far, they had merely discussed the possibilities for trying new techniques to gain entrance to the starship. Linton wanted to pick the brain of Radik, in case he had come up with some idea that had escaped Linton's notice.

Radik, on the other hand, was eager to associate with Linton, who had access to certain technology that Radik was thus far ignorant of—yet he knew this technology existed, and that Linton was holding back. It was Radik's plan to form an alliance with Linton, and when he saw his opportunity, to take steps to place himself in the superior position.

Tonar, on the other hand, was investigating the circumstances of the Pleiadean entourage. While Tyrantus was preoccupied with Dalos himself, Tonar saw that he had an opportunity to learn what the Pleiadeans knew. He was somewhat surprised that the Emperor was so disconcerned with these two hundred individuals. Had they not traveled on the same starship as Dalos? Were they not also possessed of the same scientific knowledge? What secrets might they reveal about this society, which was obviously more advanced in its technological development than their own? Certainly, they would find among these Pleiadeans individuals who could be broken down and milked for information!

Tonar's agents began to infiltrate the team of behavioral scientists observing the Pleiadean entourage. He soon learned of the restrictions that Tyrantus had placed upon these combination scientists and overseers. Tonar found this quite interesting.

So, he surmised, *Tyrantus has plans for these individuals! Why else would he keep them in such a healthy state? He must feel that they offer no threat to his government. He, perhaps, is losing his ability to think clearly! Good. I will think clearly for him. And I shall prove that he has made a grave mistake here. I shall meet with these Pleiadeans, unbeknownst to the Emperor, and I will get from them what these bumbling idiots, Linton and Radik, cannot get with all their technical doo-dads! I will merely use my mind.*

But underlying Tonar's devious plans was a desire that he did not recognize. There was now, within all four of these individuals, a driving desire to solve the equation that Dalos had presented to them on the starship. They would not rest until this incomplete picture was completed in their minds. Thus far, it existed within them as a slight disequilibrium, and a pressing need to discover its source.

For Tyrantus, that need now bordered on an obsessive mania to resolve the crack that now divided his consciousness.

Love—the Love of a Higher Being—had penetrated the enclosed minds of these four. There it would regenerate, increment by increment, propelling these individuals back to some form of sanity. But first, they would tear themselves apart in a mad search to understand the nature of this oscillating, inner beacon of Light-intelligence.

Dalos rested in his bed with this knowledge. He must wait now, and apply himself to gaining physical strength, for there was much work yet to be accomplished.

14

Incommunicado

The layers of consciousness are deep, infinite in their potential for expansion, yet finite in the contraction that the Orionites were now experiencing. Eventually, all illumination of mind would have disappeared for these souls, had it not been for the willingness of Uriel and her Lighted Brothers to extend physical bodies unto their midst to rekindle these dying sparks of Intelligence.

In the research mills of Orion, countless thousands of individuals had been basically dissected in the search for the logic and reason of the human mind. The Orionites knew that it was an electronic configuration; yet they could not find the source, the generating force for the ongoing existence of consciousness.

The Pleiadeans, however, demonstrated to them new facets of consciousness. They were unlike other planetary inhabitants the expanding Orion forces had contacted. They seemed more capable of maintaining a mental equilibrium than any other peoples these researchers had been exposed to. The behavioral scientists examining the Pleiadean entourage were as baffled as the surgeons delving into the physical anatomy of Dalos. Although the Pleiadeans had responded in certain typical fashions to the electronic stimuli directed to them by the Orionites, they exhibited very untypical behavior in other areas.

For instance, they did not quickly succumb to these electronic influences. It was over a lengthy period of time that their mentality began to deteriorate and they became restless and agitated with one another, and with the status of their now-stagnant lives in general. This was a first in the recorded annals of Orion research. Most individuals immediately felt and demonstrated the effects of these subliminal, low-frequency impingements that interfered with the workings of conscious awareness.

What the researchers did not realize, of course, was that these individuals had developed their minds to a greater capacity, and were able, through their own personal effort, to maintain a higher-frequency state of consciousness. They were attuned to those broadcasts of Infinite Intelligence that radiated from the Cosmic Fountainhead and were demodulated down through the Minds of many more-developed Beings, until they reached the lowest levels of Infinity, such as the physical earth planets and the life forms existing thereon. With this higher attunement, they were stabilized in their mental activity. They were functioning with a steady input of Intelligence that guided and directed their expressions of life. Through this attunement, they were also protected, somewhat, from these radiations of lower-frequency wave forms. However, their circumstances on the planet Tyron, in which they were not allowed to express freely the creative manifestations of this higher input, eventually caused some deterioration in this attunement process.

The Intelligence flowing into the mind needs an outlet; that is, nothing is stationary in Infinity and this energy must be continually regenerated. Without the ability to re-express that which they had received, the Pleiadeans were becoming short-circuited in their mental oscillation.

Now, the Orion citizens were short-circuited in another fashion. They no longer had this inner, higher contact with a radiating force of greater Intelligence. They were missing the first element of this mental equation; therefore, they did not experience the same problems that the Pleiadeans were now having. The problem of an Orion citizen was one of total mental blockage, with no Light to illuminate the thoughts and propel a mental growth and expansion.

For the Pleiadeans, they knew where to obtain this inner Intelligence, yet they were stymied in their ability to express, causing an extreme frustration that eventually blocked the natural flow of energy-intelligence, which must continuously re-express itself in a charge/discharge set of circumstances.

Their companionship with one another provided some measure of this need for the re-expression of Infinite Intelligence; however, this was not the purpose for which they had journeyed to Tyron from their homes on the Pleiadean planet Axiahn, and truly, from their spiritual residences as Visionaries of the world of Aries.

Dalos, on the other hand, while his physical anatomy was grossly abused and weakened, torn apart by the aggressions of Tyrantus' scientific teams, was yet able to express a portion of his purpose as a teacher and healer of Tyrantus and those few Council members whom he had the opportunity to address during their visit to his starship. This restored life within his consciousness—brief as those experiences may have been! It gave him hope, and re-stimulated his motivation to maintain this physical anatomy, for the expression of Uriel in the form of Dalos was strictly voluntary on the part of this Hierarchical Mind. She was not "required" by the principles of evolutionary expansion to re-experience life in a physical dimension. These training worlds had already been mastered by the One called Uriel; not only mastered, but she served as a generating Consciousness that provided the Life Substance for countless atomic worlds! No, her presence as Dalos was strictly undertaken for one singular purpose, and as long as that purpose was being served in the slightest degree, she—he—would remain, if at all possible!

Now that Tyrantus had ordered the cessation of all experimental procedures, Dalos' body was being given an opportunity to heal. This would mean long weeks of confinement in a bedridden state; nevertheless, the further deterioration of Dalos' physical strength had been halted, and he was now able to regenerate the Life Force within this atomic body.

The dilemma faced by his entourage posed a different set of problems. They knew that they were becoming less and less capable of maintaining a balanced state of consciousness. They knew that something must be done to alleviate this situation. They were ignorant, still, of Dalos' whereabouts and circumstances. This, too, drove a wedge into their minds, a wedge of fear, concern, anxiety, and restlessness. They were ripe, then, for further subversive influences to enter into their daily lives.

The first such attempt was made when the ten individuals were allowed to visit certain sectors of the planet Tyron and returned to the group as a whole, while the observing scientists recorded the impact this new input had upon the Pleiadeans. They were gratified to see that it had caused some further dissension among the Pleiadeans. A jealousy began to arise among those who had not been allowed to leave their captivity for several long months. They felt that information was possessed by these ten and was being withheld from them.

They were not living in squalid circumstances, by any means. Their quarters were quite beautiful by earth-world standards and they were given access to colorfully landscaped garden areas. They had the means of entertainment by which the Orionites pleased themselves, and they were allowed to gather together to speak and to record their speech for some future purpose. But they were not allowed to speak to the citizens of Tyron. Even during the tour of the ten Pleiadeans, they were only given the opportunity to observe, but not to interact with the citizens whose activities they were viewing.

Now, however, it was proposed that a group of Orion citizens be introduced to these Pleiadeans. This would provide the behavioral analysts with an opportunity to observe and record the way the minds of the Pleiadeans were affected by their introduction to a foreign culture. It was decided that this phase of experimentation, strictly controlled and monitored, would begin at a particular location that would accommodate a large gathering.

The Pleiadeans were much encouraged by this new development, for they felt that now they were about to begin their true mission! They were led to a docking area for aerial transport vehicles. For many of them, this was the first opportunity to view the capital city from an overall perspective. They were stunned by the sight of endless, identical buildings, as far as the eye could see. The ten individuals who had already been allowed this vision of Tyron nodded at the astonished faces of their companions.

Yes, they seemed to be saying, *we told you so! Life here is as stagnant and restricted as our months of captivity have been! We were no worse off than the ordinary citizen of Tyron! Indeed, we are far better equipped to manage such a circumstance, to understand its larger impact upon our evolutionary existence.*

This "conversation" did not occur in words, for the Pleiadeans communicated largely by their mental contact with one another. They had developed this compatibility over many lifetimes and were chosen by Uriel for this mission to the earth worlds due to their harmonious association and their long, long history of working as joined Mind Forces. While living in a physical body, this mental communication was hindered somewhat by the separation involved in a time-space world, yet it still functioned to a greater degree than possible among individuals of lesser mental acumen. So as they boarded the transport vehicles, the Pleiadeans were silently taking in the sights and sounds of Orion life.

They noted that all citizens dressed alike and never expressed any joy or recognition when they encountered one another, or even any curiosity about these foreign individuals. They merely passed through the motions of their particular tasks without lifting their eyes, as if in a dreamlike stupor.

The Pleiadeans had learned the Tyron language, of course, and were quite fluent in its speech. When they addressed one of these individuals, the response came in monosyllables—an affirmative or negative, or a referral to one in a supervisory position, if the question was beyond the scope of that individual's knowledge. This was frequently the case, and when a supervisory individual was addressed with this particular question, he or she very often gave the same response. In this way, one seeking information might travel up a ladder of a functional hierarchy that would not end until it reached one of those serving in the higher echelons of Orion government. Only those individuals were possessed of any true knowledge of the life they were living, for their minds had been allowed to function relatively free of the controlling frequencies that were influencing the rest of the population.

They lifted off in the hovercraft and sped across the city to a massive circular building. This building, although of a different shape, was still of the monotone, grayish color that was used in the design of nearly all structures on Tyron. They were led through a doorway and into a circular auditorium. Seats rose up in an arena form around the perimeter of this auditorium, yet the central area was composed of a large open space. Here, they found two hundred citizens of Tyron seated uncomfortably on portable, individual benches, holding liquid refreshment in their hands. It was as if they had been posed in these positions and were asked to remain there, motionless until their guests arrived.

When the Pleiadeans entered this odd scenario, the Tyronites stood and began to approach them, each one greeting one of the Pleiadeans and presenting to that individual a vessel of amber liquid. All of the motions and expressions of the Tyronites seemed rehearsed, as if they had gone through these actions many, many times before. They smiled—a rare occurrence on this world—and even laughed, yet the sound was hollow, with no true mirth to support it.

The Pleiadeans were fascinated, yet repulsed by the experience. They did not quite know how to address the Tyronites at first, so shocking was it to be suddenly exposed to an onslaught of other individuals after so many months of isolation. All together, the Tyronites joined to form a radiating force of consciousness that was not biased to a higher frequency, as was the group consciousness of the Pleiadeans. It required a mental adjustment on the part of the Axiahnite visitors and they felt immediately drained from this experience.

Apparently, it was the plan that they should mingle in this fashion for several hours, but there was little that could be discussed in this one-on-one contact, for the Pleiadeans were so unsettled by the events that had transpired that they were unpracticed and incapable of launching into some lengthy dissertation about the principles of life which they had come to teach. It was not the appropriate setting for such teaching endeavors, and they quickly realized that the individual whose vacant eyes were fixed upon them did not understand a word of their speech, although their Tyronite diction was perfect in its elocution.

By the time the Pleiadeans were allowed to leave this arena, they were exhausted. They had learned many interesting details about the lives of these individuals, particularly the fact that they had been given this task as their life's work. These were official Greeters of the Orion government. Both male and female were trained in the art of conversation, the Pleiadeans learned, and were used by government officials to entertain the arriving ambassadors from other planets. Their conversation, however, was as empty and meaningless as their laughter. It contained nothing more than scraps of information about daily occurrences of minor government affairs—nothing of any true importance, and yet somewhat beyond the knowledge of the workers who filled the endless rows of rectangular buildings, giving their very lives to keep the machinery of the Empire in operation.

All information shared by these official Greeters was carefully supplied to them by their overseers, and they were directed by the governmental leaders who supervised the propaganda released under Tyrantus' orders. This system was designed to make visiting officials feel as if they were enjoying certain privileges denied to ordinary citizens, and indeed, they were. The food and beverage provided was of a nature restricted to the use of the designated elite, and the talk was of topics not known by the general populations of Orion planets. There were many physical pleasures involved in these encounters. The liquid refreshment contained a drugging influence, and the entire arena was irradiated by certain frequencies of sound and light that supposedly relaxed the mind and stimulated the senses of pleasure.

The Pleiadeans found these external stimuli to be extremely irritating, and it caused them to exert a greater internal mental force to counteract the effects of these bombardments of sensory input. They sipped at and nibbled the refreshment provided, just enough to extend a gracious attitude to their hosts. But they were glad to be free of this cloying atmosphere, once the session was called to an end and they were returned to their own quarters.

Now the scientists watched carefully to see what effect this experience had upon them. They noted the exhaustion of the Pleiadeans and could not understand this, as most individuals exhibited a kind of euphoric exuberance when brought into one of the official greeting sessions. But the Pleiadeans merely retired to their rest upon returning to the holding area. They barely spoke among themselves. This was not the effect the behaviorists had hoped for. They had hoped to gain more insight into the deeper thoughts of the Pleiadeans, the more personal side of their natures, as they were very reserved creatures, in the Tyronites' opinions, and did not reveal much of their own individual personalities, as did many of the visiting officials who conducted business with the central government. It was through these sessions and observations that the government officials learned much about their visitors and were able to place themselves in an advantageous position based upon the information gained in this surreptitious manner.

But in the view of the Tyronites, this experiment had fizzled, with little result. Perhaps in the ensuing days they would detect some more subtle influence. Anything seemed possible among this strange group of individuals. For now, the researchers would retire to their own beds, and redirect their efforts in another vein.

Tonar, of course, had made certain that his agents were sprinkled throughout both the official Greeters and the behavioral scientists. He now was conducting his own debriefing sessions with these individuals. He demanded to know every detail, every word spoken by any one of the Pleiadeans. He was trying to detect which individual would be most likely to provide the kind of information that he sought—the kind of information that would give him an advantage over his opponents on the Council, and over the Emperor himself.

It was Tonar's plan to present the results of his findings to the Emperor, but to do so in such a way that he retained some portion of this information for himself, some facet of insight about the Pleiadeans that might serve him in his future plans. He did not yet know what this might be, or what they might reveal to him, but he sensed that he was reaching into a new level of attainment for himself! He pushed harder, and insisted that the behaviorists working under his direction return with a new plan to give the Pleiadeans greater access to citizens of Tyron. In this free exchange of conversation, Tonar would be able to find a way to pick their brains without attracting attention. He could not simply stride into their detention center and introduce himself. His actions would be instantly logged upon the screens of Tyrantus' secret police, and would be known by all those involved in the monitoring of the Pleiadean entourage. He must determine a way to carry out his plan without the knowledge of Tyrantus and his minions.

The same dilemma presented itself to Linton and Radik. They could not very well approach the Pleiadean starship, situated as it was in the midst of Orion headquarters, and blast away until some portion of the exterior was removed. They were attempting to invent some means by which to secretly enter the ship and return. They knew that anything removed from its interior would not be discovered by Tyrantus' forces, as they were thus far unable to open the starship hatch.

Linton and Radik believed that, since they had been in the interior of this starship and they had witnessed Dalos' opening of the hatch, they must certainly know something more about its design! They decided that Dalos must possess some electronic device secreted somewhere in his clothing or person that allowed him to activate the hatch. However, this did seem unlikely, as Dalos had been so thoroughly examined and re-examined by the medical technicians.

"Perhaps," Radik proposed, "this device is built into his actual physical anatomy."

"Do you not think," Linton replied, "that such a device would have been detected by Tyrantus' physicians? Would it not have been picked up by our electronic scanning? If this were the case, it would mean that this electronic device is composed of materials that are beyond the scope of our instrumentation."

"That does seem to be the case with these Pleiadeans as a whole, does it not?" Radik responded. "That is our problem—they are operating in realms of science that, frankly, we have never before experienced!"

A brief silence fell between the two. This was a rare admittance of ignorance on their part. They would never have uttered it had they not been alone in Linton's quarters, which were—like all the other Council members'—equipped with an array of sensing devices. But in this case, they served to both monitor and *screen* certain frequencies from the room. Anything said in this room was automatically recorded by Linton's own security forces, and at the same time, the probing electronics instituted by Tyrantus as a whole were kept from this particular room. It was, with the exception of Tyrantus' own quarters, the only such location on the planet, as Linton was the scientist responsible for the development of the majority of these electronic "eyes" and "ears." He knew, then, how to keep himself removed from their reach, and he knew, as well, how to operate his own system of electronic scanning and detection.

Radik was aware of this and it was a constant source of irritation to him. He himself had not yet developed these capabilities and it was his desire, through his present alliance with Linton, to steal some of these technological secrets. The more he earned Linton's trust, the more likely he was to be exposed to the inner circle of Linton's research teams.

"I propose," Radik said, "that we conduct our own private session with Dalos."

"How do you suppose we will have such an opportunity?" Linton inquired. "He is being kept at an undesignated location, under the tightest security available to Tyrantus. Even I do not know this location, and you know that I have high-priority clearance in all such matters!"

"Yes," Radik said, "but you have not counted upon my ability to squeeze information from certain individuals who shall be unnamed. I guarantee that I can pinpoint this location within a few hundred meters, and that I can find a way for such a meeting to occur! We will discover the secret of this starship! I do not care about those obscure questions concerning our Emperor, who I frankly think has lost his mental strength! I want to glean all that I can from this Pleiadean ship. It fascinates me, in a way that I have not been interested for many years."

"Yes," Linton agreed. "I know what you mean. There was something quite strange about the atmosphere of this ship—some unusual radiation, I believe, which caused us all to act differently. Did you not sense this yourself?"

Radik hesitated a moment. He wondered if Linton had experienced the same deep emotional waves that had overtaken his mind as he listened to the Pleiadean. No, he thought, he could not broach this subject with Linton; it might damage the delicate bonds being formed in this political alliance. He did not want Linton to think that he was not altogether in control of his thoughts! But at the same time, he wanted to avoid offending Linton, who had posed the question.

Radik decided on a noncommittal response: "Yes, I did experience some sense of uneasiness. But I believe that we will quickly find the source of this radiation, once we are aboard. I suspect that it is a form of security that Dalos and his crew have instituted for the purpose of keeping visitors to their ship off-guard."

"Yes, perhaps so," Linton said, and changed the subject. He, too, was curious to know how Radik had been affected but he feared to expose his own inner weakness. He would wait until his opportunity to explore the ship for himself, and perhaps, if Radik's plan was successful, he might be able to determine something from Dalos himself about this particular effect.

The two agreed, and Radik extended orders to his agents.

The machinery of deception was in full operation, then, as Dalos rested within his new quarters. For the first time in weeks he was able to sleep undisturbed, and the rest began to restore color to his features. The Light in his eyes, of course, had never gone out—nor would it, until that moment when he breathed his last. But now it seemed as if that time was not approaching! Now he believed Tyrantus was sufficiently aware, perhaps not consciously, but enough to give Dalos further opportunities to perform the tasks necessary to instill life into the Orion peoples once again.

Dalos sighed. *My dear Brothers, I deeply appreciate your Presence with me—for you have sustained me through this trial. I know that we shall succeed! My love is inflamed by your own, and regenerated to you, never-endingly. By this Illumination shall we restore the vision of these blinded ones, who know not how seriously they have affected, not only themselves, but so many, many souls.* And he lapsed into sleep.

15

The Battle Rages

Wherever the Pleiadeans went, their activities were monitored and recorded, just as Dalos' every pulse beat was being recorded by the research technicians who, although their experiments had been halted, were still keeping close watch on his physical condition.

The Pleiadeans were now all in the hands of the Orion government. It was like being tangled in a bed of seaweed, from which they would need to extract themselves if their mission was to be carried out successfully. In one sense their hopes had dimmed, for they were not able to teach as they had planned. Yet their presence on Tyron was extremely valuable, as they served to demodulate higher-frequency radiations of healing energy into that regressive world.

Dalos now spent his days staring at vacant walls, hoping for that opportunity for which he so longed. He had no purpose other than to teach. He could as easily discard this physical anatomy as blink his eyes, yet so long as such opportunities remained as the most remote possibility, he would continue breathing through the cell structures of Dalos.

Eventually, Radik and Linton found their way to the nearly inert form of Dalos. They had used a variety of techniques to secure this access unto an area that was strictly guarded and watched by Tyrantus' functionaries. Bribery, threats, and deception led them to the proper building, and with all eyes paid to be averted, Radik threw open the door of Dalos' room, followed closely by Linton.

Dalos' heart recorded this sudden intrusion with an extra palpitation—but the technicians on duty assigned to monitor the scanning machines had already been bought by Radik and their silence was assured, for any one of the Council members wielded power second only to Tyrantus' own. They, too, could bring life or death to an Orion citizen and would willingly do so with the merest provocation.

After a moment, Dalos recognized these two and was pleased to see them. He knew immediately that they had sought him out because of his previous contact with them. *So,* he thought, *they could not rest after all! Very well, we shall carry on with our lesson!*

He did not speak to them, however. He decided to await their inquiries. In this way, he would know how their minds had settled upon the vast amounts of information that they had received during their time on his starship.

"We are here, Dalos, because we know that you desire to give us certain information, do you not?" Linton began. "You have indicated this since your arrival, and we do not believe Tyrantus is treating you kindly. While we can do nothing to change this situation, we felt it most gracious to extend our open ears to you, so that you might continue to provide the information you began to give us several weeks ago."

"Yes," Radik agreed, "that is why we are here—to listen."

They settled themselves upon nearby metallic seats and waited. Dalos blinked at them for a moment. He was considering their motivations. Were they truly desirous? Yes, he believed. Although they may not have been aware of their deeper motivations, these two did seek him out because of that buried, inner pulse that had not yet died and would always seek out the source of its Intelligence. Their spiritual libido, then, still existed! This made Dalos quite joyous—although he was presently faced with two individuals who had allowed their lower selves full control over their conscious-mind activities.

He rested his head for a moment, gathering strength, then raised himself slightly, looking them both in the eye; one, then the other.

Now they had forgotten why they came. They were not consciously aware of their baser motivations. They were transfixed by this Being who had been their Spiritual Teacher, just as he had overshadowed the mind of Antares.

A long silence penetrated the room. They feared Dalos was unable to speak. Perhaps Tyrantus had gone too far? Perhaps this Pleiadean had lost his mental stability? They glanced at one another nervously, but in that instant their thoughts were pierced through by these words:

"You are not fearful to have bribed your way into my presence?" Dalos questioned.

They wondered for a moment how he knew of their means of gaining access, but they did not have time to think further.

"I shall tell you why you are not fearful—because you have been touched by the Light of your former selves! Yes, I know you both. I have known you for far longer than you can conceive! I see you as you truly are, lost in a world of your own making. But you can find yourselves—if you will it so!"

They did not know how to respond to this unusual speech. Neither moved, nor spoke. They simply stared in astonishment.

"You have both been *true* leaders of mankind, benevolent Minds who cared not for self but gave, instead, that Infinite Radiant Intelligence you yourselves had received from the Cosmic Fountainhead. No, you have no conscious memory of your former existence. You have buried it in a landslide of selfish egomania and I do not expect you to understand my words at this present time. But heed my warning: you shall be lost forever if you do nothing to change your course. You have become devourers of your fellow man. You are animals, unfit for human company!"

Dalos laid his head back again, staring up at the ceiling.

"How dare you speak to us this way!" Linton sputtered. "We did not come here for your abuse! We came to know of this 'science' about which you have made so much noise. Now, Pleiadean, is the time for you to spill your guts or I assure you, Tyrantus will have them hanging upon his wall as souvenirs of his conquest over you and your crew—which, by the way, I believe you would no longer recognize! They are becoming fine Orion citizens." He smiled, taking in Radik's own glance of satisfaction. "So truly, Dalos, you are alone now with us. If you see us as animals, then beware, for you have landed in our den!"

"We demand to know how you have secured your ship from our entrance," Radik said. "This information must be supplied, or we have our own means by which we can terminate your life."

"My life means nothing to me," Dalos said, not moving from his fixed position. "You may have it, if you wish, for I have no desire to live on this world. Only one thing motivates me to remain in your so-called glorious, super-human civilization. I have come"—and here he looked again into their eyes—"to save my Brothers from their own destruction. You no longer remember the Love that permeates all life—yet that is the Love that I bring to you! I do not 'love' you as personal beings, for you are quite despicable. Yet you are creations of Infinity and therefore deserving of the Love Force that has given you life, your very lives.

"Yet I feel I waste my breath with you," Dalos sighed. "You may be beyond this help." And he closed his eyes.

The two rose to their feet, fearing that he was losing consciousness again and they had not yet gained a single scrap of usable information—not in their minds, anyway!

Radik grabbed Dalos' arm roughly and shook.

"No, you do not need to abuse me further!" Dalos said in a strong, piercing tone. "Your physical abuse does nothing to dim my purpose! Nor will it free you from the prison that you have created of this world. Do you not know that you have distorted your own minds with all your electronic tampering? No, I suppose not. You have forgotten the very basic principles by which you came to this world! Someday," he said, "you will know, and on that day your hearts shall surely break. I do not expect to be there on that day, for when this physical body finally expires, you shall be on your own."

Something about these words chilled the two Council members. Something familiar. For a moment they looked as if they might soften their approach. But Radik soon picked up his interrogating attitude again.

"I do not care what you think of me! But, Pleiadean, you must know that it shall be your death if you do not tell all!"

Dalos just looked at him. "I am telling all, as you put it. But you cannot hear! You have sealed your ears in a vacuum, cloistered yourselves among your victims. If I were to tell you precisely how we enter our ship, it would be meaningless to you, for you cannot accomplish it, no matter how hard you try! Your present minds are incapable of such feats."

"Let us determine that for ourselves!" Linton blurted. " Tell us—now—else..." He stopped. What more terrible thing might they threaten this man with than his physical death, about which he seemed to hold no fear whatsoever? Pain? Certainly he had experienced enough of that, and still his attitude had not changed.

"No, you do not need to threaten me," Dalos interrupted. "I shall tell you. It is with our minds that we project the proper frequency that opens our starship entrance, and it is with our minds that we motivate our ships from place to place throughout the Cosmos. We have developed this capability over many, many lifetimes, polishing our lenses of consciousness to a highly refractive state, until they have become demodulating stations for an Intelligence well beyond our own development or conception. Yet the basic principles by which our minds—and yours—function are universal. They apply throughout Infinity. But you and all of your compatriots have destroyed your mental abilities! That is why we are here. We have come to lend ourselves to help you repair the damage committed."

"This man speaks in gibberish," Linton said to Radik. "Why are we wasting our time here?"

"Because," Radik insisted, "he knows more than he tells. There must be some device which amplifies their thoughts and then directs them to open this hatch! That is so, is it not, Dalos?"

"No, Radik, you still do not understand; but I do not expect you to, at this present time. If I were free to leave this bed, I would gladly instruct you in the ways of our life and science, for life and science are one and the same. That is, again, my purpose here, to teach you and your brothers on Tyron—and all those who are under your control. But my hands have been tied, have they not? So you shall not benefit from the wisdom we bring. Not until we are rejoined and allowed to speak freely. It is truly your deepest loss. We were your last chance, your hope for a brighter future!"

Again Linton and Radik were touched by Dalos' words, and by his Love, which was not, as he said, personal in nature. Nevertheless, it had a strong impact upon them. Linton motioned to Radik that they step outside the room.

"We shall return," Radik vowed, and they disappeared through the doorway.

Dalos, drained but pleased, smiled, then lapsed back into his quiet contemplation. So little had he been able to achieve; yet so meaningful, each increment in which these former Brothers of Light were reminded of their lost purpose.

Dalos' quiet solitude was again interrupted by the intrusion of Tyrantus, whom he had not seen since their last encounter, when Dalos was nearly propelled from his physical anatomy by the repercussions of that conversation. Again, Dalos did not speak but waited to hear what this one had to say.

He said nothing—just stared at Dalos' mangled body, avoiding his penetrating eyes, for Tyrantus had learned how uncomfortable they made him feel, in an indescribable sensation of exposure.

"So," Dalos finally uttered, "have you come to view your handiwork once again?"

"Do not mock me," Tyrantus said, and the strain in his voice was quite apparent.

Dalos knew then that he had undergone tremendous inner turmoil. This was a healthy sign, for this individual had much to weigh within himself and very little of it was pleasant in nature. "Why have you come then?" Dalos inquired. "Surely it is not to hear what I have to say to you, for I have made that story quite plain, I believe."

"You torment me," Tyrantus said, as if reeling in exhaustion. "Who are you? Why do you cause me so many sleepless nights?"

"Perhaps that is because you have caused so many others to suffer," Dalos replied. "Perhaps it is your conscience that troubles you, not I, for I am only one man—is that not so? You have quite clearly stated it yourself. I am but a single man who does not even have the company of his beloved brothers and sisters from his own planet! Perhaps you have destroyed their physical bodies as you are destroying mine?"

Tyrantus looked at him, then quickly looked away. "I do not know why I allow any of you to live," he muttered under his breath. "I have only suffered since your arrival here. I should wipe you out like a pack of pesky animals. Yes, that is what I should do," he said, more to himself than to Dalos.

"But you have not!" Dalos interjected. "Why is that, Tyrantus? Why do you keep us alive?"

"You know the answer to that!" he shouted back, whirling around again. "You have information that I need! And yet you deny it to me, no matter what torturous…" He broke off.

"Yes," Dalos said, "you have tortured me sufficiently for any man to tell you all that he knows, and I do willingly give you my thoughts, do I not? You do not like them. They cause you unrest. So I shall not speak again, unless you inquire of me."

"Fool!" Tyrantus spat. "Why do you think I have come to see you, you despicable man! Now you must tell me what you have done to my mind! You have pushed me, Dalos, and I do not like being pushed. I demand a response!"

"You may demand or ask. My answer remains the same. You have tormented yourself, Tyrantus, with every soul whose life you have crushed within your greedy hands. These are the night cries that keep you from your rest. These are the ones to whom you must direct your inquiry. They will tell you why you are suffering. I can only tell you that the choice is yours and always has been. Change your ways, Tyrantus, and you shall sleep at night—but I fear you cannot change so quickly. Life for you will not be pleasant, I fear. You have already done too much to ensure your torment."

Tyrantus sat heavily in a corner of the room. His face was twisted with pain, a far different kind of pain than that which wracked the body of Dalos.

Dalos knew that Tyrantus was now deeply affected by his contact with the Pleiadeans.

"What have you done with my brothers and sisters?" Dalos asked.

"Are they, like me, trussed up in one of your so-called laboratories, guinea pigs for those butchers upon whom you have placed so much of your consciousness, your desire for greater power?"

"Leave me be," he said. "You have harangued me enough already. I have not laid a hand upon your crew members—no, they have done quite well themselves at adapting to life on Tyron."

Suddenly something occurred to Tyrantus. Perhaps there was one remaining way to reach this Dalos and cause his mental fabric to shred, as he had disrupted the mind of the Emperor. The only thing that seemed to concern this one was the safety and well-being of his entourage. *Of course!* Tyrantus thought. *Why did I not realize this sooner? Of course!*

They had been separated for nearly a year. Dalos would hardly recognize these individuals. If anything could be used as a tool by which to influence this Pleiadean, perhaps it was his affection for these individuals!

Tyrantus was not thinking clearly and he did not know exactly what it was that he wanted from Dalos. His desire for technological advancements was far outweighed by his present anxiety and craving for the numbed, unfeeling consciousness from which he had lived before he met this foreign star traveler. No drug on Tyron had been able to sooth Tyrantus' mental agitation. He could make no sense of Dalos' statements, yet they did not leave him. They echoed constantly through his mind when he was least prepared to deal with these pointed truths. It was as devastating as if Dalos had unleashed an army within him, and the battle that ensued threatened to extinguish his very existence! It took all his strength to maintain his outward appearance of calm and authority when faced with his many thousands of aides and, worst of all, the twelve Council members who were like vultures awaiting his death. He could turn to no one, and yet he could no longer find clear-cut answers within himself. It had all been so simple and clearly defined for him; he knew how to maintain and increase his power, yet his greed for new technology had led him into the clutches of this Pleiadean. Despite all his attempts to fell this one physically, and to overtake his mind to wring information from him, Tyrantus had failed to influence Dalos.

Now Dalos lay in this state of exhausted pain and *still* ravaged the consciousness of Tyrantus with his words!

Yet the words of Dalos carried but one force: the Force of Good, the Force of Infinite Love. It would one day be as a soothing balm to Tyrantus; but now it was the sting of truth that had been poured into the festering consciousness of one whose mind had been deteriorated by his own deeds. There is no greater torment for a soul to undergo. This truly was "Hell." It lived within Tyrantus, and within all those who joined him in their demonic aggression upon the lives of others. He ruled this Hell, earning his title, by which generations to come would remember him: The Fallen One, Lucifer. Satan he had become.

Only one Mind was capable of meeting him on his own ground, only one Being willing to suffer at his hands in order to change his pell-mell descent into oblivion, which was dragging so many souls to their own termination.

"Tyrantus," Dalos said. "There is a cure for your agony. It will not be easy, but I can prescribe it for you."

Tyrantus looked at the Pleiadean, too tired to argue with him further.

"If you will open your mind to me, I can heal you of this inner pain. But you must allow me to speak freely! You must allow me to rejoin my crew. You must know by now that we are no physical threat to you. All you have to fear from us is your own inner change, and from your appearance, I gather that such change would be welcome relief!"

So, Tyrantus thought, he would not even need to propose some elaborate excuse for reuniting Dalos with his entourage. The Pleiadean did not know what awaited him! *Now I merely need to seem as if I am acquiescing to his wishes.*

How to do so without arousing Dalos' suspicion was quite a puzzle, but Dalos resolved it for him.

"I shall arrange for one of my entourage to work with your scientists, Tyrantus, to fully demonstrate the function of the psychic anatomy viewer, and to explain to the best of our ability the mechanics by which this device functions. Free me from this torturous existence in which you have held me captive and tested my body beyond the limits of ordinary endurance. Let me walk upright again and you shall gain all that I know. You have my pledge on this matter!"

Tyrantus looked at him for a moment, then stood, making his face as stern as possible.

"You give me no choice, Dalos." These were uncomfortable words for Tyrantus, even though he knew that, once again, his own devious plan seemed to be unfolding just as he desired. "Very well, then. I shall direct my physicians to repair your wounds in the most rapid fashion possible, and you shall be brought to your entourage for a brief time."

Dalos closed his eyes in deep appreciation. Now he felt that he had been successful on two fronts. Tyrantus had been, once again, exposed to his healing projections of Consciousness, and he, Dalos, so longed for the company of his family of Pleiadean brothers that he knew he would regain his strength once he was in their presence again!

As he left the room, Tyrantus was also congratulating himself on his latest achievement, his brilliance in determining another way by which to gain the upper hand over this enigma and threat to his mental stability. He did not realize, nor could he have detected the changes occurring within him on levels of consciousness which were now unfamiliar.

They would meet again, these forces of Good and Evil—and again, and again. The battle was in full sway.

16

Truth Revealed

Shimlus by now had fully established her leadership among the Pleiadean entourage. They all looked to her to direct their daily activities. She grew increasingly willing to serve in this capacity in the absence of her beloved Dalos.

As time went on, many among the Pleiadeans believed that Dalos was no longer living. They felt that this was why the Tyronites did not respond to their repeated questions about the whereabouts and condition of their leader. Surely if he were still living, he would have found some way to contact them through his great Intelligence!

He was, of course, always in contact with them as the Higher Mind of Uriel, but the more the Pleiadeans concerned themselves with the physical circumstances in which they were now living, the less able they were to hear the inner voice of their spiritual leader and teacher. This was fatal for many of them, mentally speaking. As they detuned themselves from their inner guidance, they were that much more susceptible to the interference of the Orion electronic controls and the many attempts that were made to detract them from their purpose by their now frequent contacts with Tyron citizens.

Tonar had added several individuals to those who were now taking the Pleiadeans under their tutelage, so to speak, rather than vice-versa. The Pleiadeans were given more tours of Tyron facilities, and they were now encouraged to engage in conversation with the citizens, due to Tonar's influence among the behavioral scientists. Of course, all this was done with Tyrantus' full knowledge and approval. It was presented to him that the scientists were gaining very valuable information about the Pleiadeans through their observation of these interactions with the Tyronites. Also, it was observed that the Pleiadeans were relaxing their rigidity and coolness. They were more frequently found engaging in some of the pleasurable offerings of the Tyron elite to whom they had been introduced—food and drink, recreational activities, and other sensual stimulations. They no longer seemed to be as united in their opinions. Many times, the Pleiadeans were observed to quarrel among themselves and they now, with their new freedom to travel about the city, were less often found in gatherings among themselves, but were scattered to various locations.

Of course, each individual member of the entourage sincerely believed that he or she was now carrying out his purpose to make contact with the Orionites, and to share of his or her knowledge of the interdimensional principles of life. As they slipped, gradually, in their maintenance of a higher-frequency attunement, this change was subtle and went undetected by many of these individuals. Always were they bombarded by the electronic influences that caused a greater and greater effect upon them. It was a vicious circle in which, the more they relaxed their mental vigilance, the more susceptible they became, and thereby further reduced their level of consciousness, which allowed a greater impact of the subliminal messages that permeated Orion society.

Soon they found themselves to be much more compatible with their hosts. They assumed this to be a natural result of their conversations with these individuals; from the Pleiadeans' perspective, they were achieving some success in bringing the Tyronites around to their way of thinking. They spoke at great length during these contacts about their own understandings of life, but this became more and more of an ego endeavor on their parts. They soon forgot to give credence to the Source of this Intelligence.

Throughout these exchanges, Tonar's listening devices were in full operation. He was, indeed, gaining information that he felt he would put to good use in the future. These Pleiadeans offered a refreshing opportunity for him; they were quite willing to speak and their words had a strong, soothing influence upon the Tyron citizens, as his behavioral scientists reported. Perhaps he could use this influence to his own benefit. That is, if he could control the way in which the Pleiadeans spoke and presented themselves, if they were working for him in some way, then he could use them as a tool to influence others. He would be the guiding force, then. He would be director of these two hundred, and they would certainly form a strong army of propagandists, would they not?

These were the thoughts that turned around in his mind like a wheel that never ceased in its motion. Beneath this turning of thought was an aberration that Tonar could not detect, nor define for himself. His warped thinking was obscuring the true fact: that he had recontacted a memory of his former existence as a Spiritual Teacher, and this memory—now stirred but not yet fully awakened—was outpictured upon these individuals. It gave him a vague image of the kind of presentation he felt these individuals could make on his behalf. Somehow he sensed that there was value in having others look to the Pleiadeans for some subtle, personal guidance that Tyrantus' cold techniques of iron rule did not provide. Tonar could win their favor by attracting their interest; he could lure them to his support, and if this were sufficiently successful, he would hold a power over the people that Tyrantus could never have achieved, with all his legions of secret police and treatment room technicians! The people themselves would do the work for him, Tonar considered. They would willingly give their allegiance to those individuals whom they regarded as superior in intelligence and abilities.

This, of course, was the direct opposite of the entire purpose of Dalos' mission. He had come to inform these people of their own potential as spiritual beings, as future teachers and leaders of mankind, for each individual soul holds this undeveloped spark of Infinite Intelligence and there are no limits to the heights that he might achieve through the application of his mind. Dalos came to free the people from the control or influence of others. He came to give their minds back to them.

His entourage, as well, had trained themselves to supply this same information in a variety of expressions. They came as artists, scientists, philosophers, engineers, spiritual physicists, and every other expression of human intelligence that could be conceived or lived upon a physical world. Through these many avenues of life, they would demonstrate for the Tyronites, and eventually many among the Orion planets, that there are no limitations when one opens one's mind to make that inner connection with the higher potential of one's own consciousness, which can be joined to the Infinite Minds to receive an endless supply of wisdom and creative force.

Tonar's plan, on the other hand, was to once again remove this inner capability from the people and cause them to turn toward others, eventually toward himself in their quest, their constant seeking for truth—which never leaves a soul until those last moments of total reabsorption, when all spiritual Intelligence has been disintegrated by lack of use. This was the oblivion toward which the Orion peoples were now headed.

He did not yet know how he would accomplish this end, but Tonar was now obsessed with his desire to follow through on this particular plan. He was convinced of its foolproof nature. He knew that it was so different from anything that Tyrantus would ever consider that his actions would not be detected until it was too late.

As things now stood, Tyrantus approved of the increased interaction between the Pleiadeans and the Tyronites. He was satisfied to see that they had weakened in their arrogant air, and that they were now proving to be as fallible and susceptible to Orion persuasive techniques as any other peoples that he had encountered in his conquest of foreign worlds.

Yes, Tyrantus thought, *Dalos will be truly surprised when he rejoins this group. It will be most illuminating to see how the Pleiadean commander responds to his disintegrating troops!*

As Tyrantus formed these thoughts, while standing in his control center built into his private quarters, Dalos was not too far distant, now regaining his physical strength. And with each day that passed in which he considered the many things that could be accomplished once he was free to stand and move about, and once he rejoined with the two hundred teachers who had come to add their positive strength to his mission, he progressed that much more quickly toward his former state of health.

Soon the time arrived for this reuniting of Dalos with his beloved Axiahn brothers and sisters.

They had not been told of this meeting. Shimlus was asked to gather the Pleiadeans in a central area in their housing sector. They were expecting a visit from Tyrantus himself.

Shimlus, by now, had learned that she could use her feminine charm, seemingly, to influence the Tyron officials and persuade them to give certain privileges to the Pleiadeans which they had been denied during their first year of captivity. She believed that the greater freedoms they now experienced were the result of her influence, and this further inflated her sense of personal importance, although very subtly at first.

Truly, these privileges were granted because of the devious plan of Tonar, who was manipulating circumstances from behind the scenes. He had thus far kept himself removed from contact with the Pleiadeans, yet his fingers were upon the pulse beat of each one through his many agents and the monitoring systems which he oversaw in his capacity as head of Orion communications.

So Shimlus was deceived in her belief that it was her own manipulation that caused a change in the Pleiadeans' circumstances. The rest of the entourage was deceived, as well. Most believed that Shimlus had acted wisely, and was using her intelligence—her *greater* intelligence, they now believed—to gain the means by which their teaching missions could be accomplished. They now heeded her words without question. They were seeing results, it seemed, and so her logic was considered to be sound.

She was supported by many who spoke on her behalf and encouraged the others to follow Shimlus' guidance in such matters. They had formed a hierarchy among themselves, beginning with that first group of ten who had been chosen so many months previously, by the Pleiadeans themselves, to venture out for that first foray into the city. These ten, from that point forward, were considered as unique or possessed of something added which gave them greater influence among their fellows. This was constantly encouraged by the Tyronites, who always addressed their communications to Shimlus or one of these ten individuals.

To the Tyronites, such hierarchal arrangements among any group were the rule. Therefore, they helped to reinforce this differentiation of status among the Pleiadeans. When they arrived on Tyron, however, these two hundred had held a balanced understanding of their positions as Light Bearers. They each held a particular expertise and had been chosen to carry out their teaching efforts in this field of expression. There was no competition or jealousy among them, nor any feelings of superiority or inferiority. They all knew of their inner connection to a higher expression of Intelligence, and they all shared this free access to the great Lens of Infinity that supplied each one with the Intelligence needed to carry out his or her life purpose! There was no cause to look to one another for guidance, nor to elevate themselves among the group as special or unique.

They did all hold the greatest respect for Dalos, for his more advanced development was recognized among them. He was truly their Teacher, and yet such was his humility that he himself did not express any differentiation from them. He treated all equally, with the greatest of respect, and they knew him—not as one to be looked up to—but as one who could serve them as a source of wisdom, for which they were deeply appreciative. This wisdom was never presented to them in an interfering or commanding fashion; it was made available to respond to *their* request for information or understanding. If necessary, of course, Dalos did extend himself to help these individuals break free of any misconception to which they may have attached themselves, but this was an ongoing process between teacher and student, and they were *all* students of Dalos, or students of Uriel. Uriel, herself, is a student of greater Minds than her own, and so on, *ad infinitum.*

Humility, then, was the byword of these individuals. But as their minds began to lose their intelligence, a certain disintegration of their natural humility set in.

Had they, for but a moment, sat quietly to make contact with their spiritual Mentors, and questioned the activities in which they were now fully engaged, they would have been given the insight that their actions were not so wisely chosen. But they did not, for the most part. They were carrying on with so much confidence in the rightness of their exchanges with the Tyronites that they never dreamed they had strayed from their initial purpose. Had they not come to teach? Were they not here to give of themselves? And how better to do so than to meet the Tyronites on their own level?

True, it was a very subtle differentiation that occurred with these individuals and began to undermine the quality of information that they were conveying to the Tyronites. It was a subtle factor of motivation that crept into their teachings. They lost their humbleness and began to believe in the superiority of their own minds. They did possess an understanding of interdimensional physics which was far beyond that knowledge of life possessed by the Orionites. As they saw the difference in their seeming states of intelligence, the Pleiadeans became more and more convinced of their own superiority. They began to deport themselves with an air of knowingness among the Tyronites.

Tonar, through his subtle means, encouraged this. He saw that they could elevate themselves further in the peoples' eyes and he, meanwhile, would give the Pleiadeans cause to eventually look toward him as a supplier of something that they individually needed. He had not yet hit upon this missing factor but in the meantime, his plans seemed to be taking their own course. He needed to do very little to encourage the worshipful attitude the Tyronites were beginning to have toward the Pleiadeans. To them, these strange, tall, and beautiful individuals offered a breath of fresh air. They were something unusual to fill the drab lives and consciousness of the Orion peoples, who were so dulled and numbed by their steady drudgery and rigid thoughts enforced by Tyrantus' controls. The Pleiadeans, to them, were colorful in their dress, and flamboyant with their words.

This, Tonar subtly encouraged through his agents. The Pleiadeans were given all that they requested in terms of special attire and other accessories to their lives. They were given privileges that many of the Orion elite did not have. Their quarters had now become redesigned into something of a fairyland by Tyron standards. They had surrounded themselves with reminders of their former existences on higher, radiant worlds of Light.

Tonar was pleased by this atmosphere, as he viewed the changes that were occurring under Shimlus' direction. He was delighted by the effect that these visual displays had upon the Tyronites. *Yes,* he thought, *I can use this natural proclivity of the Pleiadeans for colorful expressions, which seem to attract that much more attention.*

Soon Shimlus was directing the Pleiadeans to perform certain demonstrations of song and movement for gatherings of Tyron citizens. These were joyous occasions for the Pleiadeans, for to bring such illuminated expressions into such a drab world was a great relief for them and they were highly gratified by the appreciation the Tyronites showed for these demonstrations of the Pleiadeans' lifestyles. The Tyronites soon began requesting changes in their clothing and opportunities to learn these expressions from the Pleiadeans.

Tyrantus was convinced that the continuation of these activities would serve to further draw the Pleiadeans into Orion society. He was sufficiently preoccupied with his own concerns regarding his contacts with Dalos that he really cared not to dwell upon the matter of the Pleiadeans. However, he did know that Dalos would be shocked when he saw these individuals again, and his only desire was to dominate this man who had so thoroughly destroyed Tyrantus' ability to be at peace!

So it was true that the gathered Pleiadeans were awaiting the arrival of the Emperor himself. They did not know, however, that he would be joined by Dalos. By now they all believed that their leader would never reappear among them! They felt themselves to have been given the mandate to carry on with this mission in the best way they knew to do so. Shimlus had replaced Dalos as their leader, in many of their minds. For all practical purposes, this was so on a day-to-day basis.

They sat, then, in their newly decorated splendor, relaxed in conversation and at ease with the Tyron officials who joined them. Shimlus was seated in front of the group in a place of honor. She expected that the Emperor was coming to commend them for their successes in their contacts with his workers, who seemed to be showing a new vitality. This, they felt Tyrantus would approve, as it gave the workers a greater energy with which to approach their required tasks, and the Pleiadeans knew Tyrantus appreciated work flow more than anything at all.

The shock, then, that passed through this gathering when Dalos appeared caused the color to drain from their faces, and then to reappear in a great flush of emotion. They were immediately bombarded by a Force of Higher Intelligence that struck them nearly senseless with the awareness of its contrast to their own mentalities, which were now vastly deteriorated from that high-frequency awareness with which they had arrived upon Tyron.

Shimlus rose to her feet but could not speak, as Dalos strode to the raised area before them.

Tyrantus had entered the room behind Dalos. He was there to observe—and this was an exchange he wanted to witness first-hand.

"Greetings, my beloved brothers and sisters," Dalos said, tears forming in his radiant eyes.

He had lost none of his dignity and composure. He was as magnificent and beautiful as the day they had arrived, albeit pale and thin. Yet his Mind permeated their own with beams of Love.

They felt ashamed.

How could they ever have believed him dead? Why did they not know Dalos still existed upon the planet of Tyron? Why did they feel so suddenly ill and desirous of curling in upon themselves with the recognition of the vast difference in frequency that they felt, causing them this inner turmoil? And yet the turmoil was so tremendous that they could not find answers to these questions as easily as they once would.

Dalos was shocked by their appearance, and yes, he sensed the changes within them. It gave him a creeping feeling of hollow disappointment, but none so much as the sight of his beloved one, decked out in a gaudy costume of luminescent fibers that gave her a harsh appearance, to his eyes. It was the harshness of her consciousness that struck his inner senses!

As he looked about the room, his heart fell with the recognition of each of his beloved brothers and sisters, whose own countenances now reflected more dimly the Light that had once shone within them all. He knew then of their deterioration.

He thought nothing at that moment of his own long months of agony and physical torture. His entire Consciousness was enveloping these souls in compassionate understanding.

Many had bowed their heads in shame, although they perhaps knew not why they could not return Dalos' gaze. This broke his heart even more!

A great shocked silence gripped them all. There were no shouts of joyous welcome, no expressions of love and gratitude to see their leader once again! Each one was awash in self-recrimination. They had lost themselves, and they were incapable of facing the Light that Dalos now shone upon them.

Very well, he thought. *So it is, and so we must carry on with our mission, despite this terrible setback. I cannot allow myself to pity them, for they have made their own choices.*

Shimlus still had not moved, nor spoken. But finally she found the means by which to propel herself toward Dalos—but his look stopped her, and she fell to her knees before him, grabbing his hand to kiss it in a great show of forced humility.

He saw through this action, which disturbed him more than anything else. To think that this one, with whom he had shared the closest oscillation of joined consciousness, could have allowed herself to succumb to her own ego—it was nearly too much for him! He was not yet as strong as the image he presented to all who looked upon his radiant face.

As he let out a short gasping cry, Dalos' knees began to give way, but he was caught in the arms of the Tyron guards who had accompanied Dalos and Tyrantus to this gathering. They eased him into a nearby seat. He did not lose consciousness, but his sudden collapse caused the entire Pleiadean entourage to surge forward, as if to reach out their hands to break his fall.

For the first time, their thoughts were upon him and not their own selves. They suddenly realized that he was not well and they had no idea what had been done to him, where he had been for these many months in which they had felt abandoned and actually resented Dalos for his absence—although they did not, until that moment, recognize the subtly growing resentment. Even now, they would not admit it to themselves but pushed it aside with a rationalization that they had done the best they could under the circumstances and they had nothing to be ashamed about.

These thoughts began rippling through the room, as their suddenly deflated egos upon Dalos' arrival began fighting to reinstate themselves and prepare the speeches they would present to him, if approached or accused of behaving wrongly. Their self-defense mechanisms were in full working order, then.

But Dalos was, at that moment, beyond caring to hear any of it. He was now—again—fighting a battle with his physical anatomy. He knew that he must remain now, for he saw the dire situation in which these two hundred had placed themselves. Now his mission was, not only to save the souls already threatened with extinction by Tyrantus' manipulations, but to rescue his own entourage from this hell world! They had disappointed him greatly. He had no more words to say to them now. He closed his eyes, and weakly asked to be taken to a place of rest where he might regain his composure.

"I cannot speak to them now," he said to Tyrantus, who was standing near. "Allow me this time to regather my strength."

Tyrantus gave the order and Dalos was lifted, chair and all, into a nearby room.

Shimlus was stricken with shock and horror. She had been humiliated in front of the entire assemblage! She could not move for several long moments. Then she fled the room, isolating herself in her own quarters. She did not go to Dalos' side. She could not face him, and she could not forgive him for treating her this way.

The others did not know what to do with themselves. They stood in confusion, milling about aimlessly for some time, wondering if Dalos would return, or Shimlus, and feeling as if their insides had collapsed upon themselves.

Eventually, Tyrantus reappeared. "Your leader has stated his desire to be alone. He does not wish to see you. You may return to your normal activities." And with that, he turned on his heel, followed by his bodyguards, leaving the Pleiadeans to their devastated thoughts.

17

The Joining

I felt the Brother take my hand in his—almost a physical sensation. "Dear one," he said, "if you want to become well—truly well in mind and body—then you must know the full story…"

DALOS DID NOT ARISE from his resting place for several days. He had sustained yet another psychic shock. It was a nearly fatal blow to his consciousness to see the fall of his many brothers and sisters. They would be of little use to him now, for they had lost the inner link, that connecting spark that united them with the Higher Intelligence of the Cosmic Fountainhead.

They believed, of course, that all was well, and that they were carrying out their missions as teachers. They had convinced themselves that they were following their inner directives and were producing results, the results for which they had all come to the planet Tyron. They were now quite familiar with many of the Tyronite citizens and carried on frequent contacts with them, engaging in many joint activities.

But what Dalos saw through the perception of his Infinite Mind was their drop in consciousness. He saw that their Lights had nearly gone out! They were now functioning from another part of themselves, not that higher input which had so directed them all unto the surface of this physical world. It was quite easy to be deceived, Dalos knew, by the exterior appearance of life, and these two hundred had indeed succumbed to the many influences and pulls upon their conscious minds.

They, too, had evolved through countless physical planes of existence to reach their more elevated state of consciousness, that developed understanding from which they had descended into their present physical anatomies. Throughout the course of their many lives lived previously, they had mastered the lessons of a five-sense, physical body, one by one, adding unto themselves a more expanded awareness of the ebb and flow of life. But now they were rapidly regressing and forgetting their lessons learned. They were influenced by the constant subliminal pulsing of lower-frequency harmonics; yet this was not the full cause for their decline. Their own egos entered in, and began to reinflate themselves as the Tyronites continued to look up to these individuals for some form of example or guidance.

Had they maintained their inner attunement with the Higher Minds, their own Brothers of Light, they would have been able to provide these lost souls with the illumination that they so desperately needed. They would have redirected these individuals to look within themselves for their own spiritual guidance. That was the true teaching of Dalos; that was the teaching they all came to spread among the Orion planets.

Each one, individually, could have served on any one of these planets as a great, illumined Flame of consciousness that could have awakened an entire world to the reality of the spiritual nature of humankind. Had they maintained their inner contact with their own Higher Selves, they could have accomplished this in an effortless manner. But they were sorely lacking in patience and, one by one, succumbed to the wiles and machinations of the Orion negative forces. Each fell from his mental development in a unique fashion. Each succumbed to a different form of material-life temptation. They forgot themselves, and forgot that they could no longer live as did these Tyronites, else they would be truly lost!

These were the thoughts that passed through Dalos' mind as he lay once again upon a reclining surface, unable to stand or maneuver his body from place to place due to his greatly weakened condition. He had not fully recovered from his injuries and tortures before attempting this meeting with his entourage. He simply could wait no longer, and had insisted to Tyrantus that he was ready for this encounter. Tyrantus, of course, was quite willing to grant Dalos' request, for he was eager to know what effect this would have upon the Pleiadean leader.

Now Tyrantus had seen exactly what he wanted to see. Dalos had been further weakened by the sight of his entourage, who were nothing like those individuals who had accompanied him on his starship one year previously! The change within these individuals was quite remarkable, Tyrantus believed. They had acclimated themselves to his society quite readily.

Of course Tyrantus was not aware of the manipulations of his Council member, Tonar. Tonar, too, added his own devious expressions into this mix of diabolical scheming to further pull at the minds of the Pleiadeans, one by one. He had tried many methods—from personal, face-to-face encounters with his agents to certain projections of electronic frequencies that he himself had found to be particularly effective in influencing others. These included subliminal messages which would cause a certain loyalty to Tonar. This was the method by which he kept his own aides and agents loyal to him, and he fully intended to make the Pleiadeans pliant to his bidding in the future. But first of all, he was working to elevate their public images.

They were frequently seen, now, on Orion communications systems, "teaching," as they called it. He preferred to think of this as their method of gaining a superior influence over others. And they now had become familiar with Tonar himself, as he was the director of these broadcasting facilities.

Tyrantus approved. He felt there could be no harm in this situation, as he knew that the Pleiadeans were incapable of causing any permanent damage to his regime. They were quite harmless fools, Tyrantus believed, and he regarded their utterings as mere nonsense which had nothing whatsoever to do with the physical lives of the people of his many worlds.

Dalos was unaware of these broadcast images. He had no conscious idea of the extent to which his followers had immersed themselves in the lifestyles of the planet Tyron. He knew only from his intuitive and highly sensitive psychic awareness that their minds were not functioning fully. He could see by their dress and mannerisms that they no longer carried themselves as the spiritual Light Beings that they truly had been. He knew that they no longer provided the example of a higher consciousness that he had hoped to present to the Orionites through the personages of these carefully selected individuals. His heart was shattered.

Yet he could not allow this to become his defeat! Dalos' purpose was to bring a higher understanding unto these worlds and he would do so, if it required every last ounce of his consciousness! Indeed, it seemed as if it might, he thought as he struggled to maintain his alertness while his body endured the agonies of the endless medical experimentations to which he had been subjected.

He was eventually moved from the Pleiadean quarters back to the medical facility, the rejuvenation center from which he had been brought by Tyrantus. Throughout these days of his relapse, he had no contact with any of his entourage.

They now knew, however, that Dalos lived, and they were quite beside themselves with anxiety and concern. Why had he not wished to see them? How could they regain their communication with this one? Each individual Pleiadean suffered a tremendous inner turmoil, not unlike that which had influenced the three Council members who accompanied Tyrantus on to the Pleiadean starship. Yet these souls were now facing a reality that was quite crushing in its impact upon their minds. They gathered, from Dalos' collapse, that he had been affected in a negative way by their reuniting. They did not understand—nay, they would not *allow* themselves to understand, for to do so would have meant a tremendous deflation of the egos which had now re-emerged and were, each day, growing in their dominating nature over the minds of these individuals. They were thoroughly enjoying their new position among the Tyronites, and with each moment of pleasure found in their superior positioning, they were lost one degree further.

Dalos began to formulate within his mind a new plan. He would concentrate his efforts to reach Tyrantus. Now this one had, not only billions of souls of different evolutionary development under his control, but he also had made inroads into taking over the minds of Dalos' close helpers. These souls, these two hundred, could prove to be a very volatile influence, further adding the weight of their mental development to the destructive qualities of the Orion government should they fully turn their backs upon their true purpose—and sadly, Dalos believed that it was already too late, that this decline was inevitable.

He would, of course, do everything possible to prevent it, but given his restricted circumstance, the induced failure of his physical anatomy, there was but little that he, as one individual, could do in a direct, personal way in terms of aiding these fallen comrades.

Perhaps they will learn something of themselves from my absence. Perhaps this is all that I can do. They have chosen their present circumstances by their own thoughts and actions. If they desire change, then they must choose that as well, and I know that my dear Brothers of Light on the higher worlds are extending their Love to these individuals, never-endingly, as am I. Should they re-open their minds to this Love-intelligence, they shall feel the truth within them once again! Beyond that, there is little that can be done. They are, like all souls, free to choose their course. It matters not from whence they came; they are here now, living a particular existence, and they must rely upon their own inner guidance, dim as that Light has now become!

Meanwhile, the efforts of Radik and Linton to penetrate the secrets of the Pleiadean starship continued. They realized that further contact with Dalos was dangerous to their plans. They could easily have been detected by Tyrantus, and this would have given him cause to end their lives. Instead, they proposed to the Emperor that a special structure be built around the landed starship. This he readily approved, as it solved his dilemma of the public appearance of this great embarrassment.

Immediately, such a research building was constructed and Linton and Radik set up their operations within it. They had been endeavoring to analyze the radiations from this starship, hoping that from this data, they could develop instrumentation which would give them access to its interior. They were unaware of Dalos' promise to Tyrantus for one of Dalos' technicians to provide detailed information about, not only the ship, but the equipment thereon.

Now Dalos realized that this would not be wise, for that individual among his crew whom he had planned to assign to Tyrantus' scientists was already becoming a part of the negatively-biased expressions of the Orion forces. He would no doubt give them the information they required, Dalos considered, but this would not be a positive development. It would be information that could become quite destructive when wrongly introduced into the society. It was Dalos' plan that they would share their wisdom with the Orionites as a natural process of the awakening of these peoples to their more constructive natures. As they bloomed in consciousness, so would these "gifts" of intelligence be added unto them.

But now all had soured, and the giving of technological tools to these individuals would become a highly flammable circumstance. Dalos knew that it was only a matter of time before Radik and Linton, or any other among the Orion scientists, developed some way to tear his ship to small pieces in their search for the Intelligence by which it operated—just as they were tearing into his physical anatomy. He wondered how long it would be before they began to tear into the bodies of his former crew members. Anything upon this hellish world was possible!

As Dalos lay in his pained state of suspended animation, a great Light penetrated his awareness, filling the room with an oscillating Radiance that was unmistakable to him. It was a projection of Mind from his beloved polarity, Michiel.

My dear Illumined One, your Presence is so very meaningful to me, as I now feel quite alone! Yet I know such is not possible. You Beloved Ones are always with me! Do tell me how I can best proceed, for all things begin to turn dark with the taint of this grim nightmare.

Dalos felt himself warmed in the luminance of this powerful Love projection. His pains subsided as he lost awareness of them, and his consciousness was lifted to join that of his biune. He left the physical anatomy behind and linked in full Consciousness with Michiel, and even so, these Two were joined as One with Raphiel and Muriel, a Flame of Cosmic Intelligence far beyond the scope of mortal senses.

This joining filled Dalos with much-needed Power to carry on. It lasted for an indefinable length of time, as it occurred while Dalos' physical body slept and he truly rose or transcended into his more natural state of existence, rejoining the Higher Mind of Uriel, of which "Dalos" was but one clear, gleaming facet. Timeless and spaceless was this joining.

From this realm of perception, all things were visible. Dalos' time on Tyron would be extended as long as possible; yet that time was limited by the finite qualities of the physical body that he inhabited. Much could be accomplished with those individuals who held the greatest influence upon so many trillions of souls; that is, the Emperor Tyrantus and his Council of Twelve—and any others who came in contact with Dalos during his captivity.

Dalos was not yet free, for he was trapped within this limited physical body and it could be waylaid and kept from certain expressions through which he might have extended his mission. Now that the physical bodies of his entourage carried the expressions of minds who were losing or had lost this higher connection, they could not be counted upon by Dalos to further extend his access to the Orion peoples, as had been planned. They were to have served as spokespersons for the Higher Minds of which they had once been a part—but now their receiving capabilities were hindered or shut off. With each day that passed, they were less and less capable of bringing through a clear, intelligent message to the Orion peoples.

What the Pleiadeans were now doing in their expressions as so-called teachers was to spread a distorted picture of Infinity that had been partially obscured by their personal interpretations, as these personalities became more and more dominant. They were encouraged in this by the machinations and plans of Tyrantus, Tonar, and eventually others among the Council. This was seen clearly by the joined Hierarchical Minds. They would extend to these ones their hands of Infinite, impersonal assistance. All involved were sparks, children of Infinity—all thereby treated equally.

If, however, any one of them could be induced to recognize his or her drop in consciousness, then there was hope that they could still aid Dalos in some fashion. But it was recognized that this would require the direct help of Dalos himself, for they could no longer hear within, the Intelligence that was radiated to them.

This is the failing that had occurred as they awaited Dalos' return, while they were kept isolated from him and from the Tyron society as a whole. It is not surprising that the Pleiadeans so quickly adapted to the company of the Tyronites after so many months in seclusion. This produced a tremendous surcharge of energy within them, as they had been short-circuited in their ability to follow through on their teaching missions; but the overwhelming rush of information which they desired to give was now tainted with their personal aberrations of thought, which had been incurred and nurtured throughout these many long weeks—their fears, frustrations, resentments toward Dalos, and feelings of abandonment.

Still, as with the Orionites themselves, there is nothing in Infinity that cannot be reversed in its trajectory. So Dalos would request from Tyrantus another audience with his entourage. He would make another attempt to reach them.

When he regained consciousness, Dalos felt much restored in vitality. He requested to speak to the Emperor and this time his request was granted immediately.

A special communications device was brought into Dalos' room. Through it, he could both speak to and see the Emperor and vice versa. Tyrantus felt safer this way. He felt more in control. The flip of a button would disconnect his communication with Dalos, communications which still caused him deep unrest.

Tyrantus was not well himself. His face had grown increasingly haggard and the evidence of his loss of sleep was becoming quite apparent. He seemed feeble-minded, which alarmed his aides, who dared not speak of it among themselves or especially to the Emperor himself. Yet privately they feared that his own death was imminent! He was obviously ill, yet he was not seeking treatment. No one dared suggest such a thing. No one told Tyrantus how to proceed with his life!

The Council members were gratified to see this change in their leader. Although he had extended his life through many, many cycles, they greedily awaited that time when he might vacate his seat of power. Each one believed that he was the rightful successor, and they would use all means in their control to gain this seat once Tyrantus died. They, then, made no comment about his obviously failing health.

But Dalos, with the first sight of the Emperor's image, remarked upon it.

"Emperor, you do not appear to be feeling well. I hope that I have not disturbed you unduly, but I have a very important request to make."

Tyrantus looked wearily at Dalos, whose bloom of life never seemed to fully leave his countenance, no matter how much pain he must have been suffering, the Emperor thought. He was filled with a deep envy that he could not define as such.

"What is it that you require?" Tyrantus said. He had tired of any further communications with the Pleiadean. He was assured by his Council members, Radik and Linton, that they would soon have resolved the so-called secrets of Dalos' starship, so he had little need for this Pleiadean commander now, except as a bothersome curiosity which he could not fully dismiss from his mind!

He had wearied of tormenting Dalos through explorations of his physical anatomy, all of which resulted in inconclusive data that clogged his computer banks with worthless information. And he could not speak to this individual without a terrible mental indigestion resulting from their conversation. So, for the present, he was unwilling to have Dalos removed—that is, put to death—and yet reluctant for contact with him. He was not certain why he responded this time to Dalos' request, but perhaps it had something to do with his curiosity about how this one was handling the rejection of his own entourage.

Tyrantus actually had some feeling for Dalos in this. He had been capable of placing himself in Dalos' shoes as a leader of men and of sensing his own inner reactions to such a circumstance. Of course, for Tyrantus it would have been a response of terrible anger and retribution taken upon these individuals. Dalos' compassion and impersonal love was strange to Tyrantus, yet touched him deeply in a very subtle way. He now respected Dalos—although he could not admit this to himself. Tyrantus felt isolated from humanity, and truly he was, and in Dalos' present isolation he saw some similarity. He was, unbeknownst to himself, drawing comfort—or information, might be more accurate—from Dalos. It was familiar to him.

"I desire," Dalos continued, "to speak to my entourage now that I have regained some physical strength. You once granted me this opportunity. I hope that you will extend it to me now, as I was incapable at that time of fully availing myself of your generosity."

Here was an opportunity to learn more, Tyrantus thought. What harm could it do? These were truly divided forces now. They could not possibly unite against him, and he had been so comforted and his fears removed by his contacts with Dalos that he gave an affirmative response. The only fears now remaining within Tyrantus' mind were of his own mental instability. He was searching now for answers.

This was Dalos' fondest hope, and he was quite gratified to sense these changes within the Emperor. It gave him further encouragement and allowed him to turn his attention, for the moment, to the needs of his own former aides.

18

A Choice

There are no limitations for a Mind such as that from which Dalos derived his consciousness. He was soon able to stand again and as rapidly as this was achieved, his meeting with the Pleiadean entourage was arranged.

This time, the Pleiadeans knew that they were to be visited by Dalos. They were anticipating this meeting with mixed feelings—fear commingled with excitement; shame mixed with love. They truly believed themselves to have been loyal to their purposes. They did not yet recognize or admit to their loss of higher attunement. This would be Dalos' purpose, to bring this to their awareness and to help them to change the bias of their thoughts, which had drifted off center, so to speak. They had become biased to personal needs and concerns. These selfish motivations had crept in upon the Pleiadeans without their knowledge, so rampant were the many distractions presented to their physical senses by Orion society. Drugs, of both chemical and electronic structures, sex, subliminal programming, lavish feasts, and a general obsession with satisfying the physical appetites permeated the lives of the Orion elite, with whom the Pleiadeans had become very much involved.

Shimlus and the other nine who had become so influential among the entire group led this movement to adopt certain facets of Tyron lifestyles as their own, thereby, she reasoned, forging an alliance with these individuals in order to better "speak their language," that is, to reach them more directly with the teachings the Pleiadeans had come to promulgate among the Orionites. Shimlus and the others were unaware of the distortion in this thinking. By lowering their minds to the level of their hosts, they had lost the entire purpose for their being present on Tyron as Light Bearers! They were no longer capable of providing a higher reflection of life, thereby. They were merely inflating their own egos with the belief that they had some grand purpose to serve, and that purpose was becoming more and more diluted in their understanding of it with each passing hour.

It soon became a vague ringing within their ears, something indefinable that they felt pushed to accomplish; yet their goals were being obscured by their selfish motivations.

Dalos felt it best to speak with these ten individuals privately before addressing the entire group. He arrived at their homes at the designated hour and suggested that they gather in a comfortable room. Shimlus was miffed at the fact that Dalos had not chosen to meet with her individually first, yet she suppressed this reaction and pretended to feel nothing. Her coldness struck a sharp blow against the mind of Dalos but he brushed it aside as his purpose was clearly laid out for him. No such attacks upon his consciousness by these individuals could affect him. He was prepared for their negative responses to the words he had to speak to these souls, who had been his closest aides and family members.

"Dear friends," he began, "for I trust that you still regard yourselves as such."

They were startled by these words and said nothing in response. They were frozen with fear—a very strange sensation which they had never before felt in the presence of their leader. Yet it persisted.

"You have done yourselves a great disservice."

They looked at him, again with a startled expression. What could he possibly mean?

"You have allowed your own egos to obscure your vision, I am afraid. This was not unexpected," he added, "for it was known by the Hierarchy that you would face great trials and tests of your consciousness while serving on this particular mission. We did not anticipate our long separation.

However, this does not grant us any excuse for a loss of direction, does it? You, each one, know of your inner purpose and yet you have misdirected your thoughts and lost your link with the higher Source!"

The faces gazing back at him bore two distinct expressions: some dropped their eyes in recognition of the truth of his words; others looked back at him in confusion, not able to recognize the reality of their present insanity—for truly that is what they had become. Any soul who has lost his inner connection to the guiding Force of his life can be considered to be mentally deficient and does carry on in an insane, illogical fashion.

"But Dalos," Shimlus began, "we *have* been serving our missions! Have you not heard of our many broadcasts to the Tyron peoples? We *have been* spreading the message! You simply do not understand," she protested.

Dalos looked directly at her, she who had once shared his life as his beloved one. He felt the greatest compassion for her confused state of mind. It pained him to speak truth—yet that was his responsibility, and his personal feelings would never intrude upon his need to express truthfully!

"You, Shimlus, are quite mistaken, and I am sad to say that you have greatly disappointed me through your behavior. You have allowed your own selfish needs for some adulation from these peoples to blind you to the fact that you are not carrying on in a wise and helpful manner. You are giving them something which they *do not* need—that is, the image of your own personality! Do you not realize that these people are now beginning to regard you all as some form of god, to which they are beginning to look for enlightenment?

"Yes, of course, we have come to illuminate their minds, but not to elevate our own selves and place our images in the forefront of their consciousness! We have come to bring these poor, struggling souls the knowledge of their own existence as Light Beings. Have you forgotten this? Have you lost all your senses?"

Dalos' words rang through the room with an intensity that silenced them all.

"Yes, you should feel ashamed of yourselves! You have done exactly the opposite of our true purpose here! How could this have happened? I had so thoroughly trusted you, each one, to be strong in purpose, and secure in your knowledge of that radiating Light which resonates within each soul. Do you now wish to spend Eternity as god-forces for these millions—*trillions* of souls, who shall willingly give their minds to you? For they have been trained by Tyrantus and his demons to look outside themselves for direction. What you have done is stepped in and placed yourselves in the position of Tyrantus! Each and every one of you is now serving as the Demonic One who is elevated as their 'savior!'"

"This cannot be!" one individual burst out. "We have no such intention, Dalos! You do not know what we have been doing! You have not been here to see the results that we have achieved! How can you speak to us in this way?"

The others attempted to silence this individual, for they were shocked by his lack of respect for Dalos. He was flushed with angry colors, and finally was subdued, but could clearly be seen to retain his emotional reaction.

"There," Dalos said, "is an example of how far you have fallen. Your emotions are now rampantly taking over your minds, are they not? I have seen enough to know of the conflicts among you, and may I add that it is quite disturbing to me to see how you have convinced the others that you are more responsible than they for our mission here, that you are now their leaders—and what of Dalos? Have you forgotten him? Have you erased him from your minds? Truly, I believe you would wish me still to be suffering the tortures of Tyrantus' surgical weaponry!"

Again, they were stunned by these words and one or two began to tear profusely. Still, there were those among the ten who fought Dalos in their minds. They could not believe these terrible things. After all, had they not been doing their best in his absence? Had they not striven with all their hearts to carry out their missions?

What these individuals failed to recognize was the subtle way in which they had been influenced by many factors. So gradual had been their decline that they were now at the bottom looking up, and their sight was clouded by the formations of many thoughts that they had generated and regenerated during Dalos' absence.

He saw that these individuals would not be immediately turned around in their thinking. There was nothing further that he could do except to project his penetrating Consciousness, a higher-frequency beam of Intelligence, directly to them, as he was now doing through his very pointed words. Those who were accepting the truth of his words might be able to change their ways. That would remain to be seen. In the meantime, he would be forced to discontinue his associations with the Pleiadeans. This meant that they were now truly on their own. And so was he. Yet Dalos still carried the full complement of higher spiritual forces within his consciousness and this formed an entire legion of Lighted Ones that could illuminate—not only a single, solitary planet, or a hundred such planets—but a hundred thousand galaxies!

This was the Cosmic Intelligence which any one of the individuals seated so miserably before him could have tapped into, had they thrown aside their self-concerns and lifted their eyes *and* minds to join with his own. The extent of their opposition to him further indicated the tremendous impact that Orion technology had had upon them. They were so thoroughly convinced of their rightness of action! Such self-righteous attitudes were, until now, foreign to Pleiadean societies. They no longer merited the term "Light Bearers." And as for Shimlus, Dalos could see a seed of hatred germinating within her.

No doubt they shall all hate me for this, he thought. *So be it. Truth heals, if accepted. I can do no more, but I have promised to speak to the entire group and I will do so.*

Dalos rose unsteadily from his chair and the others stood quickly, reluctant to assist him and yet uncertain of his need for their physical support. They felt extremely awkward and uncomfortable with the very One whose heart had once beat in harmonious pulse with their own hearts! They felt a cavernous division and separation from him. He did nothing to soothe their feelings, for this peace of mind could only return to them as they regained their inner attunement, and that could only be accomplished when they accepted the truth of all that had been spoken.

Until that time, he felt no further desire to remain with them, for their thoughts of resentment bombarded his being and although rejected by him, they took their toll upon his mental and therefore physical strength. He asked that the entire group be alerted to his desire to speak with them.

"Of course," one of the entourage said, "we shall bring them immediately," and this gave several of the ten an excuse to quickly vacate the room and to seek relief from the penetrating Light that was now exposing their lower selves.

The two hundred gathered in the large meeting area in which Dalos had previously addressed them. They, too, were confused by their conflicting emotions. They were glad to see Dalos in one sense, and yet reluctant in another. They sensed that all was not well but they were unclear about the reasons for this feeling.

"Dear brothers and sisters, I know that you have recently been directing your consciousness to Shimlus and the others whom you have elevated in your minds as leaders among you. I wish you to know that they have not acted wisely. They have been leading you astray, and you have all been allowing yourselves to drift in consciousness from that central focus which is so essential if we are to be successful in our contacts with the Orionites! I am coming directly to the point because my time with you is limited by my physical condition. As you see, I am still not well, for Tyrantus has seen to that. He has kept me debilitated so that I would not be a threat to his regime, and I dearly hope that you can analyze your own thoughts and reactions sufficiently to recognize how you, too, have been debilitated by the influences that surround you upon this world!

"Your many expositions of flamboyant attire and coarse expressions of music and dance, your frequent carousings with the Tyronites, and your general deportment—unbefitting Lighted Ones who have come with Angelic purpose—are quite disgusting and disheartening to me! I will disassociate myself with you, because you do not represent that higher purpose for which all of you once accompanied me to this world. You are now creating a mess in the minds of the Tyronites—yet I do not blame you so much as I blame those ten individuals who have encouraged this behavior! There are no excuses, however, for each one of you knows the science of consciousness more thoroughly than most who live in physical anatomies. You knew the pitfalls before you came, and no doubt you observed the subliminal influences that are rampant upon this world during your first initiations into this society.

"These ten individuals are no different than yourselves. They do not possess some special insight. Indeed, they have now inflated their egos to such a degree that you would be quite foolish to listen to their words!

"If you desire to redeem yourselves, this shall be your task: to cease and desist with these activities which you have falsely believed were beneficial. If any of these ten are honest with themselves and with you, they will explain to you, as I have explained to them, that what you are now creating is a new form of control among the Orionites!"

Throughout Dalos' speech a shocked silence reigned among the Pleiadeans. Yet now they let out audible murmurings of confusion at this statement.

"Yes, I mean what I say! They are now beginning to look to *you* as their leaders! Of course, I do not expect that you are sensitive to this subtle change among them, but I have no doubt that there are forces operating in this world who are quite ready to take advantage of your seeming ignorance. There are ample subastral influences in play among you to divert your minds into this foolhardy expression. You may believe that you are helping the Tyronites, but I assure you, you are only helping yourselves to become gods among them! This is always a danger when one contacts another civilization, particularly one in such a delicate mental balance as this. These people have been accustomed to looking outside themselves for guidance. You have now given them an opportunity to look to you!"

Dalos paused for a moment to allow the full impact of his words to seep into the closed minds of his former followers. He could feel the repercussions of these statements, which were causing extreme agitation. These bombarding frequencies of a lower nature he ignored, and continued.

"Now it is going to be extremely difficult to undo what has been done, and I am not capable of undertaking this task single-handedly. If any among you choose to recognize the validity of my words, then you shall be directed from within as to how you must proceed. I strongly suggest that you suspend all contact with the Tyronites immediately, until you have regained your mental balance and know for certain that you are proceeding with that higher guidance of which you all seem to have lost your awareness!

"I cannot do this for you. It is now in your hands, for you have created this situation—which I might add, is extremely volatile here. Only you can change the quality of your interaction with the Orion peoples. Only you know the truth that still exists within you. If you cannot sense it now, then I suggest that you weigh these words carefully in your quiet time and come to some more intelligent conclusions.

"Now I must return to my bed, for I am not recovered, and your reception here has done little to reassure me. I must seek the company of my own mind, then, and I suggest you do likewise."

With that, Dalos abruptly left the room. He walked to the doorway but was greeted by several attendants who helped him to a wheeled transport and conveyed him to the medical facility. He was thoroughly sickened by the experience.

His physical strength had been entirely expended through his desire to awaken these sleeping souls who had so thoroughly and quickly relinquished themselves to the negative forces. A great vortex of healing energy had been projected to them; yet it would be up to each individual to take advantage of the healing help being extended to them. Time must pass before the success or failure of Dalos' contact with them would become evident. One thing was already clear: that there were those among the ten so-called leaders who had closed their minds to him. He held little hope for them. They would fall much further before they recognized the magnitude of their grave errors in thinking. Such was the way of one who loses his mind in a material plane—and certainly they were surrounded by examples of Higher Minds that had turned upon themselves and humanity in ferocious egomania! Perhaps these examples would, one day, alert the four or five of the ten who had been so reluctant to accept their Teacher's pointings-up. Perhaps. But he could not concern himself with them just now. Dalos directed his mind to Tyrantus, even as his body once again succumbed to pain and fatigue.

The Emperor had observed every moment of these exchanges through the monitoring devices. He felt that his physical absence would encourage greater openness on the part of the Pleiadeans and he might gain some insight from this observation.

By now Tyrantus was unclear as to what he was hoping for from these foreign people. He was quite confused in his daily actions and there were many Council meetings that passed without his presence. He was indeed lost in a swirl of tangled thoughts. This was the healthiest state of mind Tyrantus had experienced in quite some time! Certainly it was not productive in his physical life, and yet it indicated that his conscience had been reawakened. Feelings now stirred within him that he had suppressed for lifetimes! His feelings toward Dalos grew increasingly close with each passing encounter. Whether he observed Dalos speaking to a single attendant in the medical facility, or whether Tyrantus himself was engaged in a one-on-one conversation, he was being affected by Dalos' Intelligence. Long-hidden memories were rekindled, and yet still unrecognized.

Tyrantus kept himself isolated as much as possible. This did not affect the routine existence of life on the Orion planets but it was beginning to influence the Council members. They had seen Tyrantus' wearied countenance and deduced from it that he was gravely ill. They were already beginning to jockey for the superior position among themselves. Radik and Linton stepped up their efforts to crack the impenetrable starship, which they believed held the secrets of ultimate control, and Tonar determined to implement his plan to make the Pleiadeans his personal "calling card" upon other planets. He felt emboldened by Tyrantus' inattention, as did the others, and each of the Council members now began to marshal their resources for a takeover of power. Whatever their expertise—scientific, educational, or administrative—they began looking for ways to gain greater influence and domination over the others.

The Council meetings had deteriorated further into squabbling sessions at which little was accomplished. The steady tick-tock of life for most Orion peoples continued in its endless progression of day to night to day to night, their tasks unchanging, their orders still routinely emitted from computer screens, their "conditioning treatments" still obtained as per the routine orders, and their lives carried out with a dullness of mind that made them susceptible to any subtle influence of a stronger force. Their own physical senses were the rulers of their activities, and these senses were stimulated and prompted by the electronic and other influences devised by Council members. They now represented massive numbers of political pawns. If one Council member firmly controlled the majority of these populations through whatever means, then he or she would gain the throne of power when Tyrantus inevitably vacated it.

Now Tyrantus cared little about these maneuverings by his enemies. He was more interested to observe Dalos from a safe distance. He could not risk revealing this obsessive interest to others, yet he did find himself irresistibly pulled to speak with the Pleiadean one more time. Things that Dalos had said to him previously were haunting his thoughts and causing him to lose his concentration at the most inopportune moments. He felt that a further conversation would allow him to, once again, gain control of the situation. He believed he could in this way resolve his turmoil, by proving to himself that these were erroneous statements and that Dalos could certainly be induced to retract them!

In any case, he needed to have some further explanation for his present state of mind.

Dalos did not consciously know of Tyrantus' desire—and yet he did sense that they were soon to speak again. He was thoroughly aware in his Higher Mind of all that was now transpiring upon the planet Tyron, hotbed of negative activity for the Forces of Darkness.

19

Brothers

THE MOMENTUM OF EVENTS now surrounding the Pleiadeans had reached a point of velocity that was nearly unstoppable.

Shimlus was torn. She still felt that their routine broadcasts to the Orion peoples were extremely effective and important, and she was unconvinced of the rightness of Dalos' reasoning. She believed that his mind had lost some of its clarity, due to the endless experimental treatments to which he had been subjected. About this, she felt very sad, yet she strongly believed that it was up to her to carry on in a more integrated fashion the work that they had come to express.

Others among the Pleiadeans tended to agree with her point of view. They believed, as well, that Dalos had lost some of his ability to reason, else why could he not see the value of their frequent contacts with the Tyronites—indeed, with all Orion planets through the communications systems? Was this not the purpose for which they had come? They dismissed his remarks about the Orionites looking to them as god-forces, for they did not wish to believe the truth of this.

Dalos' mind, of course, was functioning in a more complete and integrated way than their own, but through the distortions that they had allowed to enter into their consciousness, they were convinced that the reverse was true. This presented a most difficult dilemma. No one can be persuaded to believe that which he does not wish to believe, at least not through any normal means of direct presentation of information. Certainly, the Orion Empire was about gross mental manipulation and persuasion, but Dalos was not about to impose his understanding upon others, not even those who had pledged themselves to serve as his helpers in this healing mission—which was now threatening to deteriorate completely.

Based on their misperceptions, then, Shimlus and the four or five individuals who had not been touched by Dalos' words agreed that they would privately carry on with their preparations for further informative programs to be developed and presented to the Orion planets. Most recently, Shimlus had met with Tonar to discuss this matter and together they had devised a plan by which to introduce the Pleiadeans' teachings to other, outlying planets.

This was extremely exciting to the Pleiadeans, who felt the inflation of their soon-to-be expanded reputations as teachers among the Orion peoples. They were doing exactly as Dalos had warned: they were allowing their lower selves to encumber their clear-sightedness so that now they truly were peering through the fog of ego-biased motivations. Yet they were totally ignorant and unwilling to accept this fact. That is how strongly the internal mechanism of self-defense and rationalization can work to deceive oneself. Deceived, they were! And doomed, for they were choosing the downward spiral, unaware of the implications—the true implications—of their misguided efforts.

Tonar was quite pleased with their cooperation. This was far simpler than he had imagined. They now came to him for advice and to gain access to the communications systems. They were entirely dependent upon him for this opportunity, as they saw it. He had them now firmly in his control, and he served as their link to Tyrantus. Without his influence they would not have been granted permission to carry on in this fashion.

What Tonar knew that they did not was that Tyrantus was in no position to think clearly himself, as his health was rapidly failing and he was totally disinterested in such activities. He was almost completely isolated now, and would only maintain contact with those closest to him, including those three Council members who had joined him on Dalos' starship. These three had always served as his most trusted supporters, and yet he and they knew that this was merely a relationship of necessity. They all longed to gain ultimate control over the others and thereby over the entire empire.

Tonar could now see this distinct possibility looming on his horizon. He worked to control his ecstasy and carry on in a seemingly ordinary manner. Soon he would be in the proper position to make his move, but for now he must remain quiet and do nothing to attract unwanted attention from the Emperor. The Pleiadeans were so cooperative with his own desires that he needed to apply very little pressure in their direction. They were falling into his hands at an unbelievably rapid rate. Nothing could please him more, except that day when he finally revealed himself as supreme ruler of all Orion!

Radik and Linton, meanwhile, were devising a new means by which to penetrate the starship, which still sat immobile, now confined within the walls of their research facility, gleaming in mysterious radiance. Now, however, they had measured the energy that was was emitted from the surface of the ship and had been working diligently to develop equipment which could match these higher-frequency radiations. They did enlist the aid of several of the Pleiadean entourage, as now it was quite easy to gain access to these individuals. Two Pleiadean scientists provided information which had allowed Linton and Radik and their teams of scientists to duplicate the frequency emanating from the starship. They had not yet discovered how to direct these high-frequency radiations in an intelligent manner to unlock the ship's interior, and the Pleiadeans could not define this sufficiently for them.

Truly, the two individuals who had once served as crew members upon this starship were unable themselves to unlock the ship! This they explained to the Tyronites, yet they were not believed.

"No matter," Radik said to Linton in private conversation. "We now have the information we need to solve this enigma ourselves. We do not need these Pleiadeans any longer and besides, I do not trust them. I suspect that Tonar, who has had increasing interactions with them, has some scheme in mind to use these individuals for his own private gains. I don't care what he thinks he will try—I know that once we have opened this ship, the universe shall be ours!"

Linton agreed that they need no longer attempt to pick the brains of the Pleiadeans, with whom he did not enjoy contact. Something about these individuals rubbed him the wrong way. He did not like their superior attitudes, and truly he did not like the inferior feeling that he experienced every time they were near. It was the reminder of his own former Intelligence as a Light Worker that stirred the embers of resentment within him—but he had no idea of this truth.

Dalos' words to Radik and Linton so many weeks previously were now forgotten. Yet their deep, underlying effect still operated. The oscillations of energy-intelligence which they had received directly from the One who had come to awaken them were still implementing change within the minds of these two. They were still carrying on with their desire to solve the mysteries of the Pleiadean starship due to their subconscious need to resolve the questions of their own minds!

Any mystery of the physical world which presented itself to these two scientifically-biased individuals was a "mystery" that represented their ignorance of themselves. They had once known the secrets of the universe, but as they followed Antares in his descent to the earth worlds they relinquished their own knowledge, and it fell away from them like a rapidly unraveling skein of thread.

Now they were bare of all understanding of interdimensional mechanics; yet this luminous craft symbolized their own minds. It operated by the same principles of energy. If they had understood all that Dalos and his two scientists had explained, to the fullest degree, they would have solved the questions which haunted them as thoroughly as they were haunting Tyrantus, Tonar, and any of the dozens of individuals who had by now had some verbal contact with Dalos.

Unfortunately, the Tyronites now had obtained a new weapon in the construction of this high-frequency emitting device. They had not yet recognized it as such, but this instrument was resting in the hands of souls who did not desire to use any portion of Infinite Intelligence with a positive purpose. They were driven still by their personal greed for wealth, status, power, control. They would turn this weapon upon one another when they no longer had a need for each other, and they would one day direct it unto countless thousands, millions, billions of others who populated worlds still unconquered by Orion forces. This was as Dalos had feared—that without the progressive redirections of their personal intelligence through his attempts to awaken them to their true natures and past history as Lighted Ones, they would be using this technological information destructively. Thus far, their experiments had not yet brought them to this point of development, but it was now inevitable.

The two Pleiadeans who had given them this technological data were likewise ignorant of the weaponry that they had just given to the negative forces. They, like the others, were operating under the belief that they were serving as requested and supplying the next level of Intelligence to be given to the Tyronites as part of their so-called teaching mission. By now these "teachings" of the Pleiadeans were thoroughly warped and designed to inflate the egos of the so-called teachers. They were not thinking wisely nor completely about that which they gave to the Orionites; they merely spoke all that came into their minds to speak without regard for the necessity to follow a logical progression of education. There is an evolutionary development of one's Intelligence that must occur, even for those souls who once possessed a more extensive knowledge of Infinity. Now their minds were existing at an elemental level and thus they needed to relearn lessons of Infinity from "beginning" to "end," if there were such a thing.

In giving information out of context to the Orionites, the Pleiadeans were doing just as the Orion forces themselves did when they invaded a planet of lesser evolutionary development and introduced high-tech lifestyles unto peoples who were still ignorant of the basic principles of life, who had not yet developed for themselves the wisdom to use such enhancements of life with Intelligence.

Dalos' ship, then, would eventually crumble in the hands of these mindless forces of evil. They would never learn its finer purposes, nor would they be able to restore it to its operational capabilities. What they would discover was a wealth of technical data that, in their distorted usage, would prove fatal to the lives of many, many individuals.

Dalos was unable to stop this progression of events, which he sensed was now occurring by the evidence displayed among his former entourage. He had but one hope remaining: that before his death, he would set in motion the changes necessary within these individuals to accommodate their future rebirth as helpers of humanity.

So much to be done, he bemoaned, *and so many restrictions placed upon me!*

As if in response to his cry for help, Tyrantus chose that moment to contact Dalos in his quarters. Dalos was startled, but he quickly realized that this was the prompting of the Higher Minds who were working with Tyrantus from within his consciousness, as was Dalos from without.

"Yes, Emperor, I shall be very pleased to speak with you. There is much information that we can exchange, and I believe now that we may be more successful in our communications with one another. I am stronger, as you can see, and I think you will find our conversation very enlightening and helpful to you." Dalos could see how ill the Emperor had become and he knew the cause. He knew, as well, that Tyrantus would now be much more open to his teaching. So the time was arranged, and Dalos suggested that they meet in an atmosphere that would be mutually pleasing.

Tyrantus was so disconcerned with his surroundings that he agreed to a location in the exterior gardens of his own living quarters. These areas had been designed to give pleasure to the senses through the color of vegetation and sound of running water. It was a rare sight on Tyron. Most such areas were reserved as special rewards for citizens who had performed some extraordinary service for the Emperor or the Empire (which were one and the same). But Tyrantus enjoyed such luxury at all times. It meant little to him now. He could find no comfort from any of the accoutrements of his very powerful position. He had been destroyed by these Pleiadeans, Tyrantus now believed, but he would never confess this fact to anyone. He did not even allow himself to form the thought. But he realized, in some inexplicable way, that only those who had destroyed his peace of mind could restore it. He greedily sought Dalos' company then, and could not rest until their meeting.

Dalos was able to stand and walk for short periods of time now. He settled upon a comfortable, soft seat in the midst of Tyrantus' garden while the Emperor chose to remain standing—or rather, to pace nervously about.

"Emperor, I do believe that you would be more relaxed if you joined me here in this most pleasant setting. You have truly outdone yourself in the creation of this garden. I did not realize anything quite so beautiful existed upon your planet! I have seen nothing like it since my arrival."

"Yes," Tyrantus replied distractedly. "It is the work of our finest agricultural experts. They tell me it contains specimens from planets throughout the Empire. As you see, we are in a climatically controlled area. The light which penetrates this atmosphere is generated by concealed mechanisms and it is designed to alter in different areas of the garden to allow for the growth of various botanical specimens. I once found this to be a comforting environment, but Dalos, I must confide something to you." He stopped and stood motionless for a moment.

Dalos dared not interrupt. He knew that this was an extremely rare circumstance. The all-powerful Emperor of Orion had just spoken to him in a personal, humane manner! Dalos held his breath in eager expectation; his pulse was elevated by his joy and excitement to know how thoroughly this man had changed!

"I have been deeply disturbed by your statements. I cannot recall all the specifics, and this bothers me greatly! I have an excellent memory with photographic recall, yet certain words that you have spoken to me will not return to my conscious awareness, no matter how I apply my mind to remember them. I have never experienced such a loss of memory! Day and night, I am tormented by fragments of your remarks that will not complete themselves. No one knows of this, and no one is able to hear our present conversation. I have seen enough now to convince me that you are a man of honor. You may be foolish, but you do stand by your word. If I ask you, I know that my secrets are safe with you."

"That is true, Tyrantus. I hold no animosity toward you, despite all that you have subjected me to."

Tyrantus turned away.

Dalos continued. "I am not a malicious person and in any case, there is nothing that I can do to harm you. What would it profit me to turn information over to your enemies, to see yet another harsh leader emerge in their own personality, which would crush the people beneath them as thoroughly as you have crushed others?"

Tyrantus winced at these words. He sat heavily in a nearby seat. He said nothing to rebut Dalos' statement. He was thinking now upon other matters that had weighed so heavily in his sleepless nights. "These are the statements that torment me, Dalos. Have I not been kind to my people? Have I not supplied them with all that life can offer? They are all fed well, clothed warmly, given ample opportunity to express through their work tasks and lead busy, productive lives. What more can a leader do? I have helped entire planets to elevate themselves, from the lowest, animalistic state of life in caves and mud huts, to a sophisticated, smoothly operating lifestyle that has brought them forward so much more rapidly than they themselves could ever have dreamed. I have extended their feeble lives in great health, and I have given them everything to supply their mental contentment. What more could I do for them? Why do you call me names and accuse me of wrongly treating my subjects?"

"Why, Tyrantus, do these statements bother you so if they are untrue?" Dalos responded quietly. "Can you not find within yourself this very truth? You know that I speak with logic and reason."

Tyrantus looked at Dalos. For the first time he willingly gazed deeply into the eyes of this stranger from the Pleiades. What he saw there was not strange at all. A warm, engulfing sensation came over Tyrantus as he continued this gaze. The physical features of Dalos disappeared in a light that was unworldly in its luminance. Tyrantus could not take his eyes away! He felt as if he were standing beneath a warm waterfall of golden sunlight.

Dalos held this projection of Infinite, healing Love as long as he could maintain eye contact with Tyrantus, and that eye contact lasted for several long moments. He knew then that Tyrantus could be overcome. Antares still breathed within him, buried, forgotten, neglected, but alive to this inner Light that was now restimulating his higher senses. They would now have much to discuss, and Dalos hoped that he could maintain the higher-frequency link which was now established between them. From this transcended state of consciousness, Tyrantus could be alerted to many things. It was only in this state of mind that progress could be made. But Dalos realized that he must take advantage now, while he held Tyrantus' open attention, because this opportunity might not be repeated. Tyrantus was more receptive than he ever had been to the truth of his gross crimes against Infinity—that was clear from his appearance and his attitude.

"I believe, Emperor, that you are now becoming aware of the true spiritual spark that lives within you. You are not this physical ruler whom you have so glorified in your own mind as some supreme achievement! You are not a mere mortal being, nor is any one of your subjects. You are a creation of Infinite Intelligence. You are far more capable than you could ever express in an earth-world dimension. You held the potential to light entire universes with your mind—if you had maintained and developed that spark of Infinity that resides within you! You held unlimited potential, Tyrantus, and yet you threw it away, you discarded your Intelligence to rule over the physical bodies of peoples living on lower evolutionary planes of life. You fell from your higher state of mental development, and now you are grossly deceived in your miscalculation of your mental proclivities.

"You are truly the most ignorant of all, Tyrantus, but you can change if you so desire! You can free your own self from the torment which you are now beginning to recognize. It is not that you were untormented before my arrival. My presence here has simply reminded you of your former existence. You have been as I: a teacher and helper of humankind. Can you believe this? Can you remember who you are?"

Tyrantus shook his head in confusion. "Your words echo through my mind with a strange melody that soothes and yet agitates my thoughts! I almost believe what you say, and yet it is so far beyond anything I have ever heard proposed, and I have heard nearly everything. I cannot shake these words from my head and yet I cannot fully accept them!"

"That is well, Tyrantus. Do not fret over this confusion, for your concern only worsens your inner turmoil. Listen with an open mind; let that inner Light be rekindled! Let me show you the way."

"And how do you propose to do this?" Tyrantus said, rising to his feet. "How can you change me?"

"By giving of myself, Tyrantus. That is why I am here. I came to you to help you find your way home. You are my Brother of Light, although you no longer emit that radiance which you once received from the Cosmic Fountainhead. You have blocked off all inner reception—but I know this can be changed. You must do this, Tyrantus, else you will die—truly die, in a spiritual sense. Your Light shall be permanently extinguished! You will no longer exist in Infinity. This would be a terrible thing, for there are now many souls dependent upon you. You have designed it as such, and only you can change this horrible misdirection of Infinite Intelligence."

"So I ask you again, Dalos, what must I do? I am willing to listen. I have exhausted all means at my disposal. I cannot sleep and I cannot live. I will hear you out."

"Let me approach your people, Tyrantus. Let me work with you to implement some change upon this world. It can be done, but it must be done carefully and wisely. Together we can take those first steps!"

"I don't know about this, Dalos. Now I am confused again. What am I saying? What are you doing to me? I must think about this. You have hypnotized me! You are trying to take over my position!"

Tyrantus grew increasingly disturbed and began to pace once again with a short, choppy series of movements. He was truly suffering from a schizophrenic response, and Dalos knew that their conversation for now had ended, but inroads had been made!

"I will leave you then, Tyrantus, to think about my proposal," Dalos quickly suggested. He did not wish to further stir those obsessional forces which were fighting for control within Tyrantus' mind. Dalos knew that the information now implanted by his healing energy projections would have its effect. There was nothing more that he need say at the present moment.

"Yes," Tyrantus agreed. "Leave me. I have heard enough of your gibberish and I must sort my thoughts!" He signalled for guards to come and escort Dalos from the garden.

"Tyrantus—before I go, I want you to know that your Brothers of Light do love you," and he left Tyrantus standing near a small waterfall with a startled and baffled look on his tormented face.

20

The Demon-Gods of Orion

From the planet Tyron was controlled the entire Orion Empire. This control consisted of a huge network of electronic communications that were beamed from planet to planet, over one hundred in number, with the size of the Empire growing with each new conquest of Tyrantus' military forces. These planets varied in size and population, and in the mental development of the peoples residing thereon. They all, however, soon assumed the drab, identical appearance of Orion workers everywhere. They dressed in one-piece garments of monotone coloration and passed through their days with a numbed consciousness, bombarded by these frequent broadcasts of information from Orion headquarters.

These broadcasts included instructions for their daily tasks, which had been derived from the centralized computer planet, and specific programs encoded for the instruction of a particular individual. These programs were selected by computer analysis of data received through the monitoring systems, and implemented by batteries of technicians found throughout the cities of each of these planets. Many hundreds of millions of individuals were engaged in this monitoring and programming system of control. They themselves were also being monitored and programmed to carry out certain functions, to keep all of this machinery operating smoothly.

Nowhere in any of this Orion machinery was there any consideration for the infinite variety of human qualities which should have been expressing themselves through the consciousness of these trillions of individuals. The subtle differences from person to person were being eliminated by this numbingly routine structure of life. There was no allowance for sudden bursts of inspiration derived from a higher contact with more creative and developed Minds, the minds of the Elder Brothers of all souls living in lower-dimensional worlds.

There was little forgiveness for any variation in the prescribed routine, and such variations were considered to be criminal acts by the Empire and were punished accordingly. These individuals, who had followed through on some original thought or some rare spark of inner, intuitive awareness, were strictly dealt with. They were removed from their homes and transferred to detention facilities, wherein they were subjected to a variety of brainwashing treatments, or they were taken to research laboratories where new applications of electronic controls and physical alterations to the brain or anatomy were carried out in an experimental process. They were then returned to continue in their prescribed function as an Orion worker—or if these experimental operations failed, they were taken to one of several locations. They might have been transferred to a pleasure world, where the residents were used as sexual partners for Orionites who had been given a form of holiday or reward on such worlds. Or they were delivered into the hands of those who operated the human "farms" where men, women, and children became grist for the food and fuel mills.

It is a grisly scenario, indeed, with very little regard for the spiritual nature of the human being. There was no allowance for soaring feelings of joy, true happiness, love, understanding, forgiveness, and other of the more elevated qualities of consciousness of which humankind are capable!

It was to these outer worlds of the Orion Empire that Shimlus and her followers were directing their broadcast messages under the firmly controlling influence of Tonar, who had devised this communications network. Their images presented some spark of inner recognition to the many varieties of peoples indigenous to the planets of Orion. This inner recognition caused the long-deadened spiritual libido of these peoples to be restimulated in a brief, flickering attunement to former states of awareness. Once stimulated, this spiritual spark might have rekindled their desire to think for themselves, to throw off the shackles of Orion controls—and this could have been accomplished, had Shimlus and her followers remained faithful and loyal to the greater wisdom of their leader, Dalos. But they had not.

They were themselves lost in the miasma of Orion life. They, too, had fallen under the negative influence of the electronic bombardments of lower-frequency stimulation which was distorting their inner vision and drawing out their lower ego natures, which they did nothing to counteract by their acceptance and recognition of the facts as they had been presented to them by Dalos himself.

This stubborn reluctance to admit to their failings proved fatal to their individual missions and thoroughly damaging to their soulic expressions as Light Bearers. Now they bore their selfish motivations to the Orion peoples. They fed upon that ignited spiritual spark like vultures drawn to the last remains of the carcasses of those who had once been living, oscillating expressions of Infinite Intelligence. The Pleiadeans used their own inner link to a higher Source to achieve the exterior stimulus of public admiration and acclaim. This influence upon their minds increased in its drug-like effect; they began to crave this stimulation of ego as an addict craves his particular form of drug. They were using the tools of consciousness which they had developed through countless lifetimes for selfish gain, and this drew the Pleiadeans closer to spiritual death.

So they were now blind leaders attempting to point the way for those who had already lost their sight. It caused a change to occur among the peoples of the outlying planets. This change was a subtle shift in allegiance from those imposed frequencies that were designed to secure their loyalty and dedication to Tyrantus and the representations of the Orion ideals as presented by his propaganda. Now they were turning their attention to these colorful exponents of some new ideology, which they did not understand but which attracted them due to its close alignment with their long-lost spiritual desires for inner growth and understanding. The Pleiadeans became their religion, and religion has always been a strong competitor for those who would desire political control over a nation, nations, worlds, or galaxies! Religion was simply another form of mental oppression that was imposed upon these people by Tonar and his Pleiadean cohorts, for now they had joined themselves to this Council member in a seemingly unbreakable bond of mutual expediency. They needed one another, and so another alliance of negatively-biased minds was forged.

Each of the ten Pleiadeans who had taken a step forward in the imposition of their so-called leadership over the others was among this group that joined with Tonar. Their contact with Dalos had caused deep inner turmoil for a period of time, and then, as he was removed from their sight and contact, they fell back into their newly developed patterns of ego expression.

Many others among the two hundred followed their negative example and soon the majority of the former entourage of Dalos was carrying on as if they, too, desired to take control of the Orion Empire, as did each member of Tyrantus' governmental elite. Soon they became a new form of religious hierarchy that sprang up in the place where a seed of higher consciousness should have been planted by their examples. They chose instead to become weeds that further choked off the Light that should have been penetrating, not only the single planet of Tyron, but all planets now struggling under Orion domination!

Yet this Light burned brightly in one small area of this vast empire. That was within the most unexpected and unlikely enclave, the very headquarters of Tyrantus himself, where Dalos now focused his entire interdimensional expression of Intelligence to this purpose. Here, he was allowed some free rein now. He could request and receive an audience with the Emperor, who was still failing in health and expected to leave his physical anatomy at any time. Now it was Dalos who had regained physical strength, while Tyrantus was succumbing to the horrendous internal damage that he had wreaked upon himself with his acts to dominate and control entire planetary systems in a most vicious stamping out of the inner life of the earth peoples.

Tyrantus was sickened by the scenes illuminated within his consciousness by Dalos' frequent discussions. The Emperor still suffered from fits of schizophrenic behavior in which he screamed and railed against the seeming accusations of the Pleiadean teacher, yet in his more lucid moments, Tyrantus was made to understand the reality of the words Dalos spoke to him. The Emperor had been given a nearly insurmountable task: to recognize, identify, and change all the wrong turns that he had made in his fall from a higher state of mental expression, and this fall had taken place over the course of some eighteen million years, lifetime after lifetime.

It could be done, Dalos assured him repeatedly, but it would take a tremendous effort of, not only himself, but the entire Spiritual Brotherhood who would lend themselves to help in the restoration of Tyrantus' mind—not because he individually was so deserving, although he was a spark of the Infinite Mind as was every other expression of life, but because he now influenced and controlled the lives of so many helpless individuals who could no longer function through their own mental development, as that development had been short-circuited by Orion controls.

Dalos ignored, now, the work of his former associates. He was forced to remove himself from them and to disassociate his mind in order to maintain his own inner mental integrity in his attunement to Higher Minds, among which his own served as the generating, unifying Force behind his present mission. He could do nothing to halt the Pleiadeans' current activities at the present moment, but he was hoping to convince Tyrantus to allow him to speak to the population of Tyron and of these outlying planets with his own message of truth, love, and hope. He felt certain that there would be some few who would benefit consciously from his words, and many others who would not be able to understand his message but who would be touched by the Power Beam thus projected to all the planets of the Empire. In order to accomplish such a contact with the entire Empire Dalos needed, not only Tyrantus' acquiescence, but the same assistance and facilities of Tonar as were now being employed by the fallen Pleiadeans.

"Tyrantus," Dalos said during one of their meetings, "if you could agree to allow such a broadcast, I feel it would be most beneficial for you to join me in this. I understand your reticence, but I believe you will find some relief from your present stressful condition if you make at least some attempt to speak more truthfully to all those who now look up to you as their god! They are beginning to change, Emperor, due to this subversive influence that I regret to say is occurring because of the sickened minds of those who once held nothing but love and compassion in their hearts—those whom your associates have influenced and caused to turn away from their true purpose.

"I do not blame you wholly for this, as I blame them, for they are responsible for their own minds and they were wise to the ways of life in a material world such as this. They should not have succumbed, yet they did so, and nothing that I say now has any effect upon them!"

Of course Dalos knew that a projection of Infinite Consciousness always had some effect, yet he was referring to drastic, immediate, and outward change, which would be the *only* means by which these individuals could reclaim their purpose and rejoin his mission of healing. This was not forthcoming, so his only alternative was to match force with force. As they were now aligned against him, still ignorant of this fact, he must use a greater concentration of his own mental energies to counteract their influence on the already much-abused Orion citizens. He could not explain all of this to Tyrantus, as the Emperor was drifting in and out of mental lucidity now and it did not truly matter how completely he understood the situation. What did make an important difference was whether or not Tyrantus was leaning toward overcoming his own negatively-biased proclivities, or if he was content to remain as the tyrant he had become.

Dalos watched him vacillate from day to day, week to week, until finally the Emperor uttered these words one morning as they met in his bed chamber, where he had been confined due to a wracking physical illness:

"Dalos, I have been giving much thought to your proposal. Do you truly believe that I could face my peoples in this weakened condition? What would they think, to see this failure of the one who has served as their prime example of a solid, integrated life? Yes, I know you do not agree with my ideas about the quality and consistency of life among the Orion people, but I believe my appearance would cause them to lose faith and to turn in a confused state of mind from their denoted purpose as servers of the Empire. How could they follow such as I have now become? No, Dalos, I cannot face them."

"Tyrantus, you underestimate the power of human consciousness. Do you not realize that the minds of your people are so much more capable than you have estimated? They are far more resilient than you surmise! I believe they would bounce back into a more unified state of mental health if we were to make such an approach to them—if, however, this were done in a careful and wisely-conceived manner."

"And what do you propose that I should say to them?"

"I propose, Tyrantus, that you introduce me as I truly am: one who has come to you in love and compassion, and one who now wishes to extend the same elements of my mind to them. I am here to serve as a teacher of a higher, more developed way of life. This they will understand, Tyrantus, for every soul has this deep inner desire buried within him, the desire to know of his spiritual birthright. It pulses within each mind in an ever-regenerative oscillation of Intelligence. This inner Intelligence is what I desire to help them discover. They need to know this truth, Tyrantus, else you will be the ruler of one hundred deadened worlds populated by mere skeletons of human flesh with no true life burning within!

"You do not need to fear the change I propose, Tyrantus. I guarantee you that you will find yourself to be restored by this circumstance. I promise you and give you my word of honor!"

Tyrantus looked up at Dalos, whom he now viewed with a certain degree of fear and awe. He had never fully understood this man's motivations and he still could not. Yet he found himself becoming more and more appreciative of a certain quality of intelligence that Dalos brought to him. Never before had he been able to converse so openly with another human being! He had spent his life in a cocoon of lies and deceptions. It gave him, already, a sense of relief to know that he could speak openly and truthfully his deepest concerns to this individual. Granted, he had kept Dalos as a bird in a cage, an ornament to his own life, a source of companionship and illumination to which he turned increasingly for some meaningful addition to his now miserable existence. He had selfishly insisted that Dalos remain incommunicado from all but a very limited number of individuals. He feared the influence Dalos might have upon others, and he was reluctant to change the present situation, as he feared what result the strange, elusive power this individual held over him might have upon the general population!

But after so many weeks, Tyrantus was beginning to weaken in his reluctance to let Dalos speak publicly. A part of him was strongly desirous to witness what effect Dalos might have upon the people. He was quite intrigued to consider whether or not they would be influenced as he had been, or even his three Council members who had once spoken with Dalos.

He had long ago debated and rejected the notion of bringing Dalos into a Council meeting. That would prove disastrous, Tyrantus believed, and it might unleash forces that he himself could not counteract in order to maintain his control of the situation. No; better, he now thought, to grant Dalos' request and to keep him still confined in a secret location. These contacts with the public at large would be carefully controlled and broadcast over the communications systems. He would not be given a direct, face-to-face interchange with the population as a whole; he would appear to them on the same electronic screens from which Tyrantus' own image was now routinely presented in brainwashing sessions. Then Tyrantus would instruct his many scientists to measure the impact Dalos' presentation had upon his subjects.

They would begin, Tyrantus decided, with a small control group indigenous to the planet Tyron.

"I have decided, Dalos, to test your theory." He explained the conditions to the Pleiadean ambassador.

Dalos agreed, knowing that he must accept whatever degree of accommodation Tyrantus would authorize. He felt certain that these contacts could be expanded in the near future.

A meeting was arranged between Dalos and Tonar, with Tyrantus to be present as well.

This the Emperor did not look forward to, for he had kept himself removed from the Council members as much as possible. He knew that they were carnivorous beings, anxious for his demise, and he did not like for them to see his unhealthy state. But there was no way to avoid such a confrontation with Tonar if the experiment with Dalos was to take place.

Now Tyrantus felt some bit of health returning to him, particularly his mental health. He had something to look forward to, whereas before he was lost in a wash of horrible, nightmarish images, and battles between his acceptance and denial of Dalos' truthful renderings of his reign among the Orion planets.

What had actually occurred within the consciousness of Tyrantus was that another igniting spark of his own higher self had prompted him to agree to let Dalos teach. He did not fully realize what had been set in motion by this agreement; he could not possibly have envisioned the full magnitude of effort that was being funneled through the solitary conscious expression of the man called Dalos. The network of Minds so functioning through this one was staggering in proportion, and yet this concentration of mental energies was being projected with pinpoint, laser-like accuracy through every word and visible action of Dalos. The Power thus generated and reradiated into the third-dimensional atmosphere of Tyron—indeed, the entire Orion Empire—was beyond measure. Once radiated to the population as a whole, this Power would set in motion the full restoration of consciousness for all souls who came in contact with it.

This had been the plan from the beginning; however, no one had foreseen the many horrible deterrences which had occurred in the actual unfolding of this plan. The most deeply affected by these unforeseen circumstances were the two hundred who had accompanied Dalos to Tyron. They were becoming the leaders of negative force for the Orion Empire! Such a reversal of consciousness was extremely rapid, as would be in the case of any mind which had been developed to a greater refinement and ability to refract Infinite Energy-intelligence. Their descent was precipitated by their own inner weakness, and now their stubborn adherence to self-righteous, defensive attitudes was proving to be their ultimate downfall.

Soon they would no longer be recognizable as Lighted Minds. They were already taking on the appearance of individuals who cared for little other than themselves. A certain coldness now permeated the atmosphere surrounding these individuals wherever they went, where once they had radiated the warming Intelligence of their link with the Benevolent Ones who populated the higher spiritual dimensions.

Dalos viewed their broadcasts to the Orion planets. He was heartbroken and crestfallen to know how far and how quickly they had deteriorated in consciousness.

Perhaps they will yet come to their senses. I cannot abandon them, for my heart overflows to see the grievous mistake they have made and supported among themselves! Their hatred for me is self-directed, yet they do not realize this. They have separated their minds from their own source of life; they are worse off than these poor individuals who now sleep through their days and nights as robots of Tyrantus' mechanical empire. They are far, far worse—and will suffer so much more if they do not right themselves and do so quickly! Not only that, but they are causing a tremendously damaging impact upon the minds of the Orion peoples, which simply cannot endure any further negative influence.

I must step in! I must intervene! This I shall do before some further harm befalls this physical body which has been so much abused since my arrival here. My words must reach these lost, lost souls…

21

A Breakthrough

Dalos presented an imposing figure on the Orion communication screens. His smooth, beautiful features and golden blond, shoulder-length hair enthralled the Tyronites who had been brought to a larger viewing area for this particular closed-circuit broadcast.

They looked at this luminous face with rapt attention. His words were soothing to them and yet very little of what he spoke was understood. He had been introduced by the voice of Tyrantus, which was the Emperor's solution to his fear of appearing before the citizenry in his state of weakened health.

"Greetings, Orion citizens. I bid you good morning and have a very special announcement to make to you, who have been chosen for this special occasion due to your accomplishments on behalf of the Orion Empire. You are my chosen ones. You are those who have proven loyal and diligent in your efforts to forward our Empire. I have been, for many months now, in contact with an individual who has brought a very important message to my attention. He is my advisor, and has come to me from a planet called Axiahn, located in the Pleiadean constellation.

"Recognizing the great importance of our Empire, this ambassador traveled to our planet in the company of two hundred citizens of his world. You now know them as the Pleiadean teachers who have been appearing in your daily broadcasts. However, this man, their leader, has been unknown to you previously. There is great purpose in this. I believed that it was very important to first fully analyze and detect his motivations in coming to our world. This, I have now done through my personal interviews with Dalos, as he prefers to be addressed. I can assure you that this man is very wise and knowledgeable about the life of any citizen of Orion. He brings to us new information that will help us all to move ourselves another giant leap into our future—a healthy future of productive, contented life!

"I shall let Dalos himself explain more fully his purpose here, as he is now my designated associate and prime advisor on matters of human intelligence."

The Tyronites were quite startled to hear the Emperor's voice, which was piped into the room as the image from one of his photographs appeared upon the screen. He sounded quite different than he had for other messages to them, and they found their minds filled with questions—a very unusual circumstance for these individuals! That is because there were no subliminal subharmonics oscillating into the room via this communication, as was the general practice. Dalos had insisted that such subliminal influences be eliminated, else they would learn nothing from this control group, in terms of analyzing the results of his speech to them.

"But Dalos," Tonar protested, "that is our standard procedure for all broadcasts. It provides us with an opportunity to insure the effectiveness of our messages."

"Yes, Tonar, I am quite familiar with your procedures, and I am sure that you are also including such subliminal messages with those programs you have created using the images of my former associates, have you not?"

"Yes, that is true, Dalos. We have found them to be quite productive of a certain receptive attitude among our audiences."

"Receptive to your influence, Tonar, and that is not what we are trying to measure here. I believe your Emperor wishes to know what kind of influence my own words and image will have upon his people. How can he accurately gauge this for himself if they are being distracted by your routine programming messages that urge them to give their allegiance in a particular direction? To me, this will defeat our entire purpose."

"That is true, Tonar; Dalos speaks wisely. I agree that for this particular experiment, we should suspend all subliminals," Tyrantus said.

Tonar was irritated by the lack of respect for his own knowledge of how to communicate to massive populations. But he recognized that he was not in control of this particular situation; indeed, this intrusion into his own plans by Tyrantus and Dalos had caused him some moments of unrest. He feared that his plans to institute a major coup with the help of his Pleiadean friends was in danger of upset, now that Tyrantus was introducing a new factor in the person of Dalos himself. This individual, Tonar knew, was a powerful orator, and one who carried a far greater impact than any one of his followers. Tonar himself had experienced the lasting impressions Dalos was capable of creating in an individual's mind.

Even now, as he sat with the Emperor and the Pleiadean in the communications headquarters, Tonar felt stirrings within his solar plexus. He was immediately shaken to see Dalos in such a fine state of health, at least in comparison to his weak and debilitated state when Tonar had first conversed with the Pleiadean on his starship. That was nearly a year ago, and now he could hardly believe the change in Dalos, whose eyes radiated a brilliance that bespoke of great intelligence and yes, of a forceful nature that would accomplish whatever he set out to do. This frightened Tonar. He instinctively knew that he was no match for the mind and body of Dalos. For now, he was forced to acquiesce to whatever was requested of him, and he decided to do so with an attitude of gracious accommodation, so that Tyrantus' suspicions would not be aroused.

"I am quite pleased, Dalos, that you are now going to speak to our people. They have been so overjoyed by the message of your entourage that I am certain they will be quite thrilled to know that you are the leader of these individuals. It is an honor for you to grace us with your presence in this particular way."

Dalos, of course, saw through every word uttered but he let it pass. He understood the dynamics of this political situation far more thoroughly than either of the two individuals in whose presence he now sat; and he also understood that he must proceed carefully if he were to accomplish his ends.

While the two, Tyrantus and Tonar, discussed between themselves the details of this broadcast to be prepared, first for a test group of citizens and then, if the results met with Tyrantus' satisfaction, for the entire population of Tyron, Dalos' thoughts drifted back to those whom he had loved so dearly, those who had proven traitorous to their own selves.

Perhaps my message to the Orionites will affect them as well. Perhaps they will be shocked back to their senses! Well, I cannot be overly concerned, for my work here is quite enough to keep my mind occupied. Let matters fall where they may, and if my former brothers and sisters are awakened, so much the better!

So it was that Dalos appeared to this group of five hundred Tyronites. He wore a gleaming robe of crystalline facets woven into the fabric of the garment. It was the robe he had worn when he first appeared on Tyron.

This dazzling spectacle was unlike anything the Tyronites had ever seen! They had already been placed in an unfamiliar state of consciousness by the message from their Emperor, which was so unusual in its content and left them with a strangely unsettled feeling, whereas his usual messages were quite pacifying due to the underlying, drugging frequencies imposed within them.

"Greetings, citizens of Tyron. I come to you as your Emperor has explained, in the purest oscillation of love and brotherhood. I bring a welcoming encirclement of friendship to the Orion planets from my home planet of Axiahn, where we live our lives devoted to the pursuit of knowledge and the understanding of our own minds, and the Infinite Mind which has given life to us all!

"You are by now familiar with the faces of my former planetary brothers and sisters, who also came with me from this Pleiadean planet. Yet I must begin by telling you that these dear souls have misled you somewhat in their teachings. I apologize to you for their actions, as they did not realize the inaccuracy of their statements."

A murmuring sound filled the auditorium.

"Please, do not be too harsh in your criticism of them. We are all human and we all make mistakes."

Now loud talking erupted among the Tyronites. No one had ever made such a statement! Mistakes were not allowable! Orion ideology was quite rigid in this fact. Perfection was the ultimate goal, and only perfection would be tolerated! Who was this man? And how was he allowed to speak thusly? The Tyronites were not critical of his words—they were fearful for him, and many among them were exhilarated by the sound of such blasphemy! They hushed the others so that they might hear the remainder of his speech.

"...can be taken up as your life's work," Dalos was saying. "The study of human consciousness is never-ending, as we are infinite beings created of an Infinite Source! We will never come to the end of our learning about ourselves, and so we must endeavor to keep an open mind. Our thoughts are vitally important to the healthful life of our minds and of the society which we build to accommodate our learning endeavors. Your Emperor has often spoken of his desire to provide for you a life of abundance and happiness. He has told me many times of his concerns for your welfare. This is a fine quality for a leader, and yet there are many changes and reforms which can be made upon your world, and other worlds, to give all citizens the necessary freedom to conduct their lessons in life with a greater openness and access to information about their own individual place in this infinite universe!"

Tonar was furious. He could not believe that Tyrantus had allowed this particular speech to be released to even a small group of citizens! It ran counter to all of the Orion manifesto! It was extremely damaging to the Emperor's political position, and Tonar was livid over the fact that Dalos was contradicting the words of his own entourage. Of course, Tonar had invested much time and planning into his machinations of the output of the Pleiadeans to maneuver himself into a position of greater power and influence. If Dalos' message were released to the larger populations of Orion, Tonar feared that all his efforts would come to naught! He must do something to stop this situation.

"I believe that you will find in your Emperor a benevolent leader who now recognizes that he has himself made some mistakes in the past. He now desires to correct these errors, as any intelligent individual would wish to do, and I deeply respect him for his honesty and willingness to admit his past failures. You will see, dear friends, in future cycles of time that these changes will give you much more to look forward to in your days upon this world, which is so accomplished in its technological capabilities, yet does want for a greater inflow of spiritual intelligence.

"It is my purpose to offer you my services as a bringer of this Light, this Inner Light that shines within the mind of each Homo sapiens. I am an illuminator of that which already resides within you. You do not need to seek for it any place other than within your own self! There, you shall find all the wisdom that you require to live your life in a happy and productive manner, as a part of the larger whole of Infinite Creation. Yes, your joined Empire does symbolize the kind of joining of brother and sister to which I refer. We are all children of this Infinite, Creative Intelligence and as such, we share this creative parentage with one another. Therefore, we must learn to treat one another with the greatest respect, with the same love and understanding that we must have for our own selves.

"Do not condemn your Emperor for his past failings, as he has discovered that even his own self-condemnation serves him not—it does nothing but sicken the mind and body! A more intelligent approach to one's mistakes is to recognize them quickly and take steps to correct one's actions until, once again, you are living and working in a more integrated, intelligent, and productive manner.

"I shall leave you for now, with the hope that we shall have many such opportunities to speak to you in the very near future. Do know that my words are the expression of a single man and yet they carry the full Mind Force of all of my Lighted Brothers of Spirit who no longer reside in atomic, physical anatomies, but live in higher-dimensional worlds of Consciousness wherein they have learned these principles of life-continuous and now desire only to share their wisdom with you. I am their representative and as such, I bear their Love to you all!"

As the screen faded, the Tyronites were riveted to their seats. Now the auditorium was silent. They could not move for several long moments.

When they did finally find themselves capable of moving their limbs once again, the entire gathering seemed to rise as if one individual. They spontaneously burst into shouts of approval and applause.

Tyrantus, who had carefully observed this reaction, was surprised.

Dalos sat by his side in the viewing room and smiled.

"You see, Emperor, that your people still love you. They have now recognized you as a human being—fallible, Tyrantus, as all human beings—and that is what gives us our very flexible qualities, is it not?"

"Dalos, you have always been capable of astounding me. I am no less astonished by this reaction! I had believed that this treasonous speech—for truly, Dalos, anyone who had spoken thusly in the past would be immediately executed—I thought such words would enrage them to demolish the screen and tear the seats from the floor of the auditorium!

"These people have been trained to regard such statements as the highest form of criminal activity! Many of them are employed as overseers and supervisors among groups of workers. They have been instructed to ferret out any wrong-thinking individuals and report them immediately to the authorities. Yet I have just seen these same individuals accept your words of condemnation for their Emperor with glee, and with no indication of fear after their initial shock. Their demonstration of approval is unbelievable! They lost all fear for their lives! They left this auditorium with little thought that they might be immediately incarcerated. What, Dalos, have you done? What does this prove?"

"Tyrantus, this proves that the Power of Infinite Love is unconquerable, and conquers all! Do you know why you have allowed me this demonstration of *my* power? *My* power does not threaten you, Tyrantus. It threatens only that which opposes life itself, and you, dear Emperor, are a part of that life whether you like it or not! You are beginning to sense your true nature for the first time in many thousands of lifetimes. I am very pleased, Emperor, to see the changes in you."

Tyrantus could not respond to this. He knew Dalos spoke truth, for he had been feeling stronger in recent days and he knew that his health was finally returning. He also knew that there was logic in all that Dalos spoke.

"Tyrantus, you do not need to rule these people with an iron fist. If you show them your true, compassionate, benevolent nature, which you have for so long denied yourself, they will love you for your genuine leadership qualities. They will regard you as an example of the kind of human being who cares for his fellow beings."

"But Dalos, there is so much to be done, so much to change! I despair of ever being able to accomplish this all! I have my enemies to consider. If I lift a hand to change a single process of life in the Orion Empire, I am lifting my hand against hundreds of thousands of individuals whose very positions depend upon this orderly process of distribution of justice. These people have also been trained to believe in all those qualities of life which you, Dalos, have shown me to be erroneous. They will assassinate me, Dalos. They will not allow me to make these changes—and where will you be then?"

"I am not concerned for myself, Tyrantus, as you should well know by now. I have no fear. I have only the desire to see you follow through on this plan that we have discussed. You have now seen how your people were affected by my speech. Truly, it was not my words that touched them but the Power of the Higher Minds flowing through my expressions that radiated a higher frequency to them, and this higher-frequency Intelligence does change and rectify all negatively-biased equations of life! Nothing remains unaffected by such projections of what is truly Infinite Love—not even yourself, Tyrantus, and you are my prime example!"

The Emperor smiled and allowed a chuckle to escape from his lips. Had anyone else been present, they would have dropped to their knees in total shock! The Emperor of Orion did not laugh! Nay, he rarely even smiled, except with a wry sort of pleasure in his achievement of some superior gain. But this smile was truly one of mirth and shared understanding with his Spiritual Teacher—for now that is what Dalos had become to him. There was much that Tyrantus had not yet accepted about himself, but Dalos was in no hurry to push him too far, too fast.

If Dalos could continue to teach through these visual presentations to groups of Orion citizens, he knew that a seemingly miraculous change would overtake all planets of the Empire. He merely needed to counteract all those negative forces which were now writhing in opposition to this particular breakthrough event. He knew that the full fury of these forces who had been so long entrenched within the minds and bodies of the Orion peoples would fight with all their demonic force to halt such progress. He was prepared for their onslaught, even as the Emperor

Tyrantus was oblivious to these machinations of subastral influences that were now erupting with volcanic force.

Such eruptions of explosive negation began to percolate among the Council of Twelve. They were horrified by this broadcast! They'd been privileged to view it via recordings Tyrantus had delivered to them. They were now meeting in emergency sessions with their own allies, some separately and some joined in force.

Linton and Radik were holding a special session with their own agents, and Tonar was speeding from the surface of Tyron toward a planet called Bombadzion in the third planetary system of Orion. There he had established a secret headquarters in recent months. From it, he planned to make his move upon the Emperor.

Now he must meet with Shimlus and her followers to determine how best to proceed, in view of the fact that it appeared that Dalos would be allowed further access to the Orion populations. Tyrantus had truly lost his mind, Tonar believed—or maybe not.

Maybe the old man has some scheme in mind that I have not yet pieced together, Tonar thought as his ship sped through space. *Well, I shall show him who can be clever! He does not know how strongly these Pleiadeans have wedged themselves into position in the outer planets. He has a rude awakening in store for him!*

But first, we must deal with Dalos. First, we must devise a method by which these subversive broadcasts will never reach the ears of the Orion people! And yet I must find a way to deceive Tyrantus, as well, for he seems to be quite loyal to the Pleiadean ambassador.

I fear this man called Dalos. I myself do not trust my thoughts when I am in his presence. They flicker and dance and threaten to deter me from my purpose. This man Dalos has a strange, hypnotic power that I do not understand, yet I would give anything to have it as my own!

Tonar leaped up from the console involuntarily; nervous energy made him pace around the cramped space as the ship flew itself. He needed no crew for this shuttle vessel, which suited him just fine. He thrived best beneath shrouds of secrecy, reliant only on his own wits and invention. His recent alliance with Shimlus and the other Pleiadeans may have been expedient—necessary to his ultimate plans—but it made him uneasy and he would be relieved when he could move into phase two.

But this recent demonstration by Dalos! He couldn't get it out of his mind.

He completely counteracted a lifetime of educational development! The control group turned upon all their training without a moment's hesitation! Had I not seen it for myself, I would not believe it could be done.

Perhaps I can use my friendship with his former mates to learn something more of this ability. For all their hundreds of teaching programs, I have never seen a single one of the other Pleiadeans have such an effect upon an audience! Granted, they do gain a great deal of attention and influence over their viewers but they have done nothing to change the basic qualities, to divert their viewers from the programmed responses that our finest scientific minds have worked to develop into educational programming. Yes, thought Tonar furiously, *I must work quickly.*

"Shimlus, where are you?" he growled. *Why does it take you so long to respond to my call? I sent my ship to you hours ago!*

He punched a communications device and programmed a code that would give him access to Shimlus' quarters on Tyron. He found her there in a state of mental disarray.

"Shimlus," he barked, "why are you there? Why have you not answered my request for your immediate presence on Bombadzion?"

"I cannot," Shimlus moaned. "I—" She could not speak. There were tear streaks appearing like white rivers along her rouged cheeks. "Did you not hear his words? Did you hear what he has done to us now?" She broke into sobs. "How could he? How could he do this to us when we loved him so?"

Tonar cursed in exasperation. So—Tyrantus had made sure the Pleiadeans viewed Dalos' speech in private. He must've gone behind Tonar's back somehow.

"Shimlus, get hold of yourself! Do you realize the danger of this situation? You were shown this broadcast for a very devious reason. This was meant to deter you from your work! Not everyone on Tyron saw this speech. Did they tell you that it was shown to only a controlled test group of five hundred Tyronites?"

Shimlus stopped crying and looked back at Tonar's image on the communications screen. "What? You mean this was piped into our quarters out of sheer cruelty—or—why, Tonar? What is happening? What is Tyrantus thinking of?"

"He has some scheme in mind, I am certain of that. I do not know what it is thus far, but you and I must talk in a safe environment. We must take steps to counteract this before it gets out of hand. If Tyrantus continues as he plans, these broadcasts will be shown to the entire planet of Tyron, and eventually to all planets in the Empire! You see what I mean, Shimlus—we must do something now."

"Yes, Tonar," she said quietly. "I think I understand your meaning. I shall leave now." She closed the communication.

Shimlus sat quietly for a moment, trying to collect her thoughts. They raged within her like a stormy sea that had not yet seen the worst of the hurricane that approached. She was torn by her thwarted love for Dalos, as she still believed that he had wronged her personally and many of her activities were tainted by revenge. She was not conscious of this subtle motivation. Her conscious mind led her down dark alleyways and gave her visions of grandeur and failure. These two conflicting futures collided within her mind and left her incapable of forming any intelligent conclusion about all that had transpired. She did not know what else to do but to meet with Tonar. She would not go alone, she decided, and she rose to find her closest companions—those with whom she was formulating the approach of the Pleiadeans unto the Orionites.

They were also in various stages of shock, fear, and confusion. They were glad to hear that Shimlus had some plan in mind, even it if was only to leave the planet immediately for Bombadzion to meet with Tonar, and they quickly agreed to accompany her.

As their ship sped away from Tyron, Dalos asked Tyrantus' permission to speak to his former associates directly.

"I believe that they are now struggling to understand my speech, Tyrantus. We must have compassion for these poor souls who have so thoroughly shamed themselves by their misguided actions. Please, do let me go to them now. I think I can avert further catastrophe among them."

"Very well," Tyrantus agreed. "If you wish to do so—but I must say,

Dalos, that I do not believe they have treated you kindly and I wonder at your desire to help them. Yet I never have understood you, Dalos!"

"You shall, Tyrantus. You shall indeed!"

22

To Free an Empire

There was no time to lose, Tonar explained to the small group of Pleiadeans gathered at his new headquarters on Bombadzion. They must do something immediately to counteract Dalos' message to the Orion peoples, even before it had been released to the wider population.

"Shimlus," Tonar said, "I believe that we can take steps to insure our position here, if you will work closely with me. Now please explain to me again why Dalos spoke as he did. I thought you all worked together!"

Shimlus could not respond for a moment. The others—there were four who had accompanied her—held their breath in anticipation of her response.

Each one of them was undergoing a tremendous gnashing of psychic gears. They were clutching to whatever lifeline they could find; in this case, it was their new involvement in these broadcast messages to the Orion peoples. These activities had given them a sense of accomplishment, a placating effect to restore their damaged egos, which Dalos had punctured by his words of truth—both spoken to them directly, and now, in a public exhortation in which he accused them of acting unwisely. This added further fuel to their resentment for the one who had always shown them the greatest kindness and compassion. Now they were convinced that Dalos was suffering from mental stress due to his long incarceration and that they must join forces with one another to insure their ability to carry on as planned.

So the mission of the Pleiadeans to the planet Tyron was now divided into two camps. On the one hand, Dalos, the Hierarchal Leader of the Spiritual Light Forces, continued to radiate his full Consciousness, his Infinite Intelligence into this lower-dimensional world, and the healing force thus provided for the Orion peoples was having its effect—most greatly upon those closest to him in physical proximity. At the same time, Shimlus and her cohorts were deluding themselves with the belief that they, too, were serving the peoples of Orion, but they had lost sight of their true objective when they turned their backs upon the only one who was capable of maintaining a clear and true mental link with the Higher Forces. This was proven by their actions. Dalos never lost sight of his benevolent, selfless purpose, while the Pleiadeans of his entourage were now operating in a fog of self-concerns and, truly, their motivation was no longer pure in the sense of having no personal taint.

Shimlus, herself, was divided in consciousness. A part of her knew the wrongness of her deeds, and the other part of her—her lower self—was striving hard to silence this inner awareness of truth. She could not accept the tremendous deflation that an admittance of her errors would have caused, and neither could any of those individuals seated nearby. There were dozens of others like them, still on Tyron, who could not face truth and accept the deflation of knowing that they had lost their higher consciousness.

Each day, each moment they took another step away from the Light, and the further removed they allowed themselves to become, the more difficult it was to maintain some semblance of benevolent leadership. Now Shimlus and her companions faced a critical test: if they were to continue in their activities with Tonar, the promotion of their own selves, they must take steps to oppose Dalos' teaching.

"Tonar, I cannot publicly make any statement against Dalos. You understand my position, I am sure. He has wronged us, that is clear, and yet he has been a very part of us. He is our leader; he is our teacher. He is suffering, I believe, from Tyrantus' influence, and I think that he does not speak wisely because he is laboring under some illness prompted by Tyrantus' torturous probings into his physical and psychic anatomy. But

I repeat, Tonar, I cannot say this in a public forum. I cannot speak for my brothers and sisters, but that is how I feel."

"Yes, Shimlus," one of the others said, "I agree. We cannot let the Orion people see the differences among us, no matter what Dalos has said to detract from our words! What do you suggest, Talimondia?" he asked.

"I think there must be something that we can do without exposing this to the population as a whole—isn't there, Tonar?" Talimondia responded. "How soon do you believe Dalos' broadcast will be released to the people of Tyron?"

"I cannot predict Tyrantus' actions anymore," Tonar replied. "He is himself quite ill and is not behaving according to his usual practices. I personally feel that Dalos has had some undue influence upon our Emperor. This is a dangerous situation, and I know you recognize how serious it has become. If he continues to speak this way about you, the people will lose all confidence in what you have to teach them. That is not why you are here—you have come to share of your knowledge, is this not so? And you need to have this clear opportunity to do so, without interference from some dispute among yourselves."

"What do you recommend then, Tonar?" Soretiya asked.

"I am just beginning to formulate a new plan. I think that with the help of my knowledge, we can delete these particular statements from the broadcast before it actually reaches the people."

"But Tonar," Shimlus said, "won't Tyrantus immediately recognize this fact? And what of Dalos himself? Certainly he will be watching these screens to see that all goes well. How can you conceal such tampering from them?"

"I have my ways," Tonar smiled, as the ideas began to take shape in his consciousness. "They must watch Dalos' speech as everyone else, is this not true? They will be viewing a screen in one of several locations. I can arrange it so that the broadcast they view is not the same as the message that is played out for the people."

"So you mean that you will show an expurgated version to the public, while Dalos and Tyrantus believe that the full speech has been relayed?"

"That is correct, Talimondia. It will not even be a difficult matter. And so it is settled." Tonar stood. "We shall handle this situation efficiently and without delay. I must return to Tyron before my presence is missed and I suggest that you do likewise. I am glad that you see the importance of our working together to insure our continued successes. I know how much your teaching means to you, and I will do all in my power to help you reach the people. I have seen the results of your work, and I must say, I am most pleased to know that our people are benefiting from your lessons. They have begun to show a greater enthusiasm for all of their daily activities."

Shimlus rose and as she did so, the others followed her example.

"You can save your flattery, for we know that you have your own desires to gain influence over the people as a whole. But you will see, Tonar, that even you can benefit from our teachings. You must learn to recognize a larger purpose, and we shall be the examples for all Orion peoples. They will see through our life expressions how joyful their days can become! We have given much already, but there is much more to give. If you continue to work with us, then you will begin to understand whereof I speak. So do not forget that our alliance is mutually beneficial."

She smiled sweetly at him. "We do learn from one another, and I speak for all of my brothers and sisters when I tell you that we are grateful for your greater vision in seeing the usefulness of our wisdom, which can be applied in so many avenues of Orion life. But I shall save my speech for a more appropriate time," she laughed, and Tonar returned her smile.

He was quite taken by her beauty, but did not fully trust in her sincerity. He sensed that beneath the golden tresses and radiant smile lurked an ambitious soul like himself. Indeed, he had seen this within all of the Pleiadeans who had made contact with him. They all responded to praise and commendations, as did any other individual. This told him that they had their strengths and weaknesses, and either one could be manipulated to suit his purpose.

"For now—" Tonar nodded curtly as he made his departure from the room.

"Let us hurry back," Shimlus said to the others. "We must not be missed, else we will need to explain our absence to the others. I do not think we should tell them of this plan."

"Nor do I," Soretiya agreed. "I think it would only cause argument."

"Agreed—and we do not need for them to know all the details of our activities," Shimlus added. "They have all the information they need."

Dalos, meanwhile, was traveling in the company of his Tyronite guards to the enclave of the Pleiadeans. He was uncertain how he would address them, but he knew that the words would spring to mind when necessary, for they flowed not from his conscious mind but from his mental attunement with his own higher Intelligence, and all of those Supercelestial Minds which served as a lens that focused Infinite Wisdom unto the lower-dimensional worlds.

As he arrived, the Pleiadeans were in a state of scattered confusion. Many of them were not anywhere near this sector of the city; they now all had their associations with Tyronites throughout the planet and were allowed to travel freely. They were engaged in a variety of activities, from the purely pleasurable to the more constructive—at least in an outward appearance. However, even these activities in which they taught various skills, such as music, art, science, philosophy, education, or other facets of human expression, were tainted by the egotistical qualities of their belief that they were helping others through their superior intelligence.

When Dalos appeared to several startled Pleiadeans who happened to be gathered nearby, they froze in their seats, then rose with a hasty gesture of humble welcome. But it was too late to conceal their true reactions. They were not pleased to see Dalos. He expected this, and simply brushed aside their lack of proper greeting.

"Good day, dear friends. I hope it finds you all well?"

"Dalos, we did not expect—"

"Yes, I know that you were not expecting me, but I hoped that all of my brothers and sisters could still find a moment to converse with me. The Emperor Tyrantus has been kind enough to grant me this request, and I am sure that you have questions you would like to address to me after our recent breakthrough, would you not?"

"Yes, Dalos."

"Of course."

"Certainly. We shall see if we can find the others!"

And they scattered to the four corners of the living area.

Dalos sat in a comfortable chair and thought of his Brothers of Light, whose radiated Consciousness surrounded and imbued him with a peaceful, warm sensation.

I am so glad to know that you have not forsaken me!

How could we ever, dear Beloved One? Michiel responded in Dalos' consciousness. *You are the Light shining upon this dismal planet, and you are the Light for countless trillions of souls who now depend on your success! We give our very selves to the sustenance of this Light, this healing Beacon. We are ever at your beck and call! We will be here, standing by.*

And I am so glad, Dalos thought in response, *for I truly need your assistance now. This is a most terrible, regretful circumstance, the loss of our beloved ones, our very heart and soul—those who had seemed so steadfast in their purpose and desire to aid the earth worlds. But now they have shown themselves to be weak, indeed. I do not think there is much I can do from this vantage point. I only hope that your additions of Consciousness will enable me to break through the walls they have thrown up between us. They hate me now, and I am sure that they are not pleased to know that I am now being given an opportunity to speak. 'Tis a very sad and sorry situation, but we cannot let this opposition waylay our efforts!*

No, dear one, we cannot and shall not! You have all that you need from us to carry on. It will depend upon their individual acceptance of your words of truth. This may not come easily to them, but we shall withhold predictions of doom and disaster, and let the future unfold in its natural course.

The others returned, their faces stricken pale. One stepped forward and hesitatingly informed Dalos that several among them had left the planet's surface a few hours previously.

Dalos was quite surprised at this news. He did not know that Tyrantus allowed the Pleiadeans such freedom of movement. It irked him to know how restricted his own activities had been, while these individuals who could no longer do much good for the mission were being given free rein to travel and communicate with the Orion populations. But Dalos withheld his response and shifted the conversation to another topic.

"Very well, we shall proceed without them, and I am glad to see that the majority of you are still here. From my estimation it appears as if there are only—" he counted for a moment—"fifty or so who are missing."

"That is true, Dalos," one brave soul spoke up.

"Are all fifty on other planets at this time?"

"No, Dalos," the man replied. "Some are here on Tyron but it will be a few moments longer before they arrive."

"Then they must have been at some distance—is this your habit, to be spread out around and among the Tyronites?"

"It is part of our teaching, Dalos," another replied. "We are involved in many activities with the Tyronites. We are serving as art instructors, and are now holding classes in many of the subjects that we came to teach!"

"Well, that is quite wonderful," Dalos responded, "but I fear you are not giving much of value to the Tyronites."

A silence fell upon the group.

"I suggest that if you wish to carry on, you follow the advice given to you during my last visit. You are still unaware of the harm that you are doing among these people. I sense it by your very frequency, that you are now more interested in promoting your own leadership among them than in truly pointing the way to a clear contact with their inner resources. Do not argue." He held up his hand to stop the many voices that began to speak all at once. "It will make no difference to me whatsoever. I merely state the truth. You are deceiving yourselves still, and this is a great and deep shame, for you are now working against all that you came to accomplish."

"But Dalos!" several said at once. "We are doing exactly as we had planned!"

"I think *you* are mistaken!" one woman said. "I do not believe you truly know what we have been doing! How could you? You have been kept from all communication with, not only us, but the citizens themselves. You have not seen the results of our work!"

"Oh yes, dear one, I can see the results of your work on your own face, and I hear them in your voice! If you were truly serving the Infinite in a positive, regenerative way, you would not speak so harshly, nor carry yourself with such an arrogant, egotistical air!"

The woman's face turned an angry red. She turned away from Dalos' piercing look.

"Yes, hide your face if you must, but accept what I say if you wish to make some purposeful change—and that is why I have come to speak to you. Where is your leader, Shimlus?"

There was a moment of silence while the Pleiadeans looked to one another in hesitation. Finally, one told Dalos the truth, that it was Shimlus and four others who had left Tyron without telling the others of their destination, merely that they would return shortly.

"I see. So you now have not only lost touch with the Infinite Minds who might give you some meaningful food for thought, but you are beginning to lose touch with one another. I suppose that your living situation here is quite uncomfortable, isn't it, now that you are all fighting among yourselves."

Again, many protests erupted to fill the air with a cacophony of defensive attitudes. Dalos ignored them all. He expected such reactions. He knew that his words to them were striking deep into the tenderest portions of their wounded mentalities and that was good. How else to be healed than to pinpoint the source of one's ailment?

"Perhaps when Shimlus and her associates return, you will tell her of my words to you. I do not expect her to desire to speak to me, but please convey to her and her fellows this message: that they are severely hampering the Light radiations that they themselves came to convey to this world and many others. She is now the demonic force that is leading, not only all of you astray, but the entire Orion Empire! Do you believe this? No, I doubt that you can accept this bald-faced truth, but know it to be so!

"I shall not remain here, for I know you do not appreciate my presence. I am told that you heard my speech to the people of Tyron, and so you see that the mission progresses without you—and it will continue to do so. You can still alter your course, if you choose, but I cannot do this for you. This must be your own determination, to set aside these many concerns that you have now embraced with your whole selves, to the point of losing sight of any higher purpose!

"Very well, then. Amuse yourselves with your dalliances among these mindless people! You cannot halt progressive Infinity by your simple-minded actions. You only harm yourselves. I regret that you were unable to follow through on the mission you had set up, but I cannot lose myself in this regret, for I have much work to accomplish—with or without your help!"

And Dalos turned his back on them, leaving them to argue among themselves about his words.

He could feel their animosity following him from the room. He cared not; his only concern was to do everything possible to meet the foe head-on, and to conquer the force of darkness that was engulfing this world and many others and would eventually swallow the entire galaxy if he were not successful in his mission!

This "foe" could easily appear in any form. It fed upon loose thoughts. It multiplied in selfish minds. It had as many guises as Infinity could provide, and it was opposite to all that was Light-filled, purposeful, constructive, creative, and regenerative.

Tyrantus was now beginning to awaken to the reality of this foe that had been feeding upon his own insides for many thousands of lifetimes. He was now beginning to raise a weak hand to smite this foe. Dalos was determined to strengthen that hand, and to encourage Tyrantus in his opposition to his own lower self!

Dalos returned to his quarters and applied his full consciousness to the next task at hand. That was to convince Tyrantus to allow him more frequent addresses to the Orion peoples, and to give him the same freedom of movement that his former entourage now enjoyed.

If he could only speak to these Orion individuals, Dalos knew he could help them to find their own consciousness once again. It had been severely hampered by all of the electronic implants and subharmonic frequency bombardments, but their minds were still functionable. This, Dalos now knew from his observation among those with whom he had some limited contact, and he was now convinced that Tyrantus could be persuaded to lessen these controls that were presently amplified throughout all planets of the Empire.

This would be his next hurdle, then, to talk to Tyrantus about how these controls might be carefully eliminated. Dalos knew that there could be no sudden changes in the lifestyles of the Orionites because they had become so dependent on this voice from above, this "god-force" that told them how to go about their every detail of life. Such a dependency was not easy to break, and would take time and patience, and most of all, wisdom on the part of those who would do this dismantling of the Orion controlling mechanisms.

First would be the difficult task of convincing Tyrantus that the removal of these controls would not threaten his own self. The Emperor was so filled with fears and insecurities that Dalos knew he must carefully explain why and how this process would benefit all concerned, including the Emperor himself.

Yes, this is my greatest challenge, and it will be the key to success or failure—much more so than the loss of my helpers! Now I cannot count on them, but I do have an entire Brotherhood of Lighted Minds to assist me, and what more could I require? That alone shall sustain me in this horrible atmosphere. I shall be glad to complete my work here. But until that time, I will focus upon my soon-to-be success with freeing the Orion people from this outside influence. Only then can their minds breathe the luminance of life that is their rightful state of expression! Only then can I rest from my toils on their behalf.

23

Anticipation

LINTON'S FACE GLOWED WITH the reflected light from the Pleiadean starship, which still remained intact, impenetrable, an enigma that all of the Orion interplanetary physicists could not resolve. The applications of high-frequency laser projections to the surface of the ship resulted in no deterioration whatsoever of this material, which Linton had come to regard with a mixture of awe and frustration.

It was late and he was alone, staring at this foreign object as if it might speak to him and give him the answer which had eluded them for so many months. As his face was warmed by the oscillating radiance of Dalos' ship, Dalos himself was oscillating in the consciousness of the one known at that time as Linton.

Linton's psychic memory banks were being stirred. Something in the quality of this peculiar light triggered faint echoes of his own former existence as a pilot of such craft. Linton had, indeed, traveled on starships of this mental Light creation; he had been a true leader of men. His own Angelic Mind had embraced the minds of others with that higher source of healing Intelligence that supplied their many needs for personal, spiritual growth. Now, of course, he was locked into the iron suit of his own choice to follow the one called Tyrantus in his descent from such higher states of consciousness.

Linton had become a rigid, roboticized man who sought only his own personal ego glory through the conquest of third-dimensional worlds. His particular means of conquest were the tools of scientific research and the production of technological gadgetry to accomplish this overpowering of the forces of nature. His heart was as cold as his eyes, and human beings had lost their appeal to this one. He saw them as means to an end. They were the gears that kept the wheels of progress in motion for Linton and he used them freely, discarding those who no longer had a purpose to serve.

Many of the research team that worked with Linton and Radik on this particular project had already been thrust aside in this manner and severely reprimanded for their failures to conquer the Pleiadean starship. This relieved the pressure on Linton and Radik to succeed at their pointless endeavor.

In one sense, however, their quest to solve the mystery of the Pleiadean starship was not pointless, for it drew them further into the surrounding Consciousness of Dalos, which had constructed this ship from the materials of an atomic world; yet these atomic formations were bound together with the mental additions of Consciousness that caused the ship to change in its oscillating frequency. When joined in Consciousness, the Pleiadeans themselves created a force that actually directed the oscillation of atomic "particles" and could raise and lower the frequency of the starship, thus giving them the option and power to interrelate with the electromagnetic lines of force in whatever way they so chose. They were the navigators in this fashion, through their own mental attunement. It required such attunement for one to gain access to the ship itself, for any who were not of compatible frequency could not enter this ship without causing themselves harm, or disintegrating their physical anatomies through the contrast in their personal frequency oscillation with the higher frequencies of the ship itself.

How did Dalos, then, allow Tyrantus, Tonar, Linton, and Radik to enter this ship?

He had altered the ship itself for that particular time, through his own direction of Consciousness to accommodate the lower frequency of their minds, and at the same time, he was extending a projection of Consciousness to each of these individuals to raise their own frequency to a higher level. Thus they met in-between, you might say, and the visit was accomplished.

But Tyrantus and his Council members were ignorant of these factors of their visit. They functioned from their perception of the visible world, and their abilities to use their minds in this more constructive fashion had long ago been deteriorated by their own actions and thoughts, over the course of many thousands of lifetimes since their fall from their more sublime state of Consciousness as Arian Brothers.

Linton was beginning to believe that he would not ever succeed at penetrating these impenetrable walls. He reached out a hand to touch the ship and felt a very familiar sensation now. Whenever one of them placed a hand upon this radiating surface, a warm sensation passed through the fingers, into the palm, along the arm, and throughout the physical anatomy. It was not a shocking sensation but a pleasant, warming feeling that Linton often allowed himself to experience. He could be found here many late nights, staring at the ship or touching it, as if to learn its secrets through some form of osmosis. This was perhaps the most constructive endeavor of all his many aggressive attacks made upon the ship! It would be in the silence of his own consciousness that he would find the key to this seeming mystery. He did, in some part of his being, still possess some glimmering remainder of his previous understanding of the interdimensional physics by which the starship was created and used.

"Dalos," he whispered, "you are indeed a strange phenomenon on our world. I should like to know all the secrets that your mind holds! Perhaps some day you will tell us, in a way that we can understand." He sighed. *Truly, I wish circumstances were different. I should like to speak to you in private. I do not know what you might say; I doubt that you could give me the formula that would break this impenetrable barrier that you have placed around your ship, but I feel within me, in the strangest way, that there is something I need to learn from you!*

Linton could not consciously remember his previous conversations with Dalos. They were like dreams to him now, for he was not at that time oscillating in his usual state of consciousness. The elevated frequency at which this conversation took place had such an effect upon the conscious memory, seeming as if the exchange had passed in some other realm—and indeed it had! Now his thoughts were being stimulated by this oscillation that Dalos had set up with each of these individuals. There was a linking frequency between them now. Linton's thoughts were, at such times, colored by the higher influence of not only Dalos—or the Consciousness of Uriel—but all four Hierarchical Minds and the entire Spiritual Brotherhood! They were extending their Minds to each of the Orion government leaders, and as Dalos made a physical contact with these individuals, the bonds between them were strengthened—not between these physical individuals, but between each one and the Higher Minds.

In this way, Dalos was literally securing a pipeline into the depths of this lower-dimensional world through which the flow of Higher Consciousness could once again be extended into the most needy receptacles; that is, the minds of those who were leading an entire civilization into its spiritual destruction.

Such moments of quiet thought now occurred with the several individuals whom Dalos had touched most directly: Tyrantus, Tonar, Linton, Radik, and others in the medical facilities where Dalos had spent so much time.

Dalos had yet to establish this linking oscillation with all twelve Council members and this was one of his greatest desires; but he could see that circumstances were unfolding to give him the opportunity to speak to the larger population of Tyron and, hopefully, all planets in the Orion Empire. Through this communication he would be establishing a link with each soul who heard his words and saw his face. It was an extremely important opportunity, as much as Dalos could have hoped for in this society of roboticized beings.

As Linton finally turned away from the ship and left the research center for his home, Dalos was arising from his bed with a new thought that would not allow him rest.

I must see Tyrantus now. I cannot wait longer! He is dying of his own guilt, and he is now my strongest ally upon this world! He has been most thoroughly imbued with this healing frequency and he is in the position to do something constructive to propel this mission forward. I must see him.

Dalos left his sleeping quarters to awaken one of his constant guards. "Please, I must speak with your Emperor."

The man looked at him with a startled expression. "It is the middle of the night!" he protested.

"Yes, I understand, but it is urgent, and I am sure he will be glad that you followed through with my request."

Dalos sounded so confident of this that the guard was convinced and, against all previous training, he walked to a special communicating screen and entered the access code for the Emperor's quarters.

His call was intercepted by an angry voice that demanded to know why such an attempt was being made to disturb the Emperor at an inappropriate time.

"I have an urgent message from the Pleiadean for the Emperor. He will be expecting this message, I am told," the guard replied.

There was silence at the other end, and finally a gruff voice said, "Very well, if you have security clearance."

"I do," the guard said, and entered the proper numerical codes.

Finally Tyrantus himself spoke, although his image was not yet visible on the darkened screen. "What is the meaning of this intrusion? Who are you?"

"I am Security Guard F473ZXT. I am requesting a communications completion originating from the Pleiadean Commander Dalos. Message coded 'Urgent, expected.'"

There was silence.

"I repeat, I am extending—"

"Never mind!" Tyrantus barked. "I heard you. Let him speak."

Dalos stepped to the communication device.

"Tyrantus," he said in a firm but unemotional voice, "we must talk now. I cannot wait, and I believe you will be glad to hear what I have to say."

There was no reply.

"It concerns your own self more deeply than any of our previous discussions, and it will bring some relief to you, I promise."

"Very well," Tyrantus said. "Bring the Pleiadean to me," he commanded the guard, whom he knew to be standing near and eavesdropping on the conversation, for he could see Dalos and knew that he was standing in a central security control facility.

"Yessir," the guard responded, and the communication was terminated from Tyrantus' end.

As Dalos traveled the short distance to Tyrantus' quarters, he felt a stirring within. Now events would be moving at a quick pace and he must keep his thoughts clear. It was much more difficult now that he did not have that polarity oscillation which had been so beneficial to him in his association with all two hundred members of his entourage. Not only was this polarity lost, but they formed a huge blocking mass of negatively-biased energy now, as their efforts were directly opposed to his own through their choice to sever their ties with their leader.

Yes, it was *they* who cut short their association with Dalos; he, in his disassociation with them, was merely continuing on his way in carrying out this vital mission to restore life to the Orion planets. They had chosen to turn and walk in the opposite direction—but they were not merely walking away from their own mental lives, they were forcefully applying their consciousness in an opposite direction to his own! They had made themselves enemies to the Light represented by and regenerated through the consciousness of Dalos.

As he arrived at Tyrantus' bed chamber, Dalos discarded the thoughts of his former associates. He entered the room with a strong and direct thought: *Now I shall break through this last barrier!*

"Tyrantus," he said immediately, "you must now take swift action to instigate change on Tyron and then on all planets of your empire!"

Tyrantus had obviously just roused himself from his bed. His face was lined with worry and distress; his hair, uncombed; and his attire, rumpled. He looked at Dalos with great fatigue rimming his eyes. "What is it that you ask of me now? Have you not gained sufficient pleasure from my torment?"

"Tyrantus, you know that your torment is of your own doing. Please do not require me to go back over old issues which we have already discussed. It is too important now for us both to act for the benefit of the larger whole. You know now of the mistakes that you have made in your attempts to bring a so-called better life to our people; you know of the graveness of these errors and the horrible impact they have had upon the teeming populations of planets in this constellation. Now I am going to propose to you a sure-fire means by which you can reverse the trajectory of all this negation!"

"Speak, Dalos. I am listening, for I now long only for a night of peaceful rest. I am open to hear what you have to say."

"Good," Dalos replied. "Listen very carefully. We have already begun. My speech to your people will tap into recesses of their minds which have been unused for who knows how many lifetimes. This will bring about a restorative influence upon them, and I have now realized that if we follow quickly with further information, they shall be able to take a step on their own two spiritual feet."

"I do not understand what you mean," Tyrantus said. "How can this be accomplished?"

"You shall appear to them yourself, Tyrantus—you, in your full, visible image, and you shall echo my own words! They look to you, Tyrantus, as their leader. They have been taught, and I might add, programmed electronically to seek guidance from this image of the Emperor Tyrantus. What you say, then, has great influence upon them. Thus far, all of your words and deeds have been for the purpose of maintaining your own glory and securing your power of influence over them. But if you were to speak Truth to them, Tyrantus, miracles could be accomplished, in a very short space of time!"

"But Dalos, I do not have much time, and you and I both know this is true. Until now I have not allowed myself to speak the words but Dalos, *I am dying.*"

"Yes, Tyrantus, you are dying from that pain which you have inflicted upon so many others—but I promise you, the only way to alleviate this pain is to do something to *change* what you have done! You must do this, Tyrantus, and you must do it soon, while you still have strength to stand and speak and demonstrate the reality of the principles I have explained to you at great length!"

Tyrantus heaved a huge sigh of resignation. "I am not sure..." he began

"Be sure," Dalos interrupted. "Be strong! Be the leader that you have

always wanted to be—but do so now with *true* Intelligence to guide! I will be standing by to lend my own positive consciousness, and you know, Tyrantus, that this extension of Love carries the full weight of the entire Spiritual Brotherhood. I hope by now that you have begun to see the truth of this statement."

"Dalos, I am no longer certain of any so-called truth. Much of what you say does sound logical to me, and certainly I have withered upon the vine of life. I am failing in health, but even worse, failing as a leader! I am no emperor at all! I am a sad and sick man. This is your doing, Dalos, so your Love of which you speak has not healed me!"

"You are quite wrong, Tyrantus. My Love is an Infinite Radiation of high-frequency, healing energy which is indeed healing your true Self. Yes, your physical body has been torn apart by the surging storms of your own personal battle between higher and lower self, but your true being is being revealed to you, and this is progress. You have been lost for a very long time. Do not think in terms of this one physical body that is now failing you; do not think in terms of a single lifetime. Think of the larger evolutionary picture of your existence in Infinity and you will see that what you now do will affect not only your own self, but so many trillions of others. They depend upon you, Tyrantus. They cannot be healed until you instigate this freeing of their minds!"

"But how can I do this, Dalos? I am one man, as I have told you, and there are so many others who will fight me. They have much to lose in this world. They have not been touched by your words as I have."

"This can be remedied, Tyrantus. Let me speak to them directly."

Tyrantus thought for a moment. *Why not? It could not cause any harm, could it?* He could determine no reason to say no to this proposition.

"Perhaps, Dalos, you might be right. Perhaps you can do this weighty task for me, for I have long dreaded any confrontation with the Council members, who are so full of eagerness to see me crumple in weakness and death! Yes, I shall present them with a force much greater than they have ever experienced—is this not so, Dalos? Is this not the force which you have been so tirelessly explaining to me?"

"Yes, Tyrantus, you do begin to understand. This Force is not destructive; it is the Force of Good. It is the Power of Love, the Intelligence that steers the course of all planetary systems, suns, galaxies, and universes! This Force is a part of each one of us. We can use it for constructive purposes, or we can apply it as you have, in a destructive, degenerative ambition that destroys life itself. It is a Force that will meet head-on the lower minds of these individuals. One day they must confront this Force of Infinite Intelligence—the sooner this occurs, the better it will be for the people of Orion. I say, let us arrange this contact as soon as it grows light!"

"Very well, Dalos. I shall make the proper arrangements, and I promise you I will be there, if I must have myself carried into the chair and placed upright by attendants! I would not miss this! For I shall delight in seeing these individuals meet their match. You, Dalos, have certainly conquered me! And I know that you shall conquer them with your greater power of mind!"

These words did nothing to inflate the ego of Dalos, for he had none. He knew them to be truth. He was gratified to know that Tyrantus recognized the validity of his own change in consciousness to the degree that he was able to articulate it in this way. But Dalos' mind was filled with plans for tomorrow's speech. (He knew that there would be no delay; he would be addressing the Council by the end of the following day.) It was a very necessary step in the process of making his debut, so to speak, to the larger population of the Orion Empire. His public speeches would be that much more effective if he had already extended a force to rectify the opposition of these powerful individuals, who controlled Orion life through the claws which they had clutched around the civilization.

When Linton heard of this special Council session, he was stimulated by mixed emotions. Some part of him dreaded a further confrontation with the Pleiadean. But another very quiet element of his consciousness was intrigued and eager to have an opportunity to pose certain questions.

The man who had designed the starship filling his research building must certainly hold great secrets that would, when revealed, illuminate fields of life that Linton dreamed about in his more elevated moments of thought! Intuitively, he knew this. Yet that silent flow of consciousness had become no more than a trickle buried beneath the heavy rock of Linton's material-life obsessions.

For Tonar, it was a time of high anxiety. He was on the brink of staging a revolution. Any sudden change in the operation of Orion daily life was a threat to his success—and Dalos, of all people, posed the largest threat. There was no way to alter any broadcast in this situation! For Dalos and the Council members would be seated face to face in a personal, one-on-one confrontation, he knew. It was always a "one-on-one confrontation" with Dalos, as he seemed to have the power to affect any individual present in his company. Tonar dreaded that meeting! He had everything to lose.

Radik was confused. He, too, held conflicting emotions about another meeting with the Pleiadean. He was extremely distrustful of Dalos and felt that there must be some new scheme unfolding. Tyrantus and Dalos had perhaps cooked up another method by which to disrupt the lives of the Council members and to bring about some change which would no doubt, Radik believed, wrest some influence from the Council members. It was always Tyrantus' desire to take back from them the powers he had given them, for he feared the Council, and this Radik knew. He would wait, but he would keep a watchful eye upon the proceedings. At any moment in which the concealed hand of Dalos or Tyrantus became apparent, Radik would pounce on that opportunity to blow the whole shenanigans sky-high and defeat Tyrantus' plan before it got off the ground.

Each of the other Council members was suffering their own inner battles of confusion, anxiety, and a host of emotional reactions caused by some addition of unplanned activity into their very rigid and routine schedules. They had very limited knowledge of Dalos and he represented an unknown factor. They had heard fragments of intelligence garnered through many sources about the effect he had had upon their colleagues. None of them was eager to speak to the Pleiadean. They felt him to be a bothersome entity who had disrupted their lives by his impact upon the Emperor; and yet, at the same time, this disruption was giving them opportunities and advantages which they had not previously enjoyed.

So there was much anticipation for Dalos' meeting with the Council members. Only in the solitude of his own higher mental attunement did Dalos possess the full knowledge of all that this meeting would mean—not only to these individuals, but to those countless billions whose lives were intertwined with the Council of twelve dictators.

24

The Council of Twelve

Deep in the internal workings of Tyrantus' mind, he knew that he was going to make some changes.

First, he had changed his own personal life—by necessity, for his illness had made him incapable of carrying on in his accustomed way the daily affairs of the Orion Empire. His ambition had fallen away and now his waking thoughts were entangled with the stinging words left by Dalos' many presentations to him.

But how to implement change in the civilization as a whole? This, Tyrantus did not know and he was baffled, confused, torn by conflicting motivations, and unable to conceive what steps were necessary to redesign Orion society into a more productive and healthful circumstance for all people. Dalos had told him that this was the change required, yet he could not conceive of its actual implementation. He said nothing to Dalos of this fact, for he did not wish to admit his mental lack.

Dalos was unconcerned. He knew that both he and Tyrantus would be guided in the proper sequence of steps to take to accomplish a major change in the lives of the Orion people. In his conscious mind, Dalos also had no idea how to proceed, but with a very important difference: Dalos knew the source of all wisdom and he trusted it implicitly. His own higher Mind was a very integral part of this source of Higher Intelligence and he knew this for a fact.

So he was not laboring under any concerns or anxieties when he approached that time of meeting with the Orion Council.

Tyrantus was extremely agitated and fearful of this encounter. As well as he knew them, he could not predict how his Council members would respond, for Dalos was always an unknown factor. The words that flowed from the mouth of the Pleiadean were guaranteed to be most unusual and striking in their simple yet effective form. On the one hand, Tyrantus was quite interested to know what Dalos would say to the Council; and on the other, he was somewhat concerned about the kind of response Dalos' speech to them might elicit.

He did not need to wonder long for, indeed, the meeting was arranged and took place as Dalos had felt it would, within twenty-four hours of his late-night discussion with Tyrantus. The Council members were irritated by the disruption of their usual routine but at the same time they knew something was about to transpire to which they each desired to be thoroughly alerted.

"Gentlemen," Tyrantus opened the session, and even this word caused some faces to turn toward the Emperor with total surprise. "I have not seen you all together for quite some time and I know you are aware of the illness that is keeping me confined. I am not yet well, but I am here today because of the great and vast importance of the meeting we are about to engage upon. Today, we shall make Orion history!"

He paused for the full meaning of these words to sink into the stubborn minds of the Council members.

"Yes, I guarantee that you have never before heard anything like that which you are about to hear, with the exception, of course, of Linton, Radik, and Tonar, for they have had the opportunity to speak with the Pleiadean commander, Dalos, previously—although that interview was brief."

Tonar stirred visibly in his seat. He chaffed at the thought that Tyrantus might describe his behavior during that meeting in front of the entire Council.

But Tyrantus did not. He was no longer the same man who had taunted his associate with accusations of weakness. Now Tyrantus was beginning to embrace that so-called "weakness" in himself, which was truly a spiritual strength, the strongest fiber of mentality known to *Homo sapiens!* Tyrantus did not fully understand, but this did not matter. He held the position necessary to uproot and reorganize an entire system of planetary empire.

"I shall let Dalos himself speak to you. We can discuss our plans after we have heard the words of our Pleiadean brother."

Again the Council was shocked by the Emperor's choice of words. Now the rumors that had long persisted among them seemed to take on a reality. The Emperor was not only losing his life, his mind had slipped beyond all usefulness! But they still must humor him; he still held the reins of power—for now—and each one of the Council members was counting the days until he or she could make an aggressive move toward the emperorship which they all coveted.

Dalos was signaled to enter the Council chambers. He had been awaiting Tyrantus' sign outside this special room to give the gathered leaders an opportunity to adjust their minds, however slightly, to some more open state of consciousness. This was done through Tyrantus' words to them; although neither he nor they realized what was actually transpiring. Tyrantus had been overshadowed by the higher mind of Uriel as he spoke, and this was due strictly to the fact that, for the first time in many thousands of lifetimes, Tyrantus was operating on a basic foundation of true Intelligence!

He would, from here on out, be called upon in many instances to provide this open door for Dalos' access to the Orion peoples. Tyrantus' link with them was forged so strongly that this was the only way, or the best way, that their minds could be opened to a contact with a Higher Intelligence such as that being radiated through the consciousness of the man called Dalos.

"Greetings, my brothers and sisters of Orion," Dalos said as he inclined his head slightly in a courteous gesture of respect.

The hard faces of the Council stared at him blankly. They made no move to respond in kind, but simply awaited his explanation for his presence among them.

"I regret that we have been unable to meet previously but my health, as you know, has not allowed such an encounter."

There was a stir, a rustling recognition among the Council of the reasons for Dalos' so-called "health problems." They all knew that this man had been put through many torturous experiences by Tyrantus' medical experimenters. Indeed, several on the Council had been involved in the setting up of such research facilities, although this particular "patient" was kept in a high-security, inaccessible wing of the medical centers. There was little, however, that the spies of the Council members could not eventually determine, and much was known about Dalos' captivity, much more than Tyrantus suspected.

Dalos took a deep breath. He felt as if he were addressing a room full of solid concrete pillars, so vacant were these faces that stared back at him as if he posed some unknown threat. Truly, he *was* a threat to them, but only to those lower, materialistic senses which had been overdeveloped and fed by the egos of these individuals. He proceeded to speak.

"I am not native to your planet, Tyron, nor to any of the planets of your Empire, but I have been living here for over one Tyron year and I have engaged in many in-depth conversations with your Emperor. He has told me much about life on your worlds and has shown me in many ways the qualities of the life of Orion people. Now, I understand that you all have your own interests in this society, that you each possess a particular expertise. This I do respect, for you have trained yourselves carefully to fill the positions you now hold. But I am here as an ambassador of Truth from the Pleiadean constellation. This Truth is a simple way of referring to a knowledge of the interdimensional principles of energy which sustain life on all worlds, wherever they may exist, in this universe or any other.

"These interdimensional energy principles are the very basis of life for all *Homo sapiens* and I am a teacher of this science of life. I came to your planet to offer my services as such, and the services of my entourage—but I am sorry to say that they are now incapable of providing any illuminating information to you or your many associates. Be that as it may, I remain, and I can give you information which will cause you to make sudden and rapid progress in all areas of life upon your planet!"

Expressions of doubt began to crease the faces of one or two Council members. Linton was listening carefully to each word Dalos spoke, hoping to glean some tidbit that would resolve the many questions which had arisen as he spent so many long hours puzzling over the mysteries of Dalos' starship.

"Yes, Linton, I do recall our previous discussion and I know that you have many questions about my transport vehicle, that craft which brought me to your world so many, many months ago. These questions can be resolved for you but it will take time and patience on your part. I should say that your physical attempts to discover the means by which my ship operates are quite futile. I could have saved you much toil and effort, but then I suppose you have gained something from this endeavor, if only a larger respect for the elements of science which you have not yet incorporated into your own understanding."

The others quickly glanced at Linton to see if this insult would be tolerated.

Linton did not respond with the expected words of anger or condemnation. He nodded in agreement with Dalos!

The others could not believe their eyes. They felt for a moment as if this scene were taking place in some odd, drug-influenced dream state, which was common to those of the Orion citizenry who had access to so-called recreational drugs.

"Yes, gentlemen—and women," Dalos said to the single woman seated on the Council, "I can help you to implement such change as you have never dreamed possible on your world."

"Why should we be interested in change," Radik spoke up, "when our society operates in the smoothest, most efficient manner possible, and we are constantly growing as we add new planets to our boundaries? These people are *grateful* to have our aid and superior technology to help progress their worlds into a better way of life. What can you possibly do for us?"

"Radik, we have also spoken before. I do recognize your voice, although your face seems somewhat different to me than it did before. Have you not been feeling well?" Dalos inquired.

Radik snarled a monosyllabic response.

"Well, in any case, Radik, I know that you are quite proud of your accomplishments and you have made some outstanding contributions to the physical science of your world, but do tell me, are there not problems which you have been unable to resolve? Are there not issues and difficulties among the peoples of these many broadly differentiated worlds that your technology has been less than successful in addressing? I believe the answer to this question is that yes, there are elements of life which you have yet to conquer, and may I say to you all, that these elements of life stem from one singular source: the human mind.

"I have had a very close observation of your techniques for probing and analyzing the human mind. You all know, I suppose, of the many experiments which have been conducted in your hospital facilities to determine the quality and function of my own physical brain—but you must know by now that these attempts resulted in little or no additions to your storehouse of knowledge. That is because, dear friends, my brain is like yours. It is nothing more than a demodulating station for higher-frequency radiations of Infinite Intelligence, which flow freely throughout the interdimensional cosmos.

"We receive these radiations of Intelligence through the mechanism of our own individual minds. If we have developed that mechanism sufficiently, then we receive a greater, more perfected Intelligence that is more constructive and useful to ourselves and our fellow man. If we have failed to develop our own minds, then we shall be incapable of accessing a higher source of Intelligence. It is as simple as that, and you can probe from now unto eternity into my physical anatomy—you will never find a more clear and concise statement of this principle than that which I have just presented to you!

"It is within the human mind that you will find all answers to the unsolved enigmas that have presented themselves to you, and it is in your *own* minds that you must begin your quest for a larger understanding."

Tyrantus looked carefully at the faces of the Council members. They did not know how to take Dalos' words. They were unsure whether he had just insulted them all, or whether he had said something that might be of value to them.

"Friends," Tyrantus said, "I urge you to listen carefully to Dalos' statements. I can tell you that I have been giving them much deep consideration in recent weeks. I, too, was initially unwilling to listen to what this stranger had to say. After all, who is he to come to our world and tell us how to run our lives?"

"Hear, hear!" a few cried.

"That's right! Who is he?"

"And why must we sit and listen to him babbling on? Tyrantus, with all due respect, we question your bringing this Pleiadean into our private session!"

"Calm yourself, Benertizog. If you give it some time, you will understand my purpose. I am going to implement some drastic changes. I am going to propose things which you will not understand if you do not first listen to what Dalos has to say. Please, Dalos, ignore the rudeness of these individuals, as you ignored my own rudeness when we first spoke. Do continue."

"I shall do so, Emperor, and I appreciate your kind words. If you will all try to open your minds for just a brief period of time, the information I am giving to you will have a much greater meaning. This is not strange, for you have all studied previously the principles which I am describing to you, previous to your present physical incarnation—and if the truth be known, previous to many, many thousands of your past lives lived in this empire of physical planets."

Several of the Council members had thrown up their hands in exasperation or leaned back in their seats with a distrustful air. They were sitting through this discourse but unwilling to hear. Their minds were closed by their stubborn attitudes of superiority. As expected, Linton, Radik, and Tonar were the most attentive among the group, for they had been preconditioned for this meeting by their prior conversations with Dalos.

Even though Tonar was apprehensive and fearful of the collapse of his plans for a political takeover, he found that he was fascinated despite himself by Dalos' very command of, not the language, but the situation as a whole. Here was a man of utmost dignity, a man who had suffered terribly at the hands of the very individuals to whom he was now offering his own intelligence as a gift! Tyrantus had thoroughly proven that there were no strings attached, and that Dalos was sincere in his expressions of friendship and alliance. There was a quality about Dalos that

Tonar found lacking in his entourage. He could not define it, and as much as it frightened him and caused him to tremble deep within himself, he was intrigued. He listened intently.

"I propose that you all allow me to continue with the teaching which I have begun under the auspices of your Emperor. We have recorded the speech which you all have seen, which was presented to a test group of Tyronite citizens, and my request to your Emperor is that I be allowed to make such additional contacts with, not only the people of this planet, but the people of all planets in the Orion Empire. I believe that Tonar has already made such arrangements for my former associates, and as they are now spreading misleading and erroneous information among your peoples, I trust that you would desire to have a more direct and clear presentation of these interdimensional, scientific principles presented to your people."

"To what purpose?" one man spoke up. "Why must we let the Orion people have this so-called science of interdimensions?"

"Because these people are the reflections of your very selves," Dalos replied patiently. "As you treat them, so you treat yourself, for you and they are all born of the same infinite substance of life, are you not? But if that is not sufficient motivation for you, and perhaps it is not, think upon this: If the people of these worlds are knowledgeable about their own lives, their reasons for existence and their true, spiritual, evolutionary purpose, then you will no longer need to control them with such a firm and unvarying pressure. This pressure causes many fissures in your society, and although you do not like to discuss them or have them known by the general population, I am aware of their existence. These fissures will eventually rip open the entire fabric of your empire, and you will find it collapsing upon itself in great catastrophes of all qualities!"

"How can you allow him to speak this way, Tyrantus?" Qwakillahto demanded to know. "He has no right to evaluate our lives, which we have spent many hours of careful planning and research in perfecting!"

"Silence, Qwakillahto! You have not yet heard all." Tyrantus spoke without looking at him.

"Yes, there is more," Dalos continued. "As you relieve this pressure from your people, you will be relieving yourselves from that fearsome internal pressure which keeps you all awake nights and causes you to fear for your very lives! Yes, I know of this pressure, and I believe that your Emperor is approaching that time when he will discuss it with you personally, for he has felt the greatest welling up of anxiety, as he sits in the critical position of ultimate power. Life cannot be sustained in this fashion. Eventually, any human being will crack under this internal and external pressure, and you have countless examples of this cracking all around you! Sooner or later you would need to address this problem, and I know that you are unprepared to do so. That is why I am here.

"I am a Brother of Light incarnated into this physical anatomy for the purpose of traveling to your world and presenting myself in a form that you could relate to. As I speak, I carry the power of many higher-minded ones who have joined in a Brotherhood of Spirit. They are the Brothers of all humankind, residing in all dimensions of life. Our purpose is to serve one another, to serve the larger whole. We have come to you because your empire is affecting so many trillions of individuals in a negative, destructive fashion. Their physical lives may appear to be surrounded by comfort and a certain degree of productivity, but their true Selves, their spiritual, energy-intelligent Selves, are being slowly drained of all vitality, and eventually you will have created a massive horde of unintelligent beings, swarming throughout this physical dimension and many lower, subastral dimensions of life.

"I do not expect you to fully understand all that I have just described, but these are very important facts for you, each one, to know. And there is one more that I must add. Each of you has also served as a member the Spiritual Brotherhood to which I have referred. You have all been my Brothers of Light! You have all given of yourselves freely and unselfishly in the propagation of that Infinite, Creative Intelligence which flows throughout the universes, unbounded by divisions of personality and status. You have been helpers of humankind. But you now have fallen into a most horrendous and nightmarish situation! You have lost your true mentality and are functioning through a set of misguided understandings about the nature and purpose of life itself.

"Your Emperor and I have held lengthy discussions on this matter and I believe he now understands that of which I am speaking. He will explain to you in greater depth what I have just described, for he is largely responsible for your fall from a higher state of consciousness.

"You all now have a choice: you can continue to oppress and divert the people who have fallen victim to your egocentric expressions, or you can stop to consider my words. They will mean your future existence. If you ignore this statement of truth, you shall eventually terminate your own evolutionary lives—not your single, physical lifetime, but your soulic existence in Infinity! If you can accept even one small portion of all that I have spoken, then you have made a beginning, a motion toward change—a change which is extremely urgent in your worlds!

"I cannot emphasize this strongly enough," Dalos added.

Throughout the course of his final expressions to the Council of Twelve, the Power that emanated from Dalos halted all outbursts of opposition. The Council members were taken aback by the Force that they did not sense with their physical senses and yet responded to by their lack of resistance to it. This Force of Intelligence was a critical factor in their eventual recognition of their own individual responsibility for the misuse of Infinite Intelligence, in which they had been fully engaged.

Tyrantus, by now, was familiar with this outpouring of Light-energy that flowed from the personage of Dalos. He welcomed the feeling of inner strength that it now gave him. At that moment, he knew that he could exert his own influence to make the proposals for change that he had discussed with Dalos. Now he had no fear of these individuals who surrounded him! He looked from one to the other, recognizing in their eyes the effects of Dalos' strong projections of Consciousness. He did not understand the hows and whys of this phenomenon, but he knew it well.

"Friends, I believe that we have all heard quite enough for one session," Tyrantus said. "I now adjourn this meeting, and I will expect to see you all again within five hours' time. Will that be sufficient, Dalos?" he inquired.

"Yes, Emperor, I think that is wise," Dalos agreed.

And with that, the encounter was ended.

25

Tyrantus Speaks

"Dalos, I do not believe they will all take your words to heart," Tyrantus said as he and the Pleiadean adjourned to a private chamber designed for Tyrantus' comfort when conducting business over a long period of time with the Orion Council.

"Do not judge by their outward appearance, Tyrantus, for the workings of Spirit are multifold, and not always apparent to the physical eye. You shall see in weeks and months to come how they have truly been affected by my address. Perhaps they will not be able to consciously make any change in their personalities or open their minds to conceive a new way of thinking about themselves and their fellow beings, but deep beneath the surface they are, even as we speak, beginning to change.

"This will be a long-term, evolutionary change, Tyrantus. It may not take hold as it has with you, in such a quick fashion, but seeds of their future rebirth have been planted. Now they have all been re-contacted by their own former existence as Light Beings! This will cause inner turmoil, I guarantee, and they will be confronting themselves, face to face. Lower and higher selves have now been reintroduced to one another—it is a battle that they must fight individually. The ultimate victor will be their own affair.

"But as with you, these twelve individuals are affecting so many billions of souls that our attempt to reach them had to be made, and my personal, physical presence here was the only way to accomplish that reconnecting of their minds with the Higher Minds who once served as their main source of inner guidance."

"I think I know something of what you are attempting to describe," Tyrantus said thoughtfully. "It is exactly as I have experienced: there seem to be two parts of myself battling for control over my thoughts. I frequently agree with your statements now. I do sense some memory within myself of having lived, as you say, with a purpose to serve others—and so I have attempted to do here, for all these people of the many worlds of Orion. But you have stirred grave and unpleasant thoughts within me, fears that I have not done so in the most efficient or effective way."

"Efficiency, Tyrantus, is one of your major problems. You have been too efficient, by your definition of the word. You have attempted to control and make uniform all the lives of your many subjects, and through this control you have eliminated the very life that you had hoped to provide! You have worked against your own best intentions and this, Tyrantus, was your greatest mistake, as you took upon your own, solitary shoulders the weight of the evolutionary expressions of all these souls. Each planet that you add to your empire is another weight upon *your* back!

"You have erred most grievously, for no one can live the life, the spiritual, soulic life of another human being. That is each one's prerogative and necessity! You cannot remove responsibility from these people by dictating how their lives shall be lived in some scheme that you and your associates have devised to create a false version of perfection, or utopia. It cannot be! It will not be, and Tyrantus, you know that it is not so. Your empire is crumbling within, and even as you expand your influence to greater numbers of planets, the interior lives of your people are in a shambles, and the very foundation of your government depends on the minds of, not only yourself, but your Council and all of their aides, which are incapable of supporting this foundation. They are weakened by ignorance; they are functioning from a false premise of life. They have convinced themselves that what they see, hear, taste, and feel physically is the sum and total of life—and this is not the case.

"But I know that you are beginning to recall this Truth that you once lived."

"Yes, Dalos, it does make more sense to me than when I first heard you explain these things. But I hold little hope for your ability to convince the others of this. They are in some ways more rigid than I! They are greedy, Dalos. They want my position, and their ambition blinds them to all else. For many hundreds of years this was perfectly satisfactory to me, as I could keep them under control and their ambitious ways have proven useful. But now I know they will present a major block to our plans."

"We shall not allow them to, Tyrantus. We have ways of working with them that are non-interfering, peaceful, and yet beneficial and effective. It is quite simple. You and I must simply keep our minds open to the inspirational guidance of the Elder Ones. They see more clearly than we can see through the mechanism of our conscious minds. They are far more wise and they shall instruct us as to how we must proceed. For now, I think it wise that we do return to the Council with some additional information, after they have had some time to digest that which has been presented thus far."

"This is agreeable to me," Tyrantus replied. "I am feeling a bit stronger today and I think that I am capable of speaking to them, as we had discussed—if you believe that now is the best time to outline our plans."

"I am very glad that you have brought it up, for that was exactly my thought. You see that we are already in tune with one another and with those benevolent Beings who are overshadowing our every move! It is quite a wonderful way to live, is it not? We do not need to be concerned or stressful about the best course of action. We merely need to know that all such Intelligence shall be provided."

"I wish that I could be as confident as you, but this is all quite strange to me. Perhaps I once lived as you say but I cannot fully remember, and what we are now doing is so drastically different than anything I have ever done on this world that I am quite astonished by my own words! Sometimes I think that I have lost my mind. Perhaps the Council members are correct when they say that Tyrantus has totally lost his mentality! Perhaps. But there is now a very strong motivation within me to attempt your suggested changes. I am weary of the old ways, and I begin to see how I have failed my people. So, Dalos, let us proceed before I lose my courage."

"Good, Tyrantus. We shall do that."

They stood, and Tyrantus looked into Dalos' eyes, which he was capable of doing more frequently now. Dalos returned his gaze with a beam of pure love, unadulterated by personal associations, criticisms, condemnations, or other thoughts of a material nature. Tyrantus felt the warmth penetrate his very being, and although he could not yet return such impersonal love, he was grateful to know the Pleiadean.

He was proceeding at a momentum which did surprise him at each juncture, yet he could not stop, for the compelling motivation which had been instilled within him was the growing awareness of his own, true, spiritual self that he had tried to describe to Dalos. It was not important that Tyrantus be capable of fully grasping the entire picture, so long as he was moving, now, in a progressive trajectory.

Dalos suggested that they each retire for a period of rest before the time when the Council would reconvene. Tyrantus was grateful for this suggestion as well, for he did suddenly feel very tired.

The Council members were wrestling with their own thoughts. They were quite unaccustomed to change. For many centuries, life in the Orion Empire had proceeded in its dull routine from day to day, year to year, life to life. They had mastered this routine, and it was the means by which they sustained their powerful lives as leaders among the Orionites. So foreign was change to these individuals that it caused them extreme internal agitation. They did not know how to respond to the meeting they had just departed. They could do nothing constructive in this interim period, but even their emotional turmoil was proof that constructive change was afoot!

This was a most dangerous period of Dalos' mission to the Orion Empire. Any one of these individuals, including Tyrantus, was on the brink of mental collapse. The introduction of such a powerful Light Force into their lives was a calculated risk by the Hierarchical Minds. It was radical surgery that they were performing to save these individuals from spiritual death. The slightest imbalance could push any one of them over the edge—and they each wielded sufficient force to cause considerable havoc among the people under their control, and damage to the mission of Dalos. The downfall of his entourage was proof of the power of the negative forces to oppose his attempts to restore the true lives of the Orionites.

All that could be done was to proceed as planned with the best possible intentions, and the inner help and wisdom of the Lighted Ones. Then it was simply a matter of waiting while events unfolded, hopefully in a redirected motion toward progressive change.

Linton fell into a deep sleep after the meeting had been adjourned. He dreamed of matters which he could not recall when he awakened. Truly, he was taken up on this Light beam which had penetrated his consciousness through his more open-minded state during Dalos' address, and while his physical body rested, his mind was infused with information about his own previous existence as a Light Bearer.

This was the hope of the Brothers, to be able to contact these individuals as Dalos' presence among them raised their frequency sufficiently to allow this contact to occur. Until now, they had been existing at such a low state of consciousness that such inner help and guidance was nearly impossible. But as each one was stimulated to use their minds more constructively in pondering Dalos' words, thus they opened their consciousness slightly to allow a higher influence to penetrate with even more information to help them make their personal recognition of how they were destroying themselves and others.

Radik was still fuming with indignation at the blatant manner in which Dalos had criticized the government of Orion. He nurtured this anger throughout the recess and was therefore unreachable by any higher force that would otherwise have helped this one to a greater understanding of himself, and his true responsibility as a leader of men.

Tonar was struggling with his own conflicting emotions. His plans were so near to completion, and yet the address of Dalos had kindled certain feelings and recognitions that were both foreign and familiar to Tonar. He did not know how to place them in a balance in his consciousness, and so he spent the intervening hours in a state of internal combustion. He was impatient for the session to proceed.

The others were far less affected by Dalos' words. They were just beginning their experience of contacting this higher, radiating Source of Infinite Intelligence. It had been many hundreds of thousands of years since they had been presented with such, and the shell which enclosed their minds was thick and deep. The Light now warming the exterior of this shell would need to continue in its application before any progress was made in penetrating the resistance that they held to this Light-intelligence.

When they returned to the Council Chambers, all present had undergone some readjustment in consciousness. They were now preconditioned for the words they would hear from the lips of the very one who had sealed their fates as demonic leaders of a dying empire.

"Now, friends, that you have had time to think over Dalos' words, I have a few of my own that I wish to add," Tyrantus began. "You have known me, many of you for hundreds of years, and you know that when I speak, I fully intend to follow through on whatever course of action I have proposed. So it is today. I am prepared to make a vast change in our Empire. We will no longer operate in the ways which have become familiar to you all. I suggest that you note carefully what I am about to say."

They could not have done otherwise, for each one was listening as if his life depended upon whatever might issue from the Emperor. They were expecting nearly anything, given the bizarre events that had been unfolding, and they knew that their positions depended upon their ability to adapt to whatever new rules and regulations would be imposed. But none of them could have possibly predicted what Tyrantus said next.

"We shall not only allow Dalos to teach his scientific principles of energy to our own scientists—and this is the first priority, Linton and Radik—but we shall incorporate his teachings into our own educational system. Yes, we will be re-educating the Orion people to understand a whole new facet of themselves. Of course, this facet has always existed but we, and I include myself, have all been ignorant of it!"

They were shocked. No one uttered a single word. They could not. The Emperor had just admitted a flaw in his own makeup! It was unheard of! This struck the deepest fear into each one, for this meant that all previous rules of behavior were in jeopardy. They did not know how to respond to this incredible statement.

Tyrantus did not wait for their response. With Dalos seated now by his side, he continued. "As we begin to incorporate this new understanding of ourselves, I believe, and Dalos has convinced me of this, that our people will change before our very eyes. I now realize that we have been restricting their thoughts so severely, through our good intentions, of course, but to such an extreme that they have only been living half-lives! They have not been allowed to produce to the fullest extent of their capability! They have been limited by our own impositions of control and our prescribed lifestyles. Perhaps if we allow them to flower upon the branches of our Empire, we will be surprised by what new fruit emerges!"

Such language coming from the Emperor's own mouth was astounding. He was speaking like one of those very individuals who were now incarcerated by the thousands in the research facilities, as the technicians worked night and day to correct such malformations of thought!

The Council members were now stirring in their seats and a few among them were beginning to wonder how they could bring the Emperor to his senses. If he continued along these lines, he would be in violation of Orion law and he himself would be a candidate for such treatments.

Tonar was pleased by this development. He began to see some light breaking over the darkened scenario of his previous scheme to take over control of the government. *Yes,* he thought, *if Tyrantus continues to speak like this, my coup shall be quite a simple matter. He is sealing his own fate! He is signing his death warrant! I will not have to lift a finger. The others will not allow him to continue as Emperor if he exhibits such insane behavior. It is the law, and we will be fully justified in removing him. Even his own security forces will agree to that! And so the problem shall be solved. Yes, Tyrantus, keep talking. We are very interested in what you have to say!*

"First among my priorities is to change our laws which restrict the thoughts of Orion citizens. We shall, henceforth, cease all incarcerations of dissidents, and they shall be given the freedom to speak as they choose."

The Council erupted in a large roar of disapproval.

"You cannot do this!" Benertizog shouted. "This is folly! You will destroy us all!"

"Sit down," Tyrantus ordered. "Hear me out. I do not expect you all to agree to my decrees, but they are my decrees and you must find some control within yourselves. This is my decision and I shall implement these changes, whether you like them or not! I am giving you the courtesy of hearing my words first-hand. You are my associates and I do expect your continued loyalty. But if any among you should choose to oppose my plans, then you know your fate!"

Dalos looked at Tyrantus with some concern. He could see the emotional state that was beginning to take him over, and Dalos realized it was time to interject his own influence.

"Tyrantus, may I speak a word?"

Tyrantus hesitated a moment. The color had rushed to his face and he was unwilling to give up his podium, but he looked at Dalos and saw in his face an urgent plea to exhibit some restraint. The look reminded Tyrantus of their previous discussions and he relinquished the podium. "Yes, Dalos, if you feel it is necessary. Speak."

"Thank you, Emperor. I merely wanted to interject the reminder that these changes which are now being implemented are not to remove any one of you from your offices but to alleviate the pressures which are now threatening, not only your people, but your own selves. You must be willing to try a new means of governing, else you will lose your positions through violent eruptions of conflict among yourselves!

"Do you not see the civil wars that are now forming in the minds of each one of you? It is quite obvious that you are fearful for your futures, and you will take aggressive actions to insure your security. No one here is ignorant of that fact, I trust?" Dalos looked around the room. "So let us all be honest with one another. You have a fifty-fifty chance of surviving such outbreaks of hostility. You all wield sufficient power to destroy one another, as well as countless millions of people who will be used as pawns in your battles with each other. This, I know, is not spoken of in your meetings but it has been discussed between Tyrantus and me, and we believe it is time for a new honesty among us all, if this Empire is to survive!"

They glared at him with the fiercest hostility. Not one was capable of accepting these words from a stranger, a man who was not even a citizen of their Empire. So angry did these words make them that for a moment, none could find his voice to reply. Finally, Tonar spoke.

"Dalos, you are quite fearless, I grant, but you do not understand how we work here. We have lived this system of government for many centuries and it has been quite stable. You are mistaken in your assessment of our ambitions. We hold no animosity for one another, for we all recognize the validity of unifying ourselves as a stable symbol of Orion achievement. That is how our government has survived for these many centuries. We are not going to change our system of government! This would be a most foolish and fatal mistake."

The others nodded their agreement. They let Tonar speak for them; he *did* have a way of articulating things that they did not. Of course, what Dalos had said was true, but they all perpetuated the illusion of unity because it served their political goals. This false unity permeated the propaganda released to the Orion peoples. It was a concept instigated by Tyrantus himself and reinforced at any time when some disunity threatened the Empire.

Yes, they had survived in this fashion for centuries, but the price of that survival was the very life force of countless souls, as well as their own!

Tyrantus seemed stunned by the rapid exchange of words. He was treading on shaky ground to begin with. Tonar's speech was quite familiar to him; it was born of Tyrantus' own ideas about the government of a society and it rang strong, familiar harmonics within his consciousness.

Dalos saw that Tyrantus was losing his grip on the fragile state of higher attunement that had been so carefully groomed within the mind of the Emperor. He knew that he must act to save the situation from deteriorating further. "Very well, Tonar, if that is how you feel," Dalos said, "then I commend you for your efforts to join yourselves in a positive purpose. What we are proposing here is a joining of minds to a great new momentum of positive change. How can this harm any one of you? How can it do anything but help the lives of all people living as Orion citizens, including yourselves?"

"Yes." Tyrantus finally found his voice. "That is my purpose—to give new life to this Empire! What Dalos has said previously is true. There are fissures in our society threatening our very existence, and they are not external threats from some hostile force but internal weakenings that, if we confront the facts, are a reality now. We have been unable to resolve this weakening of the minds of our people and you all know this to be true. Now what I am proposing will be a radical change, granted, but I sincerely believe that it is our only choice. We are most fortunate that Dalos has come to our world, for he has brought with him a fresh perspective and a wealth of information that will give us the added leverage we need to implement such far-reaching change.

"I am going to adjourn this session and call upon the necessary department heads to begin the implementation of these changes in our educational material. I shall have Dalos as my advisor, and any one of you who wishes to participate in this change is welcome to be present and to learn as we learn—by doing. Yes, this is new to me as well, yet I am willing to place myself in this position because I so strongly believe in its ultimate success! I know that I shall be a better leader of my people if I am giving them some greater reason to continue living, and this is the bottom line. We have not allowed our people any true motivation for their lives! Yes, we have ample systems of reward and punishment, but how long does the gratification of such rewards sustain any one of us?

"Friends, I ask you this question: Are you content with your life? And if you have any hesitation as you make your automatic, programmed response of, 'Yes, of course,' then I urge you to look beneath that hesitation. Your lives are lived with the greatest luxury that our Empire can provide. You have all advantages, and you have tremendous responsibility for the lives of others. You have everything toward which each young Orion citizen is urged to strive! But if you examine yourselves, I suspect that you will come to the same conclusion that Dalos has brought to my attention.

"I myself sit upon the pinnacle of Orion life. But Dalos helped me to recognize that I have never been truly happy, satisfied, contented, or at peace with myself. If any one of you truly believes that he possesses these most desirable qualities of life, then I salute you. You are a better example than I. But I doubt, if you are honest, that you have ever experienced more than a brief moment of tranquility.

"This inner tranquility, I have learned in recent weeks, is the goal toward which all human beings truly strive, and they need no urging to desire such peace of mind. This is the strongest motivating factor of us all, yet we have been ignorant of this fact. We have done nothing to understand this motivation. We have done nothing to give *ourselves,* let alone our people, this opportunity! That is the purpose of all changes that I am determined to make here.

"Yes, you can sit there and assume that I am a dying old man, gone crazy with illness and incapable of making wise decisions. Live in your folly if you choose, but I am going to take steps to *do* something constructive about this most dismal situation! I have seen that we have allowed ourselves to deteriorate into a state of existence that is quite abominable! We do not control life for our people—we destroy it!"

Now Tyrantus' blood was rushing through his veins for a new reason. He was stimulated by a force of Intelligence that had, for too long, been strange to his mental circulation. Now it filled him with a vigor that he had never felt! His voice had grown increasingly strong and vibrant with this Force.

Dalos smiled with the greatest satisfaction he had experienced since his arrival upon the planet. *Yes, we are now beginning the new beginning of life for the Orion people!* He was moved to tears, which formed as moist droplets in the corners of his eyes, invisible to all present for they were wrapped in their own thoughts, which raged like thrashing seas suddenly accosted by a hurricane force.

These raging seas of energy would cause their damage, but Dalos felt confident that he and Tyrantus would ultimately win them over through the logic and reason of all that was in store for the Orion civilization as it became embraced by the radiant Light of the Hierarchical Minds, which now encompassed this room and each individual seated therein.

26

Threats

A SMALL LIGHT NOW SHONE in the darkness of the minds of the Orion Council. It had been implanted by Uriel, through the person of Dalos, and securely anchored therein by her amplifications of Intelligence that were directed toward these powerful individuals.

The Council members were powerful in a material world, yet thoroughly weakened in their spiritual natures to the point that none among them could rise above these material worlds when they left their physical anatomies in death. They continued to oscillate in a close frequency relationship as denizens of subastral worlds, and there they continued their directing force, leading hordes of demonically-minded ones to carry on with their attempts to subvert the minds of others, and thereby gain control over large masses of people. To remove these individuals from their positions of power was to remove the leadership of the negative forces—and, of course, the removal of Tyrantus from his dominating role in this scenario was vital to the success of Uriel's mission.

Now it appeared as if that mission was slowly moving forward once again, despite the obstacles that had been placed in opposition to the Forces of Light by these subastral hordes.

Dalos could not have been more pleased with Tyrantus' address to the Council. If they were able to maintain this positively-biased motion for change, then all would proceed according to plan.

But even now, the forces of opposition were gathering to meld their strength to interfere in this healing effort.

Tonar would now insure that none of Dalos' broadcast messages reached the larger populations as planned. He was uncertain how to accomplish this without Tyrantus being alerted to his tampering, but he knew that he must make this attempt, else all was lost. His entire plan to overtake the government and buy for himself the seat of power hinged upon the popularity of the Pleiadeans, who were now truly *his* spokespersons, although they were unaware of this fact.

The Pleiadeans were operating from a blind ignorance. They were now drawing their information from external sources rather than from the Intelligence that resides within. They were becoming increasingly dependent upon the feedback of others for their sense of personal satisfaction. This was fatal to their true Minds. They lost their directives and lost their Consciousness; they lost all sight of original purpose. They still believed, however, that they were serving the force of goodness but in fact, they were serving none other than their own egos—and in this case, the ego of Tonar, who was using them to his own best advantage.

He planned to use them as puppets to his regime. He would easily nudge Tyrantus from office, now that Tyrantus had displayed, in full view of the entire Council, his mental lapse! They would agree, Tonar knew, that he must be removed from office "for the safety of the larger population." But Tonar's biggest hurdle to overcome would be the opposition of the other Council members who also felt they deserved to sit upon the seat of power.

Linton and Radik both fell into this category, and their efforts to secure for themselves the outstanding technology of the Pleiadean scientists was now placed in jeopardy by Tyrantus' proposal that Dalos work directly with the scientists. That would mean that any information about this advanced technology would be openly available to all who worked within this realm of Orion life. Linton and Radik would no longer hold an edge over the others by their superior knowledge of Pleiadean technology. So they were, at the moment, stymied by this new development. They had not yet foreseen how they might gain some leverage over the situation to place themselves into superior positions.

The other Council members were devastated by Tyrantus' and Dalos' words. They were still too stunned to take action, but their thoughts were churning with anger and fear—both dangerous emotions in the unstable atmosphere that now existed among the Orion government leaders.

Dalos knew that he had pushed the situation to the brink of total collapse, but he also knew that this firm push was essential. Without it, the stagnation that encrusted Orion society would have defeated any attempt he made to awaken the Orion peoples to the reality of their interdimensional lives. So the explosive material which had been distributed into the hands of each individual present at this special session could be used in one of two ways: constructively or destructively. It might detonate their old ideas and attitudes to allow for a new civilization to spring up beneath their feet, or it might be turned against themselves or one another in a violent outburst of paranoia.

Civil war among the Orion planets would be a no-win situation for all peoples. Worlds would be devastated, for the Orion weaponry had reached a level of development that was quite diabolical in its arsenal of equipment that was capable of incinerating entire worlds and all people residing thereon. These weapons, Dalos knew, would be turned brother upon brother, with extensive bloodshed as the most tangible result; and even so, the far-reaching effects of such cataclysmic warring would be untold! Not only were there trillions of individuals now living on Orion-controlled planets, but each one of them was connected to an infinite number of souls through the principles of frequency and harmonics. Each one of these interconnected soulic expressions of Infinite Intelligence would be affected by such a broad-based war.

The minds of the Orion peoples would suffer the greatest damage, for such violent deaths do inflict a serious wound into the psychic anatomy of any individual who undergoes this experience. These psychic wounds are not healed as a physical body is repaired, or exchanged for a new one through the process of reincarnation. The psychic anatomy is a creation of consciousness, and therefore it is governed and controlled by consciousness, by thought. It would require the thoughts of these very individuals at some future time, with the help of many, countless millions of spiritual Brothers of Light, to repair the damage thus sustained if they were to enter into all-out wars among the planets of Orion.

These facts were all being carefully weighed by, not only Dalos in his conscious awareness of them, but the Quadrocentric Hierarchy and the forces joined with them in this concerted effort to restore Consciousness to the earth peoples of Orion.

I must now consider each act carefully, Dalos thought as he returned to his new quarters, not too far distant from Tyrantus' own.

This was now their arrangement so that they could stay in close communications, at Tyrantus' request. The Emperor knew that he was on unfamiliar ground and was dependent upon Dalos' guidance to achieve this miraculous change in a society which had not changed for hundreds of thousands of years; which had only become progressively more restricting and vile in its use of human souls as mere bodies to propel a civilization into some kind of technological nightmare!

Dalos warmed himself with the knowledge that he was not operating alone, nor would he ever be. Those of greater vision and intelligence were guiding his words and deeds; this fact would never depart from his consciousness, and well that it should not, for if he, like his brothers and sisters who had arrived upon the planet with him, had lost sight for even one moment, then all would fail! And such failure would hold an even greater premonition of death for the Orion peoples.

But such failure was not to be. Now Dalos was preparing for his second address to the peoples of Tyron and of other worlds in the Orion constellation—for Tyrantus had given his green light of approval, not waiting for the full response from the Council of Twelve. The address made to the Council by Dalos and Tyrantus was merely a courtesy, an attempt to contact them more directly with the Higher Force that was propelling these events; thereby, their venom directed toward Tyrantus might be lessened in its poisonous qualities and their claws might be dulled somewhat. Still, Dalos fully expected them to make some attempts to halt his activities.

Indeed, these attempts were made. Tonar, as already described, was now working with his technicians to develop subtle means by which to alter the words of Dalos as they appeared on the large screens scattered throughout the Empire. He would need one key piece of information and that was: the precise location wherein Tyrantus and Dalos would be viewing these broadcasts. Once he knew this, he could arrange to have the system in this location tampered with to allow a special, one-of-a-kind showing of Dalos' speech. That would be the complete, unexpurgated version, while the remainder of the Orion people would be watching a travesty. They would see Dalos describe his former entourage as his "helpers," those who spoke truth and to whom the people should direct their minds for instruction.

Even Shimlus and her close associates did not realize how far Tonar would be going in this alteration. They assumed that he would merely remove derogatory references made to themselves. They did not know that he possessed the capability to actually insert words in Dalos' mouth and to alter Dalos' physical imagery to accommodate these new vocal expressions. They did not know of Tonar's full plans for their futures. They misguidedly believed that they were doing good and helping people. This was their most dismal failure, that they became unaware of the truth of their own motivations! If they had accepted that they were now driven by their own egos, they could have saved themselves and many souls who were now falling under their influence; but they did not accept, and they did not seek Dalos out to learn a more productive and illuminated method by which they could have followed through on their individual missions. They were ignorant of Dalos' present plans, and it should not have been so—each one of them had arranged to serve as a facet in this larger plan of healing ambassadorship!

But Dalos could not spend the amount of time he would need to spend with them to change their mental misconceptions. This, they were fully capable of doing on their own, he knew, and they must do so—*for they do have, like all souls, free choice; so I will not dwell upon this most painful subject. I will simply carry on to the best of my ability.*

He had that opportunity sooner than he believed. The piercing tone of the communications device shattered the silence of his solitary room. He reached to press the receiving mechanism and was quite shocked to see Shimlus' image appear upon the screen. She could not have known of his location or communications code unless informed by one of

Tyrantus' aides.

Actually, it was Tonar who had gained this information from his agents, and who had suggested that Shimlus make this direct contact with Dalos to attempt to restore their good relations. Tonar knew this would be important in concealing his backhanded attempts to follow through with his subterfuge, of which Shimlus was still ignorant. She was persuaded to contact Dalos by Tonar's suggestion that Dalos had asked about her and was eager to carry on a private conversation. So Shimlus believed she was answering a direct call from Dalos.

"Dalos—" Shimlus stopped before she began. The words would not come to her lips when she saw his radiant face. It filled her with a sharp sensation of fear. Her mind went blank for a moment. He seemed quite startled to see her, and in some deep recess of her consciousness, she wondered why this would be so since she believed it was he who initiated this contact.

"I did not expect ever to see you make some attempt to speak to me," Dalos said quietly to the image on the small, bluish screen in his quarters.

Shimlus looked back at him with a pitiful expression of confusion, pain, and anxiety. Dalos had never seen her look this way, and it was quite distasteful to him to see how far his beloved Shimlus had plummeted. It pulled at his heart, and he desired with all his being at that moment to help this soul recognize the truth of her present existence and opposition to her own life force. She was committing spiritual suicide, he knew, and he also knew that she was unaware of this fact. She was totally oblivious. Her mind was broken, to all intents and purposes; it did not function to provide her with a complete, unified picture of existence.

"Did you wish to say something to me?" he inquired.

"Dalos, I was told that it was you who desired to speak to me," she finally stammered, visibly trembling.

"Yes, Shimlus, I would truly love to speak to you if you could hear my words fully, but I know that you have already closed your mind and heart to me. There is nothing that I can say to you now."

Tears began to fill the eyes of Shimlus, who had once been the most beautiful vision of feminine life on the planet Axiahn. Now she was all sharpness and steel, like the civilization which she had swallowed into her very being.

"I do not understand why you want to hurt me," she cried. "I have done nothing to harm you. I have done my best to accomplish our mission here! You have only been abusive to us—you will not listen!"

"Shimlus," he interrupted, "you are very sick, indeed, and yet you are ignorant of that fact. There truly is no way for me to illuminate your thoughts now. You must do this for yourself. If you believe that I hold any animosity toward you, you are quite mistaken and, dear one, you must look within yourself. Have you forgotten all?"

She turned her face to the side. He could see the turbulent emotions pulling at the mind of this one, but there was no way to soothe them for her. He had spoken truth; he had nothing left to give to this soul, nor to her associates. They were not accepting his gifts of Higher Consciousness, so he would not squander that priceless commodity. He must reserve his energies for those avenues which were proving to be quite beneficial to his mission.

"Shimlus, I cannot bear to look upon you any longer. Please, know that within our very soulic selves, we Brothers do love you, but you must demonstrate some fiber of inner strength before this will have any meaning to you! You have lost all touch with your own higher self. You are performing the most horrendous deeds imaginable by your ignorance here; you are using your mind to bully and abuse those of lesser mental development. You are now a full-fledged member of the negative forces, and I fear, Shimlus, that you are clawing your way to a position of supreme dominance over this subastral horde!"

She turned and glared back at Dalos. "There! You have done it again! Why are you insulting me? I do not need to take this abuse!" And she snapped off the viewing screen, severing their connection.

"So it is, and so it shall be," Dalos said under his breath.

He was drained by this exchange and sought out his bed, where he lapsed into a deep, heavy sleep for many hours. When he awakened, he did not feel refreshed. He knew that this was the pull upon his consciousness of, not only Shimlus, but those to whom she had spread her animosity, and they were joining their minds with hers in a dark cloud of negative energies, stirred by the flames of emotional instability.

He rose from his bed to find a more illuminated atmosphere in the gardens to which Tyrantus had now given him free access. Here, he could feel the warmth of an artificial sun, and although it was not a real luminous orb of concentrated higher frequencies, it did remind him of his home on Axiahn and his true, inner home, as a leader of the Spiritual Forces. He settled into a comfortable seat and thought of his polarities, whose Presence filled his inner senses with Light.

Immediately they made him aware that all was not well on Tyron. There were forces now stirred and arming themselves that would cause gross deterioration of the situation. He was warned that he must be on guard at all times, for attacks upon his very person were a distinct possibility, and many would be the subversive machination of those who now posed a strong opposition to Tyrantus. They were extremely fearful of the changes the Emperor had proposed, with Dalos' assistance, and they were now convincing themselves that they must, at all costs, stop the Emperor in his madness from making significant alterations in the lifestyles of the Orion people.

Subconsciously, they knew their positions depended upon maintaining a status quo, and consciously, they were now dividing themselves up into armed camps to prepare for battle. So it would be a fight to the death for the Emperor's position, for surely he would be removed by them, and this would be but the beginning of their attacks upon the society. The very civilization which they convinced themselves that they were fighting to uphold was on the brink of destruction at their hands!

These factors were brought into the forefront of Dalos' consciousness as he made his inner attunement. The heaviness that he had felt was the surrounding pressure of these negative forces, which were encroaching upon his solitary position. And yet Dalos was not alone, as he at that moment demonstrated. His mind was illuminated by Higher Minds who could provide their wisdom in great abundance and did so.

Dalos knew now that he must seek out the Emperor and inform him of these activities. They would be put to a great test of will and determination, and Dalos was uncertain as to how stable Tyrantus was in his own consciousness. He had been teetering on the brink for many weeks now and it would be all too easy for him to relinquish his hold on his own mind.

Truly Tyrantus was now more sane than he had ever been, but that dark, swirling pit of his lower self loomed large in his consciousness and was always threatening to engulf his mind in a sea of blackness, in which even Dalos could not reach him to haul him to safety once again. The only means by which this could be prevented was if Dalos could maintain a more frequent contact with Tyrantus and keep the Emperor's thoughts elevated in a more stabilized attunement to the constructive measures they were now prepared to implement.

When they met, at Dalos' request, the Pleiadean suggested that they both adjourn immediately to the place designated for the preparation of Dalos' second speech to the Tyronites. This would give Tyrantus some productive activity to occupy his mind and help elevate him above the fears and insecurities which were released when he heard of the rumblings of opposition now posed against his seat of power.

"Dalos, this is cruel news that you bring to me. You have so highlighted a scenario of happy growth for us, I had nearly believed you! But now I see that I was foolish to think that these people could be so quickly changed."

"Not foolish, Tyrantus, for you yourself have proven that such rapid change is possible when the Power of Infinity is directed in a constructive intent. That is what we must continue to do; we cannot lose ourselves in fear or concern with what may be taking place among your enemies. They will immediately strangle you if you allow them this access into your mind! It is only through your own thoughts that you shall protect yourself, Emperor. Let me demonstrate this for you. Join me this very day, and we will keep ourselves removed from any mental battles that are now raging."

"I have no choice, Dalos, but to listen to your advice. You are my only remaining friend; you are the only one who has nothing to gain by my defeat. In fact, I believe that your very presence here would be severely threatened by my demise."

"That is true, Tyrantus. We are now allies in Spirit, as well as in our present physical joining of purpose. So, let us take full advantage of this alliance while we can. Let us speed up our schedule and get these vital, life-giving truths to the people of Orion!"

"Yes, I see your point. What else can I do? My hands have been tied, and yet you are telling me that my mind is free. Well, we shall see how truthful your statements are. I will give it my fullest and best attention."

"Wonderful, Emperor! That is what I hoped to hear! So, shall we?" Dalos gestured toward the door.

Tyrantus stood, drawing himself up to his fullest height and visibly strengthening his resolve. Dalos was glad that the Emperor could find this inner strength now more easily, when directed to it. But he was still incapable of maintaining a solid mental balance, Dalos knew, and so he must remain with Tyrantus as much as possible.

They called upon Tonar for his expert assistance, informing him that their plans had been stepped up and that they would not be waiting until Dalos' first broadcast was viewed by the entire planet before preparing his second.

Tonar responded with a curt word of agreement, but the moment he was out of their view screen, he panicked. *I am not yet ready!* He swore. *What shall I do?* But he had no time to think further, for already the signal of Tyrantus' arrival was beaming into Tonar's headquarters. He would have to think quickly on his feet, Tonar decided, humor them and look for his opportunities wherever a sign of weakness became apparent.

He straightened his uniform and entered the hallway to greet the two who now embodied his most hated enemies.

Dalos extended his hand with a warm, sincere smile. "We are appreciative, Tonar, of your quick response to our request."

Tonar could not return this friendly greeting and Dalos knew then that he was a most serious threat to their success.

27

To the Victor ...

While Dalos and Tyrantus were busying themselves with the new plans for the introduction to the Orion peoples of an interdimensional physics of human consciousness, the Council members were scrambling about to make their own plans. They were all conniving to have Tyrantus removed and to place themselves in his present position. Ultimate power was their desire, and anyone who occupied the seat of Emperor would control the lives of hundreds of billions of people. They could shape the civilization to match their own personal whims, and they could implement or deny whatever changes they desired.

These individuals controlled all facets of life on Orion planets, each of the many departments that kept the wheels of this vast machinery turning. They were an integral part of this computerized civilization. If any one of them desired to sabotage the whole, then that was fully in their capability to do. Such sabotage had upon occasion been attempted by one or more members of the Orion Council, but always such coup attempts were put down by Tyrantus and these individuals' lives taken from them. Now those who sat upon the Orion Council had proven largely loyal—at least in their willingness to maintain the status quo and to serve Tyrantus, being content with the relatively huge share of power that they were given by the very nature of their position.

Yet three or four upon the Council were not satisfied with this share of power; they desired the pure ego glorification of becoming that sole individual to whom every single Orion citizen must look for direction. It was not that their lives would change so significantly by this position of power, but that they could claim supreme achievement if they became the solitary leader of the Empire. This was a lure that proved strong, indeed, strong enough to induce these individuals to risk all for the dim possibility that they might be successful in this quest.

Tonar was one of those individuals so convinced, and Linton, with Radik close behind in his own desire for takeover; Sortiriahn was another, as was Donquill, who had controlled the transportation systems of Orion. Had they joined their forces, they could easily have succeeded in cycles past to overthrow the regime of Tyrantus. But that was not their goal, to bring about a change. Their goal was for personal victory. They would fight one another, then, for this prized possession of supreme rulership. They would use their wits and their technology and the backing of many hundreds of thousands of unnamed individuals whom they had swayed to support their particular points of view.

This all had to be accomplished surreptitiously, under the surface of the outward calm of Orion life. There were bribes promised and delivered; special favors granted; and promises for future reward should the individual in question be successful in his move against the Emperor. Many were those individuals quite willing to risk their own lives for the promised returns of ease and comfort, position, wealth, influence, and status. It was, in fact, quite simple to attract the interest of the Orion populations because their lives were geared around the satisfaction of the material nature of man. They could be swayed with anything that would give them a greater sense of inflated importance, for they had never been instructed in a more illumined lifestyle. They knew nothing other than the gratification of the physical senses.

Now, for Tonar, that gratification of physical appetites was being exemplified in the teachings of Shimlus and her followers. They were, by their very appearance, promising the Orionites a lifestyle that was filled with many diversions. Color, music, gaiety, and the indulgence of pleasurable activities were now incorporated in the expressions of the Pleiadeans, as they further relinquished their more sensitive, inner understanding of the true purpose for which a human being exists on a physical world: to learn of himself and to grow in his mentality. It was now but a matter of convincing Shimlus to lend her support to Tonar in his bid for Emperorship. With her support and the support of her followers, Tonar's victory was assured, for he would have many thousands of souls pledged in their loyalty to his regime, and their pledge would include the sacrifice of their lives in battle should his quest bring about that state of conflict.

Thus far, Shimlus knew nothing of these plans, but after Tonar's encounter with Dalos and Tyrantus, in which the second broadcast to the Orion peoples by Dalos was recorded, Tonar knew he must move quickly. He summoned Shimlus to his headquarters. No sooner had she entered his official greeting room than Tonar himself appeared, with urgency inscribed across his countenance.

"Tonar, you seem quite distressed! What news have you now for me?"

"Your leader Dalos has just prepared another speech."

She was visibly disturbed by this reference to Dalos.

"Do not expect that he had any kind words for you," Tonar added, "for he did not. He spoke quite plainly on the matter, and used you and your associates as examples of how 'one's mind can be deterred from its true purpose.' I do not believe the Orion people will have any understanding of his meaning, but Shimlus, you know that Dalos is a very persuasive speaker! Something about his presentation causes one to lose all sensibility and to be swept into his point of view."

"Is that true of yourself, Tonar?" she inquired coldly. "Do you believe that we are victims of our own misconceptions?"

"Of course not." He attempted to placate her. "I support you wholeheartedly, as you know. I believe that your messages to the people have been quite beneficial, and I fully intend to do all that I can to continue my help to you."

"That is wise, Tonar, for we do have so much to give to your people."

"Yes, of course, Shimlus. But I must caution you that these speeches made by Dalos are doing much damage to your credibility. They have not yet been released but if they were heard by the people, they would undermine your every word!"

Shimlus said nothing but her eyes became extremely cold and narrow. "Yes, I know he hates me," she finally said. "I do not understand it. But I can't let his hatred deter me from what I came to do! I know that I am right. I must simply carry on. His mind was lost long ago, Tonar. We are fortunate that Tyrantus did not apply his instruments to *our* bodies. We are still capable of speaking intelligently to the people. I have seen many methods by which we can extend our messages, and our influence. I hope that you will continue to offer your support and assistance to us. You have been most gracious in this way."

Now Tonar saw his opportunity to propose his true desire. "That is why I have called you here. We must speak privately on this particular subject, you and I."

"Yes, I am listening."

"Good. Now please keep an open mind. I have seen a weakness in the Emperor that I believe is long-lasting and has caused him an inability to govern as he once did. I believe this is most damaging to our Empire, and if allowed to continue, Tyrantus will bring destruction upon us all."

Shimlus thought for a moment. "What kind of weakness do you mean?"

"A weakness of mind, Shimlus. He recently brought Dalos into a special session of the Council and the two of them proposed the most preposterous, sweeping changes. You would not believe what was said in that session! These two madmen think that they can uproot a society that has functioned smoothly for so many hundreds of thousands of years, with strange and bizarre ideas about re-educating the people! Your proposals for our change make much more sense to me, Shimlus, as you are not attempting to destroy anything but to add to our society with a greater sense of pleasure and lightness. This is what the people truly lack! They have no joy, and you and your brothers and sisters are now bringing joy to the surface of our awareness."

"That is our desire, to fill your lives with joy and happiness. Truly, there is no need for life to be such drudgery as you now express on all planets under your control."

"That is precisely the point, Shimlus. This is Tyrantus' point of view—*he* is the one who has imposed this strict, rigid code of order. But I believe the people are thirsting for a new way of life, and I believe that we can provide that new life for them!"

"How do you propose to do this?" she asked, although she already suspected what his answer would be.

"I propose, Shimlus, that you and I can accomplish something that has never before been successfully attempted. I am prepared to step into the Emperor's position." He paused to glance at her to gauge her response to this statement, which he had never before uttered aloud. Her face was completely expressionless. She did not seem surprised at all.

"Yes," she said, "I have been having thoughts along these lines, that if only Tyrantus were removed from his damaging influence upon the people, they would be free to awaken to their new ways of life. I could never reach Tyrantus, but you have the capability to bring about many changes. Together, you and I could forge a new, thriving society for the Orion Empire. This would be our first major achievement in our mission here. I do see that our success is possible!"

"I am so glad, Shimlus, that you yourself have pointed this out. That was exactly my thought. With your influence, I know my success is assured and together we could accomplish much. You have the goodwill and admiration of the people already, and this admiration is growing day by day. The only drawback that we now face is the slanderous attack upon your person by Dalos.

"It is Tyrantus' plan to give Dalos access to our scientists, and to the people as a whole. He wishes for Dalos to institute a new teaching system upon all Orion planets. These public addresses are only the beginning, Shimlus, and from there they plan to change all structures of our society to accommodate their own vision of how life should be lived by the Orion peoples. But I do not agree with their ideas. I think this will be a dismal failure, and besides, my colleagues on the Council all have their own ideas about taking the seat of power for themselves. That is why we cannot delay, Shimlus. We must act now!"

"I am willing to follow your suggestions. How do we begin?"

"We have already begun. You and your fellow teachers should continue your work. I will insure that for you. Meanwhile, I will do as we have planned; I will make certain that these slanderous statements by

Dalos directed toward you never reach the ears of the public. I have my technicians now working on this new method for revising Dalos' speech and I am attempting to determine where Tyrantus and Dalos will view these broadcasts. Once I am certain of this, we can make sure that they believe the speeches have been relayed to the pubic as planned. But in fact they will do nothing to hinder your own public image."

"This sounds agreeable to me," Shimlus said. "I am saddened by the fact that we must make this attempt, but I sincerely believe it is the only way. We are operating with the best interests of the people in mind and therefore, our actions are justified. Yes, Tonar, do as you must, and please keep me informed as to your progress. I am glad of our conversation."

She stood and approached him, stretching out her hand. Tonar clasped it in his own and looked into her wide blue eyes.

"I shall enjoy our work together." She gazed at him pointedly.

"Yes," he responded. "It shall be a pleasure."

Sequestered in their laboratory, Radik and Linton were comparing notes. They determined that they still had insufficient information about the Pleiadean starship to bring them to any conclusive ideas about the technology that had created it.

"These are still secrets locked in the mind of Dalos, and perhaps some of his former associates," Linton said. "But it is hopeless now for they seem incapable of recalling this information. Have you noticed this?"

"Yes, I have. The Pleiadeans seem quite willing to share what they know but our technicians can make nothing of what they have to say. We have created a high-frequency emitting device, but it seems to have little effect upon the surface of the ship. The other information they have to give is so clouded by esoteric ramblings about the human consciousness that we have been led in circles by these individuals. They seem to have lost their coherency."

"This was my observation as well," Linton replied. "I think that we may as well abandon our attempts to gain information from them. It is Dalos who still holds the truth of this starship. I have hit upon an idea, Radik, which is quite far-reaching in its implications. I think perhaps *I* may be verging on the loss of my senses, but here goes. I trust you shall take this in the manner in which it is intended, as a last-ditch effort to ensure our positions and maintain our hold upon the scientific life of Orion. You realize, Radik, that we are in danger of losing this position?"

"Unfortunately I do. Speak. Nothing could be too outlandish at this point, so long as it works."

"Well then." Linton stood up, striding to a window in his elevated control center. From here he could gaze down upon the work area, where the Pleiadean starship filled a large hangar-like building. Dozens of brown-suited technicians milled about beneath the towering ship. They were still making calculations of the energy radiations from its surface and applying various instruments to determine the effect they had upon this energy field. These calculations were then entered into computer systems and slight changes in the calibration of the instruments were made, with the entire process repeated again and again, inch by inch, over the surface of the starship. Hundreds of thousands of such calibrated adjustments had been made over the past year, with this work ongoing day and night, to little effect.

"I think that once Dalos has completed his speeches to the people of the outlying planets, he will be desirous to make a personal appearance among them."

"Yes, that is quite likely," Radik agreed. "He will strengthen his position thereby, and Tyrantus seems willing to give the Pleiadean free rein."

"He will also be desirous of communicating, as Tyrantus proposed, to our scientific conclaves. This will be the most efficient way by which his concepts could be relayed to a large group of individuals."

"What is it that you are suggesting, Linton? Get to the point."

Linton turned back from the window to face Radik. "I propose that we place ourselves in charge of Dalos' activities. We shall offer our services as liaisons with the scientists—after all, we are the heads of all scientific departments between the two of us. We are the natural sources of information and access to the thousands working on all planets in the system! So far, Tyrantus has not requested this service from us. I believe he is waiting to see how our loyalties shall align themselves. He is testing us, Radik, and we must show him that we are on his side."

Radik nodded as the meaning of Linton's words sank into his consciousness.

Linton continued. "Once he is convinced of our willingness to go along with his proposed changes, then he will relax his guard with respect to us. We shall have more freedom to function and our activities won't be suspect. Then we will suggest that Dalos use his own ship for this travel, and that we accompany him on these many forays to the outlying planets."

"Ye-es," Radik said, rising to his feet. "Yes, yes, I see what you are saying!" He placed a hand on Linton's shoulder. "My colleague, I think you have now outdone yourself with your brilliant reasoning! We shall have free access to, not only the interior of the starship, but to Dalos himself. He will be in *our* hands, and this man carries with him the entire panoply of Pleiadean science! Surely we shall find our opportunity to gain that information for ourselves. Yes, Linton, I am wholeheartedly in agreement with you. I shall do my part to convince Tyrantus of our sincerity."

"Now we must realize that if we seem too eager we will again arouse Tyrantus' suspicions. He must still regard us with his usual sense of caution. We must not alert him to any underlying motivations; we must be as ordinary as possible in our 'reluctance' to support him—that is our usual habit, is it not?" Linton smiled.

"True, that is very true. I am glad that you are thinking clearly, Linton. But there is one matter that does concern me. I found it quite unsettling to be aboard the Pleiadean ship with Dalos. Do you think that he will have the upper hand, as we will be in his territory?"

"I am not going to weigh this too seriously for now. We have little choice. This may seem somewhat extreme, and yet I feel it is within our grasp to accomplish. I do not know for certain of Tyrantus' plans for the Pleiadean, but I think we can present this in a way that will appeal to the Emperor. I think it will actually be a relief to him to know that he still has two strong supporters on the Council. Certainly he must know of the unrest now brewing as the result of his proposals. It was quite apparent that our colleagues are all turning green with their desire to be rid of Tyrantus!"

"Of course," Radik agreed. "We will appeal to his insecurities. In his fear of losing his power, he may be sufficiently distracted to believe our protestations of support."

"That was my thought."

"When shall we approach him?"

"Soon—as soon as the opportunity ripens. In the meantime, we will continue here as we have been doing. We must appear normal. But we must be cautious, Radik, that we do no damage to this ship now. I suggest that you order the technicians of Unit 43 to halt their applications of the high-frequency resonator to the under section of the ship. This, to me, appears to be the weakest sector and I would hate to see us render the ship immobile now!"

"Very true. I will attend to that immediately." He reached to shake Linton's hand.

Linton brushed him aside. "No need to play the suitor to me," Linton said. "We are agreed that we have our own motivations, and that our alliance is mutually beneficial. It will serve us best if we attempt no falsity between us. I know that you would as soon be functioning by yourself as with me, but neither of us has any choice. We could quickly destroy one another if we became divided in our purposes—we both know that."

Radik was stunned by Linton's rebuke but he knew that his collaborator spoke truth. He said nothing but turned and left the control room.

Linton strode back to the viewing window, rubbing a thoughtful hand over his cheek.

I shall dearly love to watch this ship lift off from our soil, he thought. *I shall be aboard, at all costs! I must know its secrets! Radik is a fool. He cannot see his own doom. Never mind; it does not matter. If I can satisfy this raging desire within me to resolve these enigmas, I shall be content. I care not so much to be in Tyrantus' shoes; I am not as greedy for power as Radik or Tonar or Donquill or any of the others. Certainly I will assume that mantle when the time comes, but this*—he stared at the ship—*this is my empire to conquer, this beautiful example of aeronautic workmanship!*

Dalos, I am closing in upon you! You shall tell me all before I am done.

Tyrantus was in a state of high anxiety. Dalos was using all his energies to keep the Emperor preoccupied with their progressive plans, but to little avail.

"Tyrantus, you must let go of these fears and insecurities. What does it matter now if you lose your position? Or even your life?" Dalos said to him. "I care not for my physical body; it is nothing. It is my mind that truly matters and no one can touch it. Only I can influence that. And it is no different for you. Your mind has not been at rest for many, many centuries, Tyrantus, but now—now you have the opportunity to do something about that!"

"So you say, Dalos. So you say. But I feel as if my life is falling down a long tube into a bottomless pit."

"Your life fell down that tube long ago, Emperor! Only now are you beginning to climb up into a clear understanding of your true position. You must not lose heart; you have only just begun."

"It seems such a long, impossible quest. I am tired. I do not think I am the man you believe me to be, Dalos. I have not one fraction of your strength, nor conviction. My habits have been frozen into place. It is not so easy as you make it sound to change my ways! This society is now entrenched in its pattern. If we begin to loosen one small portion of that which has become familiar to all people of Orion, we shall have chaos on our hands! Look, Dalos, at what has already occurred among the Council. Your words, and mine, have unleashed forces of hostility which are threatening to devour us all. They will destroy this Empire!"

"Only if we allow it to be so. We have not yet exhausted our resources. They are inexhaustible, Tyrantus. Remember that we have at our fingertips the resources of all Infinity! There is nothing impossible when one keeps this awareness lighted within his mind. That is why I am here with you, and why I shall remain by your side until I breathe my last breath. I have no other purpose on your world. I shall be victorious—and so shall you, Tyrantus, but you must stand up for yourself and your future!"

"My future is dim indeed, Dalos. I have no future. I had invested my entire being in this Empire, and now you have shown me that it is a web of spidery misconceptions that are strangling me, and the people themselves. I do not wish to live," he moaned. "I want to close my eyes to all that now haunts me, day and night."

"Tyrantus!" Dalos spoke sharply. "You must snap out of this self-pity! It benefits no one, least of all yourself! You are a man and you must behave like one—a whole man, a man who understands his place in the entire panoply of life, and his obligation to others. You have a very serious obligation to these people! You have taken upon yourself the directorship of their lives; you cannot abandon them without giving them something meaningful and intelligent to replace this. You cannot leave them stranded, now that you have willingly taken over control of them! Stop moaning about your failures and do something to change them."

Tyrantus just sat and stared weakly at Dalos. He spoke no further.

Dalos was unsettled by his attitude. He knew that his work would be that much more difficult if Tyrantus lost hope. He must continue to keep the Emperor's mind preoccupied and distracted from his self-concerns.

What can I do? Dalos inquired inwardly. *What more can I add that will give him the motivation to follow through all that has been set up?*

The answer came immediately.

"Tyrantus," Dalos said, "we must meet with your people."

"What do you mean, Dalos?"

"I mean we must, face-to-face, speak directly to the Orion people, in person, not through some video screen, but as human to human."

"And what do you think that will accomplish?"

"They will see your sincerity, and they will be enlivened by it, Tyrantus, I promise you! They will be touched by a higher force of reason and they, the people, will give you the support that you now need. You must have this personal contact with your people; I believe it is the only way to convince you of the validity of the actions you yourself have proposed to your Council. Let yourself feel the pulse of the people, Tyrantus. Let us go to them and sense their humanity."

28

A Brewing Storm

Dalos was much taller than Tyrantus. As he stood upon the podium before a gathering of several thousand Tyronites, his face filled with compassion, his words oscillating at the higher frequency of a mind attuned to its Infinite source, the people felt themselves to be lulled into a state of peaceful transcendency. This was different from the hypnotic trance that was induced in the people by the radiating frequencies of the government's control systems. They felt alive, and yet drowsy; awakened, but ready for sleep. For each word that was shaped by the lips of the Pleiadean was an embracing radiation of healing energy that oscillated to every individual gathered in this large public amphitheater.

Tyrantus had not yet spoken to the crowd. He had introduced Dalos and then receded into the background to await his opportunity. He was frozen from head to toe with a fear that he could not shove into the background of his thoughts; but he, too, was affected with a calming sensation by Dalos' speech. Gradually, as Dalos described to the people in greater detail the same principles that he had outlined in recorded speeches (which they had now all viewed), Tyrantus grew stronger in his ability to speak when his turn arrived.

Many weeks had passed since Dalos first proposed this public address to Tyrantus. The broadcasts of Dalos' messages had been relayed now to the planet of Tyron and, as promised, Tonar had tampered with these speeches. They did not contain any damning reference to the other Pleiadeans. They still had no insertion of Tonar's own words, for he had not had sufficient time to perfect that technology, but his aides and assistants were working around the clock to accomplish this. As planned, Dalos and Tyrantus had no idea that such alterations had been made. From the private viewing room from which they observed these broadcasts, all appeared to go as intended.

No one among Tyrantus' staff was capable of discerning any difference in the broadcast speeches, so they were none the wiser. Only Tonar, Shimlus, and a dozen of the Pleiadeans knew of this tampering before the broadcasts. Once the speeches had been relayed to the larger population, the other Pleiadeans suspected something unusual about Dalos' speech, as they distinctly recalled the first time they had seen it projected into their private quarters, when the first address had been presented to the test group of five hundred Tyronites. They questioned Shimlus on this matter.

She pretended to know nothing. She evaded answering further inquiries and suggested that they all approach Tonar on this matter.

"You are our spokesperson, Shimlus," one of her colleagues said. "You ask Tonar what has occurred. Did Dalos decide that this was not wise, to put down the activities of his own planetary brothers? This is very important for us to know, Shimlus. We have not been allowed to speak to Dalos for many, many weeks. We have so little knowledge of his activities any more. Please, find out for us what his intentions are. Can you not speak to Dalos directly?"

Shimlus' face visibly changed. She was silent for a moment, not knowing how to respond to this question from Pertillion. Then she thought of a solution to her dilemma.

"Perhaps that would be a good idea, Pertillion. I will attempt to make contact with Dalos. He has ignored us for too long. We may be able to assist him in regaining his full consciousness, and we do owe him this, do we not?"

They all nodded in agreement. Yes, it would be a great relief to them to restore their good communications with Dalos, for beneath the surface of their façades of contentment they knew inwardly that something was amiss. None among them was thoroughly satisfied with his or her life on Tyron. They would suffer from this internal unrest so long as they remained in their diametrically opposed position against the very Light that they purported to be carrying to the Orion people. But their ability to truthfully analyze this situation had now been severely impaired; they were incapable of coming to any clear, rational conclusions on this matter.

Instinctively, however, they knew that they must restore communications with Dalos.

"Yes, Shimlus," another spoke up. "Please, please do ask Dalos for an audience! We cannot go on like this; he should not have abandoned us! We are his brothers and sisters and we merely desire to do our duty, to serve the Orion people."

Shimlus now turned brilliant red with emotion. She could not conceal the truth of her inner battles with this one who had once been her polarity or mate. "Yes, Silkkon, I have said that I would do so. Now let us drop this issue. I will share with you all the results of our conversation."

Of course Shimlus did not intend to contact Dalos. She knew what the result would be, and she was not desirous of hearing his further rebukes for her behavior. She would lie to the others and tell them something that would placate their curiosity. She would wait a reasonable length of time and then return to them with some report.

Those who were closest to Shimlus suspected that something was afoot in her quick agreement to speak with Dalos. They themselves were terrified of any such contact. They did not raise the subject with her privately, for they feared their own inability to speak directly to the one who had been their closest advisor and spiritual mentor. They knew the reality of their opposition in some portion of their being, but they could do nothing to accept or change this truth about themselves.

The people, in the meantime, were still being deluded by the Pleiadeans' false teachings, and they had just been denied the benefit of Dalos' truthful statements about this particular situation. Now the people were being exposed to conflicting teachings that were so subtle in their variations that these differences would not be detected by the unexercised minds of the Orionites. They were so awash in the programming to which they had been subjected that they were presently incapable of these finer differentiations of frequency. That is, they accepted the words of both Dalos and his former associates, and incorporated them in their consciousness in one large misunderstanding of the principles of Infinity that were being described. Thus Dalos' true teachings of Spirit were added to the distortions of the others, resulting in a mish-mash of concept that was thereby deteriorated in its ability to straighten out the confusion that had long governed these peoples' activities.

Still, those present for Dalos' speech were being directly infused by his higher consciousness, the Consciousness of Uriel. This Universal, Radiant, Infinite, Eternal Light wove itself into their psychic anatomies with a restorative cure for much of their mental ills, although this cure was long-term and would not exhibit its full effect, perhaps for many lifetimes into the future! It was but a small drop from an ocean of Intelligence which would eventually flood their minds. But this ocean would grow, drop by drop, sparkling in its crystalline clarity, as they were capable of incepting these drops of Higher Intelligence.

Dalos made no reference to the other Pleiadeans during this particular speech, believing that he had explained sufficiently his position on this matter and there was no need to dwell upon the negative when there were many illuminating concepts to be brought to the minds of these hungry people—hungry for their true identities as spiritual beings!

The time eventually arrived for Tyrantus' speech. Dalos extended his arm in the Emperor's direction and gestured for him to join the Pleiadean in standing before the people.

Slowly, the Emperor rose to his feet and walked to Dalos' side.

Dalos placed a strong hand upon his shoulder, saying to the people, "Dear friends, this man, your Emperor for many centuries, has now awakened to all that I have just described to you. He is now living these new truths, accepting that he was ignorant before but can become wise overnight, so long as he is willing to keep an open mind and maintain his humility in the face of the vastness of Infinity!

"He will tell you himself of his healing. He will describe for your benefit the changes that will take place in your own lives. Let his example serve you, for he is a man to be much admired for his courage and conviction!" Dalos beamed a radiant smile directly into Tyrantus' wide eyes.

The Emperor nearly lost his balance with this burst of Power that blinded him for a brief second with its brilliance and passed into his being with a swirl of uplifting frequencies.

Dalos stepped aside to give the people a full view of their new leader—for truly, he was not the man whom they had known before!

Tyrantus hesitated for a long time, as if the words were trapped in his larynx and unable to reach the surface of his lips. Finally, he croaked a greeting. "Good day, dear friends," he began awkwardly. "It is a day to be remembered."

The people were staring at him with great intensity. They were flabbergasted by this appearance of the Emperor. He so rarely made public appearances, and he seemed so different from his recorded images.

Truly, they did not know Tyrantus himself. They had always known that façade which was carefully prepared and redesigned for their consumption by his propaganda teams. His public image was created from the fabric of many minds joined in negative collaboration. They devised a perfect leader to symbolize the goals of the Orion Empire. He was not a real man at all, but a figment of the demonic minds who had joined themselves to maintain a status quo of dictatorial rulership. So even if Tyrantus, as his old self, had appeared physically before the people, they would not have recognized him.

They were now open to nearly anything, for Dalos had raised their consciousness sufficiently to elevate them above their previous limited states of comprehension. They were, thereby, relatively free of the subharmonic influences of Orion programming. Tyrantus did not realize all this, else the words would have sprung more easily into his mind. But he was making great effort to be sincere and to implement the change he had recognized as so important to his own spiritual survival, and of course, to the many people who looked to him for guidance.

"You have not seen me this way before, and I am here to tell you that you shall see me many times in the future, speaking to you about these new understandings of life that Dalos has so kindly brought to my awareness. I have many wonderful things to relate to you, if you will bear with me. I am as unused to addressing you personally as you are to having me here, among you!

"This is one of the many changes that shall come about upon our planet. I am here to tell you that, as Dalos has said, I have undergone a complete revision in my thinking. I now realize that there were many mistakes I have made in attempting to lead our Empire into a position of strength and abundance. I have used methods of accomplishing these goals which are now questionable in my mind, and I am inclined to change the process by which we conduct our lives.

"But this is another key change which must occur: I can no longer dictate to you how you should live your lives!"

A loud rustling of concern passed through the crowd.

"Yes! You must begin to think for yourselves."

They had no understanding of these words. Were they not already thinking for themselves? Did they not now accomplish at a peak rate of performance? These were the values that had been instilled in them: productivity, speed, accomplishment, efficiency, loyalty, obedience. Anything else was foreign to them. What did the Emperor mean, "think for themselves?" They were the finest thinkers in the universe! So had they been programmed to believe.

Dalos, seated behind Tyrantus at some distance, recognized the confusion among the people. He saw that this would not be easily instituted, this change of learning to think as independent beings, the independent souls that they truly were—for no one can own another. No one can own a portion of Infinite Creative Intelligence! It is not a static object which can be circumscribed, packaged, and delivered, despite the illusions of this potential in a third-dimensional, physical world.

Tyrantus, oblivious to the stirrings within the people, continued. "You will see how rapidly our planets will thrive under this new plan of sweeping change! Your Council of Twelve has added their encouragement for these changes," Tyrantus lied, and Dalos looked at him with a penetrating glance. "They wholeheartedly support my new position and agree that such changes were long overdue."

Tyrantus was succumbing to his own insecurities and padding his speech with these false statements because he believed that a single point of view was invalid; it must be bolstered by the additions of many strong figureheads.

Dalos sensed his sudden drop in attunement. This thread of thought was dragging Tyrantus off course! Dalos applied his mind to think of a way to put Tyrantus back on track without causing him any public diminishment, for this was not the time to interfere in Tyrantus' speech.

Merely the direction of Dalos' consciousness toward Tyrantus was sufficient to recharge his resolve and re-establish his attunement to a higher frequency. Tyrantus dropped the subject of the Council, suddenly feeling uncomfortable with his lies.

"But, dear people of Orion, you yourselves shall be the ones to implement these changes in the confines of your own minds, as I have done! Go to your homes and think carefully upon Dalos' words. I know that you will find many questions arising that seem unanswerable, but we shall carry on with our dialogues and through this back-and-forth exchange of information we will, as a people, eventually incorporate a greater intelligence into ourselves and our lives. Then, as we begin to function from this more intelligent perspective, we can implement the necessary changes in our societal structures to accommodate our new ways of thinking.

"Do not be concerned about the 'how's' of these changes in our way of life. Address yourselves instead to the words of the Pleiadean. They are filled with wisdom and advice for us all. I leave you now with my words of encouragement, and my proclamation that a new Orion shall emerge beneath our feet! Thank you, all." And he bowed slightly to them.

They had never seen such demeanor from the Emperor, such humility! They were stunned, and gave no response. They were waiting for the orders to tell them that it was the appropriate time to stand and leave the auditorium. No such order was given. Eventually, as Dalos and Tyrantus disappeared into the rear of the amphitheater, one or two hesitatingly rose from their seats and glanced around to see if they would be reprimanded by the guards at every entrance. The guards themselves seemed confused about their orders. None had been given!

This was Tyrantus' first experiment in freeing the controls of the people. He had given one order, to the individual in charge of such large gatherings. That order was that there would be no commands and no subliminal additions to these speeches, no "reinforcements," as they were called. That individual feared for his life should he disobey an order of the Emperor, no matter how strange or bizarre it seemed to him. He therefore deployed his guards and they functioned in their routine manner to direct the people into the auditorium, but always before were they given specific commands as to when the session had ended. They had received no such command, and they had no orders to stop the people from leaving. They would not act without orders.

Therefore, as the handful of brave souls who ventured up the aisles toward the exits began their tentative journey, the guards simply looked at them in confusion and allowed them to pass. The people were astonished! They glanced at one another with questioning looks. No one knew what to do.

Eventually, all rose to their feet and a murmuring began to rise in volume among them. They were thoroughly confused and at a loss. After some time, they realized that something had gone wrong and perhaps some system had broken down. They knew this would result in the removal of many individuals from their positions, and the fear that clutched each one was a fear for their own lives; they identified with this situation as if it had been their own mistake—and mistakes were not allowed! This brought terror to the minds of many of these individuals. They began to tremble and quake. They stumbled from the auditorium in a state of panic that was most extreme, given the circumstances.

After some length of time, the people had all dispersed from this gathering place. The only "order" they had been given was that phrased by Tyrantus himself, to return to their homes. This they did, religiously. They would remain until they received further command. They were instructed to ponder Dalos' words and they attempted to do so, word by word. They did not speak to one another; that was not a part of their instruction. They were in a most unfamiliar state of consciousness and many of them were incapable of managing themselves in this unfamiliar realm.

Others simply passed into a state of repose, and they were those who benefited most greatly from their exposure to the one called Dalos. They were lifted into specially prepared "classrooms" in the spiritual dimensions, where they received more information than they could incept while oscillating in a conscious state of awareness. Again, it was a preparation and preconditioning for future experiences that they would have while living in physical bodies upon the physical planets of Orion. This was the beginning of their healing.

Dalos was unaware of the fact that the people had been left in such a state of confusion by the changes in their routine. He knew that not all would be capable of receiving the fullness of the energies supplied to them during this address. He had not intended for Tyrantus to begin to remove the directives upon which the people had become so dependent. This was to be a gradual process, for Dalos realized how drastic this would seem to the people. They must have something within their minds to replace this exterior source of guidance before they could survive such a diminishment of the controlling factors of the Orion government.

The Council members were not present for this address. They had not been informed of this incident but they knew immediately, once the event had occurred, due to their many agents sprinkled throughout the population. They were infuriated. Now Tyrantus was operating outside their realm of control and this was a serious threat to each one of them. Things were progressing at a rate much faster than they had expected; for it must be remembered that their minds also functioned at a sluggish rate, compared to one whose consciousness is illuminated with the constant ebb and flow of a Higher Intelligence, which is the natural purpose of the mind.

Although they each had their plans of action to counteract Tyrantus' intentions, they had not moved as quickly as Dalos had inspired Tyrantus to move. That was Dalos' ability, particularly to forge a new conduit for Higher Intelligence through whatever resistance arose, whether it be in the mind of the Emperor, or in the society as a whole. This required a concentrated effort by Dalos, and a knowledge of all factors involved in bringing about such all-encompassing changes. He was capable of functioning on many levels simultaneously.

Truly, it was the Mind of Uriel that orchestrated every element of Dalos' activities, and he was so thoroughly open to this higher influence that he allowed himself to follow through on all such impulses gained from his inner contact with Uriel. Now, he believed that they were prepared to make the next step.

"Tyrantus," he said, "we must quickly follow through on all that we have promised your people. We must return to speak to these same individuals, and I suggest that we find ways to continue our personal addresses to the people. Today, we only reached five thousand, a small fraction of the people living on this planet. And how many, Tyrantus, live on the planets in your Empire? I know that we cannot speak to each one of them individually, but I will not be content until we have contacted as many of these souls as possible. Do you see what great influence you have had upon them?"

Tyrantus was oblivious to the effect of their message. He could not answer Dalos' question.

"It is not important," Dalos said, realizing this fact. "I will tell you. They are now, each one, digesting this most unusual contact from their Emperor and this strange man from a foreign planet. So much information was given to them that their conscious minds are incapable of grasping all that was said. It will be a matter of proving our words by demonstrations of actual change in their daily lives."

"Yes, Dalos, I have already begun this change!" Tyrantus perked up. "I did not tell you but I requested that their orders for the remainder of the day be suspended!"

Dalos looked at him inquiringly.

"They were not given the usual commands to leave the building, to return to their places of work, or any other of the orders which had been programmed for their daily activity."

Dalos considered this surprising news for a moment. He immediately realized what confusion this must have added to their already overburdened minds, which were so unused to functioning with this kind of mental freedom.

"I am not sure this was a wise move on your part."

The Emperor, who had seemed so pleased with himself, looked suddenly wounded, as if Dalos had struck him.

"I fear that you may have caused more harm than help. I am not convinced that your people are ready to be thrown out into the vast unknown of a world without directives for their every activity! Think for a moment, Tyrantus. You have told them from morning 'til night, and well into their time of sleep, how to perform every single facet of life. They are accustomed to this guidance. Remove it suddenly and they will fall flat upon their faces—perhaps literally so, for you have supported them upon the rigid, iron control that you have instituted over the course of many thousands of years! You cannot suddenly remove the earth from beneath their feet and expect them to remain suspended in any reasonable state of consciousness! We have already given them so much to digest that I was concerned that their minds would be overtaxed; but now that you tell me you have added this additional element of confusion, I am troubled by your action. I fear that we have done them harm.

"Now it is that much more important for us to return and attempt to allay their fears, which must even now be rising to a fever pitch within them! Please, inform your controllers to reinstitute some guidance to these poor souls' lives."

Tyrantus had turned a ghostly shade of gray. He did not move.

"Tyrantus!" Dalos said again. "This is urgent! Please, please, for the sake of these poor lost souls, do something to rectify this mistake that you have made! Please."

Dalos' words prompted Tyrantus to rise in his own confused state and walk to his panel of communicating mechanisms. He keyed in a code as if in a state of catatonia, then pushed a button to suspend the message. "Dalos." He stopped for a moment. "Dalos, what shall I tell them?" He had lost all ability to think for himself. He was as rattled by the last few moments as were those who had been gathered in the auditorium.

"You see, Tyrantus, that even now you are experiencing the confusion that you have brought about in the minds of these people. They are now attached to you with strong psychic bonds and you are receiving the feedback of what you have done to them.

"Very well, I shall tell you precisely what to do until you regain your composure. Give them orders to rest now. I imagine that many have been already in a state of transcendency, because the Power projected to them was quite sufficient to cause them to leave their bodies in a state of sleep. But for those who are still floundering in shock and confusion due to this mishap, give some benign command that will relieve them of this pressure. This will give them the security to know that they are following your wishes and they are not in violation of any of your many laws. This will remove the fear they may now have for their very lives, for I know the strictness of your regime."

Tyrantus was further wounded by these truthful statements but he complied and gave the appropriate order, which traveled down the chain of command and reached those souls who were, indeed, struggling with their many fears. It had the intended effect: they lapsed into a state of contentment. Now they had something solid upon which to brace themselves. They knew what to do; they knew how to comply with orders. They were far more comfortable doing so than they had been for the past hour!

All was well, then, with these individuals. But even as they drifted into a sleep that was permeated with the Love radiations of the Higher Minds, there were those upon the planet of Tyron who were striking out at any who dared come into their presence. These were the Council members, livid with anger, venting their hostility upon anyone and anything that crossed their path. They would get their revenge, they vowed. They would make Tyrantus eat dirt! They would see him topple from his powerful position, and they would reign supreme!

Each one of them harbored such thoughts, cursing Tyrantus' very likeness, which stared back at them from the walls of nearly every corridor and room they passed through. Their hatred generated a fierce black cloud which threatened to burst into a raging storm at any moment.

29

Hope

THE CLOUDS OF IMPENDING war hung about the planets of the Orion Empire, brooding, waiting, threatening in their destructive potential. Dalos' very life was in danger, but he cared not. He knew of the strength of those who would oppose his mission long before he came to the Orion planets. He was determined to move things forward as quickly and efficiently as possible before his time was up.

Tyrantus was now struggling in a state of mental instability. When he was placed in a more receptive state of consciousness through Dalos' influence, he was being guided to institute groundbreaking changes in the daily activities of the Orion people. But when he lapsed into his old insecurities and fears, his habits of being in control, he was capable of undoing all that had been done. He was unpredictable, a danger to himself and to society.

To the best of his ability, Dalos strove to keep Tyrantus moving with a progressive intent to free the people from the shackles of his former applications of governmental influence. Thus far, all that had been accomplished were the several addresses to the public by Dalos and Tyrantus, appearing in person, and those broadcast speeches which had now been released to the larger populations of the Orion planets. However, these broadcast speeches were reduced in their effect by the tamperings of Tonar and his cohorts.

Tonar was on the brink of implementing his coup. He would use Dalos himself to promote his cause—he would insert endorsements for, not only the other Pleiadeans who were now recognized widely as elevated minds, teachers bearing great knowledge for the Orion people, but would include endorsements for himself, Tonar, support for his bid for the Emperorship. This, of course, would not take place until Tonar was certain of his timing and was prepared to act quickly in his follow-through, for he would not be able to keep such subversive statements from Tyrantus' attention. Tyrantus' "eyes" and "ears" extended too far throughout the Empire for Tonar to engage in such blatant treason without detection.

Shimlus was aware of Tonar's desires for power, but she felt confident that he could be swayed to her point of view, that he would be like putty in her hands as compared to the inaccessible nature of Tyrantus. Besides, Shimlus knew that Tyrantus and Dalos were now working together on their own plan for the change of the Orion Empire, and she had nothing to do with that particular plan; she had no position nor place in it; she had little knowledge of it; and she had not been consulted, nor had any of the Pleiadean entourage—although they could hardly be called that now. They now resided in separate locations upon the planet of Tyron and a few had already found homes upon other planets in the Empire, where they were given positions of great influence as teachers, eventually as leaders among the population.

Tyrantus was still unconcerned with their activities. The Emperor had all he could do to maintain his balance within the scenario in which he himself was now engaged. Dalos kept him busy with public appearances, and the two of them were now preparing to travel to other worlds in the Empire to spread their message of change.

Radik had contacted Tyrantus with the offer proposed by Linton, that they be designated as Dalos' personal escorts on these journeys to the outlying worlds, and that Dalos use his own ship for these traveling purposes. Tyrantus did not trust them. He refused this offer, and Dalos agreed.

Dalos would not leave the Emperor's side; he could not allow any such separation, for Dalos knew the threats abounding within the minds of the Council members. He was not so foolish as to believe that Radik and Linton were sincere in their desire to help with Tyrantus' plan. One look at their faces gave Dalos the full picture of their true intent. They desired power for themselves and they believed Dalos could supply this for them.

Yes, he could supply Power—but not of the nature they longed for! Although there was some small portion of their consciousness that was desirous of learning the truth of their lost lives as Angelic Beings. But their transformation would have to wait until the full restoration of the mind of Tyrantus. He was Dalos' priority. He carried the greatest influence over others. Therefore, since Dalos' mission had been circumscribed by limited abilities due to the loss of two hundred members of his expedition, he could only do that which he was capable of doing.

It was decided that they would travel on one of Tyrantus' own ships. The vessel was readied for their departure.

"Dalos, I sincerely hope that you know what you are doing! If we fail in this venture, then I have surely become the fool in my people's eyes."

"Tyrantus, rest your mind. We cannot fail. We bear the Light of a new understanding for all people of Orion. Truth heals. We shall become the healers of your people! This has always been your true inner desire, and yet you had allowed this natural, selfless motivation to become distorted into a personal, egotistical quest to dominate others and to feel yourself to be superior to them. We are not superior, Tyrantus, neither you nor I. We hold the same potential as every spark of life—but we do have knowledge that has been given to us that we can, in turn, share with others, and so we have a mandate to do so."

"When you speak, Dalos, your words weave a spell upon me. You have done so from the first moment I laid eyes upon you. You were never my equal, Dalos. You have been my superior all along!"

"Not superior, Tyrantus, but perhaps more wise in my usage of the mental tools that I have been given. But you shall learn. You have come a very long way since our first meeting." Dalos smiled. "And you have far, far to go. But I am confident in your ability to persist. It shall not be easy, Tyrantus. You will face opposition at every turn, and no opposition stronger than that which resides within yourself! Surely you must know of this lower mind that would devour you in its insistence upon the rightness of your former actions."

"Yes, I am quite familiar and it does cause me some torment. But I am placing my trust in you, my friend. So far you have been a pure example of intelligent leadership. I shall study your actions closely and learn from them."

"Nothing you say could please me more than that, Tyrantus. That is how I can best serve, as an example of the words I speak. Words are meaningless unless backed by action."

Tyrantus nodded his agreement.

There were many among the Emperor's staff who were thoroughly confounded by the activities which had been taking place within their range of authority. All these orders from the Emperor himself that defied previously set standards of behavior! They could not understand his motivations. They had heard many things, that he was losing his mind, that his health was failing and his ability to rule had been weakened, that he was on the brink of death and should not be taken seriously. They were being given such information by the agents of the Council members. These carefully placed rumors were designed to weaken the superstructure that supported the Emperor's position, and they were having their effect upon his advisors.

He cared not. His only advisor now existed in the body of the man from the Pleiades. He was unconcerned about matters which had once obsessed him and driven him to institute more and more rigid controls upon those who worked most closely with him. Now they were left largely to their own devices to carry out their usual methods of keeping the machinery of Orion in operation. They would have continued indefinitely were it not for the subtle erosion of their duties by the implanted doubts manufactured by such as Tonar, Linton, Radik, Donquill, and others. These doubts were frequently accompanied by a positive word or two for these Council members. They were spreading such information throughout the planets in the hopes of gaining support for their own rulership when the time came.

It was Donquill's plan to raise sufficient armed forces to take the Emperor's position by a show of military strength. Linton and Radik were not yet defeated by Tyrantus' and Dalos' failure to support their scheme of gaining control over Dalos. They had already turned their minds to a new scheme, a more devious plan to attack Tyrantus' and Dalos' ship while it was in a vulnerable position during their journey from planet to planet. They would also use force to overtake the personages of these two individuals, and adding the factor of the weakened position of Tyrantus politically, they felt that they would easily accomplish their ends—which were to place one of themselves upon the seat of power. Thus far, they had neither addressed nor resolved the question of which one it would be. Each individually felt that he could easily subdue the other when the opportunity arose.

Tonar's scheme was slightly more complex. He was aware of the journeys of Dalos and Tyrantus to other planets in the Empire, but he knew that they could only be in one place at one time, while his broadcasts reached all worlds simultaneously. He, then, would have greater leverage than they in gaining the support of the people. He was now working more closely with Shimlus and her followers to develop their platform—the platform upon which they would all step into a position of power and influence. They believed that this could be easily accomplished due to the great popularity of the Pleiadeans with the people. If Shimlus gave her nod of support to Tonar, many, many would follow her lead. She would be given a specially developed position in the government of Orion, a newly created post for which she was eminently qualified. She would be the spiritual advisor for the entire Empire, and the others would serve as her assistants in this position. They would devise a new educational curriculum, just as Tyrantus and Dalos had already proposed—only Shimlus' curriculum would be vastly different from that of Dalos.

Her teachings now had little to do with the truth of life. They were much more involved in the outward, exterior enhancements of a physical dimension. They directed the minds of the people outside themselves, in a worshipful attitude—at least this is how these teachings were being incepted within the minds of the Orion people, for the words of Shimlus and her followers no longer carried the Power of an attunement to Higher Minds, who were far more capable of reaching through the smog of Orion propaganda and electronic controls to tap the true inner core of an individual's consciousness and reawaken the Intelligence residing therein.

Dalos' ability to touch the people in this way was being proven with each public address he made. Thus far, none of the Council had dared consider any public attacks upon his person, or the person of Tyrantus. Their fears still ran too deep for such overt actions. They felt frustrated by this restraint, yet they could not overcome their fear. Therefore, Dalos and Tyrantus were capable of carrying on, unimpeded by such subversive acts as these individuals might have devised. They spoke freely and shockingly to the people, who had been accustomed to total domination of their minds. Now Dalos was speaking of things which staggered them and Tyrantus was behaving like an entirely different man from the one they had known as Emperor!

They had many questions but feared to ask. Dalos expected their silent responses and he merely continued to speak to them in a most direct, personal manner. It was his compassionate nature that touched them most deeply. It was the Power of Love emanating from his very being that surrounded them with an enveloping energy, lifting their minds slightly, just enough for them to absorb fragments of Intelligence that could, if nurtured, develop into healthy, restored states of mind for the Orion people.

Once their tour of the Orion planets was completed, Tyrantus and Dalos planned to revise all educational curricula for these worlds, but this activity would not be undertaken until they had first made these contacts. Dalos believe this personal contact was crucial to the success of these changes. He knew that the people would be touched by a higher, healing frequency, so long as they were in his physical presence. That was why he incarnated in this physical, atomic anatomy. Then they would be more capable of understanding the energy principles of life which would be outlined for them in their studies. But first he must let them know that they were each individually important in the larger scheme of life!

This sense of self-esteem had been denied to them. It was replaced by a programmed response of total loyalty to the Empire, the belief that they were only as valuable as their work contributed to this strictly governed society. That was not true. As sparks of an Infinite Creator, they each carried an inner Light that was capable of growing to illuminate the lives of many others. This spark was their own intelligence which could be developed beyond all limitations. Even so, they were joined, linked with Higher Minds than their own, if they allowed themselves to recognize this fact and practice this method of inner questing for knowledge.

It was quite simple, Dalos explained to them. "Just as I now speak to you with the solitary voice of one man, but carrying the Intelligence of many more Advanced Minds which are now speaking through me, so can you develop this ability! You do not need to look outside yourself for answers to the many questions that life itself does raise! This is a revolutionary thought, I know. But it is nonetheless true. You are all equally qualified to receive and extend the Intelligence of great minds—minds of beings like yourselves who have traveled from life to life, through worlds such as your own, and gained great wisdom by their experiences, just as you are now doing. They are your Elder Brothers; they are compassionate Beings who have dedicated themselves to lending their Intelligence to those such as yourselves who now struggle to learn on physical planets."

Very few understood this concept, but they *felt* the hope that it held for them. None of those addressed in this way by Dalos were unaffected! They all sensed a feeling of liveliness, eagerness, and freshness, which was unusual. They had lived for so long in their routine patterns of expression that these words promised a way of life that was just beyond the periphery of their understanding, and yet, inwardly, they were accepting of Dalos' descriptions. That is because in each soul resides knowledge of Truth, and it is instantly recognizable when heard. It cannot be denied.

Dalos and Tyrantus had reached the third planet on their itinerary when Tonar's technicians made their breakthrough.

"I believe, sir, that we can now accomplish your desires," the lead man said to Tonar. "We have developed a method by which we can reconstruct the features of Dalos and manipulate them to our own specifications. There is no way to detect the difference between this recreated imagery and the original. That was the imperfection we have been striving to eliminate and now I believe you will be quite satisfied with our results."

Tonar grinned from ear to ear. He quickly escorted the technician from his control room and directed him back to the laboratory. "Bring me a sample immediately."

"Yessir," the man responded.

Tonar gleefully returned to his console and made contact with Shimlus. "Shimlus, my dear, I have something to show you. I think that you will be very, very pleased. I shall be waiting for you in my private quarters."

By the time she arrived, the sample imagery was already installed for Tonar's demonstration. Shimlus settled into a comfortable seat, draping her long, flowing skirts gracefully about her slender legs.

"Well, Tonar, I am ready. What have you now that we can use for our contacts with the people?"

"Something that you did not suspect was possible; but we have been working on this for many weeks now." He pressed a control switch.

Immediately, Dalos' face lighted the room. He was describing his former Pleiadean brothers as traitors to his cause, in no uncertain terms.

Shimlus turned fiery red. "What is the meaning of this?" She threw a fierce glance at Tonar. "Have you brought me here to insult me?"

"Watch," Tonar directed.

The insults to Shimlus and her followers were not Dalos' original words but those that had been recreated at Tonar's request in the laboratory. They were extremely vicious, which was not Dalos' way. Yet Shimlus believed them to have been Dalos' own words. That was Tonar's first test. If Shimlus had been fooled, then he could fool anyone!

Now, as they watched, Dalos' face changed to a more peaceful countenance. He began to describe Tonar in glowing terms, as a "fine man, a man who is a natural leader," and whose activities on the Council should be looked to with great admiration by the people of Orion.

Now Shimlus' suspicion was jogged. She stood, as if to touch this suspended image. "How—?"

"Yes, how?" Tonar repeated. "That is the question, isn't it?"

"These cannot be Dalos' own words!"

"No, they can't, can they?" Tonar grinned. "But they do appear to be so—do they not?" He was quite pleased with himself.

"Do you mean ...?"

"Yes, we fabricated every single word—even those directed toward you, dear lady. You yourself believed them to be genuine, did you not?"

She was furious. She had been put through a terrible series of reactions. Tonar had had his fun at her expense; silently, she vowed revenge, but outwardly she feigned her admiration for his technology.

"Well, Tonar, you have certainly caught me by surprise. I did not know you were so capable. We can use this to correct Dalos' misstatements. We can help him by readjusting his speeches to conform with our own. He does not even need to know of this, does he? You are capable of doing this without his assistance, I assume, for I know of no other way for you to have accomplished this."

"That, of course, is its great value. Of course he knew nothing of this. Neither does Tyrantus. No one except my closest associates knows of this capability. It has never before been accomplished! There were always subtle indications which gave evidence of this tampering. But now we have refined the process to thoroughly duplicate the image of any individual, and to use certain techniques to precisely duplicate the formation of words, sounds, vowels, so that entire speeches can be fabricated in this manner.

"Can you imagine, Shimlus, what speeches we might present from the mouth of Tyrantus himself? We shall have Dalos speaking on your behalf very soon, on all planets in the Empire, and when we are prepared to make our move, we will add Tyrantus himself to this display. He will never know what hit him!"

Shimlus sat back down again, quiet in her thoughts. She was a little stunned by the opportunity which had just been laid at her feet. Could it be true? Could all this be successfully carried out, with no one the wiser? She must carefully decide who among her own companions she would let in on this particular plan. Not all would agree, she felt. There were still those reluctant to take any opposing action to counteract Dalos' slanderous references to their very selves. She could not understand this, but she could not convince them that his mind had lost its true clarity.

"Tonar, I must return to my private rooms to give this deep thought. You understand the importance of the actions we are about to take."

"More than you, my dear," he responded.

"Perhaps, perhaps not. But in any case, I must carefully select those who shall know of our activities. This I know you understand, and this will require some thought on my part. One slip and we are done for!"

"That is true, Shimlus. Take all the time you require, for I know you are as eager as I, and I know that you recognize our need for expediency. Tyrantus and Dalos have now circumscribed three planets in the Empire—four, including Tyron. They are being welcomed by the people who, I am told, are left with their own lives in their own hands! Tyrantus has completely lost his mind in allowing Dalos to spread such foolishness, but he is thoroughly taken in by your former leader. He does not realize that he is standing mid-span on a rope bridge and, with his own hands, cutting the supports at either end. Soon enough, he will recognize his failing—but not soon enough to prevent his fall!" Tonar laughed.

Shimlus said nothing. She rose to extend her hand to Tonar, who placed a kiss thereupon and watched her depart in a flurry of chiffon.

He did not know how far he would continue their association, but for now she was most valuable. There were others among her entourage who could serve him nearly as well, if she proved too troublesome. He had already been grooming them to step into her position if need be. They were his security. She was unaware of his private contacts with these individuals. Tonar knew that Shimlus would highly disapprove of his close personal association with them and they, likewise, kept their silence. They did not fully understand his intentions in cultivating their closer association; they were merely thriving upon his attention and flattery.

These individuals would not know of his plans to alter the speeches of Dalos and Tyrantus—*not for now,* he decided, *not unless that becomes necessary, not unless Shimlus herself includes them in this plan. That would be most interesting,* he thought, *most interesting.*

Linton was preparing plans to depart from Tyron in his private warship. He was torn as to whether he would include Radik on this venture or not. He knew that this action must be taken swiftly if it was to be successful. He was not convinced of Radik's loyalty, even to that point of their mutual desire to accomplish the same end that had originally bound them in a tentative alliance. Now that they were preparing for a more aggressive approach, he felt less inclined to work with Radik, and yet realized that if he made an enemy of this individual it would be but one more battle he would need to fight—one he felt confident he could win, but nevertheless a bothersome expenditure of energy and manpower.

Radik was attempting to devise his own plan for the overthrow of Tyrantus' regime. He could not, despite hours of tactical calculations, come up with a reasonable plan of attack. He and Linton had already discussed the idea which Linton was now implementing. He knew that it was but a matter of time before his arch rival proceeded, with or without him.

I must include myself in this plan, Radik decided. *I must convince Linton that he requires my support!*

Linton had reached nearly the same conclusion but he hesitated. *He will be a difficult partner. He is too explosive in his responses. I do not trust him in battle; I think he reacts too harshly and quickly. I shall keep him occupied with some harmless position and thereby keep him out of my way. Then I shall deal with him at a time when it is more appropriate.*

So their pact was sealed—although there were many gaps in their bond that should have been filled with mutual trust. This weakened them both, but they were ignorant of the damage they had done to their own desires for victory.

Dalos was now speaking freely to the Orion people—it was the sole purpose for which he was living!

He was gratified and joyous at this development. He did not allow himself thoughts of impending doom, although he was keenly aware of the forces gathering in opposition. Wherever a great Light shines, clouds gather to obscure its warming rays. But Dalos was unconcerned. He was fulfilling his mission.

Most importantly, the people were being given the first sequence in the combination that would unlock their minds. They were now living with some hope for a brighter future—it was the first they had known for thousands of years, and on some planets, hundreds of thousands of years! They had never seen a Being such as Dalos, but he triggered long-distant psychic memories of their own originating Source of life. He was an embodiment of Infinite Creative Intelligence—one look at his face was sufficient to fill them with an indefinable awareness of their own potential. He signified the higher accomplishments of a human being whose spirit was illuminated by a greater Intelligence.

In Dalos' countenance, they found the missing element that had turned their lives to drudgery by its very lack. Such Love they had never known!

30

To Find a Way...

WITH THE WAR DRUMS beating their distant tremor, Dalos and Tyrantus sped from planet to planet, leaving in their wake the first carpeting of new consciousness to bloom on these worlds for many thousands of years. It was just a tiny green shoot of curiosity poking through the darkened soil of mandated lifestyles, but it was an important, tender beginning. If his mission should be cut short at that moment, then Dalos would find contentment in all that he had accomplished until then. He was very pleased with the changes in Tyrantus, and equally appreciative of this opportunity to reach so many people.

He had never seen so much uniformity before. He was shocked, as they visited world after world, to see how the Orion forces had obliterated all variety and reinstated a uniform code of living that was being strictly enforced and followed by the people, who had little or no choice. Those who disobeyed or who attempted some insurrection were quickly rounded up and brought by the hundreds into the treatment rooms. Brainwashing techniques were applied to eliminate all vitality from their minds and to recondition them to function in the robotic fashion that had been instigated among the larger population of each planet.

Of course, this process did take some period of time for each world, and many methods were used as the Orion forces made their way across the surface of each individual planet. But those now visited by Dalos and

Tyrantus in their tour of the Empire were those worlds that had been long a part of this system.

With each public address, Tyrantus was becoming more confident, Dalos noted. He was feeling the mental freedom that these actions would ultimately bring him, although this was a very, very slight step forward for the Emperor. He had an incredible amount of rectification to undertake within his own consciousness before his mind would be fully restored. Still, it was a beginning, and that was extremely significant.

My dear, beloved Brothers of Light, Dalos said inwardly to those who were always standing by. *I am very grateful to you for your unfailing guidance. You have seen me through much pain and many dim hours when I thought my mission here had been thoroughly foiled by the negative forces—but this was not so! You did not allow me to succumb completely to any form of despair. Now I know that the impossible can be accomplished, and I shall never rest until I have done so!*

We understand, dear one, his beloved polarity responded. *We feel as you do, for we are not separate.*

No, we are not, Dalos agreed, *and of that I am extremely glad! But what of these darker minds who are now applying all their energies to stop our mission to the earth planets? Are they a serious threat to our progress?*

Dear one, we would not cause you any undue alarm, but be advised that the negative forces are strong, and firmly entrenched within the consciousness of these individuals. We are speaking of the Orion Council members who are now preparing their counterattack upon Tyrantus' new position. Their lives seem threatened, and they will fight to the death to resist any alteration in their present way of conducting life for others. This power means all to them. But your words have seeped into the deeper reaches of their minds. They will have their effect, but we cannot predict at what point this re-awakening shall occur. All we can do is to carry on in our efforts to contact as many souls as possible with this healing, radiating Force of Infinite Intelligence.

Yes, of course. I know that is true, and so I shall continue to place my full consciousness on this endeavor. Thank you, dear, dear Brothers for your constant aid and support and, of course, for your Love, which I do feel bathing me in the warm sunlight of your Consciousness! May I add my own to that Light radiation?

And so it is done, Michiel replied. *And so we appreciate your extension unto us!*

These quiet times of inner contact that sustained Dalos whilst living in his physical anatomy were examples of that consciousness which he was striving to bring to the awareness of the Orion peoples, a consciousness that is aware of its many Brothers, particularly those who have developed a more refined ability to use their minds and can, thereby, lend great Intelligence if one quests inwardly of this illumined source. It is through the frequency of one's thoughts that this contact is made. Merely the knowledge that such potential exists and the attempt to derive wisdom from this inner link with the very Fountainhead of Life would bring success to them, each one.

Dalos had explained this to Tyrantus, and he seemed as if he were beginning to understand. He described to Dalos his experiences of inner illumination when he was speaking to the people.

"Is this what you are referring to, Dalos, this inner warmth and, truly, an ability to speak words that I never thought I would speak?"

"Yes, Tyrantus, this is precisely the process of making one's higher attunement. It does feel very natural, as if you are speaking your own thoughts and yet, as you yourself have identified, they carry a Power much greater than your own solitary mental development. That is how my messages to your people are bringing to them a healing Force which shall work great miracles upon your worlds, Tyrantus—although they are not really miracles when one understands the scientific process in action. In time, Tyrantus, all of your people shall understand. I promise you this."

"Dalos, I have been giving some thought to these educational changes that we shall be instituting. Do you not feel that we should return to Tyron and begin now to develop this curriculum? The people to whom we have spoken seem somewhat confused by our statements. Perhaps if we began these classes now this would alleviate their distress."

"Yes, you may be right, but I am eager to continue to contact as many individuals as we can before your enemies catch up with us! There will be sufficient time to follow through once we have completed our journeys. Do not be overanxious. Your eagerness is admirable, and yet we must be wise and patient in our actions. We must carefully consider our course and follow to the letter that which seems, to our inner senses, most beneficial to the whole."

"I shall defer then to your guidance, Dalos, for I do not trust my inner senses. They have led me astray, and I am now grateful that I have, as my friend, one who never seems to give himself a thought but is always thinking of a new way to help others."

Dalos was deeply touched by these words, for he knew they had not come easily to Tyrantus. They were evidence of the healing, the change that was taking place within this man who had become a tyrant to trillions of souls. If he could be so changed, then Dalos knew that there was hope for all those who had been his victims!

They were traveling to a world called Stytonn, in the fourth sector of Orion. Their ship cut a solitary swath through space. It was unescorted, as Tyrantus' private craft was equipped with the latest Orion technological defense developments and they were, of course, in friendly territory; that is, this sector of the Empire was strictly patrolled and guarded by Orion warships. They believed themselves to be in no danger whatsoever.

It was through their very nature as "friendly forces" that Linton and Radik slipped through these defense systems. They were able to identify themselves directly to all commanding officers in this sector and were not questioned about their presence—none dared to question these two Council members. It was assumed that they were speeding to an important rendezvous with Tyrantus' ship. This rendezvous, however, was decidedly not friendly.

Linton's ship was also equipped with the latest weaponry and if attacked by Tyrantus, could withstand any weapons that were deployed. They would be, militarily, at a standoff, and Linton's plan was to hold Tyrantus and Dalos captive by this very fact. Either of the ships which would attempt a departure would then become vulnerable, by the very nature of the design of these weapons and defense shields.

But Linton's first plan was to attempt a friendly hailing of Tyrantus' vessel and a request to board. He, with his accompanying officers, would then take Tyrantus and Dalos captive, while Radik remained behind to command Linton's vessel.

Tyrantus was alerted to the presence of this specially designated ship by his first officer. He was instantly disturbed by this development. He sensed that something was afoot.

"Dalos." He turned to the Pleiadean. "We are now in the presence of my enemies! Now is the time for your intelligence to guide. What do you recommend?"

Dalos immediately knew that they were at a disadvantage. He could not condone the use of massive weaponry but his mission was at stake. He closed his eyes for a brief second, then spoke, slowly and clearly.

"We must speak to them personally. Ask Linton to make his presence on your ship, with Radik. I believe that I can reach these two individuals. I have already had some success with them. It is but a matter of turning the bias of their consciousness, Tyrantus, just as we have accomplished with you. I see no other alternative. We must exhaust all peaceful means of resolving this situation before we resort to any destructive tactics. That is my best advice to you."

The Emperor questioned Dalos' decision but he did not speak. He was uncomfortable with such non-violent techniques. If he were on his own, he would immediately call for backup support and disintegrate Linton's ship without waiting for questions or answers. He would not take any chance. But Tyrantus was not the man he had been just a few weeks or even hours ago. He had opened himself to Dalos' influence and this time he decided to quell his personal fears of death. Dalos had worked seeming miracles before; perhaps he would be successful.

"Linton," Tyrantus responded to the Council member's contact, "it is your Emperor, Tyrantus, who speaks to you. Please state your business with me."

"Yes, Emperor. I come bearing an important message from Tyron. This highly classified information could not be entrusted to any other than personal, face-to-face communication. I submit my request to board your ship."

"Your request shall be granted, Linton, under this condition: that you bring Radik with you and leave your armed guards behind."

Linton hesitated a moment. "Very well, Emperor." He signed off with a quick cessation of their audiovisual communication.

"Well," Tyrantus said, "he took that very smoothly. Now we shall see what they are about. But Dalos, I would not trust them for an instant if it were not for your persuasive ability!"

"Do not fear, Tyrantus. We must not fear. Fear is our downfall if we allow it to overtake our minds."

"So I have always believed," Tyrantus said, but he did not add that he had never been capable of conquering the many forms of fear and insecurity which constantly plagued his true, concealed thoughts. It is quite a different matter to conceal one's fear than to actually overcome and eliminate that emotion, in all its infinite varieties!

Word came that Linton and Radik were approaching the control center of Tyrantus' ship. "Very well," he responded. "Allow them entrance."

The two Council members appeared in the small chamber.

"State your business," Tyrantus said bluntly. "We have important work to carry out."

"Yes," Linton said. "We understand. But Emperor, I must request a private meeting with you. What I have to say is not for the ears of anyone other than yourself."

Dalos stepped forward. "Linton," he said, "I do not pose any threat to you or your Emperor. We have been closely aligned in our activities here. I feel that you can speak freely in my presence."

Linton shot Dalos a withering glance—but it was he who withered at the sight of this man. Dalos' eyes projected a Light that was always a shock to one who was not accustomed to the higher-frequency Intelligence that gleamed through these windows unto the true Mind of Uriel.

Radik had already taken his position some three feet from the side of Dalos. It was the plan of these two—which had been quickly altered by Tyrantus' orders that they both appear—to separate Tyrantus and Dalos and thereby use force to hold them each in captivity, and use the threat of their deaths to subdue the forces of Tyrantus' crew. But first they must convince Tyrantus and Dalos to acquiesce to this separation.

"Linton," Dalos said, "I know that you are not pleased with the changes we are proposing." Dalos was using the most direct approach to cut through any illusion or façade and to speak directly to the heart of the subject. "I trust that you are not attempting some subversive activity here, for you shall fail to halt the progress that has already been set in motion!"

Linton took a deep breath through clenched teeth but said nothing.

"Yes, I see by your face," Dalos continued, "that you are quite angry at the thought of losing your position of power. But as I told you previously, you all have the same opportunity to restore your status in the eyes of the Infinite, to become true leaders of your people! To give them the lives that you have been taking from them!"

Now Radik could not be still. He raised a hand to strike Dalos. Instantly, Tyrantus reacted in a defensive move and Linton seized him in a firm hold about his throat while Radik took hold of Dalos.

Dalos had not flinched nor moved to defend himself. He recognized the futility of any such action and responded as he would to any ferocious animal that would throw him about its cage. He went limp, relaxing in Radik's grip so as not to cause himself further pain by resistance.

Tyrantus, on the other hand, was nearly snarling with anger and thrashing about with attempts to overpower Linton's strong hold upon him. But it was a hopeless attempt. Tyrantus had been physically weakened by his long illness and he was no longer the picture of vitality that he had once been. Linton was tall and muscular, and if he had failed, Radik would certainly have come to his aid.

"Tyrantus," Dalos said, "do not fight these madmen. They have but one thought in their minds and we are not in a position to change them at this moment."

Tyrantus cursed and spat. "You fiends! You shall die for this!"

"Be that as it may, Emperor, but we are now *your* commanders," Radik said. He shoved Dalos toward the door. "Now, Pleiadean, you will see how efficient we are! Now you will have some real leaders to contend with!"

The instant they passed through the opening, Tyrantus' crew froze in shock.

"Do not move," Linton shouted to them, "else he dies!"

"They both die!" Radik added.

Obediently, the guards backed away.

"We are taking control of this ship and we order you to return to Tyron." Linton threw Tyrantus into a seat.

Tyrantus had not said a word to his crew. He simply glared at a vacant space before him. The Emperor had never been humiliated in this fashion.

Dalos' mind was turning rapidly to evaluate this situation as it unfolded. He was looking for some alternative to the end he foresaw for this unfortunate incident, but thus far, he could determine no course of action other than to wait and cooperate.

The warship crew was in shock. Nothing of this nature had ever presented itself to their highly trained minds. They were trained in all disciplines of military tactics but they were unprepared to deal with circumstances that were unexpected. Linton and Radik had helped to design their training; they knew this about the Orion forces; they knew all their strengths and weaknesses.

Linton conveyed an order to his own ship to return as if he himself were still aboard, and the ship vanished, making its way back to Tyron.

"Now, Emperor, we shall take our own tour. We will contact the officials on Stytonn to inform them that you have made a change in your plans." He twisted the Emperor's arm behind his back. He now had a weapon placed firmly at the throat of the Emperor, and Radik was securing Dalos to a seat with steel restraints.

"I will never do as you say," Tyrantus said in a low, even voice.

"You shall, if you wish to live."

"I shall not!"

"Emperor, do you not realize that your life is dwindling in its value? One slash of a sharp blade and these men are in my command! They know the result of their failure to follow my orders. I suggest that you observe these same rules of military conduct. I am obviously the superior man here."

Tyrantus spat again.

"Yes, it is quite clear, so do as I say."

The Emperor did not move or speak.

"Tyrantus," Dalos called from across the navigational communications room in which they were now being held captive. “Do as Linton asks. It can only do us both harm if we do not cooperate.”

Tyrantus looked at Dalos and quickly looked away. He felt as if the Pleiadean had let him down somehow.

“Tyrantus please, do as they ask. We are in no position to fight. Your life does have meaning—remember that, Tyrantus. Your life has great meaning to many, many souls! Do not leave them without doing all you can to help them! Have you forgotten everything we have discussed—”

“Be silent!” Radik ordered and struck Dalos across the face. Dalos began to bleed from the corners of his mouth.

“Stop it, you vermin!” Tyrantus shouted. “Leave him alone!”

“You see, Emperor, how it is. We are in control here. So, will you give your message to Stytonn? Or shall I take the appropriate steps? Perhaps it is Dalos’ life that you value more than your own.”

“You shall rot!” Tyrantus vowed, but he jerked his head toward the communications controls. “Make your contact. I shall speak.”

“And do so with a pleasant ‘Good morning,’ Emperor.” Linton smiled as he entered the proper frequency.

There appeared upon the screen a man in military garb. “Yes, Emperor, we are at your service.”

Linton had programmed the communication so that the Emperor’s image would not be visible but his voice would be heard.

“We have a change in plans,” Tyrantus said abruptly. “You will not see us upon your planet at this time.” That was all he said, and indicated to Linton to end the communication.

Linton did so, as the man on the other end was voicing his respect and regrets for the cancellation. “Not very kind, Emperor, but sufficient.”

Throughout these events, the crew members present had been frozen with fear. None had made any move to defend their Emperor or Dalos. They were confounded by conflicting rules of conduct, and Linton and Radik had engineered this confusion. Their orders were to follow a chain of command, and second in command beyond the Emperor was any member of the Orion Council. They also feared for their lives, for it was clear that Linton and Radik were in control and the crew did not have upon their persons the necessary weapons to defend themselves. Such internal attacks were not expected from these visiting dignitaries!

Dalos had not spoken since the blow he had taken at the hands of Radik. Blood now covered the lower half of his chin and dripped onto his garment.

"Are you all right?" Tyrantus inquired.

"Yes, Emperor."

"Silence!" Radik barked. "We have heard enough from the two of you. Linton, can we proceed?"

"Yes." He ordered the first officer to program their course for Tyrantus' headquarters on Tyron.

"You will never be successful, Linton. They will not follow your commands once you leave this ship!"

"Perhaps, Emperor. But perhaps it is too late for you to be concerned about that."

The element of surprise had given Linton and Radik an advantage that they would not have enjoyed in any other circumstance. This was an ambassadorial trip, a journey undertaken, not in a warring state of mind, but as a political venture. Tyrantus' ship was fully armed, yet his officers were unprepared for battle. Certainly they had been trained, but they were lounging in a relaxed state as Linton and Radik arrived. No alert had been given. When these two burst from the control center into the communications chamber with their leader in captivity, the officers were stunned, not only by this shocking scene but by the knowledge of their own failure and incompetence! They realized immediately that if Tyrantus were released, he would order their deaths, for they had failed to protect their Emperor! That is why the crew was so willing to adapt to its new commanders and fearful of Tyrantus' release.

The Emperor knew this, of course, and he made no attempt to communicate with them. He knew that for now he had lost the battle, and he was as crushed by his own failure as were these men who had once served him. He could not allow this to be seen, of course, and he gave no outward indication of his inner ragings of thought, but Dalos knew—and Dalos' greatest concern was for Tyrantus' state of consciousness, not for his own personal welfare or safety.

As Dalos sat confined by Radik, who had now ordered the remaining crew members into a secured section of the ship, he thought of the consequences of this development. They were not good. Tyrantus was a key to opening the lock upon the minds of the Orion people. These two Council members, Linton and Radik, were not sufficiently prepared nor capable, nor in any state of mind to serve as Tyrantus had been serving, to give Dalos an open forum with the people. He realized that he could do nothing now but wait until circumstances changed. Wherever they ended up once they returned to Tyron, Dalos must endeavor to remain close to Tyrantus so that he might keep his spirits up and thus keep him alive. Dalos knew, as did all present, that there was but one option for any Orion commander who had failed in his duties, and he knew that even now, Tyrantus was bemoaning his own failure.

There was no way that Dalos could speak to the Emperor so long as Linton and Radik remained in the room. Perhaps they would leave them alone once they felt secure. But that was not to be.

"Radik," Linton ordered, "you take the helm of this ship and I shall remain with our friends here—and take these gawking idiots with you! They are bothering me."

Radik bristled at such orders from Linton. He always had considered himself to be equal. But he would not confront Linton in the presence of others. He glared at his partner and left the room.

"You see, Emperor, how quickly change does occur. As I recall, it was you yourself who said that this Empire is long overdue for change. Well, if you live long enough, which I doubt, you shall see what change can bring!"

"Linton," Dalos said, "I do hope that we will have some opportunity to speak."

"I have nothing to say to you," Linton growled at the Pleiadean. Truly he had many questions that he longed to ask of Dalos but he was fearful of this man.

He had planned to sequester Dalos in some location so that he would have sole access to the Pleiadean but he had not yet devised how that would occur. This fear that rose within him and caused him to desire to be in another room, apart from Dalos' penetrating stare, was quite a shock to Linton. He had not counted upon this reaction and until he could gain control of it, his plan—born of gut response—was to ignore the Pleiadean.

But Dalos was not going to allow Linton to ignore him—not so long as he had any voice left to speak! "Linton, do you know what you have done?"

"I said I have nothing to say to you! And I would advise you to keep your silence, else I will have Radik return to deal with you!"

"Are you fearful to deal with me yourself?"

"You are an astonishing man, but I have no fear of you," Linton lied. "You do not appear at this moment to be in control of anything, do you? So I do, with all respect, suggest that you refrain from any further statements."

"Dalos," Tyrantus said, "please. Now I ask you to not anger him. He is quite capable of killing us both."

"Yes, Tyrantus, I know you are right. An animal must kill or be killed. That is the mentality bred among your Council."

"I see that you are a stubborn man, Dalos," Linton said. "Well, we shall determine how stubborn you are. Enjoy your journey," he said to them both and left the room abruptly. It was sealed with a security device which prevented their escape, even if they had managed to break free of their restraints, which were now firmly placed around both Dalos and Tyrantus.

"I do not have any words to say, Dalos; do not even speak to me. I am beyond speaking. I am beyond caring." Tyrantus' chin fell to his chest.

"Tyrantus!" Dalos said sharply. "You surprise me! I thought you were stronger than that. I thought you were fearless! But I see that that is another of your lies."

"Do not torment me, Dalos. Nothing you say can do further harm. I am a dead man, can't you see that? There is no alternative for me."

"I will not listen to such drivel, Tyrantus! Very well, keep your silence if you wish, but I prefer to keep my wits about me! I shall not lose hope—no, there is always something that can be done, whatever situation presents itself.

"*Tyrantus, do not forget all that you have learned.* Do not forget that inner, golden key that unlocks the door of Infinity for you! *No one* can take it from you! No one can seize it! No one can deny you this inner access—*remember that, Tyrantus! Remember that always.*"

Tyrantus looked at Dalos with a pained and tired expression. "You are a phenomenon, Dalos. I shall never, never understand you."

"Do not try to understand me, Tyrantus; it is yourself that you must understand!"

"Yes, yes, my sad and sorry self. Well, I understand all too well this turn of events. It is as I had feared. No, Dalos, I am sorry that your plans did not develop in the way you had hoped. My enemies are too many. They are too strong …"

His voice trailed off in weakness. Dalos feared that he was losing consciousness but the Emperor simply sat and stared ahead.

Dalos said no more. He rested his own head as comfortably as possible. The bleeding from his mouth had stopped and he felt no pain, for his thoughts were far distant from his physical anatomy. His thoughts were with his Brothers of Light. His mind was illumined with all-knowing, all-seeing, penetrating, radiating Intelligence. If there was a way to turn the tide, Dalos would find it.

31

Captivity

Dalos awoke from his sleep with a start. He had drifted off and was shocked for a moment to find himself still restrained in the communications room of Tyrantus' private warship. Remembering all that had transpired, he looked for the Emperor and found him with his head fallen over in sleep as well.

That is good, for there is little else we can do while we await our arrival on Tyron.

He glanced about the chamber. They were confined in the midst of the very room that might have served as their link to those who could come to their rescue, but now Dalos realized that very few among Tyrantus' forces could be fully trusted. He had seen how quickly the ship's crew had turned on the Emperor in their fear and desire to maintain their physical lives. If only they were able to loosen these restraints, they might contact someone who could be of assistance—but who would that be? Which of the Council members would speed to Tyrantus' support? And if they did so, how long would their loyalty last? Only until Linton and Radik were defeated, no doubt, and then their efforts would turn to the glorification of their own positions in the government. All desired to be rid of Tyrantus now; all would as soon see him die, and Dalos as well, as to reinstate him in his position as supreme ruler of Orion.

No, Dalos realized, there was only one source of help to which they could turn, and those very Minds were already oscillating their Intelligence to both Dalos and Tyrantus. If Tyrantus could remain open; that is, if he could keep his consciousness uplifted slightly from the despair which was now pulling at the lower reaches of his mind, then he could serve them both in a fuller fashion to take every opportunity that might present itself to extricate them from this situation. For now, Dalos was glad the Emperor was lost in sleep. Perhaps he was not lost at all; perhaps he was seated at the feet of the Master Teachers who were imbuing his energy self with a greater strength of purpose!

That had been Dalos' own experience, of course. While he slept, the mind did not rest. It was free to travel the universe—free to see clearly the circumstances which had befallen them, and when Dalos returned to his conscious mind, he felt as if he had traveled a great distance. Yet truly only a few moments' time had elapsed. He wondered how long it would be before they reached the surface of Tyron, but his question was answered as Radik broke through the door.

"Well, I see that you have not managed to escape your captivity," the Councilman laughed, knowing full well that such escape was impossible, for these restraints had been designed to be impenetrable. No one had ever escaped from this configuration of steel! "You will be most happy to know that we are making our approach to Tyron. Emperor," he roughly jostled Tyrantus, whose eyes had opened at the sound of the opening doorway. "Your services will be required."

Tyrantus glared at Radik.

"Oh, no, of course we do not expect you to willingly participate, but we do have means of persuasion. Now, Dalos, you shall serve a greater purpose." Radik strode toward the Pleiadean.

"Stop!" Tyrantus said. "Do not lay a hand on him! I will comply with all your—" He stopped, unable to form the word.

"All my commands? How very wonderful to hear you agree, and to recognize your true position now!"

Tyrantus said nothing. He would not give Radik the satisfaction of hearing anything further from his lips—only that which was necessary to keep Dalos from harm.

Linton had entered the chamber, giving Radik a sternly disapproving look when he realized his cohort's tactics. "Emperor," he said, "we do not wish to harm you, for you are going to serve us well in a very short period of time. We need you in top condition. Now, if you will please inform your controllers that your vessel approaches."

The proper codes were entered and Tyrantus spoke the appropriate commands. Their access to the planet's atmosphere was cleared and an escort of ships appeared to meet the Emperor's own. It was a courtesy required by the importance of his position. No one questioned the reasons for the Emperor's unexpected return. As usual, no one dared question any of the Emperor's activities. But much discussion was carried out behind the scenes, so to speak.

Tonar was immediately alerted to this radical change in the Emperor's plans. He was alarmed, and knew that something was amiss. He ordered his agents to stand by and to report to him every activity of the Emperor.

Donquill was not on Tyron at that moment, so news took some time to travel to his outlying post, where he was making ready to attack the Emperor's headquarters and to take control by force. He was aware of Linton and Radik's departure from Tyron, but he had no idea yet of their capture of Tyrantus and Dalos.

As the ship glided into its home port, Linton arranged for a high-security transport vehicle to take the Emperor and Dalos to the Emperor's personal quarters. This, Linton knew, was the most carefully guarded, private location on the planet. Their activities therein would not be detected for quite some time, as the Emperor's personal privacy had been strictly created and was maintained by a cadre of specially trained guards. They were adept at watching but not observing, hearing but not listening. They forgot all that they saw or heard; this was their training, and that training included the routine electronic interference with their memory. Their minds were basically "erased" at the conclusion of each work shift. They were thoroughly trained to disregard whatever they witnessed, and to never, under any circumstances, question what they saw. This special force had not been infiltrated by the spies of the Council members. This had, of course, been attempted but was unsuccessful. Tyrantus' screening techniques had thus far detected every such spy who appeared among the ranks of these special agents. That individual lost their life immediately.

So Linton (through Tyrantus) had ordered this transport vehicle to be manned by these special security forces. He and Radik, with Dalos and Tyrantus in tow, boarded and set the course for Tyrantus' private chambers.

Dalos looked at them both in turn. "Now that you have us in your power," he inquired, "what will you do? How do you plan to expose yourselves to the public as the new rulers of Orion? Will you both share this position—or will you murder one another in the dead of night? Whoever is quicker, I suppose, shall be the ultimate victor."

"Shut up!" Radik snapped. "We do not need your blabberings."

But Dalos had struck a painful note. They both knew that what he said was quite likely true, and in their haste to accomplish their takeover, they had not satisfactorily resolved this question. Neither of them cared to broach the subject. They had simply done, and now they were continuing to do, without thought and with planning only in the short term.

Linton's main desire was to probe the mind of Dalos, but not in this way, in this free, one-on-one conversation. He had arranged for special treatment centers for Dalos. They were, in effect, torture rooms. The techniques used by Tyrantus' surgeons were nothing compared to that which was planned for Dalos by Linton's minions. His main purpose was to elicit technical information to finally, for himself, resolve the mechanics of Dalos' starship.

He had also made tentative arrangements to eliminate Radik. His assassination would be swift. But first they must take care of this question of Emperorship. For the present, Linton would need to continue all activities as if Tyrantus were still in full power. He did not wish to alert the other Council members to the fact that they had been successful in capturing Dalos and Tyrantus. He did not want to bring down their wrath until the situation had been stabilized.

But Radik was fearful that something might go wrong, that somehow Tyrantus and Dalos would escape their clutches and turn upon them with great and, Radik felt, deserved vengeance.

Linton attempted to quell Radik's fears. They had now sequestered Dalos and Tyrantus in a small anteroom and had departed to Tyrantus' central control facility for their private conversation. "You must keep control of your emotions, Radik; they do not become you."

"And what of yourself?" Radik boomed. "You have certainly not behaved as the calm scientist you pretend to be!"

"Never mind me. We are now concerned with one fact alone: we must not allow word of our actions to leak out to the public, or the Council at large! Are you certain that our arrival here has gone smoothly, that no one suspects?"

"Of that I am sure," Radik responded. "The first guard shift has been deprogramed and the second shift is now in place. I have made certain that this operational technique is in full force and will continue in its routine deployment. Eventually, however, we will need to issue some statement to Tyrantus' close advisors to explain his sudden return to Tyron. They are aware of his return, but they do not have any suspicion of our presence here, in his quarters. They would not dare breach his privacy!"

"That is good," Linton said. "We must think, Radik. We must continue to persuade Tyrantus to cooperate. So far the Pleiadean is falling into our hands. It is he who has convinced Tyrantus to stop any resistance. He is a very wise and brave man, Radik. We must regard him with the utmost caution. I suggest that you keep a special eye on Dalos, for I do not trust that he is as pliant as Tyrantus has suddenly become. He is much more than he indicates on the surface."

"I agree. Shall we separate them into different quarters?"

"Yes." Linton thought for a moment. "That would be to our advantage, I believe. On the other hand, it is the threat to Dalos' life that caused Tyrantus to respond to our demands. No, on second thought, Radik, let us keep them together for now. We can use such threats to convince the Emperor to issue a statement to his advisors. Now, we must discuss our next step."

"Yes, Linton, the time has come, and I suppose that you have plans to place yourself in the seat of power."

"No, you are mistaken. I feel that you should serve as Emperor."

Radik looked at him in shock.

"Yes, I believe that you are the better qualified man for this position.

I am more interested in my scientific pursuits. I do not care much for the drudgery of endless commands and orders, the constant bickering amongst the Council, the endless executions that must be carried out to insure longevity—no, Radik, I think you are more suited and, frankly, more desirous of this grand, elevated position. Besides, I know that you would quickly assassinate me if I were to take the reins of control over the Empire, and if you did not, then I would be forced to assassinate you for my own protection!"

"And what makes you believe that I will not take the same steps against you, Linton?"

"I do not know. Something tells me that you will not. Perhaps you may find me useful in the future; or perhaps you recognize that I could easily gain the upper hand at this moment and yet I am relinquishing it to you. This should convince you of my sincerity. I have no desire to be Emperor," Linton lied.

He was now luring Radik into his net and Radik blindly acquiesced. He believed Linton's deceptive statements. He could not see behind these words to detect the true twist of mind that was directing Linton's actions. Once Radik had become comfortable and relaxed his guard, then Linton would strike, and by then he would have all the information contained within the brain of the Pleiadean to back him up. His power would be absolute! With Radik to hold the position open for him, Linton could not fail. There would be no one, then, who could threaten *his* Empire—no one greater than he!

And so their arrangement was made. They would, for now, lead the people to believe that all was well with the Emperor. This was quite simple to accomplish. The weekly broadcasts of his public speeches had been prepared far in advance, and they were still being used for the routine maintenance of all Orion activities. These were one of the many facets of educational—so-called—messages that would have been revised by Tyrantus and Dalos upon their return to Tyron, had they been allowed to complete their mission. These daily directives would have been kept in force in order to keep the people's confusion and the disruption of their lives to a minimum while great, all-encompassing changes in their knowledge were instituted. But it appeared that this was not to be.

Now the negative forces were, once again, controlling the Orion Empire.

Through his agents, Tonar learned that Linton and Radik had left and not returned to the planet. He sent trackers to locate them and learned that their ship had arrived, but the Council members were nowhere to be found. He also picked up the information that Tyrantus' ship had docked and was met by an armed, high-security transport.

Could it be? Could these two imbeciles have actually—? No. He shook his head. *Not possible. These bumbling idiots could not possibly have accomplished such a coup! They do not have the audacity to face Tyrantus directly! Or do they?*

He sent a new flurry of orders with dire threats to his people to find Linton and Radik at all costs, and to report on their activities.

Many hours passed, and no such results were attained. Many lost their positions in Tonar's hierarchy of agents. He sent his backups into play but they, too, failed to uncover any data regarding the true whereabouts of his enemies.

Tonar fumed in his private command center. He had moved many of his technicians to Bombadzion to his secret headquarters to continue their work in falsifying the public addresses of Dalos and Tyrantus. It had been quite some time since Dalos and Tyrantus had required his services. *Perhaps I can learn something after all,* he thought suddenly. *I will contact the Emperor to offer my assistance!*

Now that they have returned to Tyron, perhaps he will wish to continue to speak to the people through the use of our broadcast facilities. Yes, it is a logical request, one that—now that I have thought of it—seems almost mandatory on my part, if I am to remain in the Emperor's good graces. He would expect such farsightedness on my part. It would be most unusual for me not to make this contact. There were no attempts to conceal his ship as it reached Tyron; so I assume that this was not classified information. Therefore, I am in the right to contact the Emperor!

And he rose to do so.

His attempt was met by a stony-faced functionary who relayed a pre-recorded message that the Emperor was not receiving contact from anyone, and that any urgent business be directed to the appropriate department head.

Tonar knew then that there were ill deeds at hand. He began to wonder if the Emperor still lived. Certainly, if he had been defeated by Linton and Radik, he would not be alive for long. If they had not killed him, then he would be required, by all the rules of dignity, to take his own life!

Now Tonar's need to consult with his technicians had become desperate. Here was an opportunity that he could not possibly have foreseen! He would not wait for Shimlus in this matter; he must act quickly. He ordered his private ship and left Tyron in haste.

"Dalos," Tyrantus said, "we are in grave danger. My life is over, but yours—I fear for you, Dalos. These mindless brutes will not be kind to you. You have too much valuable information, in their perception, and I do not believe they will leave you alone until they have satisfied themselves that you have told them everything."

"This does sound familiar, doesn't it, Tyrantus?" Dalos replied calmly.

"Please, please, Dalos … forgive me." It was the first time the Emperor had ever mentioned his regret about Dalos' early captivity.

"It is not I who must forgive you, Tyrantus, but you who must forgive yourself."

"I cannot," Tyrantus moaned. "I have been a horrible *demon*. I had convinced myself so completely of my rightness—I could do no wrong! I was supreme master! *Who* could question *me?* I knew what was right for my people. And I took every possible means at my disposal to prove my rightness. How can I continue? No, Dalos, don't speak; I know what you will say to me. But you do not understand the hollowness that now fills my heart. I am but a shell of a man. I have lost all reason to live, and now I have been defeated and humiliated by my enemies. This was my own doing, wasn't it, Dalos? It is the ignominious end that I deserved."

"Tyrantus, you must not continue to carry on in this fashion. You are only losing your grip, and doing yourself a disservice by allowing these thoughts to course through your mind. Now especially, you must keep your consciousness elevated above these circumstances! Yes, you are quite correct. You have made gross and harmful mistakes. You have harmed many, many trillions of people. You must deal with this fact in your own mind, but at the same time, you must recognize that if you lose yourself in despair, you can do nothing to help them now, and I mean to truly help these lost souls to find that which has been taken from them! If you allow these barbarians to take over your Empire, then you will have lost your opportunity to correct your mistakes."

Tyrantus heaved a great sigh. "All good and well, Dalos, but I see no way to regain my position now. They have us, Dalos. We are under lock and key. They are even now plotting my demise and your torture, no doubt. What can I possibly do from this inferior position to restore myself and save your life?"

"Nothing whatsoever, Tyrantus, if you insist upon this self-pitying attitude. Nothing good can come of it."

"What do I do then, Dalos?"

"Stay with me, Tyrantus—stay with me in consciousness. Think upon all that I have taught you. Use your full mind! Open yourself to the Brothers of Light; let them guide your thoughts and your words. We do not know what opportunity may arise in this situation, but if we allow our minds to become weighed down by despair, we will not recognize this opportunity when it does appear."

"I shall try," Tyrantus said half-heartedly. "But I think we are beyond help."

"Think what you like, Tyrantus. I can say nothing further to change your mind. I see that. So I shall be silent."

Tyrantus was even more miserable after this rebuke. He knew that Dalos was speaking wisely and truthfully, but he could not manage to keep his mind from falling into this downward plunge. He had complied with Linton's demand that he appease his close advisors with some false statement of his reason for their return to Tyron, and he also issued a command that they be left in peace and that no communication attempts be made by other than his high-security guard.

That bought time for Linton and Radik. But unlike Tonar, they were unaware of their fellow Council members' activities. They had no idea of the powerful propaganda weapon that Tonar had developed. This would cause great damage to their plans, but they were oblivious and carried on with the next sequence of their efforts to place Radik in power. They alerted a large squadron of fighter ships to stand by. Such orders were directed through Linton personally, as he held the proper position to command the fleet at the request of the Emperor. The fleet officers had been trained to obey Linton's orders and they did so without question. The entire Orion military force could be controlled in this way.

But there were those who had formed rebel forces and these individuals were now falling under the influence of Donquill's own quest for power.

Donquill had been, for several weeks, marshalling these forces from the most recently annexed planets in the Empire, where minds had yet to be fully adapted to total Orion loyalty, and where Donquill himself had implanted certain subliminal influences to cause these military forces to lean in his direction. He was required by his position to institute changes on these worlds as the Orion way of life was introduced to them, and so his activities were beyond question. This was his golden key of opportunity, he believed. For quite some time he had harbored these dreams of takeover, and when Tyrantus' illness presented a weakened façade to the Council as a whole, Donquill knew that the time was ripe for his coup.

He, too, was oblivious to Tonar's activities, but he had heard reports of the movements of Linton and Radik. Like Tonar, he did not believe that they could be successful in the way that they actually had been! No one would have believed the ease with which they had stepped in and taken over control of the very persons of Tyrantus and Dalos.

Donquill moved his forces into an advantageous position, just beyond detection and under the cloak of a falsified scenario of battle that was planned to overtake yet another world on the outskirts of the Empire. Linton had been so preoccupied by the events unfolding that he was uninformed of this movement of squadrons of starfighters. He was aware, however, that the announcement of Radik's emperorship would bring some forceful resistance from their enemies and was taking routine precautions to prepare for the inevitable battles that would ensue.

Meanwhile, new quarters for Dalos' incarceration were in final preparation. Once this shift in power had been accomplished, Linton would order Tyrantus' execution and Dalos' confinement.

32

War

THE REPERCUSSIVE BLAST OF a nearby explosion shook the room in which Dalos and Tyrantus were now being held. Full-scale war had broken out as Donquill's forces attacked the capital city of Tyron.

Linton's announcement of Radik's emperorship had evoked the expected response; yet Linton was unprepared for the fact of Donquill's amassment of rebel forces. He knew that there were fighting ships available to his enemies on the Council—there were always ships to be had from some outlying source—yet he was stunned at the vast numbers of warships that met the Orion forces, who were now following Linton's commands.

Radik was a mere figurehead, fearing for his life as he witnessed with shock the explosive response of their enemies. He realized that his time was limited. Now that the strong bonds of Tyrantus' long-held control over the Empire had been shattered, the position was up for grabs; at least that was the belief of all Council members. And now that war had begun, all opposing forces entered into the fray.

It became a mass confusion of brother fighting brother, with ships of similar insignia engaging in aerial battles that obliterated the physical bodies of soul after soul, and eventually spread to the surface of many Orion planets.

This warring would continue for quite some time, but for now Dalos was most concerned to keep Tyrantus alive, if possible. So long as he lived, there was some hope of his reinstatement. He had been successful in uniting these now-fragmented factions created by individuals of strong and dominating personality. It was possible that, as the warring took its toll upon the Orion people, some among them might look to Tyrantus, their former figurehead, as a solution to this horrible scenario that was now playing itself out among them—and many of the Orion people would become victims of these wars among the Council members.

So far, Linton had not separated Dalos and Tyrantus. It was believed that Tyrantus was dead, and Linton was preparing to make that belief a reality. He also was aware of the threat Tyrantus posed so long as he still lived. Linton's reasons for maintaining the life of Dalos were still in play; he still hoped to gain information from the Pleiadean, information that was even more vital to him now, as he believed that if he could gain a technological edge, then his ultimate victory over the others would be a matter of due course.

So it was that Dalos was moved to the torture rooms prepared for him by Linton's orders and the applications of these painful enforcements were begun.

"Linton," Dalos said to him as the Council member prepared to leave the Pleiadean in the hands of his torturers. "You realize, of course, that this is not necessary—there is a better course for you."

"There is no course but this one, Dalos. I have tired of your vague and deceptive expressions among us. You have promised us knowledge, and yet what have you delivered? Chaos, Dalos. Our Empire is now in chaos! It is your fault, can you not see that?"

"No, Linton, it is not my fault. I came to help you resolve the very circumstances which have now erupted around you with volcanic force. If you recall, you will recognize that I described this very situation to the entire Council, and yet you have all ignored my plea to you to take steps to correct the problem before you ended up destroying yourselves and your precious Empire!

"Now you have me in your control, and I know you will do with me as you please. I do not care for this physical body. Torture me, if you like, but I am telling you that you will find nothing more than what I have already told you, and what I am willing to spend my entire life to demonstrate and prove to you!"

"This is nonsense," Linton replied angrily. "I will not listen to any more of your gibberish. I want facts, Dalos, and I will have them. We will see what you have to say to me in the near future!" And he left the room.

Dalos sighed deeply and looked at the technicians surrounding him. They were oblivious to the true harm that they were about to perpetrate—not upon the body of this individual being, who had come to their world with the purest, most compassionate motives, but to themselves and their people as a whole. If they destroyed his physical life, it would do no harm to the true person expressing through the body of Dalos, but it would embed within their own psychic selves the horrific, negatively-biased frequencies which they were about to regenerate by their actions.

Yet their faces were blank canvas; no personality remained within these poor souls who had been programmed to carry out these dastardly tasks. Dalos knew that it was pointless to speak to them and yet he did so.

"I shall not hold you in contempt, yet I have the deepest sorrow for what you are doing to yourselves. If only I had been allowed to continue in my teaching, there would have been hope for you all! Now, you are compounding your spiritual death …"

As they applied the electric shocks to his restrained body, his words were halted, but his love for them never ceased.

Tonar's headquarters on Bombadzion had become a beehive of frenzied activity. He was on the brink of nervous exhaustion and exploded at anyone who crossed his path. He had but one objective at the forefront of his consciousness: to produce a speech by Dalos that would name Tonar as the rightful successor to Tyrantus, and point to Shimlus as a recognizable and important spokesperson for the new teachings that Dalos would bring to the Orion people, just as they had been promised.

Now Tonar did not care if Tyrantus or Dalos lived or died. He had them in his hands, "alive" in his laboratory—that is, their physical imagery, recreated through certain methods which he himself was solely capable of producing. He had a weapon that would win this battle that had broken out among the Council members, and they knew nothing of it!

Yet timing was of the essence and he must reach certain planets before the spreading wars preceded him. He would thereby enlist the loyalty of the now-fragmented military forces and step into the lead position.

Shimlus and her close consort of Pleiadean advisors had been brought to Bombadzion by Tonar. They were fearful for their lives and totally shell-shocked by the attacks upon Tyron, which had awakened them from their slumber. They were grateful to have made the alliance with Tonar, for it was through this association that they were whisked from the surface of Tyron, skirting around the warships and finding safety on Bombadzion.

Now their loyalty to him was quite secure, Tonar knew. They had nowhere else to turn, and he was offering them a position of leadership, which they could not refuse. It was not their nature to sit by idly and relinquish that influence which they had so recently come to enjoy among the hundred-plus planets of the Orion Empire! No, they could not revert to some oppressed state of life; they were destined to become leaders, and he was the only individual who could provide them with this opportunity.

Now they would do as he bid them to do, and now he had the upper hand over Shimlus, who had been feeling somewhat superior to Tonar and expressing this arrogant attitude more frequently. On this day, however, she was frightened and submissive.

She and her companions were working closely with Tonar's technicians to duplicate the exact inflections of Dalos' mode of speech. They now believed him to have died at the hands of Linton and Radik, along with the Emperor. They were therefore willing to recreate his image and place words in his mouth as a way of insuring their own ability to continue with what they still believed to be their primary objective, as "saviors" for the Orion people. They were thoroughly deluded in their belief in this state of "deity-ship," for that is the quality of mind which now obsessed these individuals.

Tyrantus was left alone in the room which had once been his private quarters. He was under guard but unrestrained and able to pace the floor in his deep state of despair. He knew that his life would be over in a matter of hours, and it was his choice to die by his own hand. It was the last shred of dignity left to him, he believed. He was oblivious to the fact that, by so doing, he would explode a very part of himself, his true self, and cause much damage to his psychic structures that would need to be repaired in order for him to follow through with the plans which he and Dalos had devised.

Tyrantus was not yet aware of the fact that these plans *would* be carried out, no matter how long such endeavors might take, or how many lifetimes into the future! He had not yet fully grasped the larger picture of his responsibility for the downfall of the people who were now dying by the hundreds of thousands as warships strafed the planets of his former Empire.

The explosions that rocked his headquarters proved to him that all was crumbling, all was hopeless. He was overcome by bursts of ferocious anger, smashing his fists into the objects that had once signified the grandeur of his office and causing himself bodily harm in the process. He felt no pain. He felt only inner, mental agony, and worse than this, he had once again failed by allowing this sequence of events to occur, thus bringing harm to the only soul who had ever truly shown him friendship and love! Sobs wracked his frame.

I have failed you, Dalos. I told you—you were wrong about me! I am a total failure, and so I shall remove this blot upon the lives of these people!

A sudden numbed sensation overcame his thoughts. He felt a deadened calm at the core of his being.

Linton had arranged for all means of his demise to be available to the Emperor. It was poison that Tyrantus chose, and as he ingested the fatal capsules, crumpling to the floor, the room closed in upon him in blackness.

It was the end of nothing but his physical life on Tyron! He was not free. He, like the others, had merely compounded his problems and reinforced his responsibility for the eruptions of negative force that were now engulfing the lives of the Orion people. He had relinquished and thrown away his opportunity to breathe through a physical anatomy and thereby to always have the option to add to the life surrounding his own, or to detract from it. That option is always available, no matter what one's circumstances may be, and Tyrantus had thrown this potential to the wind, throwing his own consciousness into the chaos that thrived upon the hatreds now devouring the remaining leaders of Orion.

At that moment, there was no leadership; there was only the blackness of destruction, the fury of enraged minds gone insane. Whoever emerged as the ultimate victor would rule over a burnt-out forest, where once there had been a thriving civilization, but now would remain only the charred embers of opportunities lost through ignorance and disregard for the true Intelligence of each individual soul.

Radik had barricaded himself in the Emperor's control center. From here, he screamed orders to his squadrons to attack, attack, attack, and he was determined to obliterate his enemies with a show of force that would instill fear in them for all time.

Linton had departed for his own private headquarters, from which he too was directing the movements of military forces, but these forces were truly those whose loyalty to Linton alone had been secured. Now, he thought, he must make his move. But he was uncertain, as he had not yet learned the secrets he hoped to gain from the mind of Dalos.

Thus far, the Pleiadean starship was unharmed in its bunker-like research hangar. Linton hoped that it would remain so, for it might prove to be his sole escape from Tyron, should the flames of war engulf the capital city, and from the ship's vantage point of superior technology, he would return to rule the day.

Dalos was delirious from pain when Linton entered the so-called treatment room. The man in charge informed Linton that this effect would not last much longer and that he would be able to question the Pleiadean in a short while.

"Good," Linton said. "I shall return." He did so, after waiting impatiently until he was given the signal that Dalos was able to speak more coherently.

Dalos stared at Linton without recrimination but with a penetrating gaze of one who sees to the very depths of his enemies, and knows the larger truth of the hell they have created for themselves through their hatred and disregard for the spiritual nature of their fellow beings.

Linton looked away and addressed his interrogation to a bare spot on the wall behind Dalos' fractured body. Dalos' bones had been irradiated with a shattering force of electricity—not all, but in key locations so as to cause the greatest agony.

Pain coursed through his body and nearly caused him to lose consciousness but Dalos knew that he must speak truth to this one. There was always hope of contacting that higher nature which was now so totally dominated by the lower, demonic mind of Linton.

"Tell me, Dalos, how to gain access to your starship."

"Certainly, Linton. You must possess a consciousness capable of activating itself at a higher frequency," Dalos said weakly. He could barely form the words and Linton was forced to step closer to hear them.

"And how can this be done?" he demanded to know.

"It is a process of soulic development. You must apply yourself in a positive consciousness to learn these principles of energy, about which you are vastly ignorant."

This angered Linton but Dalos did not care. He continued, slowly and painfully. "I came to teach you this psychic science, but you are killing me now, so I will be unable to serve you in this way. That is a great shame. You are killing your own self."

"Bahhh—he is still full of gibberish!" Linton uttered under his breath. *I can make nothing of this nonsense! I shall return when he is more willing to give me these formulas. I know that I can open this ship if he will only supply me with the key to its mechanics!*

"Yes, Linton, I have already given you the key, but you refused it."

"He is babbling again!" Linton shouted. "Do something!" he directed to the lead man.

"We can attempt a drug injection," the man replied.

"Then do it! And call me when you have been successful!" He stormed from the room.

"Yes," Dalos said, "you will learn, but you will learn the hard way ..." and he lapsed into unconsciousness as the injected serum took its effect.

Far across the galaxy, in a sector that was still relatively free of fighting—for now others among the Council membership had staged their own attacks and were spreading their defensive lines among the planets—Tonar's technicians were meeting with some success.

The speech of Dalos was now complete, and they were attempting to develop the *coup de grace,* the speech from Tyrantus himself that would name Tonar as the new Emperor of Orion.

Of course, none among the Council would believe this fabricated statement, but it would serve Tonar to gain the loyalty of many unsuspecting heads of departments who were programmed to believe all they saw beaming at them from the huge projection screens. Their training had been quite sufficient to prepare them for this subtle manipulation, and Tonar knew that the others would be unable to counteract this immediate reinforcement in the minds of hundreds of thousands of loyal servants of the Orion government. It would require his enemies to enter in with a counteracting force, and this would need to be a physical de-programming and re-programming of the minds of these individuals, which Tonar knew that the other Council members were unprepared and unequipped to perform. They were all busy with their warships and their land wars, and they were too preoccupied with killing one another to dabble in such esoteric and delicate, clean operations. This was Tonar's superior hold upon the minds of the Orion people.

Soon, he was prepared to release these speeches over the broadcast network which extended throughout every planet now annexed as part of the Empire. There were some whose communications had been damaged by the fighting, but many, many others were still capable of receiving these electronic messages beamed from planet to planet.

"Now, Shimlus," he said, "we shall step into our true roles."

"But Tonar, what of Radik? He now holds control over Tyron and Linton is supplying him with backup military force."

"Yes, that is a most interesting development, isn't it?" Tonar replied. "These two, who would as soon devour one another for dinner as shake hands in friendship, are now supporting one another. How long do you think that will last? No, Shimlus, Radik poses no threat to us. His life is going to be very short-lived, I promise you. Linton is no fool—he has placed Radik in this dummy position because he has the greater foresight. He knew that the first idiot to step into the Emperor's shoes would be immediately destroyed by those who are stronger. Linton's miscalculation, however, is that his military force can defeat any others on the Council; that is true, but he has not counted upon our ultimate weapon, our weapon of words, Shimlus—words and pictures! They will clear the way for us!"

Shimlus was unconvinced but had no choice. Her life now depended upon the life of this Orion leader. She and her followers were agreeable to all that he spoke, at least for now.

Among the two hundred who had accompanied Dalos to Tyron there now remained a dozen or so scattered among the planets. The remainder had lent their support to Shimlus as they witnessed the breakout of war among the Council members and realized, from information provided to them by Tonar, that Tyrantus and Dalos had most likely been killed in this uprising. They, in their fear, flocked to Shimlus to ask her advice, and when Tonar's ship arrived to rescue them from the clutches of these warring factions, they quickly agreed to accompany Shimlus to Bombadzion.

Those who remained behind were sought out by various Council members to add whatever knowledge they might, in terms of technical know-how, to their own bids for emperorship. It was commonly believed, and quite true, that the Pleiadeans had an advanced understanding of science. Thus far, it had not been fully appropriated by the Orion leaders, who were busy with their own plans for elevating their positions.

Some among the Council knew that it was futile to attempt the emperorship for themselves. They were those who were in a weaker position, or who did not have access to military force. They knew of Linton's superiority in this area of Orion life and now they were all aware of Donquill's surreptitious means of amassing large fleets of fighting starships, so they were attempting to align themselves to the faction most likely to be successful. Tonar eventually contacted one or two of these individuals, those who he felt were just ignorant enough to be useful to him without posing any serious threat to his plans. They were easily swayed to his support, and now his faction consisted of three Council members and one hundred and seventy-five Pleiadeans. This was a strong position, as the others were still fighting solitary battles.

Yes, Tonar was fully armed for his takeover.

As his fabricated messages from "Dalos" and "Tyrantus" spread their propaganda, word of these public broadcasts filtered back to Radik and Linton. They were stunned. They could not, for a moment, understand what was happening. How had these speeches been recorded? And then, as the two met in the Emperor's old headquarters to view hastily accessed samples of these speeches, Linton's eyes were opened. He recognized the advantages Tonar had. For the first time, a fear crept through him. He instantly calculated the support these false statements would gain for his enemy and he knew that his time for action was running out. Now he must get rid of Radik. Linton himself must portray to the Empire his superior might!

Radik was still unapprised of the full meaning of that which he had viewed. "What is the meaning of this, Linton?" he sputtered. "Who authorized these speeches—and when were they prepared?"

"Can you not see the hands of Tonar's technicians on these supposedly real images? These are not genuine, Radik. They are a total and complete fabrication. Think, Radik. When would Dalos ever have spoken on behalf of Tonar? And Radik, this speech of Tyrantus, resigning his office and handing the reins of power to Tonar on a silver platter! Think, man! Do you believe a word of it? Of course not!

"But there are many who will. They are mindless, vacant-headed idiots who hold key positions in the hierarchy of, not only the government, but all departments of Orion life! They now think that Tonar has been named as their new leader. They think that Tyrantus has retired to some paradise in which to spend his declining years, and they have seen Dalos, a man known to speak with the greatest integrity, endorse Tonar's puppet, Shimlus. What havoc she will wreak upon our plans I do not know, but she is as much a threat as Tonar—of this I am certain!

"I do not like these Pleiadeans. I do not like them at all. But I know one who can save us." He looked at Radik. He had been thinking aloud. No matter; Radik would not be around much longer to cause him trouble. He must keep him preoccupied.

There was terror in Radik's eyes. It filled Linton with disgust, for he was looking into a mirror of his own fears, which he had thrust deep into the depths of his mind and refused to face or admit.

"You should return to your private quarters, Radik. Leave this control center. It is now a prime target for Tonar's attack. He will attack, you realize, now that he will have behind him the new converts he has just won through this propaganda war. Flee the Emperor's lair, Radik, flee for your life!"

"And what of you?"

"I will make myself scarce. But first I must pay a visit to Dalos. I believe he is ready to help us."

"And when shall I hear from you?"

"You can contact me in my own quarters in approximately three hours. Until then, I recommend that you keep your communication screens silent."

"Yes, of course. I do not wish to leave a trail for Tonar to follow, or Donquill, for that matter."

"Yes, Donquill. He is an interesting proposition, but I feel that his little uprising is about to be squashed by minds greater than his own. No, he is no bother to me. Tonar and Shimlus are our number one threat."

The two parted, Radik to the false security of his former headquarters and Linton to give orders for Radik's death, which were hastily enacted.

Before he announced his claim upon the emperorship, Linton would speak to Dalos.

33

Peace

With cascading love, the Brothers of Light rained their Consciousness upon the planet of Tyron. Dalos was still held captive in the torture rooms of the Orion Empire and he had spoken nothing but Truth to those many individuals who came to question him. So long as he could still voice the words, he would give of his Mind unto these lost souls, for that was his entire reason for enduring their hatreds and ignorance—to help these souls heal their minds. He knew this help, instilled in some forgotten recess of their consciousness, would one day blossom and restore their minds.

Many long years passed as these "wars of the worlds" continued. Souls came and went in physical bodies, rulers appeared and disappeared, and the plans set in motion by Linton, Radik, Donquill, Tonar, and all the others had their successes and their failures. Those who rose to a position of power oppressed those beneath them, and those oppressed, if they were capable, plotted their revenge and followed through to whatever degree they were able to accomplish.

Tyrantus, meanwhile, was but a vaporous configuration of his former self. He was now being attended to by souls in higher astral worlds who exhibited great mastery of the healing arts—the true, psychic healing of the energy body that contains all the information impounded within its structure through the experiences of a physical lifetime.

Tyrantus' suicide caused untold damage to his energy self, but this damage was gradually and painstakingly being repaired by Those who gave of their own Essence to supply him with the missing elements of true consciousness so that he would be able to, at some future time, recreate a physical anatomy; for this one, the "fallen Angel" who became in legend Lucifer, Satan, Beelzebub, Tyrantus, had much work to complete.

He had now been illuminated by the Higher Mind of Uriel, his true spiritual mentor, friend, teacher, guide, the only one who loved him in her infinite compassion and wisdom! He would never be that same individual who had led countless trillions of souls into psychic and physical destruction. He could not!

He would, henceforth, be unable to express the full demonic roar of his lower mind without the subtle reminders of his spiritual nature, soft and nearly inaudible as they might be. Yet gradually, this inner chime of consciousness would increase in its volume, swelling to a loud clanging that could not be ignored, and this soul, who had once been known as Antares, would have no choice but to recognize this chime of Infinity swelling forth within his own consciousness!

There would be an added harmonic to this ringing celestial sound, a note of purest Love, the clarion call of She who had embraced him within her very Consciousness. She would never give up her efforts to awaken the mind of Antares that resided within this being, no matter what physical form he took upon himself, and no matter how often he fell again to the depths of his lower mind and returned to his old habit of control and domination. Always would she be alerted to his needs, and always would her hand be extended in his direction.

Sometimes, and quite frequently, that hand was physically embodied in the person of an earth being who took on the shell of an atomic anatomy in order to speak directly to the conscious mind of this leader of negative force. Uriel appeared in many, many subsequent civilizations. Dalos had many names, in many times, on many worlds, and still does!

You know this Being of Light! You too have been enveloped in the Love of Uriel! You yourself have lived this history now unfolded for your own illumination of consciousness. There is no end to this tale that is filled with sorrow and victory, triumph and regret. It is the story of your own evolution. It is your life that has been dramatized upon the screen of your consciousness!

Have you not found your role in this scenario? Have you not heard the sounds echoing from your distant memory of lives once lived, mistakes made, crimes perpetrated upon another?

These are the lessons which become your golden tools to rebuild your future with a clearer understanding of your role as a spiritual being, an endless expression of life force that serves a great purpose in the larger whole of Infinity.

Were it not so, the Hierarchial Minds—Uriel and Michiel, Raphiel and Muriel—would not have endured the many incarnations which they have lived upon planets that you have inhabited. They understand your true purpose, and they know of your value to one and all as a spark of Creation, a growing entity of consciousness, a Light that can spread to illuminate life for many, many others.

What of Dalos, whom we have left suffering at the hands of his enemies? His true survival rests within your own minds. His Mind has lodged itself within your psychic structures!

Even as you extended a hand to this negative force and became a facet of that opposition which would crush the physical being of this Angelic One, you were being infiltrated by a higher-frequency, healing radiation of Infinite Intelligence, directed to you by the Mind of Uriel and introduced to your conscious awareness through the personage of Dalos and his many successors upon the earth planets.

Yes, many have been those Higher Minds who have rained physical anatomies upon your civilizations, and who have brought this Lighted way of life to your very midst. Many have been those who have suffered in a similar fashion. Many times, your own life has been recharged by such Presences among you.

Do not bemoan your ignorance and your failure to recognize this Illumined Gift of Love in times past. Do not follow the example of Tyrantus, who allowed his own despair to cause further destruction to himself and to the many souls whom he might have yet touched with his own example of overcoming! Know that, as he has now proven, life can be redesigned by your own desire to improve your understanding and mend your ways. This cannot be accomplished if you give up, if you despair of ever achieving your goals!

Now you must elevate your thoughts from this gloomy scenario and realize that you have returned to your present lifetime, where you have golden opportunities at every moment to look upon your brother and sister with love and understanding, to see in their eyes the long history that you have shared among yourselves, and to recognize therein the same potential for growth and change, which Uriel has now brought to your awareness. Her Love now binds you in this unity of conscious recognition.

No, Dalos did not fail in his mission! He was supremely successful! He touched the mind of the demonic one and wove therein a healing frequency which had its immediate effect, and which has forever thereupon radiated a message of Love eternal. Yes, Dalos touched the minds of many in this fashion. His mission was completed, and when he could no longer serve in this capacity, he relinquished his association with the atomic structures that held him in the lower-frequency atmosphere of a physical planet. The Mind of Uriel, never divided, never separate from the Minds of many Illumined Ones, saw all, knew all, and carried on with this long plan to restore life upon the earth planets.

If you can recall the lighted face of Dalos as he presented to you, in that long-distant past, a ray of hope, an example of Infinite Intelligence manifest in human form, then you will recognize your present responsibility. You carry within you the seed of his great love for humanity, in all its diverse forms. You must water and nurture this seed of Higher Consciousness. If you have been moved by our tale, then allow your love to join with our own and soar to the widest reaches of Infinity!

As the peace gained from this journey descends upon your heart, know wherefrom it originated. If you always keep this knowledge of your Spiritual Brothers close to you, you will be constantly warmed by their radiant Minds. You will not lose touch, as so many of Dalos' brothers and sisters lost their inner contact with this illumined source of wisdom. You shall become a server of humankind, a Light Bearer, one who has conquered the demon that lives within his own mind and now recognizes the Angelic pulse beat that has become a very part of himself. So shall you, too, become an Angel Being, not born of ease and comfort, but emerging from the flames of your own hellish past through your own effort to join your Brothers and Sisters who have already made this journey.

You are joined in your history by many other souls who live on other worlds in your galaxy. They, too, have been ground beneath the wheels of Orion technology and they, like you, have emerged from their dark night through the Love and constant aid of the Lighted Ones. They too know the story of Dalos and Tyrantus. They, too, played their own roles in this scenario; they, too, are desirous of overcoming and proving their new existence as Light Beings!

You will all be rejoined in your mutual recognition of your true past history, the journey that you have shared with one another as enemies and allies, friends and foes. You will have many opportunities to recontact elements of these long years of war and strife, oppression and degeneration. But these shall be joyous experiences—for you will be digging through the sands of history to retrieve the gems of wisdom buried therein! You will be working elbow to elbow, shoulder to shoulder with one another, now eager to be done with your task and to use these gems of wisdom gained to rebuild your civilization into a glorious monument to those of Illumined Consciousness who have led the way back to your true state of evolutionary development!

It was a long detour that you have taken, but now you are rejoining the main highway of life. You are prepared to speed ahead to a new spiritual understanding of your place in the continuity of Infinite Intelligence.

As you identify your brothers living on other planets, you will recall your last encounters with one another. Remember always that there are many Hands guiding you all mentally, and that you shall be protected from any replay of the harms you have committed upon one another, if you keep your mind alert to this history that we have related to you.

Nothing is done by the Higher Minds without great purpose. Every word spoken by Dalos as he met the Orionites proves this fact. Every action taken was carefully designed by the Higher Mind of Uriel to accomplish some facet of her mission to the earth peoples.

Now that mission has become your own, and that joining of Higher

Minds who have been guiding and directing this healing plan is available to you to point the way, and to make visible to you all that which you can contribute to the restoration of peace among the peoples and planets of your galaxy!

Enduring peace originates within the mind of every individual. It is self-developed and maintained by a constant state of humility and openness to continued spiritual and mental growth. As the people of your planet learn of their past, they will desire to share in this inner peace, and they will have made a most valuable beginning in this direction.

The words of Dalos still echo Truth and always have, down through the ages of humanity on Earth. They are gilded examples—not to be worshiped nor raised as icons among you, but to be taken in and made a part of yourselves.

Dalos' mission has continued, unceasing, unbroken by the birth and death of the many physical anatomies this One has prepared to carry out particular facets of this mission. It shall not come to an end, so long as there are still souls suffering from damage that was incurred more than eight hundred thousand years ago, on planets scattered throughout the Orion constellation!

Now you know your own true story. What will you do with this information?

You can brush it aside as so much "imagination." That is your choice. Your choice has always been a free choice. You are and always have been the master of your own life. But now perhaps you recognize that life does not extend from a single birth to a single death, but from life to life, through the course of many cycles of evolution, and that there are many dimensions of Infinity upon which one's mind exists and either grows, expands, extends its intelligence—or diminishes and shrinks in its ability to function as a facet of the larger working Mind of Infinity.

To grow or diminish—that is truly the question! To continue, or to cease in one's soulic existence? If you perceive yourself as this small, microscopic speck of atomic dust, then so you shall be. But if you are capable of reaching deep within your consciousness to find that softly glowing luminance of Infinite Intelligence, then you know of your own true self, and when you "know thyself," then all things shall be added unto ye!

Yes, many are the Minds who have brought these messages of Love and Truth to you. Now they chime in scintillating harmony within your consciousness. Touch upon these Truths from any of their many facets and you shall hear the larger swell of symphonic harmonies, formed by the many radiating Intelligences who have recognized their own true selves!

You are a part of this Infinity; you have your own notes to play in the Symphony of Life!

You, dear soul, have asked to know of Truth. So we have told it to ye, and so it is yours to use in the most constructive method available to you.

No end shall ever be found, for there is no end to this Love that regenerates infinitely, eternally, within each soulic expression of life. Live each moment with this Love uppermost in your consciousness and you shall be fulfilling the mission of Dalos, the mission of Uriel—the Universal, Radiant, Infinite, Eternal Light—the Liberator of the dark forces!

And so the Brother left my consciousness, leaving behind a part of himself. He let me know that he was not one, but many, and their Love encompassed me with Peace, Hope, and Truth. They would always remain as my Illumined Companions.

A Letter

To those who have recognized
themselves in this story:

"Dear Reader:

"We wrote this book for the purpose of awakening the people of Earth to their prehistory, as it were, to show them some of the roots of their current conflicts and dilemmas. We knew at the time that this material would not reach them until some years into their future, perhaps at a time when they most need to understand from whence they have evolved and to what future they might aspire.

"This aspiration for a better life is the motivating force that has drawn the people of Earth together as a conglomerate population on this singular planet—for in the past, you have all lived in a great diversity of planetary systems. However, your lives were not diverse. You lived as citizens of that Orion Empire described within the pages of *The Liberator:* that conformity and uniformity and suppression of true mental function that has haunted your existence down through the ages, all the way until your present day, when the last vestiges of this mental numbness have come to the forefront and caused great unrest on your planet as it stands today.

"This battle is not the battle being fought on the plains of Africa or the jungles of Asia or the dunes of some Middle Eastern country. No, the battle we are most concerned that you comprehend is the battle for your own mental function, for the full reclamation of your birthright as offspring of the Infinite Creative Intelligence, for the complete functioning and functionability of your minds as interdimensional transceiving devices. Without your full mental powers, you were easily duped and led into lives of routine existence by the Orion leadership, over a period of many thousands of years. So we are not being hasty when we say that you will soon overcome the last of this Orion influence. It has been a long-fought struggle to reclaim your place in the Infinite scheme.

"What you see now bursting forth upon your planet are the memories carried by many individuals of their previous positions as dominating forces or rulers of various factions and planetary bodies. On the other hand, you also see the memories of individuals of having been oppressed, suppressed, and limited in their ability to counteract this negative force.

"However, in actual fact at the present time, these limitations no longer encumber all the peoples of your planet. Many are substantially free and capable of self-determination; yet they have failed to recognize that potential. They have become, through the course of many thousands—hundreds of thousands of lifetimes—so accustomed to being directed by some outside force for every moment of their daily lives that they do not fully comprehend how to use their own mental capabilities to direct their own lives.

"A few are beginning to tap into this higher power. Yet many, many millions are still lost in the fog of their Orion memories.

"We have visited your planet countless times to further this awakening of the remnants of the Orionites who have been sequestered on your world for their own protection and for the protection of others. We helped to arrange this global healing ward, you might term it, and have served as its counselors and healing advisors ever since.

"It was determined that the individuals brought to Earth would need to fulfill their destinies as members of the larger humanity, and we speak of a humanity that spreads throughout unnumbered galaxies. These individuals would be required to use their own inner strength to rebuild what had been torn apart by their actions in the Orion Empire—whether they served as overseers or whether they served beneath the thumb of Orion control.

"The drug abuse, alcohol abuse, violence, sociopathic tendencies, mental illness, insanity, and greed evidenced on your planet are all carry-overs from these Orion lifetimes. They are but echoes of the past and as such, they are actually hollow. You might say they are 'holographic' in nature. That is, they can easily be dispelled once a full understanding is reached by an individual of the position he or she truly holds in the Infinite scheme of life.

"You have created on your planet many works of art that lead the mind forward and backward simultaneously; that is, that offer some form of enlightenment or clue to this negative, destructive past history. We are referring now to a film called 'The Matrix,' which, although quite trendy in its exterior trappings, still carried at its heart a message for the liberation of humanity. The science fiction involved in that story may have seemed far-fetched and yet it is not that far from the truth, if the humanity, the population of planet Earth were to be seen from the broader perspective of a true image of *interplanetary* humanity. The people of Earth have been as if they were trapped within the machinery of Orion yet, and have been sleep-walking through their existence, playing out their roles on the various stages of your political and historical unfoldments. And yet all has been as a continual psychodrama.

"The illusions portrayed by your life on Earth are *nothing more* than illusions. They are in the larger sense harmless to your soulic development. Indeed, they are necessary in your repair work. Let us explain more clearly if we can.

"Each re-enactment of a battle, let us say, offers the opportunity for the individuals involved to stand up and recognize that they are not participating of their own free will, and yet at the same time, to recognize that they do have a will to be exercised and that they do have the choice to walk away from this battle re-enactment and to take their place elsewhere in Infinity!

"The death of a physical body is a minor event in the course of a soul's evolution. Bodies come and bodies go. What *is* of great significance to each individual human being is the inner mechanism of thought; the control or lack of control or lack of knowledge or understanding of one's personal, emotional involvements; and the deep, inner striving for a greater awareness and sense of Oneness with the positive forces of Infinity. These elements of life are what truly matter in a soul's growth and development. So the participation in a battle offers that individual the opportunity to vent the destructive force that he or she has absorbed from others, to reflect it back out to his or her fellow man—or, to turn aside and *choose a different path:* To recognize the infinite force within every other individual, no matter where they stand on some political, religious, or cultural platform! To respect that individual's differences, and to do all possible to encourage and support that individual's own personal, soulic growth.

"If *all* the soldiers on *all* the battlefields on *all* the planet Earth were to lay down their weapons of death and destruction and take up the hand of their enemy…yes, what a shocking and brilliant future Earth would then have! What a mass upheaval of consciousness would ensue! If each young man and woman on your battlefields turned to look into the eyes of the enemy and saw therein the reflection of himself or herself—where would your generals and presidents be then?

"*This* is the soulic opportunity we are describing. We have chosen a battle scenario for its dramatic effect. But this battlefield extends into every city in every home in every country across the globe. At every moment of every day, you all face similar opportunities. When you begin to see the Light of Infinite Intelligence in the eyes of those around you, no matter their exterior, superficial differences, *then* you have begun to reclaim your mental birthright! You have begun to recognize the great flow of Infinite Intelligent energy into and throughout and interpenetrating the vast universes beyond end!

"It is your first step to joining with this centrifuge of intelligent Love.

"In that moment of decision, each and every time you face such a moment and make your choice, some broken aspect of your old Orion mentality snaps back into place. Your circuits reconnect. You rejoin the Family of Humanity, and for those brilliant, shining moments you light up a portion of planet Earth. Your consciousness joins with the Advanced, Higher Minds of countless trillions of souls who have likewise joined in this unity.

"And for those moments of peace, you comprehend who and why and what and where and how.

"Over the eons, many who have lived on planet Earth have made this connection, have restored their consciousness, have regained their true, functioning mental abilities and have disappeared from your planet. They have reappeared among us, or on other physical worlds more highly evolved than the healing ward of Earth, there to carry out the soulic development that had been diverted and short-circuited through their encounter with the Orion military forces so very, very long ago. They have become helpers to humanity, servants of the progressive way of life.

"But that is for your future, and you will comprehend that state of existence fully as you achieve it.

"Is there an epilogue to our story? A happy ending to soothe the heart and mind, which has been deeply disturbed by our telling of the story of Dalos and his Pleiadean entourage?

"The happy ending will be yours alone as you make this connection with your past participation and your future as a member of the entire human family.

"Now we say 'human' and use that term in a broader sense than you envision. You no doubt envision bodies such as your own expressions, very similar to those that you find around you. But do not limit yourselves to this concept, for there are more expressions of humanity in the vast universes than you will ever comprehend from your third-dimensional, conscious awareness!

"And what of the soul, Antares, who fell to become Lucifer, Tyrantus, Satan in your mythology? Has he reversed his trajectory and regained his place among the Lighted Ones, serving humanity instead of destroying? Did he choose correctly?

"We would not wish to leave you in suspense, so we will tell you that he has made great progress in this direction, yet his work is not complete—nor will it be until all those souls who were influenced by his actions have reclaimed their Infinite birthright. He cannot rest until this reclamation project has been completed. So we do not make such demarcations of 'success' and 'failure' as you tend to do in your circumscribed lives. We see a broad continuum. We do not accept limitations such as 'failed' or 'succeeded.' We understand that life is a continuous process of growth and development. The hardest fall is often followed by a triumphant climb to a new level of awareness.

"So we do not view your 'failures' as such. We see them as perhaps the turning point in your evolution, either personally or globally. Always opportunity awaits, in every second that you draw breath on planet Earth! Your world was designed as a place of healing. Therefore, true spiritual, mental healing is constantly available to you despite outward appearances to the contrary! And while you may not individually be capable of healing the planet or even others in your close proximity, your turnaround in consciousness does reflect a great beam of Light and serves as a beacon to guide others.

"So do not fret so deeply when you see the tragedies unfolding on your planet from hour to hour. They do wrench and tear the heart of any soul who bears some compassion for others, and yet we must view these turns of event as opportunities for the individuals involved to restructure their lives, their minds, their attitudes, their perceptions, their values, their understanding of what is truly important and what is not.

"We cannot fathom these turnings of thought within another individual's mind. One cannot predict how rapidly an individual can reverse his or her trajectory and become the opposite of what he or she once was! If we condemn the actions of others so vehemently that we become locked into this limitation of judgment, then we ourselves have turned our faces back to the past and begun our own descent back into the pits of hell or Orion—the terms are fairly well interchangeable. For as that individual awakens, opens his or her eyes and views a new perspective and gains an illumination that changes his or her course, we may be left behind with our harsh opinions!

"It is easy to pinpoint leaders on your world who are making choices that are harming others. It is more difficult to pinpoint within your own self wrong choices, wrong choices being made at the present moment—and even more difficult to admit that perhaps you have not made the right move and must now choose another direction. This humbling exercise gives strength to the mental faculties that were damaged by the electronics and drugs and surgical interference practiced in the Orion technology. These moments help you to reclaim your humanity.

"If we could offer one last word of advice—although with our history you can well expect that it will not be the last, for we always seem to be coming up with new ways to approach our Earth brothers and sisters, one 'last' attempt to foster their reawakening. But let us say this: look to yourself as the seed of global change. You have heard this countless times. Yet it still rings true, and is still largely unheeded.

"Have the people of planet Earth made *any* progress? you often wonder. Perhaps as you read this book, you saw the parallels with your present society and were dismayed to factor in the number of years that have passed since our story began. How could so much time have gone by with so little evident change?

"But we will remind you that you are now looking at one planet, one solitary world among countless numbers. What was once the Orion Empire has now shrunk to a single planet. You live in the eye of the hurricane, only the hurricane itself has vanished and this hardcore nucleus remains.

"Do not be alarmed, for the exits are not barred. You can achieve your personal liberation at any moment you choose, in a countless stream of moments in which you choose to fuse your mentality with ours, with your Brothers and Sisters of Light, with the Elder Ones who will show you the way back to wholeness and goodness!

"In your heart, you know what those choices are. And the fact that you can find them there *proves* the magnificent progress that has been made by Dalos and many others who followed after him, carrying out his healing Mission to the lost souls of the Orion Empire! Within your heart and mind are planted the seeds of Truth, Honor, Respect, Compassion, and Unity. When you find them there, you will know that you have personally been touched by the many Light Beings working on your behalf who have never ceased their contact with you. You have only to raise your mind to their level and behold the Light they hold aloft for you.

"Your exit from planet Earth will be far easier now than ever in your memory! You will not be drawn immediately back into the melee upon your physical demise, as you had been when you lived as a citizen of the Orion Empire. You will ascend to higher-frequency worlds to further your education, and if you do return to Earth, it will be with this Light burning brightly within your deepest layers of consciousness, where it can be accessed now and drawn forth to light your own path and the path of others.

"This is the great change that has been wrought among the Earth people. They are no longer confined in the earth or third-dimensional realms. They have regained their ability to levitate to higher frequencies when out of the physical body. This objective has been achieved for the majority of the population on Earth, although there are those who have refused to relinquish their hold on the physical life. In time to come, there will be many more who join you in this new level of enlightenment, and then the changes on Earth will become exponential—eventually reaching the exterior manifestations on your globe!

"Hold, then, to this Light within you. Fan the flames of love and compassion wherever you go. And remember the story of Dalos, the Liberator, and the boundless compassion he has demonstrated in all his many incarnations among you. The spirit of Dalos is no longer a singular being, but a conjoined Brotherhood of Minds who hold humanity in the highest regard, extending their Life Force as a bridge to aid you in your evolutionary climb.

"With these words, we close our communication but leave our beepers on, so that you may contact us at any time you choose. It takes but a single thought in our direction to activate that signal, and we promise to respond immediately!

"Your Brothers and Sisters of Light,
in Love, Truth, and Peace."About the Authors

ABOUT THE AUTHORS

PAST-LIFE (OR AKASHIC) READINGS are fairly well-known: the information is relayed to the questing individual from a psychic channel or reader (such as Edgar Cayce), usually in response to some urgent need for healing from a physical or emotional problem in the present lifetime. This can result in a healing episode, often fraught with tears of psychic release signifying the changing of old, perhaps ancient energies stored within that individual's energy body, also known as the "psychic anatomy." The present-life problem can appear to lift or vanish so naturally that it is usually quickly forgotten by the individual, who has become completely liberated from the carryover effect of a past-life, negative experience.

Among modern truth-seekers, this concept of past-life therapy is well known. Although they cannot explain why or how it works, many professional therapists or energy psychologists now use this method for particularly difficult cases.

What's far less common is what you are holding, a psychic-spiritual history, if you will, a past-life reading for an entire civilization produced for exactly the same reason: global healing.

This reading of the akashic record of collective, interplanetary history was accomplished exactly as a reading for an individual would have been. The psychic channel, not in a trance but in an elevated state of consciousness and receptivity, voiced on audio tape the words and descriptions given to her, including the conversations among the people you will soon read about. The tapes are lodged in an archive as proof that this psychic history was received "whole cloth," in toto, through this feat of mental communication. The sensitive listener can even detect the slight variations in vocal quality as various individuals spoke during this transmission and re-enactment of certain crucial scenes in this history. The tapes also carry a few tears and muffled sobs, evidence that the psychic transceiver herself was being healed, as her own past-life history was revealed along with all others. Although she played but a small role in this sequence of historical events, to her the impact was significant and has carried through, over hundreds of thousands of years, into her present lifetime, when she was given an opportunity to serve, again, the Forces of Light, by mutual agreement prior to her present incarnation.

She accomplished this feat only through the steady, strong, and powerful influence of her spiritual mentor and Master Teacher, Ruth Norman, also known respectfully as Uriel, who overshadowed this physical incarnation once again in this world for the purpose of finalizing her Mission to help such individuals as this book's channel.

Uriel's full Consciousness, of course, exists only as a denizen of higher-dimensional worlds. Her story never ends, as all our stories continue eternally, endlessly, infinitely. But her victory over Tyrantus was at last assured, with only the final pieces to fall into place as Earth entered and marked its New Millennium and Earth's peoples became more receptive and eager to discover realities beyond their former limitations and restrictions of mind, imposed in the dark and distant past described in the tale of the Liberator.

The true Authors of this book were many, although by prior agreement they spoke through one voice in order that the tale might be recorded, reproduced, and distributed to the people of Earth. In their vast wisdom, they have concurred that this is the right time and cycle for the Earth people to begin to reawaken to knowledge of their prior history among the star-filled galactic horizons.

Many are the planets previously inhabited by the Earth peoples, which accounts for their striking differences—and for their persistent, if vague, memories and affinities with all things cosmic: tales and fantasies of space travel, galactic warfare, great heroes and heroines, and inexorable villains whose deeds were so vile, and sometimes so successful, that they have managed to keep the truth of these "fantasies" locked deep within the subconscious minds of the individuals who lived them, long, long, long ago, in a galaxy NOT so far away …

Acknowledgments

MY DEEPEST GRATITUDE TO my Cosmic CoAuthors who brought me through this story for my personal healing benefit, all the way to its printed conclusion. To Ruth Norman, who drew me out of my traumatized shell and nudged me back into the Light, and who does so still. To Joseph, who nurtures me in every way. To Al, whose support and confidence and accomplishments have driven me further than I thought I was capable of going with this manuscript. And to William and Chelle Doetsch for their special friendship and commitment in helping me bring the book into print.

Lianne Downey
August 18, 2009

Other Books by Lianne Downey

Fiction:

Perception: A Novel
The Butterfly Carriage: A Novel of Life Between Lives

Non-fiction:

Speed Your Evolution
Biography of an Archangel

Lianne Downey began her writing career covering theater for *The Los Angeles Times, San Diego Union-Tribune,* and various magazines before she transitioned to writing, editing, and publishing books. She holds a BA in Mass Communication (theater/film/journalism) from the University of California, Davis, but credits the work of Ernest L. Norman (1904-1971), and the personal mentorship of his widow, Ruth E. Norman (1900-1993), for her life-long education in the fields of non-local consciousness, reincarnation, and interdimensional science. She lives in San Diego with her husband Joseph and enjoys ballroom dancing, watching the wild pets in their back yard, and taking dictation from her Cosmic CoAuthors. She has high hopes of finally learning to play the hammered dulcimer.

ISBN 978-1-953474-07-0 HC
ISBN 978-1-953474-08-7 Pbk
ISBN 978-1-953474-09-4 eBook

www.ingramcontent.com/pod-product-compliance
Lightning Source LLC
Chambersburg PA
CBHW020946310726
48980CB00001B/68

* 9 7 8 0 9 8 2 4 6 9 1 0 1 *